the
child's
SECRET

Amanda Brooke is a single mum in her forties who lives in Liverpool with her daughter, Jessica, two cats and a laptop within easy reach. Her debut novel, *Yesterday's Sun*, was a Richard and Judy Book Club pick and *The Child's Secret* is her fifth novel.

www.amanda-brooke.com
@AmandaBrookeAB
www.facebook.com/AmandaBrookeAuthor

D1018842

Also by Amanda Brooke

Yesterday's Sun
Another Way To Fall
Where I Found You
The Missing Husband

Ebook-only short stories
The Keeper of Secrets
If I Should Go

the
child's
SECRET

AMANDA
BROOKE

HARPER

Harper
An imprint of HarperCollins*Publishers*
1 London Bridge Street
London SE1 9FG

www.harpercollins.co.uk

A Paperback Original 2016
1

A catalogue record for this book
is available from the British Library

ISBN: 978-0-00-811649-1

Set in Sabon LT Std by Palimpsest Book Production Limited,
Falkirk, Stirlingshire

Printed and bound in Great Britain by
Clays Ltd, St Ives plc

MIX
Paper from
responsible sources
FSC® C007454
www.fsc.org

In memory of Donna Hall

'What you see depends on what you're looking for.'

Anon.

1

Wednesday 7 October 2015

The muscles in Sam's calves screamed with pain as he turned the last corner. His legs were shaking but he didn't slow as he started up the hill that would take him home. He was in pretty good shape for forty, and more than used to pushing himself to the limit as if training for a marathon, but there would be no finishing line for Sam McIntyre. He had never been able to outrun his thoughts and today was no exception.

'Not far to go now, boy,' he promised the dog trotting alongside him.

Jasper, a chocolate-brown cocker spaniel, was little more than a pup and he had been struggling to match his master's stamina. At one point that morning Sam had thought he would have to carry him, but the dog had picked up the scent of home and was now straining at his leash.

Sam put his head down as they entered the final stretch and it was only when he stumbled to a stop on the driveway that he registered the police car parked outside the house he shared with his landlady. There were two policemen waiting on his doorstep and while the one in uniform spoke quickly into his radio, the other approached Sam.

'Mr McIntyre?'

Sam glanced only briefly at the warrant card DCI Harper was showing him. He was more interested in checking the house for signs of the catastrophe that would explain the need for a police presence. The drive was covered in a thick carpet of sodden autumn leaves with the exception of a small square next to Sam's Land Rover. His landlady had left in her battered old Mini earlier that morning and hadn't yet returned home.

'What's happened? Is it Selina?'

'Selina?'

'Selina Raymond. My landlady.'

'No,' Harper said dismissively. 'Could we have a word with you, please?'

'About?' Sam asked as he raked his fingers through his short-cropped hair that was more salt than pepper around his temples.

'Perhaps we could go inside first?'

Sam wasn't so much followed by the police officers as he was escorted up the handful of steps to the front door of the large Georgian house. Stepping into a wide communal hallway, Selina's ground-floor apartment was on the left and at the far end there was another door that accessed a shared utility room and the rear gardens. The curved staircase with its painted white spindles and polished oak handrail leading up to Sam's apartment was among many of the original features which gave visitors a grand first impression of the house, but both policemen remained impassive as they headed upstairs. The only sound came from heavy police boots and Jasper's laboured breathing.

Once inside, Sam turned to Harper who was a few years younger than Sam and a fair bit shorter and wider too. He had a round face and the kind of smile that would earn him a fortune as a used-car salesman.

'Are you going to tell me what this is about now?'

Harper appeared more interested in taking in every detail of Sam's living quarters than answering the question. The door to the apartment opened directly to a living room that had access to a small kitchen, a bathroom and a bedroom. The room was wide and spacious and there was plenty of light, albeit grey, coming from a large picture window to the front of the house and a smaller one to the rear. The furnishings were sparse: a small dining table, two armchairs – only one of which showed any signs of wear and tear – and a bookshelf which was almost as bare as the room itself. The floorboards were polished, but there was no rug or any other homely touches to speak of, except for a couple of garish crocheted cushions.

While he waited, Sam watched Jasper disappear into the kitchen and the sound of frantic lapping from his water bowl quickly followed.

'You live here on your own?' Harper asked eventually.

'Just me and the dog.'

'And you've been out for a run?'

Dripping with sweat, Sam opened up his arms and invited the detective to take in his attire. 'Aye,' he answered in his soft Scottish lilt, his voice sounding pleasant enough despite his instincts telling him he should be cautious.

'How long were you out for?'

Sam glanced at the clock on the mantelpiece, which was showing half past twelve, and he did a quick calculation. 'A couple of hours, maybe.'

'I thought runners wore watches to time themselves?' Harper said, glancing at Sam's bare wrist.

Sam shrugged. He had long since lost all desire to track the passage of time and hadn't worn a watch in six years. 'I don't,' he answered bluntly, having decided that he wasn't going to give any more information than was absolutely necessary until the detective explained what it was he wanted.

Harper was nodding as he drew his own conclusions. 'Two hours. That must have been some run.'

'Nothing unusual.'

'So how far did you get?'

'Not that far. I ran towards Allerton, then Garston, before sweeping around towards Hunts Cross. It was the first time out running for Jasper so we walked for a while too.'

'Did you go through the park?'

'Calderstones? Yes, I cut through it on the way out, but we came along Menlove Avenue on the way home,' he said as he rubbed his clean-shaven chin and neck where the sweat had begun to dry and tickle. 'Has something happened there? I work in the park.'

'Yes, we know. And you only left the house at about half ten, you say?'

'Yes.'

'Not before?'

'It could have been nearer to ten but no earlier,' Sam said as he sat down heavily at the dining room table, which was clear except for a single sheet of silky smooth paper.

4

The six-inch square was dark green with a pattern of yellow flowers and he played with a corner while waiting for Harper to explain himself. His patience eventually paid off.

'At approximately nine o'clock this morning, an eight-year-old girl was reported missing. While you were out on your run, Mr McIntyre, her parents have been frantically searching for her,' the detective added helpfully.

Sam's slowing pulse gathered up speed. 'What little girl?'

'Jasmine Peterson.'

The name was like a direct jolt to the heart but Sam kept his voice surprisingly steady when he asked, 'What's happened? Has she run away? Do you think she's been harmed?'

'That's something I'd like to find out as quickly as possible for her parents' sake.'

'Have you spoken to them? Is her mum all right?'

'Mrs Peterson is distraught, as I'm sure you can imagine,' Harper said, and then his eyes narrowed, changing not only his demeanour but the nature of the interview. 'When was the last time you saw Jasmine, Mr McIntyre?'

A flicker of guilt crossed Sam's face but he hid it well. 'It was a while ago. Two weeks, maybe.'

'That long?' Harper said, less concerned with hiding his own reactions. 'But you had become very close to her, hadn't you?' Before Sam could respond, he added, 'And yet you haven't known her very long at all.'

2

Six Months Earlier

Thursday 23 April 2015

'Does it hurt?'

Scanning the group of schoolchildren, Sam searched out the owner of the fragile voice which had been difficult to hear above the whispers and giggles of her peers. A small cluster of girls to the back of the group had turned around and he followed their gaze. The girl standing behind them was taller than many of her classmates and yet so insubstantial she was hardly there at all. Her head was dipped and her long blonde hair fell poker straight over her shoulders. Her blue eyes fixed directly on Sam and worry hung like a veil over her face.

'Sorry?' he said. 'Does what hurt?'

'The tree. Does it feel pain?'

A frown furrowed Sam's brow as he considered his answer. He had given countless tours of Calderstones Park in his time and the Allerton Oak was one of the highlights, for him as much as anyone. The behemoth was estimated to be a thousand years old and had remained rooted to the spot while the human race rushed past towards bright futures that had quickly receded into the dim and distant past. Had the tree been an impassive observer or did it somehow absorb the trials and tribulations of the people who had taken shelter beneath its heavy boughs? Was that what the girl was asking? It was a good question if it was.

One of the boys nudged his friend and Sam knew instinctively that there was a derisive comment on its way. The Allerton Oak was the last stop of his guided tour and he had already worked out who were the troublemakers – they were easier to spot than the quiet ones. The boy in question had taken a deep breath and was opening his mouth when Sam beat him to it. 'It does look like it should hurt, doesn't it?' he agreed, looking from the girl to the tree, his eyes drawing the children's gaze away from her willowy figure and towards the giant oak with its fresh green buds that were only just peeking through gnarled branches.

The group took a few steps closer and one or two leaned against the painted iron railings that formed a square to guard the oak from the more inquisitive visitors. The trunk of the tree was at least six feet in diameter but was by no means solid. The hollow at its core was large enough for a small child to stand up in. Some said it had been a gunpowder ship called the *Lotty Sleigh* exploding on the Mersey in 1864 that had split the tree asunder, but age had also played its part. Like an old man leaning on crutches, the oak's boughs were held up by giant metal props to keep it from tearing itself in two.

'This old gent would have been around long before Calderstones was a park and even before this land was part of a great estate – long before Calderstones Mansion was built. In fact, the tree is older than Liverpool itself,'

Sam said. He looked over towards one of the teachers. 'Isn't that right, Miss Jenkins?'

'Yes, and when we get back to school we'll be looking at some old maps which show how the area has changed over the centuries,' she said.

Miss Jenkins was standing in amongst her class and when they had first met a year ago, Sam had thought her not long out of school herself. He had said as much to her and was surprised when she told him she was twenty-eight. The teacher was slightly built with dark hair and almond eyes that always seemed to be smiling and they were smiling at Sam now, making him uncomfortable. He scratched his tangled beard, which, in contrast to Miss Jenkins, made him look older than his years.

'Why don't you tell the children about the tree's special powers, Mr McIntyre?' she asked.

Sam raised an eyebrow. 'Now you know I'm not supposed to do that.'

The statement sounded like the perfect ruse to leave the schoolchildren intrigued, but Sam had been told on numerous occasions by his managers not to make up stories but to keep to the script approved by the park ranger services. He was meant to explain how the tree was reputedly the medieval meeting place of the so-called Hundred Court, but that wasn't going to impress a group of eight year olds. Sixteen faces – nineteen if you included the teaching staff – looked at him expectantly. What harm could it do? he asked himself.

'Can you keep a secret?'

When the flurry of yeses ebbed away, Sam made a point of looking around to make sure they wouldn't be overheard.

'Legend has it that this is a Wishing Tree. For centuries, people have written down their secret desires and placed them inside the trunk.'

'Where?' someone asked.

Sam pointed to one of the gaping wounds in the trunk. 'Right there.'

'So you just stick a bit of paper in the tree. Then what?' said the boy who had caught Sam's attention earlier.

'Manners, Matthew,' Miss Jenkins scolded.

'And then what, Mr McIntyre?' he repeated, sounding even less interested in the answer than he had the first time he'd asked.

'And then,' Sam said before clearing his throat, stepping back, and opening up his arms. He tilted back his head. 'You close your eyes and listen.'

'To what?' whispered one of the girls closest to him.

Matthew blew a raspberry and the whole group convulsed with laughter, even the teachers. Sam wasn't sure how he kept his face straight but it helped that he still had his eyes closed and his face lifted towards the gargantuan spider's web of branches. 'You listen for the answer!' he said, loud enough to shock the children into silence. 'Listen to the tree's creaks and groans and it will tell you if it's going to grant your wish.'

'Let's do it,' someone said and they all began scribbling on their clipboards. A few children compared notes and a couple of boys broke out into an argument, but after a few minutes they all held their wishes in their hands.

'We can't reach the hole,' one of the boys said and they all looked at the railings that formed an impassable barrier.

'I can,' Matthew announced and before anyone could

stop him, he had scrunched his note up into a ball and threw it with perfect aim into the hollow. A dozen or more paper balls rained down in quick succession, some hitting their mark while others littered the ground among the haze of bluebells surrounding the base of the tree.

Sam sighed as he looked over towards Miss Jenkins. 'That's why I'm not supposed to tell anyone,' he explained.

The teacher held his gaze a little longer than was absolutely necessary. 'Sorry, I didn't mean to get you in trouble.'

Sam smiled and shrugged off the comment. 'It's all right, the boss will be happy that I've added litter picking to my long list of duties, because I do everything else.'

'Shush,' one of the girls said in a loud whisper. 'We haven't listened for our answers yet.'

Matthew and a few of the boys grumbled amongst themselves but eventually they all raised their heads to listen to the tree. It was only then Sam noticed that the girl with blonde hair had slunk back into the shadows of her own making. She was the only child who didn't lift her head.

'Didn't you want to make a wish, Jasmine?' Miss Jenkins asked when she noticed too.

Jasmine shook her head. 'My dad says I'm too old to believe in wishes now.'

The little girl wouldn't be persuaded and so Sam wrapped things up by thanking the children for being so well behaved and encouraging them to come back to the park. He challenged them to give their families the same tour and to see how much they could remember. It was fast approaching lunchtime and the next stop for the children was a picnic, so they all began trooping off in the direction of the walled gardens. Miss Jenkins kept one eye on her class and the other on Sam.

'I'd better go,' she said without moving. 'But if you're still around later, I wouldn't mind a quick catch up. I'd love to see the sketches you said you've been working on, if that's all right?'

'Yeah, sure,' he said, although he wasn't in the least bit sure.

'Good. Once I've loaded the kids back on the coach, I'll come and hunt you down.'

The teacher's words left him feeling slightly uneasy. He had left Edinburgh almost four years ago to make a fresh start, to begin a life that was a drastic deviation from the one he had once mapped out. He still hadn't worked out what his new life should comprise of and his only ambition, which was a vague one at that, was not to give into the overwhelming desire to keep running away from everything – and that included very attractive young women.

Once the children and teachers were out of sight, Sam looked at the mess they had left. There was a padlocked gate to access the enclosure but he never carried the key so resorted to using a low-lying branch as leverage to climb over the railings. Before picking up the litter he stopped to rest his palm on the Wishing Tree, as if by doing so he would feel its pulse. Its bark felt warm, and as his skin melded into the wooded knots he imagined that the tree was attempting to ground him too. With his hand still pressed against the wood, he took a moment to look around, peering through the fir trees that crowded around the oak to catch glimpses of visitors pushing prams and walking dogs. He felt no connection with the world passing him by and was only aware of a constant fear that there was an axe poised somewhere out of sight, ready to cut him down – again.

Moving away, Sam wiped his hand on his trouser leg. 'You shouldn't be here, Sam,' he muttered to himself as he imagined how much simpler life would be if he had chosen instead to hide away in the Highlands as a recluse. Gathering up the scraps of paper and stuffing them into his pocket, Sam had no interest in the fifteen wishes in his possession; he thought only of the one that was missing . . .

With his park ranger responsibilities at an end, Sam was forced to return to some of his more mundane duties, which today included potting bedding plants into various containers to brighten up the public areas around the Mansion House. Sam was a skilled horticulturist and had developed his craft working on grand estates in and around Edinburgh, and although the job in Liverpool wasn't as senior or as well paid, it covered his living expenses and it offered its own challenges – working with inquisitive, entertaining, demanding and soul-destroying schoolchildren for one. But, in recent times, budget pressures had meant cutting back on nonessential services and Sam now spent more time on park maintenance than he did on ranger duties. In fact, the only way he managed to keep the service at Calderstones Park going at all was by volunteering some his time, but that wasn't a problem for Sam McIntyre. He had plenty of time to give.

'Have you had your lunch yet?' Jack asked when Sam showed up in the courtyard to the rear of the old Coach House.

12

Sam gave his supervisor a shrug and proceeded to slip on his protective gloves. He picked up a spade, intent on helping Jack shovel compost into a wheelbarrow. 'I'll grab something later.'

'Over there,' Jack said, tipping his head towards a brown paper bag that had been left on top of an upturned plant pot. 'Sheila made extra and I can't go home with so much as a crust, especially since I might have mentioned how you've been skipping lunch lately. You know how she likes to mother you.'

Sam smiled and knew there was little point in arguing. He had met Jack's wife only a handful of times and she was no older than he was, but she had felt compelled to take him under her wing. She had looked at him and recognized a lost soul who needed saving. Sam had seen the same thing that morning on the face of a little girl.

Taking his lunch, Sam chose a bench to the side of the Coach House and took out the small sketch pad he always kept with him. He had been working on the collection of illustrations for Miss Jenkins for weeks, having made the mistake of showing off his sketches one time and, as was so often the case, had agreed when she asked for a favour. He had promised to come up with some drawings to accompany the worksheets she was producing for a nature project.

And he wanted to impress her, even though he knew he was making a fool of himself. She was interested in his drawings and nothing more and that was probably for the best. Not allowing his mind to wander, Sam took out a pencil and worked on some last-minute touch-ups to sketches of pine cones and earwigs, daffodils and dandelions, seedlings and, of course, the Allerton Oak. He was working on one particular drawing of a family of ducks when someone banged into him. His hand jolted in surprise, adding a crooked smile to an unfortunate duckling.

'Jasmine's gone missing!' Matthew said. He was with another boy and both were panting heavily. 'Miss Jenkins is outside the Mansion House and she's asked if you can help look for Jasmine.'

Sam abandoned his lunch and ran at full pelt towards the imposing nineteenth-century Mansion House that was one of the main focal points of the park, only slowing when he realized he was in danger of losing two other children. He waited for the boys to catch up and it tore at his heart not to speed off again. Eventually they reached the path between the house and the walled gardens where Miss Jenkins was watching over her depleted class.

'Leon and Amy have gone looking for her,' Miss Jenkins explained, referring to her teaching assistants, 'but I feel so useless. I want to be looking too but I can't leave this lot. Do you think we should call the police?'

There were gasps and a couple of girls began to sob.

'Has she been missing long?' Sam asked.

'Ten, fifteen minutes.' There was a flicker of guilt as Anna Jenkins added, 'No one really noticed.'

'Then yes, phone them!'

She looked hurt by Sam's sharp tone and he wanted to tell her they were probably panicking over nothing but he didn't; in his experience that wasn't always true. He managed to soften his tone when he added, 'OK, give it a few minutes. Wait here and I'll take a look around too.'

They swapped mobile numbers and then Sam took off again at a sprint, his mind buzzing as countless scenarios came to mind, each of them pulling him in a different direction. For every large open space there were countless nooks and crannies for a child to disappear into and, God forbid, there was the lake too. There were also numerous outbuildings that had once been part of the landowner's substantial estate; some were still in use while others had been abandoned, making them all the more enticing for a child with a mind to explore. And then there were the busy roads surrounding the park, the busiest being Menlove Avenue, which was where the school bus had disembarked. If Jasmine had decided to leave for whatever reason, she might head that way.

With his heart hammering in his chest, Sam bolted in that direction. Racing along the main throughway, he looked from left to right, desperate for some reassurance that she hadn't left the park, and all the while the distant hum of traffic grew louder until it was deafening. He started to zigzag from one side of the path to the other and he was moving so fast that he went a dozen extra steps before his body was able to react to what he had just seen. He did an about turn and darted through the fir trees towards one of the park's oldest occupants, which had not only captured *his* imagination.

Jasmine stood with her forehead resting on the railings as she stared at the exposed heart of the tree. The wood was rotting and crumbling along the exposed edges of the trunk where the mighty oak had split in two. She wished she could stand there all day watching over the tree and she didn't think anyone would miss her if she did. Even her best friend, Keira, had been too busy swapping lunch with Jenna Rose to notice when she slipped away.

Wondering how cold and creepy the park might become if she stayed through the night, Jasmine looked up at the gnarled and twisted boughs above her. They reached out in every direction, some strong enough to support themselves while others needed the assistance of the metal props, reminding her of the crutch her mum had hobbled around on when she had fallen and broken her ankle last year. But it wasn't the boughs lifted high out of reach that caught her attention, but the one that rested its weight on the railings to save it from falling to the ground.

When Jasmine touched the sagging branch, she could almost believe she was taking the old tree by the hand.

'Hello,' she said. 'Do you mind if I get a bit closer?'

The Wishing Tree didn't complain when she climbed along the branch; in fact, she was convinced it was giving her a helping hand. Once over the railings, she stepped carefully through the cloud of bluebells until she was within touching distance. She reached out her hand and placed her palm tentatively against the warm, wrinkled bark. When she flinched, she wasn't sure if she had felt the tree's pain or her own; it was as if the two had become intertwined . . .

Sam could see no more than a wisp of golden hair and the sleeve of her chequered school pinafore but there was no doubt in his mind that he had found Jasmine. He came to a halt twenty feet away from the Allerton Oak and took a deep, shuddering breath that caught in his throat. If he didn't know better, it had sounded like a sob. This, he told himself, was why he wanted to be a recluse. People were too much of an emotional investment, and Sam was already spent.

As a seasoned runner, it didn't take Sam long to catch his breath, but his pulse was still racing as he dipped beneath the shade of the oak. Jasmine was standing on the other side of the railings. She had her arms open wide and her eyes closed.

'Can you hear anything?' Sam asked.

The girl stumbled back in surprise and the notepad she had been holding dropped to the ground with a flutter of pink paper. 'I didn't do anything,' she said, backing away.

'Hey, it's OK,' he said. 'And I'm sorry if I gave you a wee fright.'

The girl reluctantly collected up her things and clambered back over the railings while Sam remained at a safe distance. He waited until she was standing on the correct side of the barrier, her head bowed with guilt, before he broke the bad news. 'I'm afraid you've got Miss Jenkins in a bit of a flap. I'd better ring her and let her know to call off the search.'

Jasmine's head snapped up. 'She won't tell my dad, will she?'

The sudden look of horror on her face was difficult to ignore and Sam did his best not to reflect her concern but to give her a reassuring smile. 'I'll see what I can do,' he promised.

After making the call and telling Miss Jenkins they were heading straight back, Sam was as reluctant to escape the shade of the tree as was Jasmine. 'So,' he asked, 'did you get a reply from the Wishing Tree?'

'All I could hear was it groaning,' she said before shaking her head. 'I shouldn't have done it.'

'Run away?'

'Asked for a wish,' she corrected. 'I think it does feel pain, you know.'

Sam considered telling her that the Wishing Tree was only a figment of his own imagination and that it was no more aware of their secret desires than the pink paper she had used to scribble her wish on. But one look at her told him that she needed something to believe in and so instead, he found himself saying, 'I don't think it feels its own pain, Jasmine, but there are times when I think it feels ours.'

Jasmine looked thoughtful for a moment as she glanced from Sam to the tree. 'Maybe we should leave it in peace then,' she said, and Sam didn't argue.

Rather than welcome arms, Jasmine's classmates greeted her with scowls as if disappointed that the drama had been drawn to a close without an exciting climax.

'I wanted to see the scuba divers going into the lake,' Matthew muttered as the teaching assistants gathered everyone into line for the final trek to the school bus.

Miss Jenkins was bringing up the rear and only when she'd finished counting her charges for the third time was she satisfied. 'Sorry, I'm not going to have a chance to ask you about your sketches now,' she told Sam. 'We're late getting back as it is.'

'I could always drop them off at school for you,' he offered.

She tilted her head and snared him with her smiling eyes. 'I do have a life outside school, you know.'

Anna Jenkins was ten years his junior and although he could remember being thirty, he had nothing in common with the man he had been back then and for the life of him couldn't see what this young woman saw in him,

18

assuming she was interested at all. The answer to that question came soon enough when she added, 'You have my number, Mr McIntyre. Why don't you invite me out some place where I can call you Sam and you can call me Anna?'

The flush rising in his cheeks was obscured by his beard, but he wouldn't have been surprised if Anna could feel the heat of his embarrassment. His eyes darted from left to right until he found his means of escape. Gesturing towards the fully loaded bus, he said, 'I think your group's about to lose their teacher if you don't hurry up.'

Anna was forced to leave without receiving her answer and voiced her regret at not casting her own wish into the Wishing Tree.

3

Sam's flat: Wednesday 7 October 2015

'It seems like Jasmine made quite an impression on you,' Harper said.

The detective had remained standing in the middle of the room, his feet wide apart and hands shoved in his trouser pockets as he looked at Sam with his head cocked to one side. He couldn't yet appreciate the effect Jasmine had had on Sam – and why would he? Sam had been deliberately vague about that first meeting, skimming over the details of the Wishing Tree story, playing down Jasmine's earlier disappearance and only briefly mentioning that she had made a wish. But he wasn't the only one who knew more than he was letting on. Sam couldn't yet tell how much Harper had been told and so, for the moment at least, he would have to be cautious about volunteering any information that might only add more substance to the detective's potted theories. It wouldn't bring the little girl home to her mum any sooner.

'She was just a lost little girl,' he offered.

'Until you found her.'

An image came to mind of Jasmine standing amongst her classmates beneath the Allerton Oak. She had looked so insubstantial that Sam had thought that if he blinked she might have disappeared completely. 'She must have run away again,' he said with unshakeable conviction.

'Why do you say that?'

Sam blinked, and this time Jasmine did disappear. 'Because the alternative is unthinkable.'

Harper stared at the polished floor and battled with his own thoughts. 'I hope you're right, Mr McIntyre, but in my line of business the unthinkable happens more often than you'd imagine.'

Sam was starting to cool down after his run and his sweat-sodden T-shirt felt ice cold against his skin but when he shuddered, it had nothing to do with the temperature. His mouth was so dry he could barely speak. 'Can I get a drink of water?' he asked, already getting up from the dining table.

Harper stopped him. 'We'll sort that,' he said and nodded towards the uniformed policeman who had been standing guard by the one and only means of escape.

'Thanks,' Sam said, not quite sure why he should be grateful for the offer of a glass of water in his own home. What was quite clear, however, was that the police were making their presence felt that little bit more.

As he waited for his drink, Sam played nervously with the green square of origami paper. If he weren't careful he would start folding it into the shape of a crane, so he pushed it out of reach and clasped his hands together . . .

'Now,' Harper continued, 'tell me why one little girl amongst an entire class should catch your eye.'

Sam refused to be goaded. 'Shouldn't you be out searching for her rather than wasting time with me, for pity's sake?' he asked.

Harper didn't appear fazed by Sam's reaction and took a step towards the bookshelves, which held little more than a thin scattering of books and journals. He briefly scanned the titles, which were exclusively related to gardening and horticulture, then his eyes settled on a shoebox that had been decorated in brightly coloured paper squares.

'Look,' Sam said, 'I want to help. If Jasmine's missing, then I'll do anything I can. When was she last seen? Where was she?'

When Harper turned back to Sam, he was smiling – although perhaps smirking might have been a better description. 'And there I was thinking I was the one asking the questions.'

Sam offered up his hands in supplication. 'Fine, ask away.'

Harper moved closer to Sam and rested his hands on the back of a dining chair but didn't take a seat. 'What I'd really like to know, Mr McIntyre, is how you became so deeply involved in her life so quickly? And, perhaps more importantly, why?'

From the kitchen, Sam could hear the other policeman talking to the dog, offering to refill his water bowl while Sam was left waiting. His lips were painfully parched and if Harper wanted answers, he needed that drink. Not that Sam had any idea how to answer the detective's question. Why *had* he become so involved? Would Jasmine be missing now if he'd had the good sense to stay away?

He refused to let his gaze be drawn to the bookshelf and the shoebox which contained a growing collection of origami cranes; paper birds of varying colours and sizes. Some were pink . . .

4

Thursday 23 April 2015

The spring day was still clinging to the sunshine when Sam set off for home, although he had somehow managed to take the shadow of the Allerton Oak with him. He liked his job and, within certain boundaries, he enjoyed being around people. Up until today he had thought that the limited contact had come without risk, but when the girl had gone missing, when he had raced through the park with his heart pounding with terror, he had realized he wasn't as insulated as he had thought. He was starting to think that the cutbacks at work that pulled him away from his ranger duties were a blessing in disguise. Planting, sowing, pruning . . . these were far safer activities, where the only casualties would be seedlings lost to the frost. Perhaps he should speak to Jack about giving up the tours so he could put all his energies into the job he was actually being paid to do.

Calderstones Park was close enough to walk the short distance home and he strolled up the hill with his head down and his hands in his pockets. When he stepped onto the drive, he found Selina busily dusting the windowsills. The wiry and wily octogenarian was barely five foot tall and with the sills almost at head height, cleaning them was a difficult and somewhat pointless task. She pretended not to hear the heavy clomp of his work boots on the block paving and gave a start when Sam tickled her waist.

Swiping him with her duster, she cried, 'Sam, you gave me a fright!'

'What are you doing, Selina? I told you I'd wash the windows at the weekend.'

She twisted the duster in her fingers, which were swollen with arthritis. 'Oh, I can't sit inside on such a lovely day,' she said, 'and I can't sit in the garden doing nothing. You don't exactly leave me much to do, but staying busy is what keeps me alive.'

'That and the whisky,' he said smiling.

She swiped him again. 'I've told you, it's medicinal.'

Sam laughed. 'Anyone who's reached the ripe old age of . . . What is it now? Sixty?' he asked, deliberately knocking quarter of a century off his landlady's age. 'You deserve at least one vice, Selina.'

'For that compliment, I'll have to invite you to dinner. I've made a lovely cottage pie and it'll go to waste if you don't help me eat it.'

Sam had moved into his lodgings soon after arriving in Liverpool and the setup had suited him perfectly. Selina was a widow and had converted her oversized house into two separate apartments many years ago. She lived on the ground floor while renting out the upper level. There was a basement that could easily be converted if she wanted another lodger but Sam's rent was sufficient to plug the gap in her income and they were comfortable in each other's company. They liked their own space while knowing there was another living being close by. Over time, they had let their lives overlap far more than either intended, although they respected each other's privacy. Selina wouldn't push her offer for dinner or be offended by Sam's refusal, which he gave rather reluctantly.

'I'm sorry, Selina, can I give you a rain check? It's been a tough day and I want to go for a run. I need to clear my head.'

'I understand,' she said with a nod. 'I'd go with you if these hips didn't keep seizing up on me. I'll put some dinner on a plate for you and you can heat it up when you get back.'

'Thank you, you're a sweetheart.'

The old lady tried not to let the worry show on her face when she said, 'And don't stay out too long. You don't want to wear yourself out or *you'll* be needing a hip replacement before I do.'

'I won't go too far,' Sam said but it was at best a half-truth. He would probably be out for a good hour at least and still it wouldn't be long enough. He had spent years trying to outrun himself and tonight he would fail once again.

Later, as Sam dragged himself up the stairs, his legs felt leaden and his T-shirt was soaked in sweat but it was only when he entered his apartment and checked the clock that he realized he had been out for at least an hour and a half. He went into the kitchen, which was little more than a cubbyhole with enough room for a cooker, fridge and sink but little else. It was sufficient for his needs which right now involved the bottle of water he had left to cool in the fridge. He poured a glass and downed it in one then quickly refilled it before resting it on his forehead to cool down.

By the time he made his way back to the living room, his pulse had begun to slow. He felt completely depleted which wasn't a bad feeling; in fact it was the reason he pushed himself so hard. The exercise gave him time to get his thoughts in order and left him too tired afterwards to let them wind him up again. He went out for a run at least three times a week whatever the weather although the distance depended on his state of mind.

As he took a sip of water, a beeping noise caught his attention. It was a voicemail alert on his mobile, which he had left on the dining table. He checked the missed call, stared at the caller ID for a second or two, and then deleted the message.

By the time Sam had showered and changed, it was eight o'clock. He didn't feel hungry at all, despite his stomach rumbling, but he knew he would have to eat something and it wouldn't be his choice. As if on cue, there was a knock at the door.

'Perfect timing,' he said opening the door to Selina who was holding a tray. The cottage pie was so hot it was steaming.

'Hungry?' she asked as she marched past him.

'Famished,' he lied.

He left Selina in the living room and marched back into the kitchen.

'I won't stay if you want time on your own,' she called after him as she set about laying the table. Along with his dinner, she had brought all the condiments and a slice of cake for afters.

Sam emerged from the kitchen with two cans of brown ale. 'Could I tempt you?' he asked, already knowing his old friend wouldn't refuse. The ale was more to her taste than his and he kept a supply in the fridge as repayment for the countless offerings she served up.

As Sam tucked into his dinner, Selina occupied herself by flicking through the sketch pad he had left lying around. He watched her suspiciously. They knew each other better than either was willing to acknowledge. Selina had listened out for him returning home from his run; she had heard the shower running and had known how long to give him to get dressed before bringing the dinner he wouldn't have bothered to heat up for himself. She knew how he worked, just like he knew how she did. Selina had something to say but was biding her time.

Putting down the pad, she turned her attention to a small heap of scrunched-up balls of paper. 'What are these?' she asked, picking one up.

'Don't,' he said, when he saw her about to unfurl it. When she raised an eyebrow, he added, 'I gave a tour to a group of school kids today and made the mistake of telling them about the Wishing Tree. They're the children's wishes.'

'So why bring them home if you're not going to look at them?'

Sam's eye was drawn to one particular ball of paper. It was the only pink one in the pile. 'Hiding the evidence?' he tried.

Selina took a sip of her ale straight from the can; they had long since dispensed with social niceties in each other's company. She smiled when she said, 'You want to look, don't you?'

'I shouldn't,' he said, but having cleared his plate, he set the tray to one side and let Selina gather up the wishes to place between the two of them. They each took a handful but only Sam was selective, making sure he held onto the only one he really wanted to read.

'A PlayStation,' she said rolling her eyes.

'A bike,' Sam said, equally unimpressed.

They took it in turns to read out the rest which were equally uninspiring until Selina found one that made her laugh so hard she had to take a sip of ale before speaking. 'I'd like you to drop a branch on the bearded wonder's head!' she read, still crying with laughter.

Sam was at first shocked that one of those nice children would think such a thing but then remembered Matthew. 'Cheeky sod,' he said.

'What about that one?' Selina asked. She had noticed the pink ball of paper that Sam had palmed but was reluctant to open.

'I don't know if I should,' he said and then went on to explain how Jasmine had gone missing and how he had found her making her wish in secret.

'She's got to you, hasn't she?' The mischievous smile had disappeared and there was a pained look on the old lady's face. 'Could it be that she reminds you of someone?'

He shook his head. 'I'm overthinking things, that's all. I'd like to believe her wish would be something important, but more likely than not she's just another young lass who wants to grow up to be a film star. I'd rather leave it unopened and avoid the disappointment.'

Selina offered up her palm. 'Let me,' she said. When Sam didn't respond, she added, 'You can't fool me, Sam. You've cleared up the mess after telling that Wishing Tree story plenty of times but you've never brought the notes home with you before. Maybe you don't want to read it – but you want to know what's in it. If you feel it's against your principles then let me look. Believe me, my conscience has had to deal with far worse.'

Reluctantly, Sam dropped the ball of pink paper into her hand but he couldn't watch as she flattened the creased paper to reveal its secrets. 'Ah, bless her,' Selina said. She waited for Sam to look up from the can he had been peering into. 'She wants a job for her dad.'

'Really?'

Sam took the unfolded piece of paper from Selina and stared at it as he tried to keep up with his emotions. He had known the serious little girl wouldn't have wished for something trivial and felt vindicated, although now he had to deal with the consequences of giving her a dream to hang her hopes upon.

'I feel guilty,' he admitted. 'I spun her a story and now she's expecting the Wishing Tree to grant her wish.'

Selina shrugged. 'You never know, chances are her dad will get a job anyway.' When it became clear his conscience couldn't be eased, she added, 'We're *supposed* to tell children white lies, Sam. Childhood has equal measures of reality and fantasy and that's not necessarily a bad thing. If she believes in the Wishing Tree then she still believes in a world where good overcomes evil and we all find our happy endings. What's so terrible in that?'

'Because it's not true,' he said, not thinking of Jasmine any more but his own sorry existence.

Selina chose her moment perfectly. 'Your wife phoned,' she said.

'Ex-wife,' he corrected. 'She left me a voicemail message. I didn't play it back and—' He stopped, only now realizing what Selina had meant. 'She phoned you too?'

She nodded. 'When you were out on your run. She thought you might not listen to the message so she asked me to tell you.'

The break-up of Sam's marriage had been amicable enough. For the last two years of their marriage, they had barely talked and so he had decided to walk away before they learnt to hate each other. That had been four years ago and, after leaving Edinburgh, he had initially broken off all communication with Kirsten. They had only finalized the divorce a year ago when she had come down to Liverpool to agree the terms. That was when she had met Selina and his landlady had learned more about her lodger in a single weekend than in all the time they had been living under the same roof together.

Sam busied himself flattening out the pink square of paper in his hand before folding it carefully, this way and that. He took care with the corners and pressed down the creases with practised ease. 'What did she have to say for herself?' he asked at last.

'She's . . .' The old lady paused long enough for Sam to lift his gaze. 'She's getting married come September.'

Sam tried to smile. It could have been worse. 'I thought the next time she'd phone would be to tell me she was pregnant.' He continued turning and folding the paper until he was ready to unfurl the wings of his origami crane. 'I suppose that will come next. She's moving on.'

'You might be right,' Selina agreed, 'but it can't be easy.'

'Really? Do you think I don't already know that?' Sam asked, although it wasn't a question, but a suggestion of the anger building inside him, anger that would have been directed at his ex-wife if he had spoken to her. She wouldn't have deserved his wrath and he was glad he hadn't spoken to her directly. He raised his hand to stop Selina replying. 'Sorry, that was unfair.'

'She knew you would find it hard, which is why she asked me to break the habit of a lifetime and interfere.'

Sam smiled as he turned the paper crane over in his hand. He had travelled hundreds of miles in an attempt to escape the past but it was the woman he had left behind in Edinburgh who had managed to find a way to move forward. Perhaps he should follow her example.

'I've been asked out on a date,' he said, knowing full well that Selina would give him the final push he needed.

'Is she nice?'

'Out of my league,' Sam said, thinking of Anna's dazzling smile and sparkling eyes that saw in Sam something he could not. He scratched his beard. 'I might have thought I stood a chance once, but I'm not the man I was. I think she's going to be disappointed.'

'That's the problem with you, Sam McIntyre. You think too much.'

5

Saturday 2 May 2015

Sam had thought Anna pretty when they had first met, but when she walked into the restaurant she looked stunning. Her dark hair had been swept to one side, falling softly over her shoulders, and the black-and-white sleeveless jersey dress hugged her figure dangerously. Following Selina's advice, Sam had gone for a smart casual look and, wearing chinos and a checked shirt, felt distinctly underdressed. They were in a lively Indian restaurant in Woolton Village and even if the other diners weren't wondering what an odd pairing they made, Sam was.

'You found it all right then?' he asked standing up to pull out Anna's chair for her.

Anna assumed Sam was getting up to give her a kiss and offered her cheek. There was an awkward moment where Sam didn't know what to do and by the time he plucked up the courage to kiss her, she had moved away and the fumbling only added to his nerves.

'Yes, I can't believe I've never been here before. I love Indian food.' She took her seat and watched Sam intently as he struggled to settle back in his chair. 'You don't do this often, do you?'

'No,' he admitted, 'I'm more used to heating something up in the microwave. In fact, if it wasn't for the Christmas do at work every year, I don't think I'd eat out at all.' The traditional Christmas dinner dance was one of those annual events that Sam forced himself to attend if only to prove that he could socialize, although without fail he would slip away while the plates were still being cleared.

Anna was laughing at him. 'I meant going out on a date.'

Hearing the word date only compounded Sam's anxiety. 'Oh, erm, yes. I doubt I could even remember the last time,' he said, which was only partly true. He wondered at what point going out with the woman who was to become his wife could still be considered a date.

'Well, try not to worry,' she said softly. 'Things won't have changed that much. The idea is that we both relax and enjoy ourselves. No expectations, no strings attached – and before we order our food, I want to make one thing clear: we split the bill.' When Sam looked horrified, she laughed again. 'What? Were you expecting me to pay for everything? I thought it was just a myth that Scotsmen were tight-fisted?'

Sam couldn't help laughing, which settled his nerves, if only a little. 'You know that wasn't what I was thinking at all. And while I don't want to start the evening with an argument, I have to insist on paying. It wouldn't be right.'

Anna scrutinized his face. 'OK, but only if I'm allowed to pay next time.' Before Sam could object she was extending her hand towards him so they could shake on the deal.

They placed their orders for food and soon after the waiter brought their drinks. Sam had ordered a pint and was tempted to down it in one but made do with generous gulps as Anna sipped her wine. 'So what made you come to Liverpool in the first place?' she asked.

'I was travelling through,' he said, although travelling aimlessly might have been a better description. 'And then I somehow fell into a job I enjoyed, found a nice place to stay and so here I am, still here four years later.'

'And yet you haven't put down roots.'

'What do you think I do for a living?' he asked.

The waiter arrived with their starters and they sat in silence for a while. From the look on Anna's face, she was waiting for a proper answer, which he did his best to ignore. As the silence stretched in front of them, he was forced to accept that they risked spending the rest of the evening sidestepping the past unless he shared at least some of the baggage he carried with him. He wasn't good at sharing information, but accepted that the sooner he got it out of the way, the sooner he could give his undivided attention to the beautiful young woman sitting opposite him.

'I lived in Edinburgh all my life, right up until the day I decided to leave. My marriage of fifteen years was over bar the shouting and I decided that I wouldn't hang around long enough for that to happen. I left and I haven't been back since.'

'I take it there were no kids, then?'

Sam felt every nerve in his body tense but his voice was surprisingly level and gave no clue to his real feelings. 'The divorce, unlike the marriage, was uncomplicated.'

'You're very fortunate; in my line of business you see

35

the fallout to a lot of acrimonious divorces,' Anna said. 'But here you are, young, free and single.'

The laugh wouldn't come but he managed a smile. 'Young?'

She shrugged. 'I have a sneaking suspicion that there's a youthful complexion underneath that beard. You might think you can hide behind it, but I see you, Sam McIntyre.'

'You think I should shave it off,' he concluded.

Anna tore at a piece of naan bread then pushed back on her chair as she took a bite. She considered her response before she said, 'Unlike you, I have plenty of experience of the dating game. My last relationship ended three months ago and now I'm back home, living with my mum and dad, with my ex-boyfriend's words ringing in my ears. He told me in great detail how I tried to change him rather than adapt, and while I think that was a little unfair, there was some truth in what he said and I intend to learn from my mistakes, Sam. If you like your beard then far be it from me to tell you how much better looking you'd be without it.'

Sam wasn't sure how to take Anna but her honesty was refreshing and as she had been keen to point out, they were out to enjoy themselves; that was all. If something came of it then that would be more than nice. It had been a long time since Sam had had some excitement in his life and he couldn't deny that he missed it. And if things didn't work out then Sam could return unharmed to his comfort zone. 'So you *don't* like it, then?' he asked her with the broadest smile.

'Oh, now you'll definitely have to keep it,' she exclaimed. 'Otherwise I'll think I've pressurized you and that would make me feel awful.'

Their chatter continued as their main courses were served and eventually the conversation turned to the one thing they had in common. 'I'm sorry I ever got you to mention that Wishing Tree story,' Anna admitted. 'I never imagined the trouble it would cause – other than a bit of littering, maybe.' There was a mischievous glint in her eye but it quickly disappeared. 'We were so busy focusing our attention on the kids we expected to misbehave that we let one of the quiet ones slip through the net.'

'Did she get in trouble?'

'Jasmine? No, it was me who got hauled over the coals!'

Sam didn't look moved. 'Don't expect sympathy from me when I was the one left to clear up after you all.'

'Sorry, was there much of a mess?'

Sam thought of the screwed-up ball of pink paper which he had transformed into a soaring paper bird when he said, 'It's all in a day's work – and the way things are at the moment, I suppose I should just be glad I've got a job.'

'Actually, I think that could be behind Jasmine's behaviour,' Anna said, making the link with Sam's comment far more quickly than he could have hoped. 'Her dad was laid off a few months ago and since then she seems to have slunk deeper into the shadows. I wouldn't have thought the family are in dire straits; her mum still works but that might be part of the problem. They both worked at a builders' merchants but only she got to keep her job. They're not a happy family by any stretch of the imagination.'

'You sound like you know them quite well.'

'Oh, only to say hello to really. I see Laura – the mother – at parents' evenings and they don't live too far from where my parents live so I've seen them around. Jasmine's dad,

Finn, drinks in the King's Arms and I think he's practically living there these days.'

Thinking how the troubled girl could have more disappointment in store when the Wishing Tree failed to deliver her heart's desire made Sam lose his appetite. He didn't want to hear any more and began playing with his food, a curry that was so hot it had made his eyes water.

Anna watched him chase the same piece of lamb around his plate until she stabbed at it with her fork. 'Sorry, you'll have to get used to this,' she said. 'If I see something I like, I go for it.'

Sam waited for her eyes to start watering but Anna dealt with the spiced heat better than he had. 'I'm impressed,' he said.

'That was the plan,' she confessed.

6

Sam's flat: Wednesday 7 October 2015

'It was through Anna that I got to know the family,' Sam told Harper.

'And Anna would be Jasmine's teacher?'

Pursing his dried lips, the skin tore when Sam opened his mouth to speak. He was tiring of the cat-and-mouse game Harper was playing and said, 'You already know she is.'

'Yes, of course, Anna Jenkins. The girlfriend,' Harper said and then began leafing through his notebook, although Sam suspected it was more for effect than to check any particular facts.

The silence that followed made Sam uncomfortable, as Harper no doubt intended. Sam was becoming impatient for a drink to quench his thirst and was ready to stand up to get it himself, when the uniformed policeman reappeared with his long-awaited glass of water. Jasper had been following him, but stopped at the doorway when he saw Harper standing over Sam. The puppy looked to his master for comfort then shivered nervously.

'Go lie down, boy,' Sam told him softly but firmly.

Jasper took a hesitant step forward as if he were going to ignore the command but then, dipping his head, he disappeared back into the kitchen. There was the brief sound of scratching as the puppy settled into his bed.

'I couldn't help notice that all your cupboards are bare, Mr McIntyre,' the police officer said as he handed Sam the glass.

Harper looked up from his notes. 'Really?' he asked and shared a look with the other man before writing something down. When he looked up again, he said, 'Right, Mr McIntyre, back to this morning. You left the house when?'

Sam had been expecting a whole new set of questions but relaxed a little. After taking a long drink, he said, 'About ten o'clock, maybe ten thirty.'

'Not before?'

'I've already told you. No.'

'And is there anyone who can corroborate your story?'

'It's not a story, and no, I can't.'

'Not your landlady?'

'I haven't seen Selina this morning. I heard her leave, maybe an hour before me.'

'And do you know where she is now?'

Sam craned his neck to look out of the window. The parking space next to his Land Rover remained empty. 'No,' he said.

'And no one else lives in the house?'

'No.'

Harper was looking around the room again. 'No offence, but it hardly looks like even *you* live here. Has Jasmine ever visited?'

'No, never.'

'You met her quite often in the park, though.'

'A few times, yes.'

'And the last time you saw her was . . .' Harper said, pausing to consult his notes, 'two weeks ago. Where was that?'

'At the park,' Sam said.

'Where in the park?'

'By the—' Sam went to say Wishing Tree and only just stopped himself. 'By the Allerton Oak.'

Harper tapped a pen against his notepad and then took a quick breath as if a thought had only just occurred to him. 'Ah, yes, I'd almost forgotten about the Wishing Tree. Is there a reason why you haven't yet mentioned that you knew about Jasmine's wish to find a job for her dad, Mr McIntyre? Or why you felt compelled to fulfil it?'

7

Friday 29 May 2015

Heading away from the Mansion House, Sam and Jack looked up at the same time as the sun made a late appearance through the slate grey cloud that had hung over Calderstones all day. Lifted from the shadows, the park came to life; the verdant greens of the lawns and foliage took on a new vibrancy and the late spring blooms were dazzling.

Sam shook his head. 'Now the sun decides to come out! If they'd hung around a bit longer, they would have seen the gardens in all their glory,' he muttered, referring to the group of councillors who had been touring the city's parks to help decide how best to use some recently acquired European funding. Sam had helped Jack put together a project for Calderstones that, amongst other things, would reinstate the full-time role of park ranger.

'Oh, I don't think a bit of sunshine would change anything,' Jack said. 'You mentioning how you volunteer your time out of hours – now that didn't help our cause. Why pay for a ranger when there's someone daft enough to do it for free?'

'They have to know the service is still needed, still used.'

'Sorry, I know it's your baby and good on you for keeping it going,' Jack said. When he saw Sam's jaw clench, he put his hand on his shoulder. 'You need to find something else in your life, mate. No one should love their job as much as you do. It's not natural!'

Sam tried to look offended but then smiled. 'Someone has to keep this place going while there are so many others leaving like rats from a sinking ship.'

Jack bowed his head a little. 'I never thought I'd be one of them, but I would have been mad not to take the job when it came up. And I'll be honest, I'm looking forward to having a landscaping budget that won't be slashed before I've signed off the first order.'

'You know what they say about the grass being greener,' Sam warned, although his heart wasn't in it. Jack's new job as landscaper for a construction company sounded ideal for his friend and he wished him well.

'I know, and between you and me, I'm terrified. I'm already working up my first scheme and I'm going to have to put a team together pretty quickly when I start in a few weeks. I want to hit the ground running so if you're looking to move on yourself . . . ?'

Sam was already shaking his head. 'No, thanks,' he said, and then his words caught in his throat as a thought struck him. 'But if you're taking people on, give me a shout. I may be able to put someone your way, if only for general labour.'

'Sure, but it was you I was after, Sam.'

'Sorry, Jack. I'm not looking for a new challenge. I'm happy where I am, you know that.'

'You're easily pleased, I'll give you that. You don't ask much from life, do you, Sam?'

It was a rhetorical question and a subject that Jack had raised regularly. He couldn't accept that Sam should be content with his minimalist existence. 'Would it shut you up for once if I told you that I'm courting a young lass?'

Jack came to a stop and began stumbling over his words. 'You're joking? You? No, I don't believe it. Sam McIntyre has actually asked someone out on a date?' he asked, then laughed when he caught the look on Sam's face. 'She asked *you* out, didn't she?'

'Anna,' Sam said by way of an answer. 'One of the teachers from St Mary's. We've gone out a few times.'

'So it's serious, then?'

'It's a handful of dates,' Sam corrected. He wasn't yet sure if he was doing the right thing. He couldn't deny he was enjoying Anna's company and looked forward to their dates, but there was a long way to go before he would feel worthy of stepping out with a young, beautiful woman on his arm. The first time they had kissed, Sam had wanted to pull back and ask Anna if she was really sure she knew what she was doing, but he hadn't been able to resist her, which she undoubtedly knew.

They carried on walking towards the main gate and Sam was too busy squirming under Jack's cross-examination to even register that he was looking over in the direction of the Allerton Oak, not until he saw a small figure running away, her blonde hair billowing in the breeze like the sail of a ship. A month had passed since he had seen Jasmine, although she had played on his mind more than he would like to admit. She might not have realized but she had put her trust in Sam by believing everything he had told her, just like another little girl had once done, and he didn't want to be proven a liar, not again.

'Why don't you invite Anna to my leaving do?' Jack was saying. 'It's only a few drinks, no pressure, and the pub has plenty of exits in case the interrogation gets too much for you. Everyone, and I mean *everyone*, is going to want to meet her, including Sheila, and my wife will not forgive you if you don't come.'

'Maybe,' Sam said, but he wasn't even listening now. He made a rash promise to ask Anna along and then told Jack he had remembered something that needed checking before he headed home.

By the time Sam reached the tree, the only sign that the girl had even been there was a small ball of pink paper. When he read the note, it tore at his tender heart.

To my Wishing Tree,

I'm sorry Tree! You're too old to be granting a stupid wish from a stupider girl so please don't feel bad about it.

And I'm not making any more wishes because I'm going to help Mum and Dad myself. I don't even care if I have to work all day and never ever sleep and I can't sleep anyway because I keep hearing Mum crying. I'm going to make Mum and Dad brekfast I'm going to make Mum smile and maybe Dad will see I'm not a useless lump like he says and he'll be happier too.

So don't worry about the job for Dad and if you

45

do have any power left to grant wishes then use it to
make yourself better. I know you still hurt.

With all my love,

Jasmine xxx

Sam thought there was more than enough light in the apartment, but at Anna's insistence he got up and moved towards the door where his finger hovered over the light switch. The cooling sun remained strong enough to pick out the scattered pieces of furniture and the slender figure of the woman who had arrived like a tornado in his life, spinning his head and his emotions and, at that particular moment, scattering pieces of paper across the dining table.

Anna's dark hair fell loosely over her shoulders and she had a daisy tucked behind her ear, taken from the posy he had given her earlier. She had put the rest of the flowers in a pint glass, the nearest alternative he had to a vase, and they had been placed in the centre of the table while they ate dinner, only to be relegated to the window ledge once they began looking at Sam's drawings. Anna opened up another sketch book now and squinted at the first page, only then noticing Sam's prevarication. When she fixed him with her steely glare, he was forced into action and flicked the light switch, which chased away the shadows he hadn't even been aware existed.

'Let's spread ourselves out,' she said.

Scooping up a pile of Sam's drawings, Anna proceeded to lay them out on the vast open space provided by the apartment's bare, polished floorboards. Next she picked up the two wine glasses from the dining table and motioned Sam to sit amongst his drawings before joining him.

'You *have* to do something with these,' she told him. 'And I don't mean pasting them onto a worksheet for the Year Fours.' Her eyes soaked up every detail of the countless sketches of squirrels and magpies, primroses and azaleas. He had even found beauty in the litter strewn along the paths, but his most impressive collection of sketches was of the thousand-year-old tree. Sam had recorded its life through the seasons, up close and from a distance. In one he had drawn bare branches that exposed its age, and in another captured its strength as it raised its heavy, green canopy towards the life-giving sun.

'Such as?'

Anna lined up the sketches of the tree. 'We could create a story about the Wishing Tree.'

'We?'

Taking a sip of wine, Anna was thoughtful for a moment. 'I could write it and you could do the illustrations. We could make it into a book and even if we couldn't get a book deal, we could self-publish.'

Sam scratched his beard. 'Yeah, and circulate the story so even more kids can come along to throw litter at the tree.'

'We could adapt the story so that the wishes don't need to be written down.' She nudged him. 'You should bear that in mind next time I make you tell the story. Just tell the kids they have to touch a branch and it will read their mind and hey presto, no litter.'

The frown had appeared on Sam's face before he had a chance to hide it.

'What?'

'I don't want to give the children false hope,' he said.

He looked into Anna's eyes and tried to soak up her enthusiasm, but his conscience wouldn't be eased as he thought of a small shoebox he kept tucked beneath his bed out of sight. It was decorated with sheets of origami squares and was one of the more colourful of his possessions, if not the most precious. It was where he kept all the paper cranes he had made over the years, hundreds of them . . . and the last two were made from bright pink paper; one containing a wish and the other a declaration that had felt more like a plea aimed directly at Sam's heart. While he understood that feeble wishes were no replacement for action, he couldn't leave such a burden on the shoulders of an eight-year-old child.

Every time he met Anna, he had wanted to hear news of the little girl, but so far he had resisted asking directly and, of course, Jasmine was not one of Miss Jenkins' most notorious pupils and so hadn't been mentioned since their first date.

Anna put down her glass and inveigled herself into Sam's arms with little resistance. 'Is it such a bad thing to have a little magic in our lives?'

The warmth of her body melted Sam's resolve and he found himself saying, 'What about that girl who went missing from your class? She went home thinking her dad was going to get a job because she had asked the tree.'

'You read her wish?' Anna asked. She had placed her hand on his face and, feeling the glow of his cheeks, found her answer.

'I'm sorry I did now because I feel responsible,' he confessed. 'Which is why I've been thinking of a way I might be able to help.'

Sam then went on to tell Anna about Jack's plans and how he might be persuaded to offer Jasmine's dad some work. Anna confirmed that Finn was still a regular in the pub so she didn't think he had found a job yet. Sam already knew this from Jasmine's second note but he said nothing; he had shared enough of her secrets and would share no more.

'Maybe that tree of yours does have special powers after all. What if it wasn't a coincidence that you found a job opportunity? Maybe you're a vessel, carrying out the tree's wishes,' Anna said. She was trying to sound mystical but the effect was lost when she laughed.

Sam wasn't about to be drawn into a world of the supernatural but neither was he ready to give up on the idea of granting a little girl's wish. 'So will you help me then?'

'Seriously?'

'You know this Finn a bit, so you could engineer a meeting,' he said as if the idea had only just occurred. 'I'm going to Jack's leaving do in a couple of weeks. We could meet up in the King's Arms first and, if the gods are on our side, Finn might be there too. I could mention where I'm going and drop into the conversation how my pal is taking on labourers. You said he worked in a builders' merchants so I'm guessing he's got some transferrable skills that Jack could put to good use.'

'You've got this all worked out, haven't you?' she asked as she took the glass from Sam's hand and set it down on the floor next to her own. She leant into him, pushing him back until he was pinned down against the hard surface of the floorboards. Anna's body was supplicant by contrast but just as immovable. 'So am *I* invited to this leaving do?'

'Actually, Jack did mention it, but I thought it would be a bit too soon,' he added, not sure if he was still talking about the invitation. Their relationship so far had amounted to only half a dozen dates and while there was plenty of kissing, they hadn't taken it further, not yet.

'I would like to meet your friends,' Anna said as she leaned in to brush her lips lightly over his. 'I'd like to get to know you so much better.' She kissed him briefly.

He wanted Anna, of that there was no doubt, but there would always be a part of Sam that resisted getting closer emotionally. But Anna was already close physically and he had no desire to push her away.

'Invite me, Sam,' she whispered in his ear.

Aware that Anna hadn't agreed to help with Jasmine's wish yet, Sam was done for. 'Do I have a choice?' he asked.

Anna could sense victory and kissed him again, more deeply this time. When she lifted her head, her nose was wrinkled. Pulling the flower from her hair, she trailed it across Sam's chin. 'That beard of yours is going to leave my face red raw by the morning,' she promised.

8

Sam hadn't known what kind of trouble he had been stepping into when he had decided to offer a helping hand to the Petersons, but he refused to feel guilty about trying to grant a little girl's wish. If he regretted anything, it was telling Anna about that first one, but at least he hadn't shared any more. 'I didn't tell you about the wish because I fail to see how it would help find Jasmine.'

'Let me be the judge of that,' DCI Harper said.

'All right then, yes, I knew Jasmine wanted her dad to find a job. Is it a crime now to want to help someone?' Sam demanded.

'I suppose that depends on the motive,' Harper said. 'What was in it for you, Mr McIntyre?'

Before Sam could reply, static crackled through the air as a police radio came to life. The police officer who had returned to his sentry duty by the door stepped out onto the landing to speak to his colleagues.

Sam took a look out of the window and noticed another

51

police car drawing up outside. 'Has something happened?' he asked.

Harper didn't bother to look outside but took a seat opposite Sam, having decided he was going to be there for a while. He checked his notes again, if only to kill time while he waited for his colleague to return. He didn't have to wait long, and when he did come back into the room, the officer slipped Harper a note while avoiding any eye contact with Sam.

'Would you mind if we searched your apartment, Mr McIntyre?' Harper asked Sam.

'You won't find her here.'

'I'm starting to think we won't find much of anything here. Were you planning on going away, by any chance?'

A flush rose to Sam's cooling cheeks, but before he could reply, the detective followed up his question with another. 'Is that why you called your employers this morning and told them you were handing in your notice with immediate effect?'

Sam didn't look at Harper but stared into the depths of his half-empty glass of water. 'I'd simply decided it was time to move on. I never intended remaining in Liverpool long-term and I'd already stayed longer than I ever expected.'

Harper leaned back against the dining room chair, which groaned under his weight. 'So you'd really had enough of all those schoolchildren flocking to the park to hang off your every word?'

'I've given guided tours for years to people of all ages, here and in Edinburgh.'

Frowning, Harper lifted up the note the policeman had given

him. 'But your actual job is as a gardener at Calderstones, not a park ranger.'

'Yes, but I started volunteering my time when the ranger services were cut back. It was still an official duty and I've been DBS checked, if that's what you're wondering. I don't have a criminal record.'

'Oh, I already know that, Mr McIntyre. No one's suggesting otherwise.'

'Then what exactly are you suggesting?'

'Absolutely nothing,' Harper replied and immediately changed tack. 'Do you have family back in Scotland?'

'I was married yes, but we're divorced now.'

Harper nodded and Sam couldn't tell if he was noting the answer or confirming it was correct. 'Children?'

'No.'

There was a moment when Harper held his gaze and Sam didn't know what he was going to ask next but he dreaded it anyway.

'I might want to speak to your wife, sorry, your ex-wife,' Harper said at last. 'Do you have her contact details?' Harper had lifted his pen to his notepad in readiness.

'You might have difficulty there. She was going on her honeymoon this morning so she'll probably be mid-flight by now,' Sam said. He was getting to know Harper and had the answer to his next remark before it left his lips. 'But of course you can have her details if it helps.'

'You haven't had much success with relationships, have you, Mr McIntyre?' Harper said. 'Why did you break up with Miss Jenkins, by the way? She's young and pretty by all accounts. What went wrong? Wasn't she your type, either?'

'We dated briefly and it didn't work out, that's all there was to it,' Sam replied, not sure how he was remaining calm.

'Was it something specifically that caused a rift in that particular relationship?' Harper asked, and then cocked his head before adding, 'Was she worried about your obsession with the Petersons?'

'You'd have to ask her that,' Sam answered, too quickly to see the trap.

'We will,' Harper replied with a satisfied smile. 'But it's good to hear that at least you recognize your obsession – which wasn't only limited to Jasmine, was it?'

9

Sunday 31 May 2015

Sam pressed his chin against his chest as he concentrated on pushing the mower steadily down the length of the garden towards the house, careful to keep in line with the neat stripe of newly cut grass he had already made. He had wanted to begin the task hours ago but knew his neighbours might have taken exception to being woken up by the buzz of a lawn mower on a lazy, hazy Sunday morning. Even at ten o'clock, he suspected some would think it too early. He looked towards the house for signs of life. The curtains were still drawn on the ground floor, but as he cast his gaze higher, he spotted Anna sitting on the ledge of his bedroom window with a cup of coffee in her hand, wrapped in nothing but an old shirt she had taken from his wardrobe. Her smile warmed his heart more than the sun on his back.

She had transformed his life in such a short space of time. His previous existence had been little more than a long list of chores with his future laid out like a to-do-list. When he wasn't working, either in his official and unofficial capacity, Sam helped Selina with jobs around the house and if she didn't need anything doing then he had been known to extend the offer to her friends. The time he had left was focused on either running or sketching.

That wasn't to say that he was completely comfortable with his newly acquired social life. He tried to tell himself he was out of practice and it would take time to adapt, but there was more to it than that – there always was. Anna was distracting him from the memories that might otherwise haunt him, but rather than a blessing, it made him feel guilty. He *deserved* to live with the pain.

Sam reached the edge of the lawn and promptly did a U-turn before steering the mower across the next strip of grass waiting to be cut to within an inch of its life. He could feel Anna's eyes boring into him. She was unlike any woman he had ever met. Kirsten had been calm and considered, a mirror image of Sam in many ways, whereas Anna came across as not only sure of herself but of him, too. He could feel himself being swept along by her enthusiasm for the potential of their relationship. Unlike Sam, she wasn't interested in the past. Yes, they both had histories, but she looked only to the future and was helping Sam lift his head to the horizon too.

When he turned the mower again, he looked up to find Selina standing on the decking area that ran the full length of the house. The old lady was bent double, with one hand banging desperately against her chest. Sam was horrified to see her face contorted and tears flowing down her cheeks. He cut off the engine and was about to rush over, then stopped himself. He had to wait a full minute for his landlady to compose herself and bring the gales of laughter under control.

Sam scratched his chin as he waited, which only made the old lady crease up again. 'Stop it!' she cried, wiping the tears from her eyes. 'Oh, Sam, you're such a sight!'

Clenching his jaw and refusing to even smile, Sam asked, 'Why? What's wrong with you, woman?'

Selina bit her lip. 'I'm sorry, really I am. You look . . .' There was another burst of laughter. She took a deep breath. 'You just look so different without a beard.'

Sam glared at her but couldn't wipe the smile from her face.

'I suppose we have Anna to thank for that,' she said, still giggling.

'I practically had to lock him in the bathroom,' Anna said.

She had appeared from the house behind Selina and the two women smiled at each other. 'He looks so young without it,' Selina said, then started breaking up again. 'That's it! He looks baby-faced!'

'He has this hang up about me being ten years younger – but look at him now, you'd never guess the age gap, would you?'

Selina came towards Sam and put her weathered hand softly against his cheek. 'He's like a new man.'

'So what was so wrong with the old one?' he said.

The off-the-cuff comment hung in the air as the old lady held his gaze. 'He wasn't the real you,' she said. 'He was just someone to help you forget the person you were and could be again.'

'What did she mean?' Anna asked when Selina had disappeared into the house, promising to make them a cooked breakfast to give them some energy for the run they were planning later that afternoon: Anna's promise to go out for a leisurely jog with him had been part of the negotiations for Sam's traumatic shave. She wasn't keen on exercise, but she had wanted to please him, just as he had wanted to please her the night before.

'Oh, pay no attention to her. I think she was a white witch in a previous life.'

'And what were you in your previous life, Sam? A devoted husband who should never have given into his midlife crisis and walked out on his wife?'

For a moment, Sam was stunned. Anna had been inquisitive about the break-up of his marriage but hadn't pushed him on the matter. Had she thought that shaving off his beard would reveal a little more of the man beneath? What she didn't – and couldn't – know was that his wife of fifteen years had already tried and failed to break through the outer shell he had acquired in his later years. Anna didn't stand a chance, but he could at least allay one of her fears. 'I'm not still in love with Kirsten, if that's what you were wondering.'

Anna was still wearing his shirt, her bare legs exposed and her toes digging into the sun-warmed decking. For someone who came across as so confident, she looked suddenly vulnerable. 'Yes, I suppose I was,' she admitted. 'You're a hard man to get to know, Sam. You may not realize that you put up barriers, but they're there, and it would be nice to know that one day I'll be able to break through them.'

The comment, rather than help Sam open up, only served to push him away and he stepped back. 'I just need to take it slowly. Is that OK?' he said, grabbing hold of the mower and preparing to start it up again.

'OK,' she said, sensing the not-so-subtle withdrawal. 'You set the pace and I'll follow.'

Sam had started up the mower but Anna was talking again and so, reluctantly, he shut it off.

'You still want me to go with you to Jack's leaving do, don't you?'

'Could I stop you?' he said more harshly than he intended.

Anna narrowed her eyes in response. 'No, Sam, you couldn't.'

When he saw her lip quiver, he felt awful. He reminded himself that she was a rare blessing in his life and deserved better from him. He abandoned the mower and came over to wrap his arms around her. 'Good,' he said.

Anna didn't immediately respond and kept her hands by her sides. She had acquired a pout. 'I suppose you still want to go ahead with your harebrained idea about bumping into Finn in the pub first.'

'You don't think it's a good idea, do you?'

'I think you're a lovely, kind-hearted man,' she said. 'But Finn's a proud one. He wouldn't take kindly to an offer of charity.'

'It's not charity.'

Anna placed both hands on his chest as if getting the measure of his heart. 'No, it's a little girl's wish.'

'Exactly,' Sam said and then pulled Anna closer until she was bending to his will – and yet still he felt her resistance.

Anna had talked a lot about her local. Apparently they had held quite a few family wakes in there and it was where her dad had taken her for her first legal drink. Sam had pictured a quaint little pub but the reality was somewhat different. Although the imposing facade had all the trademarks of a Victorian public house, the interior had been transformed into a modern eatery that was full of light, although at five thirty on a Saturday evening, not particularly full of life.

Staff flitted between empty tables, tidying up as they went to take advantage of the lull before the evening rush. While Anna searched out a clear table, Sam scanned the faces of customers as if he would recognize Jasmine's father instinctively.

'Is he here?'

Anna looked momentarily puzzled. Clearly, Sam's mission was playing less on her mind than it was on his. 'Oh, you mean Finn. Are you sure you want to do this?' When Sam nodded, she tutted quietly before looking around. She waved at a couple of regulars at the bar but then quashed Sam's hopes by saying, 'No, it doesn't look like it. It's usually heaving at this time during the football season but I suppose it does get quieter over the summer. Sorry, we can always try again.'

'I'll get us some drinks,' Sam said, trying not to let his disappointment show. Meeting Finn had been the only part of the evening he had been looking forward to; the rest of the night would be filled with dread as he introduced his new girlfriend to his colleagues.

Standing at the bar, he ordered a glass of wine for Anna while debating whether to have a double whisky for Dutch courage or a soft drink to make sure he kept his wits about him. He settled on a pint, only to be told the barrel needed changing. As he waited, he leafed through a discarded newspaper on the counter and didn't look up when a man squeezed onto the bar stool next to him until he realized he was being watched.

'Sorry, is this your paper?' Sam asked, closing it up and offering it back before the stranger could reply.

'It's all right, mate. I've read it from cover to cover and the news won't get any better second time around.'

'Aye, it does seem like the only news these days is bad.'

The man nodded then turned his attention to the last two inches of beer in the glass he had left on the bar. 'And there'll be more bad news waiting for me at home if I don't get a move on.'

From the corner of his eye, Sam spied Anna giving him the thumbs-up sign which confirmed what he had already suspected. Jasmine hadn't inherited her father's dark looks or his rather squat stature but there was something about Finn that was a reflection of his daughter, if only the shadows under the eyes.

'I envy you,' Sam said as he scrambled for something to say. He tipped his head towards Anna as he added, 'I'm being dragged into town but I'd rather be heading home myself.'

'Anna's your girlfriend?' Finn asked to which Sam nodded. 'Don't tell me, she's forcing you to see some high-brow play or something educational.'

'Actually, it's a leaving do for a friend of mine.'

Finn shook his head and cursed under his breath. 'Don't tell me it's someone else who's lost their job? It's getting tough out there.'

The barman had returned from the cellar and promised Sam he wouldn't keep him much longer. Time was running out. 'Actually, he's moving on to pastures new after looking after Liverpool's parks and gardens for the last twenty-five years. How about you? What do you do?'

'Nothing. I do nothing,' Finn said with a snort before downing the last of his pint. 'I was a foreman at a builders' merchants, there ten years and then they let me go, just like that.' He snapped his fingers to drive the point home. 'Been looking around for ages, but you know . . .' He shook his head. 'It gets to the point where you think – why bother?' Finn stared at the dregs of his glass. 'But I *do* bother because I'm supposed to provide for my family.'

If Sam had any doubts about helping, they disappeared in that instant. 'Any good at landscaping?'

Finn smiled. 'I've an eight-year-old daughter at home who'd like to think she can do a better job mowing the lawn given half the chance. The wife's mostly in charge of the garden, but I'm good with a shovel. I couldn't even guess how many tonnes of sand I've shifted in my time,' he said before turning to Sam, the look alone asking why the question.

Sam rubbed his chin, the touch of warm flesh still a surprise to him after two weeks of being clean-shaven. He did his best to look as if the thought was only just occurring to him and managed to sound dubious when he said, 'I might be out of order here, and I certainly can't promise anything, but the pal I'm off to see is taking on labour. His new job is with a building contractor, working on new-build projects all over the city and I could always put in a word if you're interested?'

By the time the barman had placed the beer in front of Sam, the deal was done. Finn and Sam swapped numbers and Sam promised to do his best to help.

'And if I do get a job, then I want to see you back here so I can buy you a pint. Hell, if the job pays enough, I'll treat you to a meal!'

Sam only realized how anxious he had been when his nerves started to dissipate after leaving Finn at the bar. While Jasmine's father looked nothing like what he had imagined, in all other respects he had met his expectations. He was someone who was down on his luck and had lost his way because he couldn't support his family; a man who was reluctant to go home to his wife because he felt like a failure – and Sam knew that feeling better than most. He was going to do his damnedest to persuade Jack to take him on, so Sam's spirits were high, but nowhere near as high as the man who gave him a wave as he left the pub to go home to tell his eight-year-old daughter that maybe, just maybe, her wish had come true.

Sam's runs were getting more frequent and longer despite the summer heat, and the latest had been a gruelling one. He was leaning over with his hands on trembling knees as he tried to summon up the energy to drag himself up the last few steps to the front door. He was still a little hung over after Jack's party the night before and the run had left him even more dehydrated.

Sweat trickled down his nose and dripped onto the block paving, creating dark crimson splodges that quickly evaporated upon contact with the sun-scorched cement. His lungs burned and his heart thumped so loudly that at first he didn't hear the sound of the yard brush being swept across the ground. Its rigid bristles appeared in his peripheral vision as Selina swept up nothing but dust, and by the time he had straightened up, she had stopped what she was doing and was leaning on the brush handle watching him.

'That was a long one,' she remarked.

'About an hour.'

She looked at her watch and said, 'Try two.'

'You must have been out here a while then,' he said between gasps for breath. 'I'm surprised you haven't worn away the paving stones.'

Without even trying to deny that she had been loitering, Selina asked, 'Did I hear Anna leaving before?'

Sam managed a nod.

'She's not coming back today?'

He shook his head.

'I've got a roast in the oven, enough for two which is lucky because it looks like you've built up quite an appetite. There's beer in the fridge too.' Selina could see the refusal forming on his dried lips so added quickly, 'Right, that's settled then. I'll give you a chance to cool down and get showered, so shall we say four o'clock?'

Sam leant back to stretch his spine and allowed himself a smile. 'Yes, that would be lovely,' he said, glad that the old lady had stopped him spending the rest of the day retreating into the safety of his apartment and sealing the door on the outside world. Too much time on his own would do him no good. He had thought the run would help but he had only managed to tie himself up in more knots.

After years of becoming accustomed to living in the ruins that constituted his life, the world around Sam was transforming before his eyes. To some degree he had been a willing participant, but the pace of change was overtaking him and he didn't know how to adapt, or even if he wanted to. What he really needed was to talk it through and there was only one person he had come close to opening up to in recent years and she was standing there in front of him, resting her elbow on her broom with a satisfied look on her face that eased the wrinkles of her concern if only a little.

But there were more pressing needs to deal with first, such as a long drink of water and a shower so Sam left Selina to her sweeping and heaved himself upstairs as fast as his aching legs would carry him. Within minutes he was stepping into a strong spray of water that was cold enough to make him gasp. He dipped his head and let the water run down his back and, despite chattering teeth, refused to turn up the temperature.

Arriving with Anna on his arm at the party had caused quite a stir, not surprising given that the majority of his colleagues hadn't even been aware of her existence. Everyone was at pains to tell him what a lovely couple they made and, from his beardless appearance alone, how she had already had a positive effect on him. But while Anna had taken it all in her stride, Sam had become increasingly uncomfortable and had drunk far more than he had intended.

The shower helped ease Sam's muscles, although it hadn't been quite cold enough to numb his thoughts. Once dressed, he headed back downstairs, his heavy footfalls giving Selina warning of his arrival and she was at the door before he had the chance to knock.

'Much better,' she said with a nod of approval as she invited him in.

Selina's apartment, although more or less the same size as Sam's, had a different configuration. Most notably, she had sacrificed living space in favour of a large and homely kitchen with enough room to accommodate a family-sized dining table. There were other differences too. Selina was by no means short of homely adornments and had accumulated enough bric-a-brac to cover every available surface, making the décor as demanding of attention as the woman herself. There was no discernible theme to her collection of china figurines and carved animals, nor any co-ordination of colours or styles. Likewise, the paintings on the walls were an eclectic mix and obscured so much of the wall space that there was little evidence of the wallpaper Sam had helped Selina put up six months earlier. The only thing Selina did have in common with Sam was an absence of family photographs on display.

'Sit yourself down,' she said and returned to the oven where the makings of a roast dinner was ready to serve.

It smelled delicious, as always, especially compared to Sam's usual diet of defrosted ready meals, but on closer inspection the roast potatoes were crisp to the point of being charred and the vegetables were on the verge of disintegrating.

'I know,' she said, 'it's a little overcooked.'

'Sorry,' he said, knowing full well that Selina's timings had only been off because he had stayed out so long.

Selina put her own plate on the table, her portion sizes dwarfed by those she had imposed on her guest, before taking a seat opposite Sam. 'So what kept you out so long?'

'I had a bit of a heavy session last night and needed to sweat it out.'

Selina narrowed her eyes. 'You can't fool me, Sam McIntyre. So which was it? Were you trying to punish yourself or make your mind up about something?'

Sam played with his food as he wondered how to begin. 'A bit of both,' he said at last.

Not satisfied with the answer, Selina waited patiently for further explanation.

'I knew I'd get comments when I turned up at the party with Anna, but it was her reaction more than anything that bothered me,' he said. 'She was talking about her ideas for publishing that children's book she's been going on about and it only took one comment about a partnership for Jack's wife to jump to the conclusion that we were practically engaged. And even though Anna kept telling her it was early days . . . I don't know, it was the way she looked at me, as if we were keeping our plans a secret rather than there not being any plans at all.'

'But there could be one day,' Selina said, posing the statement as a question.

'I like Anna and I keep pinching myself that someone like her could be interested in me,' he said. 'I enjoy her company, Selina, but if I'm being brutally honest, I can't see us taking things beyond what they are now.'

'Never?' Selina asked, genuinely surprised.

Sam had taken a mouthful of his dinner and chewed as hard on his answer as he did his food. 'I keep trying to convince myself it's too soon to tell if the attraction is simply superficial. We've been seeing each other for less than two months and we barely know each other.'

'There's one way of solving that, Sam: talk to her. Tell her about your feelings. Tell her about *you*.'

Sam reverted to playing with his food again. 'No,' he said firmly. If he had reached one conclusion during his run it was that he shouldn't be encouraging Anna any more than he already had. 'I'm not even sure I should keep on seeing her. She's young and she needs to be with someone she can build a life with. That isn't me, you know that.'

'You're a good catch, Sam, and she'd have to be a fool not to want a future with you. The only fool I can see right now is you. What if she could make you happy?'

'But I don't want her kind of happy!' said Sam as he stabbed at a carrot and immediately turned it to mush. 'I'm not sure I want happy at all. And yes, I *am* a fool; a fool for getting involved with her in the first place. It would have been better if I'd just been left in peace.'

Selina had been nibbling at her dinner as if oblivious to Sam's growing agitation, but when she looked up there was a glint in her eye. 'You've got no chance of that, I'm afraid.'

The comment made Sam smile. 'Ah, but I can always close my door and ignore *you*,' he said but then reconsidered his answer. 'Actually, no I can't do that either, can I? But you're different, Selina. You don't want anything from me. OK, that's wrong too.' Sam was almost laughing now. 'Yes, you play on my good nature, use my body for your own purposes—'

'And don't forget my friends.'

'Yes, let's not forget the services I provide to half the octogenarians in Liverpool!'

'Pat's only seventy-five,' she protested.

Exasperated, Sam held aloft his knife and fork in submission. 'Look, I am willing to accept that we've become the weirdest couple in Liverpool but we still live alone, Selina.

68

You've chosen your way of life and I've chosen mine. I thought going out with Anna was the right thing to do, proving to myself that I've still got a pulse, but I never wanted to give up my old way of life completely. The problem is, it's all about satisfying my needs, not Anna's. I should have thought about her and what she might want – what she *does* want from our relationship.'

'For the record, I didn't choose my lifestyle,' Selina reminded him.

Sam dropped his head in shame. Of course it hadn't been Selina's choice to live what would have been an otherwise lonely existence for the last fifty years if it weren't for the good friends around her. She certainly hadn't chosen to be involved in a car accident that would see her lose both her husband and her unborn child. At only thirty-one she had buried them both, along with her ability to ever carry another child. 'Sorry, that was a stupid thing to say.'

'I'm not going to be around forever, Sam, and whilst I have a long list of friends who would happily take my place in your life, that isn't the answer either. You may think you can go it alone, but you can't. It isn't in your nature.'

'You're not going anywhere and neither am I,' Sam said.

Selina folded her arms as she faced Sam's stubbornness head on. 'Do you like Anna?'

'Yes, of course.'

'If you weren't so worried about not being able to live up to her expectations, would you still want to carry on seeing her?'

'Yes, but—'

'That's settled then. If you can't have Anna on your conscience, then put her on mine. I'm telling you to carry on seeing her, Sam. And that's an order,' she said and before he could continue the argument, added, 'Now, is that it or is there anything else playing on your mind?'

Shocked at the swift resolution of his relationship woes, in Selina's mind at least, Sam was too stunned to reply.

'What else, Sam?'

He shrugged. There was something, or to be precise someone; a little girl who had sneaked into his heart. 'Remember the trouble my Wishing Tree got me into?' he said. 'Well, I think I've managed to grant one wee girl her wish.'

'Not the one who wanted a job for her dad?'

Sam laughed. 'Well, I haven't been handing out PlayStations, if that's what you were thinking!'

At last he was starting to relax and tucked into his dinner with an appetite he had thought was beyond him. By the time he cleared his plate, he had explained to Selina all about meeting Finn and how he had already put in a good word with Jack.

Stretching back against his chair to give his expanded girth some room, Sam picked up a paper napkin from the table. It was crisp white tissue paper and perfectly square, ideal for origami and his fingers worked their magic with barely a conscious thought. 'I'll give Jack another ring tomorrow just to make sure he hasn't forgotten,' he explained. 'He was a little bit worse for wear when I mentioned it, but he seemed keen enough to take my recommendation.'

'But you don't even know this Finn person,' Selina warned. 'How can you recommend someone for a job when you have no idea if he's a good worker or even a decent bloke for that matter?'

Anna had been voicing her doubts as well, but Sam couldn't be dissuaded. 'I'd like to think I'm a good judge of character and I wouldn't have asked Jack if I thought I was landing him with a shirker. Besides, the work's only general labour and it's not even permanent but at least it's a job.'

'Which satisfies the wish.'

Selina had been the only other person to actually read Jasmine's note and there was a look of delight on her face that removed any remaining doubt Sam might have had. 'Sometimes all a person needs is a step on the first rung of the ladder. It's for Finn to make of it what he can.'

'Another one for your collection?' Selina was looking at the crane Sam had brought to life from a simple paper napkin. 'You must have hundreds of them by now.'

Sam folded its wings back up and slipped it into his pocket where it would remain until he returned back upstairs to add it to his collection. At the last count, there were six hundred of the things in the shoebox. 'There's an ancient Japanese myth that if you make a thousand then you'll have your wish granted,' he told her.

Selina had seen him make countless birds in her time, but he had never before explained himself and he wasn't sure why he chose to do so now. He had told the same story to a young girl many years ago. She would have been a little older than Jasmine at the time and a lot less gullible, but if she had doubted him then she hadn't let it show and they had started on the project of making one thousand cranes together. He felt compelled to carry on although he had no idea what he would do when he reached the magical number. 'And before you say it, no I don't have a wish.

All the mumbo jumbo in the world couldn't give me the one thing I want. What's broken can't be unbroken, and while there are many things I will never come to terms with, that's not one of them.'

'Fair enough,' she said.

There was a lull in the conversation until Sam broke the spell. 'So where's this beer you promised?'

Selina produced two cans of Guinness from the fridge and poured them into glasses.

'You're pushing the boat out, aren't you? Isn't smart-price bitter good enough for you these days?'

'I didn't buy them. They're off Pat.'

Sam caught the look Selina was trying to hide and asked, 'What's she after?'

Selina handed Sam his glass and then sat down purposefully. 'Well, now you've asked,' she said, 'there is a little job she wouldn't mind your help with. You know she's bought a caravan?'

'Is this the one she took you to in Wales?'

'Yes, Pantymwyn,' Selina replied. 'It's only about an hour's drive away. It's a lovely little site in the middle of some stunning countryside – it's more like a little village, really. Everyone takes care of their own little patch of land and their gardens are their pride and joy.'

'So what does she need doing in this pretty little place that's only an hour's drive away?'

Selina took a sip of beer that left a trail of foam on her upper lip then wiped it away with the back of her hand. 'A bit of decking and a general tidy up, I think, in time for a family get-together over the August Bank Holiday. I've already told her she couldn't expect you to do it in a day.

"Pat," I said, "that man hasn't had a holiday in all the time I've known him. If you're expecting miracles then let him have some time to relax too." We were thinking a week would be enough.'

'I don't need a holiday,' Sam warned, 'not even a working one.'

'Everyone needs a holiday.'

'When was the last time you went on one? Oh, don't tell me you're planning on coming along too?' He was laughing again and so was Selina.

'As tempting as it is to go off to foreign climes, someone has to stay here to look after the house. No, I was thinking . . .'

Sam knew exactly what Selina was going to say. The scheme she had been conjuring up with her friend's help was based on the same presumption everyone had made at the party the night before: that Anna had become a permanent appendage to Sam's life. But that was before their recent heart to heart and now Selina knew better. He could tell her mind was whirring by the twitch in her eye.

'I was thinking,' she continued, 'that you could go on your own. I don't condone you spending the rest of your life in seclusion but you do need to recharge your batteries.'

'When I'm not digging up Pat's garden,' Sam added, but Selina didn't need to argue her case any more. 'Actually, it's not a half-bad idea. I could go for some long walks and clear away the cobwebs. Of course, I'd have to check out the job first to make sure I know what I'm letting myself in for, but yes, all right then. Tell her to give me a call and we can set something up.'

At last Selina had found a way to settle his mind, although possibly not in the way she had intended. He had gone out on a run because he was starting to feel that same urge to escape that had made him leave Edinburgh. He was trying to resist it because he didn't want to run away again so perhaps a temporary break might give him the space he needed.

10

Sam's flat: Wednesday 7 October 2015

As they sat facing each other across the dining table, Sam could feel a trap closing in around him and he had to work hard to keep his breathing steady and his expression neutral.

'Remind me again, Mr McIntyre,' Harper said, 'when did you first meet Jasmine?'

'During a school trip to the park.'

'No, I mean *when*. What time of year?'

Sam tried to think back. 'There were bluebells around the tree, so it would have been spring time.'

'You can still picture it in your mind, can you?' Harper asked. His eyes had widened like a cat's watching its prey.

'I'd guess it was late April,' Sam clarified. 'But there'll be a record of the visit at work if that would help.'

Harper looked thoughtful and his eye was drawn to the green square of paper on the table. He reached out without warning and turned it over. There was a look of disappointment on his face when he discovered it had a white underside that was blank and otherwise nondescript.

Returning his attention to Sam, he asked, 'And you met Mr Peterson when?'

Sam scratched his head, which felt flaky with dried salty sweat. 'Early to mid-June. It was the day of Jack's leaving party, so again, it will be in a diary somewhere at work.'

'And did you see Jasmine again during that time?'

'No, I didn't.'

Harper sucked in air between his teeth. 'That's quite a gap. Did you *want* to see her?'

The detective knew Sam wasn't going to answer so continued where his train of thought was leading him. 'So you meet Jasmine in April and her dad in June. You realize at this point that while you can bump into Mr Peterson any time you like in his local, it wouldn't be so easy to engineer a meeting with Jasmine again. Would that be right?'

Sam was shaking his head. 'This is sick! There's a child missing and I don't know where she is. I would never harm Jasmine, if anything I only ever wanted to protect her. Stop wasting time here, DCI Harper, and go out and find her for pity's sake!'

Harper continued as if Sam's outburst hadn't happened. 'Are you still refusing to allow us to search your apartment, Mr McIntyre?' Harper asked. 'We can wait for a search warrant but I'd rather have your co-operation.'

'I don't recall saying that you couldn't,' Sam said. He could feel his clenched jaw aching now. He let out a frustrated sigh that he wished was powerful enough to knock the smug detective off his chair. 'Go ahead, do what you want.'

'Thank you, Mr McIntyre.' Without breaking his gaze with Sam, Harper lifted his hand and signalled to the police officer behind him. 'So, where were we?' he asked as his colleague slipped out of the apartment, presumably to organize a search team. 'Ah, yes, we know how you met Jasmine and her dad, but what about her mum? How did you manage to inveigle your way into *her* life?'

11

Saturday 20 June 2015

Selina had instructed Sam to continue seeing Anna, as if that alone would allow him to keep his conscience clear, but it wasn't that simple. It was inevitable that Sam would hurt Anna at some point and the longer he let her believe they had a future together, the deeper that hurt might be. He had to at least try to stop that from happening, but as the couple strolled down the road together on a warm summer's evening he didn't know where to begin. Anna was beautiful and lively and enthusiastic about life in general, and while he didn't think for a minute he would ever be able to immerse himself completely in her kind of world, he couldn't deny it felt good to pay a visit now and again. If there was a way forward, one thing was clear: it would have to be on Anna's terms and not just his own.

'I can't wait for school to finish,' Anna said as they made their way towards the King's Arms. 'One more month and then I can relax for a while. Mum and Dad have a villa in Spain and it's free for a couple of weeks in August if you fancy it?'

When Sam didn't immediately respond, she squeezed his hand tightly as if to force an answer from him. It worked, although it wasn't the answer she was hoping for.

'I'm not too sure about that,' he said hesitantly as he scrambled to think up a believable excuse. 'With my Celtic blood, I'll be burnt to a crisp.'

'Really?' she asked.

Anna made a point of looking at his deeply tanned arms – an occupational hazard from his outdoor lifestyle. He squirmed under her scrutiny and then, fortunately for Sam, his phone began to ring.

The call was from Pat, and Sam tried not to look at Anna as Selina's friend explained a little about the work she wanted doing at her caravan in Pantymwyn. He continued to walk as he talked and by the time they reached the pub, Sam had made arrangements to meet Pat at the site to check out the job.

'So who was that on the phone?' Anna asked after they had found a table in a quiet corner.

'One of Selina's friends wants me to do a job for her.'

Sam was being deliberately vague, but Anna had already heard one half of his conversation and evasion was futile. 'So where is this caravan, then?' she asked.

Sam hadn't yet taken a seat and played for time. 'Let me get the drinks in first.'

Before he could move, a pint and a glass of wine were placed down in front of him. A hand clamped around his shoulder. 'No need, mate – these are on me.'

When Sam turned around, Finn was smiling from ear to ear. The two shook hands. 'And I know I promised you a slap-up meal but I'm afraid I haven't had my first wage packet yet. When I do, though, I promise to take you both out.'

Sam already knew from Jack that he had taken Finn on. The job was only going to be over the summer but there was always the chance his contract might be extended.

'You really don't have to thank me, Finn. All I did was put you in touch with Jack, no more.'

Finn was shaking his head. 'No, you did more than that. I'd reached the point where I'd all but given up, and if I'm being honest, I was in a pretty bad place.' He patted Sam on the shoulder again. 'Anyway, I won't disturb you now but maybe I'll see you at school. I take you're being dragged along to see the play?'

Sam looked a little nonplussed as he turned to Anna, who raised an eyebrow. 'I told you all about it, Sam,' she scolded. 'We're putting on an adaptation of the *Wizard of Oz* in a couple of weeks.'

Finn was laughing. 'I was the same, Sam. The wife's been going on about it for weeks because our Jasmine's in it, but I took no notice. Now, thanks to you, I've turned over a new leaf and I promised Laura I'd go. And if I'm going, then I don't see why you can't bite the bullet too.'

'We could all go out for that meal afterwards if you can get a babysitter,' Anna suggested.

When Finn agreed, there was little Sam could do to object to the plan, although he wasn't giving his approval willingly. The idea of stepping inside a school hall packed with excited parents and nervous kids made his insides twist in knots, and yet there was a part of him that wanted to see more of the family he had helped, if only to remind himself that he wasn't completely selfish and self-absorbed.

When Finn returned to the bar, Sam and Anna chatted a little about the play and he feigned interest as best he could. He had assumed she had forgotten all about the phone call from Pat until she said, 'So, tell me more about this caravan. Where is it?'

'Wales.'

Either Anna hadn't picked up on Sam's reluctance to involve her in his plans or was ignoring it and said, 'I'm not so busy with the play that I couldn't fit in a quick trip to Wales.'

'Oh, it's not any time soon. She doesn't need the garden finished until the end of August.'

'In the school holidays, then, that's even better. The only time I get to go to Wales these days is on school trips and believe me, it's never a fun day out.'

'Neither will this be,' Sam said. 'So far I've only committed to pay a quick visit so Pat can show me what she has planned and to work out what supplies we'll need.'

'People do take advantage of you, Sam. I bet she isn't paying you for your time, is she?'

Sam wasn't looking at Anna but towards the bar where Finn was deep in conversation with a group of men. They looked as if they were part of the fixtures and fittings, Finn included. 'I like helping people,' he said. 'What else would I do with my free time?'

'Spend it with me,' Anna suggested, leaning in closer so that her face was only inches from his. 'It would be good for us to get away, if not for a holiday then a long weekend somewhere. I'd even settle for a day trip to Wales.'

Putting down the pint he had been cradling, Sam turned to give her his full attention. He asked himself again why setting out a future with Anna should be such a bad thing. He couldn't deny the attraction and the excitement she brought to his life, but there was something missing and it was missing in him, not her. All she wanted to do was please him and make him happy and, in response, the best he could do was try to lessen the hurt. His pulse began to race. 'Look, I think you're a lovely person, Anna—'

Her face fell and she recoiled as if his words had been a slap across her face. 'You're not dumping me, are you?' She gave a nervous laugh as if expecting Sam to immediately tell her not to be so silly.

Nausea was added to the unpleasant mix of feelings Sam was experiencing. 'How can I break up with you when we barely know each other?'

'So far,' she added quickly.

'I enjoy being with you, Anna, and I would love to keep things as they are, but I can't help feeling guilty.'

Anna's eyes were glistening when she asked, 'Guilty in what way?'

'I don't see my life changing, not in the way that I think you might be expecting it to, in the long term at least. I don't want you investing your time and your emotions in me because I can't deliver what you want, Anna. You're young and you'll want to settle down one day and do the whole family thing.' Before she had a chance to respond, he added, 'And I'm sorry, but I can't give you that. I don't think I can give anyone that.'

'Again,' Anna reminded him.

'I won't deny that my past experiences have affected me. They changed my perspective on life, so if you're looking for a happy ending then you need to find someone else. I'm sorry, Anna, it's not going to be me.'

'Why? What happened that could be so bad that you can't even talk about it? What is it about your ex-wife that holds you prisoner in the past, Sam?'

There had been more venom than balm in Anna's words and if ever there was going to be a time when Sam would feel able to explain everything to her, it most certainly wasn't now. 'I can't give you what you want.'

They both held their breath a moment. They were standing at a crossroads and each was trying to decide which path to take. Sam could feel himself drawn to the route that would take him back to the lonely life he had become accustomed to, but Anna took his hand.

'I don't understand it, but I accept that you have your reasons for not wanting to commit. I won't deny that I would like a brood of kids one day, and my head is telling me to cut my losses and run, but I like you, Sam. I *like* you a lot.'

If her words were meant to reassure Sam then they didn't. Anna's declaration gave Sam the distinct impression she had invested a lot more emotion in him than he had appreciated.

'I already have a long list of failed relationships under my belt,' she continued, 'and I can't believe I'm living back home with Mum and Dad but it's only temporary. Maybe I would like to think we could make a go of things but it's too soon, I realize that. And what if your stubbornness could work in my favour – it might be what I need to make me think more about being an independent woman for a change and not someone who has to rely on a man.

You're a good thing in my life, Sam, so stop feeling so guilty.'

There was a certain logic to Anna's argument and Sam did his best to ignore the flaws. They had reached an understanding and, for the moment at least, his conscience had been satisfied.

'So, if it's not too terrifying a proposition,' Anna said. 'Can I come with you to Wales in the holidays? I could hold your tape measure while you size up Pat's garden.'

Sam smiled. 'I would love you to.'

As Sam stood in front of the school entrance, he could hear laughter coming from deep inside where Anna's play would be drawing to a close. It was a warm summer's evening and yet Sam hunched his shoulders against a bitter northerly wind that was no more than a memory of a dark Scottish winter. He shuddered as he made his way inside and followed the Blu-tacked signs to the Land of Oz.

When he entered, the school hall was in darkness except for a single spotlight on the stage as Dorothy called out to the friends she had lost in the woods. She kept looking at the stuffed dog tucked under her arm, almost as if she were reading her lines from notes hidden in its fur. Apart from the little girl's voice, the only other sound came from the creak of the door as Sam closed it behind him. A handful of silhouetted heads turned in his direction and he winced by way of an apology.

It took a moment, but once his eyes adjusted, he found an empty seat on one of the back rows but didn't immediately move towards it. It wasn't only his eyes that were adjusting. His pulse was racing and his mouth was dry.

The stage was set ablaze with light as a dozen or so children began stomping about, tripping over the scenery and fluffing their lines. The mixture of pride and tolerance, excitement and nerves coming from the audience was palpable as Sam shuffled along to the empty seat he had spotted. Once settled, he tried to blank out everything that was happening around him by concentrating on an invisible point on the wall to the left of the stage, but this coping strategy simply left space in his mind to be filled with memories that he knew better than to resurrect. He gritted his teeth and flicked his gaze towards the stage, reluctantly accepting that the safest option was to follow the story.

Dorothy had tracked down the Wicked Witch of the West and Sam was quietly impressed by the set. It was clear that more time had gone into making the props and costumes than learning lines. Although it was difficult to recognize faces beneath the elaborate make-up and head-gear, it looked as if one of the winged monkeys was none other than the hard-nosed boy who had wished for a branch to fall on Sam's head. Jasmine was possibly on stage too but according to Anna, she was only a bit player, one of half a dozen Munchkins and without any lines of her own to deliver. There were two Munchkins taking centre stage now and another hiding behind a cardboard tree. The more the shy Munchkin receded into the background, the more convinced Sam was that it was Jasmine.

When the lights went up after the last curtain call, Sam was still staring at the spot on the stage where the little girl had stood. He felt a sense of pride that surprised him. Anna had kept him up to date with the daily dramas surrounding the rehearsals, and while the leading actors had been the focus of her attention, she had occasionally mentioned Jasmine, saying that if she managed to get on stage at all, there was a good chance the poor child would remain there, immobilized by fear. But the stage was empty.

Sam stayed where he was and watched the proud parents milling around until the hall began to clear. He spotted Finn at the front, talking animatedly with one group of parents and then another, his exit continually thwarted. It was quite remarkable to see how Finn was so comfortable being the centre of attention while his daughter was a complete contrast, but then Sam caught a glimpse of the woman walking in his shadow and it became clear where Jasmine had inherited her personality traits as well as her looks. Laura looked to be in her mid-thirties. She was tall and slender with sleek blonde hair pinned up in a twist that looked both casual and elegant. Her eyes were cast down but Sam had no doubt they would be deep blue like her daughter's.

While Finn chatted away, his wife appeared to take no part in the conversation and when they eventually came level with Sam's row, she was all but obscured and forgotten by everyone except Sam.

'Hello, mate,' Finn called, reaching across the empty seats to shake Sam's hand. 'Did we wake you up there? These things do drag on, don't they?'

'It was very enjoyable,' Sam said although the smile gave him away.

'Are you still interested in going on for something to eat? There's plenty to choose from along Allerton Road or we could go into town, if you like?'

Sam made a good impression of looking as if he hadn't

given Finn's offer much thought. 'Don't feel obliged if you have other plans.'

'Nonsense, I've been looking forward to it.'

Standing up, Sam made his way to the aisle. 'There's just the small matter of dragging Anna away,' he said as he drew nearer.

It was only when Sam made a point of peering over Finn's shoulder that his newest friend took the hint and remembered to introduce his wife. When Finn stepped to one side, it was the first chance Sam had to see Laura up close. She was wearing a simple wrap dress and held a hand modestly to her chest. Her eyes remained cast down and unfathomable, which gave her the same power of presence as her daughter, there and yet not there; a beautiful soul that was easily overlooked and yet completely captivating.

When Sam stretched his hand out towards her, they locked eyes and he stumbled over his words as he said hello.

'So are you ready?' Finn asked Laura.

'To go out to dinner? I don't know, Finn . . .'

'Oh, come on, Laura, this is the man who got me a job and I have to repay the debt. I'd like to treat you too,' he said, then turned to Sam. 'I don't know how she's put up with me these last few months.'

'But what about Jasmine?' asked Laura.

Finn remained unfazed, and then his eyes brightened as another group of parents shuffled past. 'Hey, Natalie,' he said, catching a woman by the arm, 'Laura's forgotten all about our plans to go out for dinner tonight. Is there any chance you could have Jasmine? We'll return the favour, honest.'

'You mean Laura will,' Natalie said as she looked from Finn to his wife. 'And you don't have to return the favour but yes, of course she can stay over. She's never any trouble and I've still got a pair of her PJs from last weekend.'

'Sorry, Natalie,' Laura said.

'Don't you worry about it. I'm heading for the main entrance now to pick up Keira and Jasmine's bound to be with her. Do you want me to take her back now or did you want to see her first?'

'I want to see her first,' Laura said quickly and started following Natalie out through the door before Finn had a chance to argue.

Finn rolled his eyes. 'Sorry about this, Sam. The joys of parenthood, eh?'

Sam couldn't bring himself to respond to the comment and changed the subject. 'It's all right; Anna said she'd meet me at the main doors too. She shouldn't be too long,' he said, and she wasn't. Anna was leading the charge with a handful of exhausted Munchkins bringing up the rear.

'Aren't you getting changed?' Keira whispered when she found her best friend loitering outside the changing rooms while the rest of her classmates created havoc for Miss Jenkins inside.

Jasmine gave her the best scowl she could manage given that her face had been painted bright orange. 'I'm staying in character.'

Keira spun around in the pretty silver dress that Jasmine thought a bit too sparkly for one of the townspeople of Oz but her friend had insisted on being noticed. 'Then so am I,' she announced before coming to an uncertain stop. 'But won't we get in trouble?'

Lifting her nose in the air, Jasmine said, 'Of course not. I asked Miss Jenkins and she said I could. And if I can, so can you.'

Jasmine was riding on a high and couldn't have been more proud of herself. She had conquered her fears, and even though she had been shaking like a leaf she had stepped out on stage. Her newfound assertiveness had made it impossible for Miss Jenkins to refuse her request to stay in her costume that little bit longer.

'Come on, my little Munchkins,' Miss Jenkins told them as she led the remaining cast out towards the main entrance. 'The sooner I get you lot handed over to your parents, the sooner we can all go home.'

Jasmine and Keira were holding hands as they stepped through the last set of double doors and were almost trampled over when the group surged forward while Jasmine became rooted to the spot.

'Come on, Jazz,' Keira said, tugging at her hand.

'Look,' she said, still refusing to move. Her eyes were fixed on the tall man with broad shoulders standing with her dad. 'It's Mr McIntyre.'

'Who?'

'Don't you remember? He's the man who told us about the Wishing Tree.'

Keira looked at him suspiciously. 'But that was an old man with a beard.'

'It's him,' Jasmine said without a shadow of a doubt.

'What's he doing here then?'

Jasmine bit her lip. 'Do you think it has something to do with the Wishing Tree?'

'Oh, Jasmine, why do you keep going on about that stupid tree?'

'Because it has special powers, *stupid.*'

'I'm not stupid – you're stupid. And the Wishing Tree is just a stupid story that's been made up like Father Christmas and the Tooth Fairy.'

'It is not! How do you explain how my dad got a job then?' Jasmine replied with a frown that made her brow itch. When she rubbed at it, the orange face paint flaked beneath her fingers.

Keira swatted her friend's hand. 'You're making a mess of your make-up.'

Jasmine scowled again. 'The tree made my wish come true, Keira,' she persisted.

'Then how come it didn't grant my wish then? I asked for Leah to take me with her when she went to see the new Avengers film in 3D, but she didn't.'

Keira's fourteen-year-old sister, Leah, was regularly called upon to babysit her younger sibling and occasionally Jasmine too since the two often came as a job lot. 'She took us to the park though.'

'Only because she wanted to meet her boyf—' Keira's voice broke off and her mouth was agog as she stared in the direction of Mr McIntyre. He wasn't talking to Jasmine's dad any more. 'Oh. My. God.'

Jasmine followed her gaze. 'What?'

'Did you see that?'

'No,' Jasmine said. 'What was it?'

'Miss Jenkins has just kissed . . .' she began but then felt the need to repeat herself and said with a hiss, 'She just kissed the Wishing Tree Man.'

'Yuk!' the girls said in unison.

Leah appeared from nowhere and gave Keira a shove. 'Will you two get a move on! Mum's waiting for you!'

Before being dragged off by her sister, Keira turned back to Jasmine one last time. She stuck a finger down her throat to demonstrate her disgust but Jasmine remained straight-faced and solemn as she approached the group of adults that included her parents. Her mum was the only one who wasn't deep in conversation and she was waiting with a smile.

12

Jasmine's home: Wednesday 7 October 2015

Laura's muscles had tensed to the point where she could hardly breathe. She was sitting on the edge of her seat, her arms wrapped around her body as she rocked back and forth. Her nose was still blocked even though she had managed to hold back the flood of tears for the past half an hour. She was staring at a stain on the rug where Jasmine had spilled some blackcurrant juice the night before. It had been a minor mishap and yet, at that moment, it felt as if that grey mark she had tried so hard to scrub away was all she had left of her daughter.

The only other tangible link Jasmine had left behind was her Minnie Mouse umbrella, but the police had taken it away for tests. Her daughter had been hiding beneath it while Laura told her not to splash in the puddles, to behave herself for Natalie, and to hold Keira's hand on their way to school that morning. She hadn't bothered to step out into the rain herself to make sure Jasmine reached their neighbour's house, despite there being a knot of anxiety in her stomach. She had been sick with worry about other things – everything except Jasmine arriving safely at school – but what if it was the last time she would see her daughter? What if whoever had taken her had been watching her careless farewell?

Don't, she told herself. Don't give up – not yet.

Her head pounded as she tried to find a more palatable answer. What if Jasmine had walked past their neighbour's house on purpose and had run away? Then why had her umbrella been shoved into a nearby hedge? Natalie and Keira had found it when they had given up waiting for Jasmine and had called at the house to pick her up.

The door creaked open, pulling Laura away from dark thoughts that were too terrifying to contemplate. Her hand went to her throat and she pulled at her polo neck dress to give her more room to breathe. 'Any news, Michael?' she asked the family liaison officer as he poked his head into the living room.

The answer was apparent from the sympathetic look on his face. 'Sorry. I just thought you'd like to know that DCI Harper is with Mr McIntyre who says he hasn't seen Jasmine this morning.'

'He's lying,' Finn said with snarl. 'Give me five minutes with the bastard and I'll get the truth out of him.'

Laura could taste the tears she was holding back, but it was the bile rising in her throat that made her gag. It was the last shred of hope she had been clinging onto, and, unlike her husband, she firmly believed that if Jasmine had been with Sam, she couldn't be in safer hands. But if Jasmine wasn't there, then where was she? If she had run away, where else would an eight-year-old child go? And if she hadn't run away . . . As a sob tore from Laura's lungs, she felt intense pain like a red-hot poker stabbing into her ribcage, making her gasp.

'Are you all right, Laura?' Michael asked.

Holding a hand to her left side for support, she took a few juddering breaths before speaking. 'Sorry, just a twinge. I'll be fine in a minute.'

Oblivious to his wife's distress, Finn's rant continued unabated. 'I told Harper how Sam must have known what he was doing from the start,' he said to Michael. 'Anna – Jasmine's teacher – told me how he actually tracked me down after meeting our Jazz. Who helps a complete stranger get a job unless there's an ulterior motive? I should have seen it coming. If anything I blame myself,' he said, shaking his head.

Laura was staring at the rug again. So do I, she thought and almost said it out loud.

'Looking back, it's so bloody obvious,' Finn continued. 'All that nonsense he told Jasmine about the Wishing Tree. Has Harper asked him about that? It was a sick and twisted trap to lure little girls. He'll know where she is and if he's so much as touched a hair on her head—'

'If Sam says he hasn't seen her then I believe him,' Laura said, unable to hold her tongue a second longer.

'Yeah, but you're just as gullible as our Jazz when it comes to the wonderful Sam McIntyre. You were even more infatuated, and don't go denying it. Well, I hope you're pleased with yourself, Laura,' Finn snapped back before the two resumed their vigil in silence.

13

Thursday 9 July 2015

Laura crouched down as the little girl with the bright green wig and orange face ran into her arms. The flaking paint on her daughter's face would leave a dusting of colour on her dress, but Laura couldn't have stopped Jasmine hugging the life out of her even if she had wanted to.

'You were amazing,' Laura whispered in her ear. 'I'm so proud of you.'

'I was so nervous I was nearly sick! Seriously!'

'Well, you weren't. Well done, Jasmine.'

They both became aware that all eyes were on them and Jasmine would have continued clinging to her mum like a limpet if her dad hadn't spoken up.

'About time. Can we get going now?'

Laura gave Finn what she hoped was a meaningful look. It had taken all her powers of persuasion to convince him to come in the first place and she didn't want him to get this moment wrong. Finn didn't usually take much interest in Jasmine's schooling but she had told him that the school play could be an important step forward for their daughter. Jasmine had been too quiet of late, making Laura painfully aware that when Finn had lost his job it had been the whole family who had been affected. Even with the temporary job there was still a good measure of insecurity in their lives and Jasmine needed to know that, despite that uncertainty, she had two parents who loved and cared for her.

When his wife's piercing blue eyes pricked his conscience, Finn quickly added, 'And well done from me too, Jazz.'

'Did you work out which one was me, Dad?'

'Of course I did, honey. You were the star of the show.'

Jasmine did her best to look sceptical but her eyes sparkled.

'You did really well, Jasmine,' Anna added. 'And you should be very proud of yourself today.' She then looked to Finn as if to say, can we go now?

Finn didn't hesitate. 'Me and your mum are going out for a meal now,' he said to his daughter, 'and you can stay over with Keira tonight as a special reward.'

Jasmine looked crestfallen and turned to her mum in the vain hope that she would overrule him. That look pulled at Laura's heart and she wanted to tell Finn that perhaps they should put off the meal for another time. Finn hadn't even mentioned going out and she had already eaten with Jasmine earlier. But she couldn't risk Finn deciding to go out without her because, given half a chance, he would turn it into an all-night session and forget the small matter of getting up for work in the morning. Reluctantly, Laura cupped a hand around her daughter's face. 'Natalie will take you to school in the morning as usual, but I'll see if I can leave work early and pick you up,' she said softly. 'We can have a special tea to celebrate, I promise.'

Tears stung Jasmine's eyes and she wouldn't look at her mum, choosing instead to glance towards the man who had been watching her and her mum intently without saying a word.

'You remember Mr McIntyre, don't you?' Anna said. 'He took us around Calderstones a few months ago.'

'Is the tree all right?' she asked.

Sam cleared his throat. 'Stronger than ever.'

'Don't tell me you're the park ranger who spun Jasmine that yarn about a tree with magical powers?' Finn said with a laugh.

'It's the Wishing Tree,' Jasmine corrected.

'Is that so?' her father asked. 'I bet it didn't grant your secret wish, did it?'

Jasmine gave a small shrug but said nothing.

'You should know better than to fill your head with that kind of nonsense. It's time to grow up, Jasmine,' Finn said and then, realizing he had an audience, added gently, 'You're a big girl now.'

Jasmine's lip trembled but when her dad winked at her she managed a smile and Laura knew she couldn't put off the inevitable. 'Go on,' she said. 'Natalie's waiting for you.'

After a final hug goodbye, Jasmine scraped her heels along the floor towards Natalie. To Laura's relief, she immediately started up an animated conversation with Keira, her disappointment apparently forgotten, and the two friends paid no further heed to their respective parents. When Natalie turned and waved at Laura to go it was all the encouragement that Finn needed.

While her husband was deep in conversation with Anna as they headed towards the car park, Laura trailed behind with Sam. Her daughter wasn't the only one who could suffer from stage fright and, as they walked, Laura struggled to think of something to say to break the awkward silence. She knew very little about this man who wouldn't realize how much he had turned her family around and she wanted to know more.

Sam had a powerful frame that could have made him appear intimidating, but looking at his face she didn't think he was the type who would raise a hand in anger, not at all. A woman would feel protected in his arms and it had been a long time since Laura had felt like that with Finn. Her husband was a good man deep down, but there were times when his moods became so dark that he could see nothing but his own pain, and that was how it had been since he had lost his job at the builders' merchants. Sam McIntyre might only think he had put in a good word to get Finn a job but he had been a shining light in their lives and Laura wished she could find the courage to tell him.

'Thank—' she began but Sam had also started to speak.

'Did I get Jasmine into trouble—' he began then stopped. 'Sorry, what were you saying?'

'Nothing,' she said with a shake of the head. 'I – I just wanted to say thank you for helping Finn get the job.'

'Ach, it was nothing, honestly.'

There was another pause and Laura could feel herself becoming flustered. It wasn't so much his deep voice that she was drawn to, but its gentleness, although she had the good sense not to close the distance she was deliberately keeping between them. 'You asked about getting Jasmine into trouble?'

'By filling her head with stories about the Wishing Tree.'

'She has her head in the clouds most of the time and her dad thinks she needs pulling down to earth now and again, but it's not an easy task,' Laura said with a smile as a picture of her little Munchkin came to mind.

'I'm guessing you didn't know about the meal tonight,' he said.

'Oh, don't worry about it. Finn does it all the time. It's hard to keep up with him sometimes.'

Hearing his name, Finn turned around. 'We were trying to decide where to go. How does Italian grab you?'

'Fine by me,' Sam said.

'I don't mind,' Laura added, 'I had something earlier so I'll probably only pick at my food anyway.' An expert at spotting the annoyance hidden behind the smile her husband was giving her for Sam's benefit, she tried to sound a little more enthusiastic. 'I'm sure I'll have an appetite once I smell all that garlic, just don't blame me if I end up like a big Italian Mamma.'

Sam gave her a self-conscious smile as if he wouldn't want her to read his thoughts. 'I can't imagine that happening.'

An arm went around Laura's waist and Finn pulled her away. 'We'll meet you there, shall we?' he asked as Sam unlocked his Land Rover, and after confirming the restaurant and the route, they all set off.

It was Laura who drove and with the restaurant only a few minutes away Finn was quick with his questions. 'So what do you think about Sam, then?'

'I think they make a very nice couple,' Laura said, choosing her words carefully. Her husband's insecurities weren't only restricted to his job prospects and it didn't take much for Finn to convince himself that someone had designs on her. It made Laura especially cautious about even looking at another man, let alone having an opinion about one.

'He's a bit old for Anna, though, don't you think? She could have the pick of them all but you can't blame a man for trying and he does seem like a decent bloke.'

'I've hardly said two words to him,' Laura said, 'although he must have had a good eye to spot you in the pub and know straight away what a good worker you can be.'

'Yes, he definitely has a keen eye,' Finn said, giving her leg a squeeze as Laura parked the car outside the restaurant.

They were the first to arrive and Finn ordered drinks even as the waiter was leading them to their table. Laura didn't want to spoil Finn's mood but she needed to say something before the others joined them. She took a deep breath and then, almost casually, said, 'You need to be on your best behaviour tonight, Finn. Sam might be able to put in another good word with his friend to extend your contract beyond the summer.'

'Why do you think I'm doing this?' he said and they both smiled, Laura hiding her anxiety almost as well as Finn his irritation.

When Sam and Anna walked in, the waiter was arriving with the drinks.

'Sorry, I'm driving,' Sam told Finn when he saw the beer.

'You can have one, surely,' Finn persisted, pushing the pint across the table until it was within touching distance.

'Honestly, no,' Sam said firmly. 'I'd rather not.' He pushed it back in Finn's direction and out of temptation's reach.

Finn shrugged. 'Can't you get Anna to drive?'

Anna was already lifting her glass of wine to her lips.

'Even if I was on his insurance, which I'm not,' she said with a meaningful look at her boyfriend, 'I deserve this and I'm not giving it up for anyone.' She took a gulp and rolled her eyes in pleasure.

'You'll have to get this one trained up pretty sharpish, Sam,' Finn said.

Anna spluttered her drink. 'Excuse me! We're not domestic animals and I hope you weren't suggesting that's what women are.'

'No, I was simply trying to get a reaction from you,' Finn said with a widening smile. 'And it worked.'

While Finn and Anna had their faux stand-off, Laura exchanged a look with Sam who was sitting diagonally opposite. It was only the briefest of connections, nothing that would risk Finn's attention, but it was enough to get the measure of Sam. He hadn't shared Finn's joke and she suspected he had a very different view of the world to her husband. His green eyes had a softness and depth that made Laura envy Anna, and even when she looked away she could still feel the warmth of his attention, or perhaps she only longed for it.

'Joking aside, it would make sense if I went on your insurance,' Anna was saying. 'I could share the driving when we go to the caravan in Wales. Sam! Are you even listening?'

'What? No, Anna, there's no point in being on my insurance. It's only an hour's drive,' he said.

'You're going on holiday?' Finn asked. 'I can't remember the last time we went on one, can you, Laura?'

A smile appeared on Laura's face as she summoned up the memory. 'It would have been that trip to Ireland. Jasmine was only a toddler at the time,' she said.

'Yeah, a lifetime ago,' he said.

'Don't get too jealous, it's not a holiday,' Sam told them. 'I'm doing some work for a friend of a friend and I promised Anna I'd take her there for the day to measure up the job.'

'He never stops,' Anna added. 'He deserves a break.'

'Unlike you teachers,' Finn said playfully. 'You have it made, don't you? I wish I had six weeks off over the summer.'

'You've just had plenty of time off, even if it wasn't your choice,' Laura reminded him. 'And you complained nonstop about being at home all day, Finn.'

Finn was nodding. 'Yeah, I hated it, which brings us nicely to why we're here. Even though you're only on orange juice, Sam, I'd still like to make a toast,' he said and waited for them to raise their glasses. 'Here's to my new best mate, Sam McIntyre, who got me out of a hole and back into work.' He was laughing as they all took a sip of their drinks. 'Although right now that's exactly what I *am* doing – digging holes.'

'You used to be a foreman, didn't you?' Anna asked.

The smile on Finn's face was replaced by a scowl. 'Yeah, until my boss stabbed me in the back. I gave him ten years of my life and had the yard working like clockwork.'

'What happened?' Sam asked.

Finn shrugged. 'A difference of opinion; and then, when redundancies were mentioned, I got bumped to the top of the list.'

Although Laura knew there was far more to the story than Finn was letting on, she said nothing and watched as the others reacted to the apparent injustice.

'I hope he gave you a good pay off. Ten years is a long time,' Anna said.

Finn snorted. 'Not a penny. He squirmed out of it.'

'That's not right,' Sam said. 'You should have been owed something, surely.'

Finn raised his hands. 'I could hardly make a fuss. Laura still works there and we needed at least one person bringing home a wage packet. Anyway, it's all water under the bridge now. We're here to celebrate new beginnings.' He raised his glass again and demolished the first of the two pints in front of him.

'So what about you two?' Laura asked. 'Have you been together long?'

'No, not really,' Sam replied.

'Getting on for three months,' Anna said in a tone that suggested she was correcting him.

Laura couldn't help notice Sam shifting nervously in his seat. Anna had seen it too and said, 'But we're still getting to know each other.'

'You watch,' Finn said to Sam, 'she'll have a ring on your finger before you know what's hit you.' He tapped the side of his head and then closed his eyes. 'I predict a long and productive union.'

'Oh, right, you're a psychic now, are you?' Anna said, laughing.

Finn reached out a hand. 'Would you like me to read your palm, madam, or does the future scare you?'

Anna immediately took up the challenge and offered her upturned palm. Finn held her hand in both of his and took his time turning it this way and that. Unlike her husband, Laura wasn't the jealous type and was only slightly bemused by the performance. She was more than used to Finn's party tricks but glanced over at Sam to check his reaction. It was impossible to tell if it was the sight of Finn caressing his girlfriend's hand that caused Sam's apparent discomfort or fear of what Finn might say next.

'Hmm,' Finn said. 'I see many, many children in your life. Schoolchildren? Maybe, maybe not . . .'

He looked up and winked at Sam before continuing, 'Ah, now this – this is your love line,' he said and trailed a finger along the centre of Anna's supple and supplicant flesh. He gasped dramatically. 'And what is this I see?'

'Go on,' Anna asked with more than a hint of cynicism. She hadn't fallen for Finn's charm or if she had, she wasn't letting it show.

Finn peered closer until his nose was only inches away from the creases of skin that held the secrets of the school-teacher's heart. 'I think it's . . .' he whispered. 'Yes, it is, it's a hook! You'd better watch out, Sam!'

Anna pulled her hand away and swiped it at Finn but he was too fast. They all started laughing and when they settled down again, there were smiles on everyone's face except Sam's.

'So what's up, Sam, have you been bitten once before?' Finn asked. 'Now I come to think of it, you do look like someone who's been kicked in the guts once or twice already.'

Sam turned the glass of orange juice in his hand and looked into its depths as if deciding how to answer. 'I was married when I lived up in Edinburgh,' he said at last, 'but I left Scotland to make a fresh start and here I am.'

'Was it a bitter divorce, then?' Finn asked.

When Sam lifted his head to answer, his eyes revealed the pain that his words would not. 'It was just the two of us, so it was all quite painless in the scheme of things,' he said. 'Anyway, that was a long time ago, and I thought we were here to celebrate new beginnings?'

Finn raised his second pint. 'You're not wrong there, Sam. There's no point in looking back, it's what we do tomorrow that counts.' He gave Laura a meaningful look as he spoke and the smile on his lips tempted one from hers. 'Isn't that right, love?'

Despite Finn's wise words, he spent the next couple of hours regaling them all with endless anecdotes about his life. Taking up the challenge, Anna told some of her own and the two enjoyed a battle to see who could come up with the most embarrassing or hilarious story. Sam seemed reluctant at first to dip into the past but with a little encouragement from Anna, he too started telling them about the practical jokes he and his colleagues had played on each other when he worked as an estate manager in Edinburgh. Laura was the only one not to take her turn centre stage, but she was no less enthralled by the story-telling, which kept them all entertained long after the other customers had left. The waiters had started clearing the tables around them, but their little group made no move to leave. The bill was produced and Sam insisted they share it, which eventually Finn was forced to accept and Laura was grateful for. In financial terms, they weren't out of the woods by any stretch of the imagination.

'We'll have to do this again,' Anna said. 'I'll need something to occupy me while I'm a lady of leisure over the summer holidays.'

'There she goes again, rubbing it in,' Finn declared.

'But the end of term isn't for another fortnight,' she said, 'and in case you've all forgotten, tonight is a school night. We'd better be off.'

Sam had a frown on his face as if he didn't quite believe the time showing on the clock on the restaurant wall. It was past midnight. 'I can't believe how fast the time has flown,' he said, 'and yes, Finn, let's do it again.'

'Do we really have to end the night so soon? It's still early,' Finn complained when Laura began gathering up their things. 'How about you both come back to our house and we carry on?'

Laura's heart sank. It wouldn't be the first time that Finn had brought people back to the house unannounced, although usually she was at home tucked up in bed when such offers were made.

Sam put his arm around Finn's shoulder. 'You seem to be forgetting that I'm stone-cold sober while you, unless I'm very much mistaken, are a little the worse for wear. And as Anna has just pointed out,' he continued firmly, 'you have work tomorrow.'

Sam looked over at Laura for support but she had made her views known to her husband earlier and wouldn't repeat them, not now that Finn had been drinking. She simply shrugged her shoulders and, to her relief, Finn gave Sam a drunken hug.

'I suppose I had better be on my best behaviour. I can't risk getting my marching orders again. I don't want to let you down, mate.'

It was Anna who pulled them apart. 'We'll have to watch these two, Laura. It looks like there's a bit of a bromance going on. You take yours and I'll take mine.'

If there had been any tension at the beginning of the night, it was all but forgotten as Laura walked back to the car with Finn. He had his arm around her and was contentedly humming to himself. Finn was quick to make friends, but other than his constant drinking companions, he found it difficult to keep them. Most people couldn't cope with his mood swings or his petty jealousies, and while common sense told Laura that Sam would be another casualty, she hoped that he would be around for a good while yet. If tonight was anything to go by then he was a good influence on her husband and Laura could do with an ally.

Driving away from the restaurant, they drove past Sam's Land Rover, which was still parked. The interior light was on and she could see Anna with her head on Sam's shoulder, gazing up into his face. Sam was looking out of the window and, as Laura passed, she caught his eye and he smiled at her. She felt something come alive inside her that shouldn't be there and it made her glance guiltily at her husband, but Finn was already dozing. A deep sigh left her body as she refused to listen to the voice in her head that told her that there might be a price to pay for the arrival of their knight in shining armour. Trouble inevitably followed good fortune in the Petersons' lives as surely as night followed day.

14

Friday 24 July 2015

It was the long wisps of hair that gave her away, like thin strands of gold floating in the late-afternoon breeze. Sam had spent the day working on a landscaping job and, despite feeling exhausted, he had been checking around the park one last time when he spied the telltale signs that the Allerton Oak had a visitor.

He could have left without Jasmine ever knowing he had seen her but he didn't need much of an excuse to extend what had already been a busy day; so busy that he hadn't yet had the chance to reply to a text from Anna asking if he would like to meet up for dinner – or at least that was what he was telling himself. School had broken up for the summer, and if these first few days were anything to go by, then Anna was intent on spending as much of her free time with Sam as she possibly could. The open and honest discussion they had had about their relationship hadn't changed a thing and it would be down to Sam to protect them both from falling too deeply.

A dry twig crunched underfoot as he approached the

tree and the wisps of hair quickly disappeared, as if the trespasser had been swallowed up by the great oak. He half expected her not to be there as he walked around the circumference of the tree, but Jasmine's bright blue eyes were on him as he came into view. Despite his noisy approach she looked startled and not a little guilty. He stopped in front of her and rested his hands on the railings that kept out everyone except a determined eight-year-old.

'You're not supposed to be in there.' He was trying to sound firm, but a part of him was glad to see her keeping the old tree company.

Jasmine was wearing a yellow summer dress that had stains the same shade of green as the moss-covered branches. There were similar coloured stains on her knees, which she had pulled up to her chest as she watched him. She blinked at Sam but otherwise didn't respond.

Afraid that she might burst into tears if he spoke too harshly, he added, 'Does your mum know you're here?'

As she shook her head, Jasmine's hair fell in front of her face but didn't hide her completely. The similarities between mother and daughter were striking and although there was a little of Finn there too in the set of her mouth and the dimple on her chin, Jasmine's nose and eyes were a reflection of Laura's. He hadn't seen either of them since the night of the school play although he had shared more than the odd pint with Finn who always seemed to be in the pub when Sam met up with Anna. But, like Jasmine, her mother had been playing on his mind too despite his best intentions.

'Are you here with someone?'

'No.'

'Are you allowed to be in the park on your own?'

'I usually come with Keira and her sister but Leah's staying at her friend's house and Keira didn't want to come. She says the Wishing Tree is just a lump of old wood and doesn't believe it has special powers. She'd only be a nuisance if I did bring her anyway,' Jasmine said so quietly that it was difficult to hear her above the gentle soughing of the tree's branches which heaved its lush green canopy of fresh leaves to the skies.

'So you're *not* allowed here on your own,' Sam concluded from her evasion of the question.

'I don't live that far. Just over the road.' She tipped her head in a westerly direction.

'Aren't there busy roads to cross?' he said.

'I used the pedestrian crossing.'

Sam wasn't reassured. 'I know this is your local park and I expect it's very familiar to you, but you shouldn't come here on your own, Jasmine,' he said, then wondered how to proceed with the lecture. How was he meant to tell her that she shouldn't trust strangers while at the same time get her to trust him long enough to get her home safely?

'I wanted to make sure the tree was all right,' she said. Jasmine glanced over her shoulder as if she were inviting the oak to join the conversation.

'It's lasted a thousand years and I think it's going to be safe for a good while yet.'

'It is still really strong, isn't it?' she said, placing a hand against the bark as if she were giving the gnarled wood some reassurance.

'Yes, it is, and now that you know it's safe, how about

110

we get you out of there and on your way home? If your mum doesn't know you're here then there's probably a search party out for you as we speak.'

'Mum's at work. Natalie was looking after me and she probably thinks I'm still in the garden with Keira. Keira won't tell and I wasn't going to be away long.'

'Maybe we should phone and let Natalie know,' Sam suggested.

Jasmine had her pink notepad wedged between her chest and her knees and, poking from behind it, what looked like a mobile phone. She pulled it out to show him. 'It's my dad's old phone and I only use it for the camera. It doesn't have a SIM card any more.'

'We can use my phone.'

'I can't remember her number.'

'All the more reason to get you home, then. Someone will be missing you by now.'

The curious look on the lost girl's face sent a shiver down his spine. It was the same one he had seen on Laura's face when he had spied her that very first time in the school hall, as if she was used to people looking right through her and was shocked to discover that she wasn't a ghost after all.

When Jasmine stood up, it was with noticeable reluctance, and even then, rather than go towards Sam, she turned to face the tree. She appeared indecisive as she moved her hand towards one of the trunk's open wounds and then quickly withdrew it again. Sam didn't need to see the note to know she had slipped it inside the hollow, but as she tilted her head upwards and waited for the tree to make its decision, Sam strained his ears too. He wasn't sure what answer came back, but the little girl seemed happy enough as she scaled the overhanging branch with ease and refused the guiding arm Sam had offered.

'You're sure it's strong, aren't you?' she asked, needing Sam's confirmation before she allowed him to lead her away.

'When you look at the Wishing Tree, all you see are the massive branches that have to be propped up because the poor old trunk can't take the strain,' Sam told her, purposely using the name he had christened it with because he knew that was how Jasmine thought of it. 'But have you ever wondered how much of the tree is underneath your feet? Its roots reach out wide, at least as wide as the tree itself and some of those roots will be as thick as branches.'

Jasmine looked down as her mind built up an image of the network of roots that kept her tree firmly anchored. 'You mean like an iceberg? Only one third of an iceberg is visible above water,' she said as if reciting from a book. 'We did about them in school.'

Sam smiled. 'Yes, exactly like an iceberg.'

'But there are loads of trees in the park that have fallen over,' she said, looking around her and settling her eyes on a gap in the fir trees where Sam knew there was a toppled tree just out of sight.

'They're different species of tree. Oaks can't be felled quite so easily,' he added, which was closer to a white lie than he would like.

Jasmine followed Sam to the main path although she kept looking back as if she was still unsure, but the further they went, the more sure-footed she became.

Sam took out his phone and noticed another text message

from Anna that he duly ignored. He checked the time and said, 'It's half past five. Maybe your mum or dad will be home by now. Do you know your home number?'

'Mum doesn't get back until six and we never know when Dad will come home. He's got a new job and he's working *really* hard,' she said proudly.

'I'm glad,' replied Sam.

'It's hard to find work these days,' she said knowledgeably. 'It's not the best job in the world, but Dad says it's a miracle he found anything at all.'

'It just goes to show that you shouldn't give up hope,' Sam said. It felt like another white lie.

There was something in Mr McIntyre's tone that sounded so very sad, and as Jasmine glanced up at him she was consumed with guilt. Had he realized she had been taking another wish? Did he think it was wrong? Jasmine had thought long and hard about making another one. It was greedy, she knew that. The tree didn't give out wishes to anyone; it hadn't granted Keira's wish and none of the other kids in her class had said anything either. It had picked her above everyone else and now she was back asking for more.

But she needed the Wishing Tree's help and she hoped she had left a long enough time for it to have built up its amazing powers again. It had found a job for her dad and that had made everyone happy, and not just normal happy but *really* happy. Her dad wanted them to do family stuff together, things he'd always been too busy to do before, or that they couldn't afford. She had heard her mum and dad talking – and by talking, she meant the kind of conversations

113

that you never quite knew whether they would turn nasty or not. Thankfully, they hadn't, but Jasmine could tell her parents were still worried about money and the future. She was frightened that their happiness and the peace that came with it wouldn't last. She was scared that her dad would start feeling bad again and it always started with the kind of sad look that Mr McIntyre had on his face now.

'Have you ever asked the tree for a wish?' she asked.

A smile softened the creases on Mr McIntyre's forehead, but the lines were there to stay. 'I'm a lost cause,' he said.

'What does that mean?'

'It means there's nothing within the tree's powers that it could grant me,' he said simply as he quickened his pace.

'You should try,' Jasmine said. She was a little breathless as she tried to keep up. 'You might be surprised.'

They had turned a corner and the playground came into view. It wasn't as busy as it had been when Jasmine had skipped past earlier, but there were a handful of children and their parents around, some of whom she recognized but no one who might be looking for her or wondering why she was being escorted out of the park by the park ranger.

'I can find my own way home from here,' she said, hoping that Mr McIntyre was wrong and that no one had missed her yet. Keira would cover for her if she had to. She had done it before and she knew Jasmine would do the same for her.

'I'd rather stay with you until I know you're safe.'

Jasmine had no time to argue because the park ranger was striding onwards and Jasmine's little legs couldn't keep up. 'If you're so mad keen to look after me then slow down,' she told him, making a grab for his hand.

Mr McIntyre didn't so much slow down as stumble to a stop the moment she touched him. They were near the rose gardens, on the path that led to the Four Seasons Gate and home. Jasmine's grip on his hand was strong but his was limp and lifeless by comparison.

'Uh oh, I think that's Natalie coming towards us,' Jasmine said, tugging at Sam's hand to get him moving again.

It wasn't so much that he was being pulled forward along the path as Sam was being pulled back in time. He wanted to tear his hand away but he couldn't bring himself to break the connections his mind was making. He closed his eyes briefly and, in the darkness, he sensed the vast open spaces of Edinburgh's Inverleith Park rather than Calderstones. If he had the courage to give his memories free rein, he could believe he was back there, but the pain was too much to bear and his mind and body recoiled. Snapping his eyes wide open again, he found the world as he had left it and the little girl holding his hand was unaware of the desolation that Sam saw everywhere.

When Jasmine released her grip, she abandoned Sam somewhere between Liverpool and the one place he had never wanted to return to.

Natalie looked equally unhappy and suspicious of the stranger who had been holding her charge's hand. 'Where have you been, Jasmine? You're not allowed to go wandering off on your own, especially here. You know the rules. I've been back and forth to the playground twice and was just about to phone your mum.'

'Sorry,' Jasmine said.

'I was telling her the same thing,' Sam offered.

Natalie looked at Sam and at first didn't appear comforted by the sight of his uniform, but then she relaxed. 'We met at the school, didn't we?'

'He's the park ranger,' Jasmine said.

'I am,' said Sam, 'and Jasmine, I don't expect to see you back here unless someone's with you.' He gave the little girl his sternest look then nodded at Natalie. 'But if she does go missing again, come straight to the Coach House and we'll send out a search party. Again.'

There were promises and thank yous before Jasmine was hauled back home. Sam refused to watch her go and kept his head low as he set off in the opposite direction and, for the second time that day, deviated from the path home and found himself standing in front of the railings that guarded the Wishing Tree – most of the time.

Looking around to make sure there was no one close by, Sam cleared his throat. 'If I was to ask for a wish, it would be for people to leave me the hell alone,' he said with a mixture of anger and frustration. 'Maybe it wouldn't be such a bad idea to head for the Highlands and find some godforsaken mountain to take refuge. I'd feel the cold but little else.'

The boughs of the tree swayed in a breeze that was as warm and gentle as the breath of a newborn snuggling into his neck. 'What am I doing here?' he gasped. 'Why did I think I could get close to people and not feel the pain?'

Sam clenched his hands into fists but he couldn't force away the sensation of a child's hand in his. He squeezed his eyes shut and could do nothing to stop his mind resurrecting the past this time. In a juddering heartbeat he was back in Inverleith Park. His hand slackened and a space formed between his palm and curled fingers, which was quickly filled by a memory that was more precious than life itself. Thinking about holding *her* hand made his pulse race and it throbbed at his temples as he held his breath. If he exhaled, he knew his imaginary world would disappear into the ether and that was exactly what it did, collapsing almost as quickly as he did.

He took hold of the railings to keep himself from dropping to the floor. 'Leave me alone,' he begged, speaking quietly while the scream he was holding back tore at his throat.

Ignoring his plea, his memories continued to crowd around him and he opened his eyes to stare at the tree where a more recent image came to mind, that of a little girl sitting beneath its boughs, a little girl who had hopes and dreams that might come true if only someone would notice her. 'Run away, Sam,' he told himself. 'Run as fast as you can.'

Eventually he stood up straight and inhaled deeply until his lungs were ready to burst. The muscles in his legs tensed as he prepared to push off at a sprint but at first he took only a handful of steps away from the tree. He turned quickly and ran at full speed back towards the railings and grabbed hold of the spikes that would give him the leverage he needed to jump over, landing perfectly.

When he approached the tree, he considered placing his palm against the gnarled trunk to feel the strong and steady pulse that had kept the ancient oak alive for a thousand years, but found he couldn't do it. He was afraid that instead he would feel the kind of pain that was strong enough to fell a mighty oak, the kind of pain he had carried inside him for six years. And so, without touching the tree, he peered into its hollow. There was only one screwed-up ball of paper waiting to be found and it was pink.

To my Wishing Tree

I thought you weren't strong enough to carry on granting wishes but you ARE strong and good and clever and very very powerful and you granted my wish and my dad got his job and he's soooo happy. And Mum's happy too and I want us to be this happy forever so can I ask for something else? Maybe you could find a way for us to go on holiday. Am I being a greedy guts?

Oh I am. Sorry, forget I asked!!!

But maybe sometimes making people happy makes you happy too and that takes your mind off your trunk being pulled apart because that must hurt no matter what Mr McIntyre says. Anyway I've changed my mind. My wish is that you make yourself better.

Your loving friend

Jasmine xxx

15

Sam stared at his empty glass and took in every detail, from his grimy fingermarks to the droplets of water on the sides of the glass. He was trying not to let his mind fill with images of Jasmine, or to let Harper's intense stare get to him. He was doing his best not to look guilty, but the more Sam tried to act normally, the more awkward his movements became. Not that it made any difference to the detective who had one theory and he was sticking to it.

'You met Jasmine quite often in the park, didn't you?'

'I work there, remember?'

'Mrs Harvey says she saw you walking hand in hand with Jasmine,' Harper said and then seeing the look of confusion on Sam's face, added, 'She's the Petersons' neighbour.'

'I was taking Jasmine home after finding her on her own one day, that was all,' Sam said.

'You seem to have a habit of tracking Jasmine down, Mr McIntyre.'

'If you have something to say, then just say it,' Sam said with a sigh of defeat.

Harper considered the offer and asked, 'Do you know where we can find her this time?'

'No, I don't, but the sooner you finish questioning me, the sooner I can go out looking for her. God knows I'd do a better job than you lot seem to be doing,' Sam said, letting his frustration get the better of him.

The uniformed policeman appeared back in the apartment a moment later. 'Forensics have arrived,' he said.

Harper smiled. 'Good. Any news on the search warrant?'

'We're almost there,' the officer replied.

'But I've given you permission to search the flat,' Sam said.

'This isn't for your flat, Mr McIntyre,' Harper replied. 'We intend to search the whole house and we can't keep waiting for Mrs Raymond. Do you have a mobile number for her?'

'Selina doesn't do modern technology.'

'And you're sure you don't know where she is?'

'I've told you; I haven't seen her today. She's probably at one of her friends'.'

'I hope you're right, Mr McIntyre. I don't know what I'd think if two people you knew had gone missing in one day,' Harper said.

Not rising to the bait, Sam said, 'I can give you the contact details of a few of her friends if that would help.'

'Yes, that would be useful. Thank you,' Harper said. 'And to speed things along, would you mind if my colleague took a quick look around now while we wait for forensics?'

'Go ahead,' he said and tried not to look nervous as the police officer disappeared into his bedroom.

Whether it was all the comings and goings, or simply

Sam's growing agitation, but Jasper sensed something was wrong and poked his head out from the kitchen. He looked warily from Harper to Sam then proceeded to creep slowly into the room with his tail between his legs. Before he could reach Sam, Harper bent down and when he began stroking him, the puppy rolled onto his back. Sam couldn't help but feel a little betrayed.

'I've been looking after him, but technically he belongs to Selina,' Sam said to the detective. 'I presume that was your next question.'

'Actually, it wasn't. I was going to ask you what you and Jasmine talked about during your little meetings in the park. Did you promise her anything, Mr McIntyre? Holidays? Puppies?' Harper said, giving Jasper one last energetic rub before straightening back up.

'Sir?' The policeman had reappeared from the bedroom. 'The bedroom is pretty clear – and by that I mean that the wardrobe's empty and Mr McIntyre's bags are packed.'

The smile from earlier, the one that might be a smirk, reappeared on Harper's face. 'So, you hand in your resignation and plan to leave home on the same day. Sounds like you were in a rush Mr McIntyre. Had you promised to take Jasmine with you?'

'No.'

'But you have taken her on holiday before, haven't you? You're a fast worker, I'll give you that.'

16

Sam kept his eyes focused on the road ahead while Anna sat next to him, chatting away. They were on their way to Pantymwyn to meet up with Selina's friend, Pat, and Anna was telling him how she had been sketching out a few storylines for the children's book she was still insisting they write together. She was using her spare time over the school holidays to put it together and was keen to get some input from Sam, but each time she pushed for his opinion, he gave only a brief response, claiming he needed to concentrate on Pat's directions to the caravan site.

The stories Anna had been making up about the Wishing Tree were never going to grab his attention and Sam's thoughts turned easily to the girl who believed in it. He knew he should ignore Jasmine's latest wish and was starting to think Finn had the right idea. The child had to learn one day that wishes didn't come true; not from throwing coins into a well; pulling on a wishbone; or making a thousand origami cranes – and certainly not from leaving notes in the trunk of a decrepit oak tree.

Sooner or later Jasmine would realize that life wasn't fair, but the more Sam focused on the cruel and harsh world he had long ago accepted, the more he wanted something better for Jasmine and her family. And how could he be so cruel when an opportunity might just be presenting itself to help the Petersons one more time? It was almost as if it was meant to be.

'There's the Crown up ahead,' Anna said pointing out the small country pub that Pat had mentioned. 'So we need to take the next right turn.'

They were soon driving along a narrow country road with tall hedgerows on either side. Sam followed the curve of the road until he spotted the next marker, a small red post box. 'Let's hope this is it,' he said as he drove the Land Rover up a steep incline. A couple of twists and turns later and they were there.

'It is just like a little village, isn't it?' Anna said as they drove along a single track road that meandered through a scatterings of caravans, each with its own distinctive character and treasured plot of land.

'And this one's definitely a doer-upper,' Sam said as he pulled up outside the plot number Pat had given him. The caravan itself looked relatively new, as was the wide balcony that ran along its length. But the open piece of land beyond the raised platform looked reminiscent of a building site.

A curtain twitched and Pat's face appeared at the window. She gave him her broadest smile and then, following Sam's stricken gaze towards the mess of a garden, shrugged an apology.

'I never suggested it was going to be easy,' she said in

her defence when she came out to greet them and the introductions had been made.

'I think you'd better tell me what it is you're expecting me to do. Apart from performing miracles,' Sam said.

Pat pulled out a bundle of papers from her apron pocket and laid them across the bistro table at the far end of the balcony, a safe six feet above the chaos of earth and rocks. 'Here, take a look at these. I drew them up myself,' she told Anna, who seemed the more likely of the two to be impressed. 'They're not to scale and I've had to put labels where it's not clear.'

Sam's jaw dropped as he flicked through the pages of spidery scrawl that mapped out Pat's dreams. In addition to the general landscaping he had been expecting, she wanted to cram in a patio large enough for a barbeque and a picnic table, a generous play area and a garden shed too. He shook his head. 'I'm sorry, Pat, but if you want all of this doing then it's going to take a lot more than a few days to get it finished.'

'I'm not expecting you to do it all on your own, Sam. I've told the family that if they want to come here in the future then they'll have to help with the preparation works. All I really want from you is to give me a plan of action. Tell me what needs ordering and I'll get it delivered. Tell me what needs clearing and what, if anything, can stay.' Pat peered over Sam's shoulder then added, 'OK, there's not much to salvage but I'll leave that to your expertise. And if you think there's something in my plan that doesn't work then tell me and we'll change it.'

Sam turned around to take a good long look at the garden. He was scratching his head, not because he was wondering how to make it all work but because he was trying to find a way out of it. The job was more construction than landscaping, and in all the schemes he had ever taken on, he had been able to contract out that type of work.

'I'll make us all a cuppa while you have a think about it,' Pat said and then added, 'Would you like a guided tour of the accommodation, Anna?'

Sam could hear the women chatting and giggling while he walked around the patch of earth and rubble in which only Pat could see the potential. The land dipped steeply towards the far end and, to Sam's horror, extended the garden to twice the size he had originally thought. He consulted Pat's childlike drawings again which made more sense now that he knew the full extent of the space involved.

Anna appeared from the caravan with two mugs. After walking down the steps, she struggled to find a path through the clumps of mud and occasional boulders in her flimsy sandals and was forced to give up.

She waited for Sam to reach her. 'You could have had something stronger if you had put me on your insurance,' she said as she handed him his tea. 'I wouldn't have minded driving you home.'

Sam glanced over his shoulder. 'I think I need to keep my wits about me. If I'd known how much work was involved I would never have offered.'

'You didn't offer,' Anna reminded him. Her body became as tense as her words when she added, 'Everyone just assumes you have nothing better to do.'

He took a breath and was about to say he *didn't* have anything better to do, but guessed Anna wouldn't see it that way. 'It is a lovely place though, isn't it?'

Anna relaxed into the smile growing on her face. 'Yes, it is. Pat says you can walk to Loggerheads from here. I've been there on school trips more times than I care to count, both as a kid and a teacher. There are some lovely walks, and if the weather's right the view is stunning from Moel Famau – plenty of inspiration for an artist like you.' When she scanned Sam's face, there was the merest reflection of her enthusiasm but it was definitely there. 'I know there's a lot to do, Sam, but Pat's told me that if you wanted to spend a week or two here to get the job done then the place is yours. And you wouldn't have to do it all on your own.'

Sam dug his heels into the baked earth as he considered his options.

'I know you were ready to run to the hills when I suggested going on holiday together,' she continued, 'but this is different.'

Intent on looking at the dust he was kicking up with his feet, Sam refused to meet Anna's gaze. He too was thinking that he wouldn't have to do the job on his own, if not quite in the way Anna imagined.

'The caravan looks pretty big,' he mused, still not sure how far Jasmine's belief in the Wishing Tree would take him.

'There are three bedrooms in all, two doubles and a smaller one with bunk beds, and it has all the mod cons. Pat says there's a club on site and a laundry too,' Anna said before catching a glint in his eye. 'Why? What are you thinking, Sam McIntyre?'

'I was thinking I'd like a tour of the caravan. After that we can take Pat to the pub for lunch and talk over the options,' he said but would say no more until his head had caught up with what his heart was telling him to do.

It had taken the combined efforts of both Anna and Pat to extract the plans that were forming in Sam's mind. Anna repeated her offer of help but even she had to admit that while she was ready and willing to get stuck into hard work, she didn't have Sam's physical strength or stamina. Suggesting that they invite Finn and his family along wasn't an obvious option, but one that Sam justified by stating Finn's knowledge and experience in the building trade, and all without revealing his real motives which were, of course, to give the Petersons the holiday Jasmine dreamed of.

Anna was reluctant, to say the least, but she was forced to concede after considering Sam's other alternatives, which included commandeering a couple of the lads from work with the promise of turning it into a 'boys' only' break. Sam actually made a good show of wanting to ask the lads from work first, so it was no surprise that, when he turned up at the King's Arms a few days later to lure Finn into a trap, it was with Anna's full support. It was six o'clock and she was due to meet him at seven, by which point Sam was banking on Finn having made an appearance.

'That looks interesting.'

Sam tried to look surprised as he looked up from the collection of plans he had laid out across the table. 'Hi, Finn. How's it going?'

Finn put down his almost empty pint of lager that was still cold enough to leave beads of condensation around the glass, then showed Sam the palms of his hands. 'Look at these segs,' he said with a note of pride. 'If that isn't a sign of hard graft then I don't know what is.'

It wasn't exactly the opening statement Sam had been hoping for. Tempting Finn to spend precious holiday leave doing hard labour, which would only add more blisters to his war wounds, might not be as easy as he had hoped.

'I spoke to Jack the other day and he says you're doing a brilliant job.'

Finn took a seat opposite. 'Yeah, but all good things come to an end. I can't help thinking that the harder I work, the quicker the job'll be finished and I'll be back on the dole. He didn't mention anything about keeping me on when this housing phase is complete, did he?'

Jack had mentioned it and the news wasn't promising. The current landscaping project would be completed by the end of September and Jack didn't think he'd be taking on any extra labour again until the following spring. 'Sorry, Finn, he didn't. But don't let that put you off. Even if your current contract does come to an end, I'm sure he'll keep you in mind for future projects.'

Finn drained his glass. 'My thoughts exactly. So, what's this, then?' he asked, returning his attention to the papers that had piqued his curiosity.

'A rod for my own back, that's what,' Sam muttered. He shook his head. 'I get on really well with my landlady and her friends. They're a bunch of sweet old ladies who can wrap me round their little fingers, although this latest job is beyond me.' For effect, he rubbed his temples as if he didn't know what to do next. 'Pat, who's the youngster of the bunch at a mere seventy-five, has a caravan in North Wales, the one we said we were going to see. It's on a lovely site in the middle of some stunning countryside and the caravan owners all take very particular care of their gardens. I think Pat is trying to outdo her neighbours, so she asked me to do a bit of landscaping, but I'm telling you, Finn, it's going to take a fair bit of work to transform her plot of land into anything like the garden she has her heart set on.'

Before continuing, Sam pushed his papers wider across the table so Finn could see them more clearly. 'She wants a patio in front of the caravan with a path that leads down to the lower-level section which will be a bit of an adventure playground for her grandkids, complete with rope swing.'

'And these are the plans?' Finn asked picking up one of the scraps of paper Pat had given Sam.

'Those are the drawings Pat drew up and I'm in the process of translating them into something that will work. Oh, and this is the state the garden's in at the moment,' he said, picking up his phone which conveniently had a selection of photographs at the ready.

Sam waited for Finn to skim through the slideshow and watched the look of horror growing on his face. 'Rather you than me, mate,' he said eventually, which was another response that Sam didn't need.

'I've been working on a proper plan,' Sam said, trying to sound more confident than he felt so he didn't frighten Finn off completely. He pushed the sketch he had just been working on towards Finn. 'If I can lower Pat's expectations and, as long as her family come through on their part of the deal and prepare the site, I think I could do this in a week.'

'You think?'

'I'd like to try. Anna thinks Pat is taking advantage of my good nature but I honestly don't mind. She's a lovely lady and she's not the type to sit back expecting people to run around after her. She'd be out there digging up the garden herself if she could. Actually, I think she will end up having a go if I don't get there first. And even Anna has to agree that the offer of staying there for a week is enough of an incentive to give it a go.'

'Anna's going with you?'

'Yeah, she wants to help and, like I said, it's a fantastic site. Loggerheads is close by and we're planning on going out and about trekking when we're not knee deep in mud.'

'So *just* you and Anna?' Finn asked. When Sam nodded, he couldn't help but laugh. 'The two of you are mad.'

Sam frowned as he considered the idea he would have Finn believe had just occurred to him. 'I suppose I could try and enlist more help. The caravan's an eight-berth and it's fully kitted out. Here, look.' He passed his phone back to Finn to show him a set of photos that showed off the caravan to its best advantage.

'When?'

'In two weeks,' Sam said and then held his breath.

Finn finished off his pint and then wiped his mouth as if to hold back the offer he was about to make. 'The site I'm on is on closedown around then so I suppose I could lend a hand.'

Sam already knew when Finn was free and had scheduled the work around him. He had even rehearsed the wince that would give Finn the impression he couldn't possibly let him give up his holidays. 'I couldn't pay you, or at least nothing more than food and lodgings and a slap-up meal at the Crown – which is top-notch, by the way.'

'Can I bring the family?'

'Don't see why not, there's plenty of room.'

'I've been promising Jasmine I'd take her on holiday but we can't really afford it while Laura is making us put every spare penny away for a rainy day.'

'Apparently Pat's grandkids all love it so I imagine Jasmine will too. Does that mean you're up for it?'

Finn was shaking his head as he pushed his empty glass across the table. 'Buy me a pint and we've got a deal.'

'Deal,' Sam said, shaking Finn's hand and picking up the glass although he waited until he was standing at the bar with his back to Finn before he let the smile spread across his face.

17

The weekend before they were due to leave, Selina invited Sam for Sunday dinner, and not only Sam, this time. With her inimitable timing, his wily landlady had caught him on his way out with Anna the previous night and had extended the invitation to both of them – Anna accepting before Sam could even draw breath.

'He's been in a world of his own this last week,' Anna complained. 'I might as well be talking to myself half the time. When I ask him a question, it's obvious he hasn't got a clue what I've just said.'

Sam scowled at her. 'Classic teacher's trick.'

'Ah, you were listening this time, then?'

Selina tutted as she placed a mountain of perfectly crisp roast potatoes, buttery chicken and al dente vegetables in front of Sam. 'Men,' she said with a shake of the head before serving up what were slightly smaller portions of her signature dish for Anna and herself. 'Now eat up. You need to build your strength up for next week.'

After the obligatory praise for her cooking, Anna asked, 'Were you married long, Selina?'

'Ten years.'

'Sam says you lost your husband at a young age. I'm really sorry. It must have been awful for you.'

'Yes, it was. And it's not a time in my life I like to revisit.'

Sam heard the pain in her voice and knew well enough that while Selina could never escape it, she would do her best to ignore the hurt. She had become adept at pretending her grief had been left behind in the past and she wasn't about to resurrect it. 'Have you heard from Pat this week?' he asked, in a chivalrous attempt to bring the current topic of conversation to a swift conclusion. 'I tried phoning her to ask how the work's going but there was no answer.'

'She's at the site now.'

'Ah, that explains it then,' Anna said. 'We couldn't get a mobile reception when we were up there.'

'I don't have time for those new-fangled contraptions myself,' Selina said.

'I don't blame you. They can be more trouble than they're worth,' Sam said, thinking how many texts and calls he had been getting lately.

Oblivious that the comment had been directed at her, Anna said, 'Well, at least when we're away, no one will be able to bother us. No distractions. No favours to call in.'

'We have to get there first,' Sam warned. 'I've already told Pat that there's no point in going on Saturday unless the ground has been prepared and all the supplies delivered.'

'Oh, don't worry,' Selina told him. 'Pat's family have been working at full pelt to get everything ready and she wouldn't let them get away with anything less than her exacting standards.'

'I hope she isn't expecting too much from me,' Sam warned. 'I'll do my best but I'm no miracle worker. I'm just glad Finn's going to be there to help.'

'And let's not forget the girl power,' Anna added. 'I bumped into Laura the other day and she's really looking forward to it. She says Jasmine is beside herself, even if she does have to share her holiday with her teacher. None of us are afraid of getting our hands dirty, and if the extra effort means we can have a few days off, it'll be worth it.'

'A few?' Sam asked. 'I think we'll be lucky to get one.'

'Don't underestimate this girl power,' Selina said. 'I never did agree with women being chained to the kitchen sink and I'm glad to see the younger generation aren't settling for it either.'

'Ach, wait until Anna chips a fingernail,' Sam said, laughing when both women cast him the cutting looks he had been expecting.

After facing down the backlash, Sam went on to describe all the plans he had made and how Finn had helped him work out the exact quantities of all the building materials they would need. Pat had asked Sam to do the job with good reason. Planning a garden was second nature to him and, after the initial shock, he had been able to see past the quagmire and was ready to bring the land to life. He loved establishing a new garden, selecting the right mix of evergreens and perennials, spring flowers and late bloomers. He had settled on a mixture of plants for their stunning colours and exotic fragrances as well as the more hardy plants and self-seeders that would give Pat and her family pleasure for years to come.

'I hope she'll invite us back there next year when everything's established. Do you think she will?' Anna asked.

Selina was at the stove attending to the sticky toffee pudding she had made for them. She glanced over her shoulder and, looking at Sam rather than the person who had posed the question, she said, 'I don't think *Pat* would mind at all.'

'Let's not count our chickens,' Sam warned. 'We haven't even started yet.'

'I hope you know what you're letting yourself in for,' Selina mused.

Sam said nothing and the conversation moved on as they devoured their dessert. It was only later, when Anna excused herself to go to the bathroom, that Selina framed her comment as a direct question. 'Do you know what you're letting yourself in for, Sam?'

'Hard work never hurt anyone.'

In no mood for Sam's evasion, Selina said, 'After years of being a recluse, you're going to spend a week in a relatively confined space with a lot of people.'

'I need to come out of my shell. Isn't that what you've been telling me?'

'You didn't want to get involved with Anna and now you're not only going on holiday with her, but Jasmine and her family too – the idea of something like that would have filled you with horror not that long ago.'

'It still does, Selina, but I thought you of all people would approve.'

'Don't get me wrong, Sam, I'm happy that you're not

sitting upstairs alone folding bits of paper and pretending the rest of the world doesn't exist.'

Sam looked down at the paper napkin in his hand. Expert fingers that had a mind of their own were making an inverse fold to give the crane a head and neck. 'I wasn't that bad.'

'No, you were worse.' Selina narrowed her eyes as if she were weighing up what she should and shouldn't say, but at that moment her actions were to speak louder than words. She stood up and went over to a kitchen drawer where she pulled out an envelope made from luxurious cream paper. It had an embossed rose on the back.

Sam's eyes widened. 'She sent you one too?'

'Of course. You don't think Kirsten was relying on you to extend the wedding invitation to me, do you? She's presuming I'm your plus one, given she has no idea about you and Anna.' Realizing she had rendered Sam speechless, she continued. 'She would like you to be there, and if you don't want to take Anna, I don't mind being there to give you some moral support.'

Rather than open his mouth, Sam pursed his lips. He had received the invitation to his ex-wife's wedding weeks ago but still hadn't opened it. The cursive hand-writing, along with the fancy envelope, had told him all he needed to know and, when he had shoved it into a drawer, he had pushed the news to the back of his mind too, locked away along with all the memories and emotions he would be forced to confront if ever he returned to his hometown. 'No, Selina. We've both moved on,' he said at last.

'What's this?' Anna asked, appearing suddenly while

Selina and Sam had been giving the cream envelope their full attention.

Selina fumbled briefly as she returned the invitation to the drawer. 'Oh, nothing,' she said, as if the secret were hers and Anna shouldn't ask.

Sam knew Anna better. She might let the matter go unchallenged now but she would only ask him later and she would keep on asking until he gave in. 'It's an invite to my ex-wife's wedding.'

'Oh,' Anna said, and was momentarily confused. 'I didn't realize you and she were friends, Selina.' She looked from one guilty expression to the other, settling her gaze on Sam's face. 'You had one too?'

'I'm happy for Kirsten, but I won't be going. I don't want to go back, Anna,' he said and hoped he sounded sincere enough to ease his girlfriend's insecurities.

'Oh,' she said again.

For someone who had claimed to have doubled in size since being force fed Selina's roast dinner, Anna looked small and fragile. Sam stood up and slipped an arm around her waist but when he spoke, it was to Selina. 'Could you reply on behalf of the both of us? Wish Kirsten and Rob all the best for the future but tell her I'm otherwise engaged.'

'If that's what you want,' Selina said.

'Yes,' Sam said, and pulled Anna a fraction closer. 'Yes, it is.'

Sam was comforted by the certainty in his words, but while he felt Anna relax too, Selina remained stony faced and unconvinced.

18

Saturday 15 August 2015

For the peak of summer, the temperature wasn't particularly warm and the seamless white clouds covering the sun had also sliced off the top of the Welsh mountains. Sam and Anna said very little on the drive to Pantymwyn but the silence between them was a comfortable one. They were looking forward to their week away, Sam eager to raise a garden from the sodden earth and Anna just as keen to nurture their budding relationship.

Looking through the rear-view mirror, Sam peered through the jungle of plants that had been packed into the back of the Land Rover to check the road behind them. He was searching for the red Volvo that had been following them, but as the Crown pub came into view, the Volvo had fallen back in a queue of traffic. Sam flicked his indicator and kept one eye in the mirror as he made the turn. The cars that had been immediately behind the Land Rover carried straight on and Sam slowed as he waited until the Volvo caught up to him. Finn was behind the steering wheel, wearing sunglasses despite the lack of sun, and he reached his hand out of the window and waved. When Sam lowered his own window and waved back, he could hear the noise coming from the Petersons' car. They were all singing about being wild rovers.

Anna started laughing. 'I remember singing that on the school bus when I was a kid,' she said. 'I tried getting my class to sing it on one of our trips but the head wasn't too keen on teaching impressionable young children a song about drinking whisky and beer.'

When Sam drove off again, the roar of the engine silenced the family sing-song and he tried not to notice the anxiety that made his chest feel tight. He was wondering, and not for the first time, if he was doing the right thing. He had been so determined to fight against his urge to retreat that he was in danger of pushing himself too far in the opposite direction. And at the forefront of his mind was Jasmine; the little girl who had resigned herself to living in the shadows; the unseen child that Sam had found impossible to ignore. And not only the child, but the mother too. He had seen Laura only briefly that morning when he pulled up at Finn's house and waited for the family to pile into their car. Who needed sunshine when there had been so much light in Laura and Jasmine's eyes? What the hell was he doing?

'Here's the moment of truth,' Anna warned when they came to a stop outside the caravan.

Sam had expected to see Pat's car parked outside but it was nowhere to be seen. They didn't have a key and for a moment he thought they might be stranded, but then Pat emerged from the caravan. She was practically skipping.

'I can't wait for you to see the work we've done, come on,' she cried as she pulled Sam from the car.

The ground was still drying out from heavy rain showers that had blighted the country for the last two weeks, but at least it had made the earth more malleable for the preparation works. Rather than trail across the mud, Pat and Sam stood on the balcony to take it all in and Sam had barely had time to react before Finn and his family arrived. The cacophony that had been coming from the car was cut off along with the engine and soon after, the head of the Peterson household made his entrance.

'Hello, I'm Finn,' he said extending a hand to Pat. 'This is my wife, Laura, and the little pixie hiding behind her is my daughter, Jasmine. We're Sam's reinforcements.'

'I'm so grateful for your help,' Pat said, 'and I hope you have time to relax while you're here. Hopefully, we've made a good start. What do you think?'

Finn pushed his sunglasses to the top of his head as he joined Sam. They both stood with their arms folded as they assessed the situation.

'Looks pretty flat,' Sam said, still stunned by the transformation. The area immediately in front of the caravan had been completely cleared. There were huge sacks of sand, gravel and cement and a pallet of flagstones to the front but the rest of the land on the upper level provided the blank canvas Sam needed. He craned his neck to look down the slope towards the furthest end of the garden.

'We did that too,' Pat said, reading his mind.

'What's with all this *we*? I hope you haven't been doing any of the heavy work.'

The old lady slipped her hands into her apron pockets and out of sight, but Sam had already noted the dirt under her fingernails. 'I might have picked up some of the smaller rocks, that's all,' she said.

Sam looked over at what was more like a collection of boulders than rocks. 'I can make good use of those,' he said. 'How about we add a rockery to your design?'

'It's your design now and I'm happy to hand it all over to you. My bags are packed and there's a large pan of scouse on the stove so if you don't mind, I'm going to love you and leave you.'

'Are you sure you can't stay?' said Finn. 'We could do with more general labour and I'm not sure this lot are up to it.' He tipped his head towards Anna and Laura who had been unloading the supplies from the cars while their better halves were busy surveying their domain.

'Don't you start,' Anna said. 'You two have to be nice to us or you'll have a strike on your hands by day two.'

Before a war of words could break out, Pat was slipping off her apron and retrieving her bag. 'I parked down the hill so you could get your cars in,' she explained, 'and now I'm off unless there's anything else?'

Pat had already gone through all the necessary operating instructions to keep the fires burning and the lights on when Sam had visited previously. All she had to do now was hand over the keys. 'And there's an envelope on the table in case you need to buy anything else, with enough spare for a nice meal at the Crown for all of you.'

'You didn't have to do that,' Anna said for them all.

Pat was already scurrying down the steps before anyone could argue. 'It's the least I could do.' It was only when she reached the gate that she noticed Jasmine who had been loitering by the car. 'Ah, I'd almost forgotten about you,' she said. 'There's a job for you too, young lady. See that caravan down there?'

Jasmine followed Pat's extended finger and nodded. Her eyes were wide with fear and trepidation.

'Mrs Hayes has sprained her ankle and she has a dog who's going to miss his walks unless some kind volunteer can take him out once a day. Interested?'

Jasmine still hadn't found the power of speech but nodded furiously.

Pat hadn't finished with her yet and pointed to the back of the caravan where there was a small gap between her plot and that of her neighbours. 'There's a shed behind there that may look like it's falling down but it's jam-packed with all kinds of stuff. There are bikes, tennis rackets, footballs, board games and tonnes of other junk the grand-kids have amassed. You have my permission to use them as much as you like.'

Jasmine narrowed her eyes for a glimpse of the metal shed half-buried beneath bracken and a sprawling silver birch. She managed to say thank you before Pat said a final goodbye and left them to it.

'Right then,' Sam said. 'How about we work up an appetite and get stuck in?'

'Good idea,' Finn replied, only for his attention to be caught by the oversized shopping bag Laura was about to take into the caravan. 'But how about we crack open a couple of beers to get us in the mood first?' He reached into the bag and pulled out two cans, handing one to Sam.

'Cheers,' Sam said, knocking his can against Finn's.

Anna tutted as she went past with another bag. 'Typical,' she said. 'But no more beer until I see sweat on your brows.'

142

Sam and Finn saluted obediently, much to Anna's annoyance but they were both raring to go and left half-empty cans on the bistro table as they slipped on their work boots and got stuck into the work.

At the end of that first day the perfectly levelled ground was looking a little the worse for wear after four adults and, occasionally, one eight-year-old girl trampled the earth to mark out the patio area and move supplies. The weather was ideal for hard labour with no sun to bake the earth or the backs of their necks, nor was there any rain to transform their efforts into a mud bath. By day two the gang had established a routine and the first flagstones were laid, and by day three the patio was complete.

Despite being relative strangers, everyone was getting on surprisingly well. Sam and Finn worked together with ease. When there were decisions to be made about who would do what or what should be done when, they inevitably came to the same conclusions. The only friction arose when Anna tried to make suggestions that were occasionally rational and reasonable, but mostly intended to rile the two men. Either way, they completely ignored her.

Of the group, it was Laura and Jasmine who were the quietest and most accommodating, and Sam found he had to make a concerted effort to involve them in the conversation. Not that there was much opportunity to chat because, other than at meal times, the group didn't stop, and by the evening their heads were too full of the next day's tasks to concentrate on small talk.

'My segs have got segs,' Finn complained as he dropped down heavily into one of the chairs on the balcony. As usual, they had worked through to the last rays of sun although there was still enough light to reveal the latest board game Jasmine had set out ready on the bistro table. Despite their collective aches and pains, each evening Finn and his daughter had played challenge after challenge with noisy enthusiasm and much to the amusement of the rest of the group. He eyed her choice of game with suspicion, suggesting Jasmine had chosen tiddlywinks to take advantage of his injured fingers.

Sam was sitting on the edge of the steps watching them. 'I was glad to drop that last flagstone into place,' he said, tearing his eyes away from the idyllic family scene to assess the day's progress. 'I don't think my back could take any more.'

'Digging tomorrow,' Finn reminded him as he flicked his first counter, missing the pot entirely.

Anna came out of the caravan with cans of ice-cold beer and handed them out, keeping one for herself. 'I've just checked the weather forecast and we might get rain in the morning.'

Sam nodded gently; he was only half listening as his mind made final adjustments to the planting scheme they were due to start. 'That's not necessarily a bad thing,' he said. 'Less watering for Jasmine to do.'

Jasmine had scored her first hit and had a beaming smile on her face as she looked up. 'I don't mind,' she said. 'I like watering the plants, Mr McIntyre.' When Sam gave her a challenging look, the little girl blushed. She was finding it difficult to adapt to calling her teacher and the park ranger by their first names. 'Sorry, I mean, *Sam*.'

'I must say you've done a good job so far, Jasmine,' said

Anna. 'If I were in charge, the plants would be shrivelled up in their pots by now.' She opened her can and took a swig before adding, 'The point I was making was that the weather's going to take a turn for the better after tomorrow. Assuming the forecast is right, then Wednesday will be glorious, and in my opinion, for what it's worth, I think we all deserve a day off.'

Sam wasn't convinced. 'I don't think I'll be able to relax until I know the job's done.'

'But if we leave it until the end of the week, it might never happen,' Finn warned.

Laura had appeared at the door but so far no one except Sam had noticed her. 'What do you think, Laura?' he asked.

She was surprised and a little flustered that Sam had asked her opinion, but if she had one, she kept it to herself and deferred to her husband. 'Finn's right, it might not happen otherwise.'

Finn looked from his wife to Sam as if there was something in the exchange he hadn't liked. It was the briefest of moments but an uncomfortable one until Laura gave her husband a reassuring smile. He didn't return it but continued with his argument. 'And it's not fair on our Jazz that the first holiday she's had in years will be spent hauling a watering can around all day, Sam. The only time she's been out so far is to take that little mutt up the road for a walk.'

'I don't mind. I like taking Nando for a walk.'

'Yeah, but it's not the same as getting out and about.'

The girl's face lit up as a thought occurred to her. 'Maybe we could go for a bike ride, Dad.'

Finn laughed. 'I haven't been on a bike since I was a

kid, unless you count the time I had a go of yours and bent the stabilizers.'

The memory didn't evoke the same sense of nostalgia with Laura. 'Just remember that these aren't our bikes, Finn,' she said. 'If you do use them then you'll need to be careful.'

Finn put his can down and picked up a counter. 'I think she means, I should be sober,' he said, winking at Jasmine.

'Good, it's agreed then,' Anna said. 'So my next idea is that, rather than wait until the last day before we go out for a meal, why don't we go tomorrow night? That way we can have a late night and a guilt-free sleep-in on our day off.'

'So you're planning on spending Wednesday in bed?' Sam asked, then blushed when Anna gave him a sultry smile.

She laughed at his embarrassment. 'No, of course not. I was thinking that we might go for a walk to Loggerheads together. You could take your sketch book.'

His girlfriend had read him perfectly and Sam's eyes lit up in much the same way as Jasmine's had earlier. Although they had gone for short walks when time allowed, he was eager to explore the countryside; to relax beneath the shade of a tree and sketch the leafy ferns and knotted roots; or sit down on a rocky outcrop high upon the mountainside and immortalize the view on paper. 'And what will you do while I'm sketching?'

Slipping onto the step next to him, she rested her chin on his shoulder. 'I'll be watching you,' she said while Sam squirmed, making her laugh again. 'I'll take my notepad and do some writing. I have the storyline all set out but I need to hurry up and make a start if I'm ever going to turn our book into a bestseller.'

'You're writing a book?' Finn asked without taking his eyes from the board. His tongue poked out of the corner of his mouth as he flicked another counter. It glanced off the side of the pot and the curse he muttered under his breath was all but drowned out by Jasmine's screech of delight.

'A children's book,' Anna told him. 'I'm writing the story and Sam's going to illustrate it. It's based on the thousand-year-old tree in Calderstones and it's a collection of tales about people who visited the tree over the centuries. That way it will appeal to the educational market too.'

Finn took a slurp of beer and had a smile on his face when he said, 'It sounds riveting.'

'It is! Because it's not just any tree but the Wishing Tree.'

'Oh, God, not that again,' Finn said, raising his eyes in exasperation.

Anna was undeterred. 'I'll have you know that tree has extraordinary powers. You place your hand against its bark, feel its power rising up from its roots, and let it read your mind.'

As she spoke, Anna had closed her eyes and raised a hand as if the tree was right there in front of her. No one could argue that she knew how to draw people in and even Finn had leaned forward slightly, although, in fairness, he didn't need much of an excuse to admire Anna and kept telling Sam how lucky he was. Sam was more interested in Jasmine at that moment and watched her out of the corner of his eye. She had been temporarily distracted from the game at the mention of her favourite tree and found the courage to speak.

'But that's not how it works.'

'Well, we don't want everyone knowing the real secret,' Sam assured her. He sensed Finn about to give his daughter another lecture about not believing in fairy tales, so quickly continued, 'The book is one of Anna's harebrained ideas, nothing to do with me, Finn. I'm not so sure it'll work.'

'It's good to have dreams,' Anna said, leaning into him.

Sam pushed his shoulder against Anna's while his mind resisted her ideas. The only dreams he had were ones that would forever lie out of reach. That was the trouble with the past.

19

Sam's flat: Wednesday 7 October 2015

Jasper remained on his back and was pawing the air in the hope that Harper would rub his tummy again when another dog began barking outside. The frightened pup twisted around and scraped his claws frantically against the polished floorboards until he reached Sam's side. He scratched at his master's bare legs in a desperate bid to reach the safety of his lap.

With a gentle push, Sam helped him up and Jasper licked his face appreciatively, all the while shivering as the barking continued. Through the window, Sam caught a glimpse of a dog handler unit parked on the now busy road. It wasn't the disciplined working dog at his handler's side that was causing the commotion, but rather a West Highland Terrier on the opposite side of the road. Its owner had stopped to gawk at what was happening in and around the house and Sam wondered how long it would be before the press arrived and, for that matter, how long the public interest would last once it got going. Whatever was going to happen, Sam was sure of only one thing: he wouldn't be staying in the house much longer.

Harper looked temporarily distracted too and then asked, 'You say Jasmine has never been to the house?'

Sam pushed Jasper's face away from his so he could speak. 'Yes, I do.'

'Have any of the family?'

Opening his mouth to reply, Sam was already forming the word no but held back from the lie. He was trying his best not to get too anxious by thinking of Jasmine, but he couldn't keep Laura from his thoughts so easily. He was walking a fine line as he tried to figure out how much he should reveal and how much he should hold back. He was as concerned about defending Laura's position as he was his own, more so in fact. What had she told the police? What had she told Finn?

'Can I remind you that there's a small girl missing, Mr McIntyre, and the longer she remains missing, the less likely we are for this investigation to reach a happy conclusion. Have any of the family been to the house?'

'Laura,' Sam said, his voice cracking with the effort of breaking her trust. 'Mrs Peterson has been here.'

From the look on Harper's face, this was evidently new information and Sam immediately regretted telling him. 'Just Mrs Peterson?'

'Yes.'

'She's an attractive woman, wouldn't you say?' the detective said, speaking his thoughts out loud if not his suspicions.

'Yes, I suppose I would,' Sam said with a degree of honesty. There were some feelings he was already tired of denying.

'Were you having an affair?'

'No.'

'Then why was she here?'

Sam pursed his lips as he tried to figure out how much more he should tell Harper. He needed to convince the detective to redirect his enquiries elsewhere without putting Laura in an untenable position. 'I wanted to help the Petersons, that's all. I saw a family down on their luck and I assumed that the only thing behind Jasmine's unhappiness was her dad's struggle to find work, but first impressions can be wrong, can't they?' he asked without waiting for confirmation. He doubted the detective would admit to what might prove to be a flaw with his current investigations. 'While we were at the caravan, I got to see first-hand why Jasmine and her mum tried so hard not to draw attention to themselves. They were frightened, Harper.'

'Mrs Peterson wasn't just frightened this morning, Mr McIntyre, she was terrified,' Harper said, refusing to be drawn off track. 'She's facing her worst nightmare and the real possibility that she may never see Jasmine again. I can't imagine what that's like, can you?'

'Have you spoken to her?' Sam said, ignoring the question that suggested Harper also knew more than he was letting on. 'Have you spoken to Laura alone?'

'Why would we need to do that, Mr McIntyre?'

Sam raked his fingers through his hair, which had dried into sweaty clumps. He felt a wave of nausea the moment he thought about Jasmine and his heart filled with fear. 'Haven't you worked it out yet?'

20

Anna had been right about the rain, which arrived overnight as predicted. Tuesday morning was wet and wild, but by midday the summer storm had passed and by late afternoon golden sunshine had broken through the silvery clouds. Spent raindrops glistened off the broad leaves of newly planted hostas and the air tasted damp and metallic.

Finn was standing on the balcony watching Sam, Anna and Laura as they planted various sections of the garden, all bent double as they worked. Jasmine moved awkwardly between them with a heavy watering can thumping against her legs so she could pour extra moisture into the warming earth and gradually lighten her load.

'It's almost five,' Finn called over to them.

Sam put a hand on his back as he tried to straighten his crooked spine. It was a long and painful process and by the time he was able to turn towards the caravan, Finn had opened a can of beer from the four-pack he had taken from the fridge. The other three dangled from his raised hand. 'Anyone care to join me?'

'Maybe we should be thinking about getting ready,' Anna said with a painful groan as she too struggled to straighten up.

'OK,' Sam agreed. 'Why don't you two start getting ready and me and Finn can finish off?'

'Are you suggesting we'll take the longest?' she asked.

Sam smiled. 'Yes.'

Anna shrugged. 'Fair enough.'

While she and Laura kicked dried mud from their boots, Sam's focus was on the remaining plants lined up on the newly laid patio. 'I'd say we could get this lot in the ground in half an hour, wouldn't you?'

Finn downed his beer in one before detaching another from the pack and throwing it over to Sam who caught it perfectly. 'You're on,' he said and jumped into action by opening a second can. He raised an eyebrow at Laura as she passed, daring her to challenge him. She said nothing.

'What about you?' Sam asked Jasmine. 'I can finish the watering if you want to go with your mum.'

Jasmine didn't look up but concentrated on gently sprinkling life-giving droplets over the spindly shrub Sam had just planted. 'I don't mind staying to help.'

Finn laid down his beer on the corner of the balcony and, jumping over the last few steps, landed on the ground with a heavy thud. 'Right, back to work then.'

The sun was still warming up despite the lengthening of the day and when Sam pressed the soil snugly around the very last plant, the earth was warm and dry. Jasmine's arms trembled as she carried the newly filled watering can towards him. Her foot caught on the edge of a flagstone and she stumbled, dropping the can heavily and only just stopping herself from toppling right over it.

'Watch what you're doing!' Finn shouted. He was over by the balcony again and put down what would be his third can before going over to check for damage to the patio. 'I've told you before that those flags are still settling in. I don't need you knocking them out of place.'

'Sorry, Dad,' she said and flinched when he approached.

'Here, give it to me,' he said gruffly, taking the watering can from her. 'Now go in and get cleaned up.'

'I was going to take Nando for another walk first.'

Finn's face had turned puce. 'Don't argue! Get inside now!'

Jasmine scurried up the balcony steps, but in her haste tripped on the last one and this time she did go flying. Her arms flailed in front of her and she knocked over the collection of beer cans Finn had lined up. Two empties were sent spinning across the floor but the third was heavier and rolled sluggishly across the decking, leaving a trail of foam that filled up the grooves in the wood with beer.

'Jesus! What's wrong with you, Jazz?' Finn snapped. He took a step towards her, but his daughter was already sprinting into the caravan.

'It's all right, Finn. No harm done,' Sam said although he was trying to keep his own anger under control. 'She's just tired after working hard all day.'

'Fucking kids. You don't know how lucky you are, Sam. Don't let Anna go talking you into having them, they'll be the bane of your life for bloody years,' he said savagely.

Sam didn't respond and would say little else for the remainder of the evening. The short exchange between father and daughter had been just another symptom of the mood that had been darkening all day. Working in the rain hadn't made for the best of starts, although the storm clouds over Pantymwyn had been nothing compared to the one they could all sense on the horizon and when the sun had arrived, it had brought more shadow than light.

Taking a day off in the middle of the week wasn't turning out to be the best of ideas after all, because even though they were making progress, there was still so much more to do. They had yet to make a start on the far section of the garden and there was still the rockery and the brick barbeque to build, which was a new addition to Sam's plans when they had felt a little more optimistic about the week. One of Pat's neighbours, who had taken a keen interest in their endeavours, had offered them a pile of bricks he had cleared from his own garden and it had been Finn who had suggested building the barbeque.

And while all of those outstanding jobs were worrying Sam, he didn't think it was the heavy workload that was bothering the others. Although he couldn't quite put his finger on it, something felt wrong, particularly between Finn and his family. There hadn't been even the hint of a disagreement between man and wife, but Finn kept looking at Laura as if he sensed her disapproval. Laura, by contrast, had spoken less and less because even the most innocuous of comments managed to antagonize her husband. And while Sam soaked the ground around the last planting of the day, it was that sudden insight that played on his mind. Laura was frightened.

Sam peeled his eyes open slowly as if pulling a sticking plaster from sensitive skin. He couldn't move anything else because Anna was lying with her head on the crook of his arm; an arm that was completely numb except for the vague sensation of the drool slithering like a slug trail from her mouth. They were in the smaller of the caravan's so-called double bedrooms – the bed was little more than a single and the room itself only marginally wider. The air was thick with the smell of stale alcohol.

The meal at the Crown the night before had been delicious but the evening itself hadn't exactly been the reward Sam had had in mind. Reminiscent of the first time the two couples had gone out together, the conversation had been loud and boisterous but the laughter was forced at times and the talk more animated than was entirely necessary. It was as if they were all trying to convince themselves there wasn't an atmosphere.

Jasmine had behaved impeccably, spending much of her time out in the play area, but she came back into the pub regularly so her parents didn't have to go looking for her when the food arrived. Even so, Finn had found reason to complain about having a child in tow, especially when Laura announced it was past Jasmine's bedtime and that while she was happy for the rest of them to stay out, she was taking her home. It was the only time Sam had seen Finn's wife stand up to her husband and after they had left he was sullen, but only until the next round of drinks arrived. And they had kept on coming as Finn refortified the numbers of their group by making friends with the staff and regulars until he looked for all the world like he had been drinking there for years.

Rubbing his face with his free hand, Sam's skin felt sandpaper rough and his head throbbed so much that he could feel the pulsating pain in his temples. He pulled out his earplugs which, thanks to paper-thin walls, were a necessity Pat had warned him about. It stopped being woken up by woodland creatures scraping claws across the roof and it also meant that snoring from other rooms wouldn't keep anyone awake; apparently her son-in-law was renowned for it. The only sound Sam could hear now was a blackbird singing which made him crave fresh, damp country air and the dappled shade of the woods.

When he groaned, Anna shifted in her sleep giving Sam the opportunity to rescue his dead arm. He was busy wishing it was his head that was devoid of feeling when he heard one of the external doors being pulled open, making the caravan shudder. It closed again with a gentle click and then there were urgent whispers, which Sam presumed would be Laura and Jasmine. He couldn't imagine Finn being up and about yet. As if proof were needed, there was a single, guttural snore from the next bedroom.

The warm sunshine filtering through the closed curtains was heating up the stale air in the room to toxic levels and forced Sam into action. He raised himself up onto an elbow and the pain in his head sharpened and thickened at the same time, but when he picked up his mobile from the table to check the time, he was even more determined to keep moving. He wasn't going to let their one day off go to waste. He nudged Anna.

'Are you awake?' he asked taking out one of her earplugs.

It took another nudge before she mumbled, 'What?'

'It's almost nine o'clock. We'll have to get moving soon if we're going to make the most of the day.'

Anna's response was more of a whine. 'I can't move. It hurts!'

Not to be thwarted, Sam eased himself out of bed. He ignored the wave of nausea and slipped on a T-shirt and a pair of jog pants. 'I'll get you some water. You can see how you feel then.'

'And paracetamol,' she whimpered as Sam left the room.

Laura and Jasmine were in the kitchen making sandwiches and they looked up in alarm as he opened the door that separated the bedrooms from the living quarters. He ran his fingers through his unkempt hair. 'Sorry,' he said and then winced as the echo of his voice boomed inside his head. He lowered his voice as he continued, 'I didn't mean to give you a fright.'

Laura took a step back. She was wearing canvas shorts and a white vest top beneath a bright yellow cardigan with the sleeves pulled up, and a flowery chiffon scarf around her neck to complement the outfit. Her usually pale skin looked a little more tanned than it had been at the beginning of the holiday while her hair, pulled back in a pony-tail, appeared a shade lighter. Her face was make-up free and, despite the hint of dark circles under her eyes, she managed to look stunning. Sam's reactions were sluggish and his wide, unblinking eyes gave away the attraction he had been hiding from himself as much as from her.

Laura held his gaze and her face softened. 'No, I'm sorry. Did we wake you?'

'I was already awake. I wanted to be up and about by now anyway.'

Jasmine had turned away from them both and Sam assumed she wanted to carry on making her sandwich but she had picked up a glass and filled it with water, which she passed to Sam.

'Thank you, Jasmine.'

'You need to drink plenty of water,' she told him.

Sam closed his eyes as he greedily downed the glass of cold, clear water. When he opened them again, he was being watched by mother and daughter. Jasmine took the glass and immediately refilled it.

'So what are you two up to today?'

'We've just got the bikes out of the shed and we're going to go on a little adventure,' Laura said, keeping her voice low. 'I was thinking we might ride into Mold. One of the neighbours has just said there's a market in town today.'

'And there's an ice cream shop there too,' Jasmine piped up.

'Finn isn't going with you?'

Laura shook her head. 'He'll be sleeping it off until at least lunchtime.'

'And he'll be like a bear with a sore head when he does get up,' Jasmine added knowledgeably. 'We keep out of his way then, but you could come with us if you want, Sam.'

There was an awkward pause when Laura tried not to look at Sam but he fought for and held her gaze. He wanted to say yes, that he would like nothing better than to spend the day with them, and for a moment he thought Laura might say it too, but the spark between them was a dangerous one and she was the first to extinguish it.

'I'm sure Sam and Anna would rather have some time on their own,' she said with a smile that held more than a hint of regret.

'Anna's probably in a worse state than Finn,' Sam said, deftly avoiding the answer. 'And I am sorry about keeping him out late last night.'

'If you haven't worked it out already, Finn is the architect of his own downfall,' Laura said bitterly before turning away. 'I'd better get on with our packed lunch. I'd rather be gone before he does get up.'

Sam reached over the small counter where Laura was standing to take another glass from the cupboard. He could smell her hair, which had soaked up the fresh air and sunshine. 'Anna's after some paracetamol if there is any.'

Jasmine was already on the move when she said, 'I'll get it.'

She disappeared towards the bathroom and Sam occupied himself by filling the second glass with water. Laura was still only inches away but this time she wouldn't look at Sam. 'Sorry about Finn,' she said.

'No need to apologize. After everything he's done this week, he deserved a blowout. We all did.'

Laura was slicing cheese in gentle, tentative scrapes as if her mind were not on the task. 'Once he's got the taste, it'll be hard for him to stop. He might not be as productive from now on.'

Sam resisted putting a comforting hand on Laura's shoulder, but only just. 'I'm hoping there's not as much work left as it looks. We'll manage with or without him, don't worry.'

He could sense Laura holding herself as if her whole body were one tight knot of worry and when he returned to the bedroom, he could feel his own anxiety building.

He gave Anna her water and watched as she swallowed her pills while his ears were tuned to the sounds coming from the kitchen. There were more urgent whispers and after a few minutes the caravan shuddered once more as a door opened and then Laura and Jasmine were gone.

'Who was that?' Anna asked in a hoarse whisper.

'Laura and Jasmine are going on a bike ride.'

'Not Finn?'

'Did you see the state of him last night? I don't think he'll be going anywhere today.'

Anna had been leaning up on her elbow but let her head drop back down on the pillow. 'Me neither. I'm sorry, Sam, but I feel awful. I can't go climbing mountains. Not today, please.'

She had closed her eyes but peeled them open to check why Sam hadn't spoken. 'Sorry,' she said again. 'I'm an awful girlfriend, aren't I?' When Sam still wasn't willing to reply, she added, 'I gave you a hard time last night, as I recall.'

'What do you mean?' He knew exactly what she meant.

'About Kirsten. If you don't want to go to the wedding then that's up to you. I shouldn't have been badgering you, not in front of Finn.'

'I can't be forced into something I don't want to do, even if it was two against one. Three, if you include Selina's previous attempts.'

'I just thought it would be a good way for you to draw a line under the past. If turning up with your new girlfriend at your ex-wife's wedding isn't closure then I don't know what is.'

'I already have drawn a line under it, Anna: a line that

161

separates Scotland from England and the past from the present. It's my very own Hadrian's Wall.'

Anna was trying to keep her bloodshot eyes open but there was pain etched across her face. 'OK, fair point. I won't mention it again. Oh, God, I feel wretched,' she complained as she put a hand over her face. 'I really, really need to sleep this off. You could always go out on your own. I wouldn't mind.'

'By that, you mean: can I leave you alone now?'

She peeked at him through splayed fingers. 'Would you mind? You didn't want me peering over your shoulder as you sketched anyway.'

Sam had to agree that it wasn't a bad idea and he was normally happy enough in his own company – but not today. Today he was wishing he had joined Laura and Jasmine on their ride into town, but no one was more aware than he that wishes were dangerous things.

21

When Finn jumped up off the sofa, the sudden movement made Laura flinch. She had withdrawn completely from the world around her and had been staring at the stain on the rug again. The pain in her left side flared briefly, although it was nothing compared to the pain in her heart.

'Is there any news?' Finn asked, pouncing on Michael the moment he came through the door.

'No, we haven't found her yet,' the policeman said, directing his reply to Laura who, he had surmised, was the most in need of answers.

Finn cursed first under his breath and then louder. 'Then what the fuck are you doing out there?' he roared.

Michael's only response was to sit down in an armchair. He motioned for Finn to do the same and refused to say a word until Finn was settled back on the sofa next to Laura. She didn't want Finn sitting next to her, but he had refused to leave her side since the police arrived. He gave her no comfort but he played the part extremely well.

'DCI Harper is still interviewing Mr McIntyre and he's

163

asked me to clarify some points and gather a bit more information,' Michael said.

Finn folded his arms. 'Such as?'

'For one, we'd like more specifics about Jasmine's clothing.'

'Have you found . . .' Laura said with a strangled gasp. She didn't want to think about what might have been found or where, so let her words fall into the abyss that she was only one step away from being pulled into herself.

'No, no,' Michael said quickly. 'We haven't found any clothing but we would like more details about the shoes Jasmine was wearing. We're conducting a thorough search of the park and—'

'And what about Sam's house?' Finn interrupted. 'Please say you haven't fallen for his charm offensive too. If you want to find her, then that's where you should be looking, not the park.'

'Did any of you ever visit Mr McIntyre's house?'

'No,' Laura answered quickly.

'Is it possible that Jasmine could have visited on her own?'

Finn took a breath, but before he could answer, Laura said, 'She wouldn't even know where he lived.'

'Oh, don't be so naïve, Laura. He'd find a way of getting her there,' Finn said, not willing to let the trail he was convinced would lead to his daughter go cold. 'He had plenty of opportunity to tell our Jazz where he lived; he probably told her it would be their little secret. Sam has a way of manipulating people, Michael. The job, the holiday . . .' Finn laughed bitterly. 'We all played right into his hands. Me and Laura, even Anna. You don't get a looker like her interested in someone like Sam unless you know how to play the game.'

Laura's body tensed and she closed her eyes as she listened to her husband talking about the schoolteacher in such glowing terms. It wasn't that she was jealous; she had got more than used to Finn's infatuations over the years, some of which had been foolishly reciprocated. What she didn't like was having a police officer bearing witness to her humiliation.

'And you certainly don't kick her out of bed unless your tastes lie elsewhere,' Finn said, continuing with the vitriolic attack.

When Laura peeled her eyes open, her husband was looking directly at her.

'Sam came across as the real gentleman,' Finn said slowly, 'but he was conning each and every one of us all along, so he could groom my daughter.'

'Stop it!' Laura said, unable to hear any more against the man whose only desire had been to protect them. She couldn't bear any suggestion that Sam had wanted to abuse them, especially not from someone like Finn. Unable to sit next to him a moment longer, Laura jumped up and the pain in her side hit her with the force of a gunshot wound and she cried out.

'Are you all right, Mrs Peterson?' Michael asked and was at her side in seconds.

When the family liaison officer slipped his arm around her, Laura was thankful that neither of the men with her could read her thoughts. Michael wasn't as tall as Sam but he gave her the same feeling of being in the arms of someone who would never do her harm. She refused to accept that

Sam was involved in her daughter's disappearance. She hadn't been taken for a fool: she had surely learnt her lesson after falling for Finn. Hadn't she? 'I just want my baby back home,' she cried and didn't care how the pain intensified with her sobs. She deserved the agony. She had failed her daughter. 'I want to know where she is. Please find her. Please, Michael, just bring her home.'

'We're doing our best and we won't rest until she's found, I promise you that.'

Finn had stood up too and he pulled her to him, most likely to prise her away from the police officer rather than to console her. She shrugged off both men and drew herself up straight. She wouldn't let Jasmine down again. She would do whatever was asked of her. 'What do you want to know? I've given you her shoe size, what else do you need?'

'The model of shoe would be useful. Can you remember where you bought them?'

'I can do better than that. Her friend Keira has the same pair, they both insisted,' she said with a sad smile.

'Perfect,' Michael said.

Laura nodded. She was helping. They were making progress. 'So, what else do you need?'

'How did you hurt your side, Mrs Peterson?'

22

The road from Mold to Pantymwyn dipped and fell, and as Laura pushed the broken bicycle up the side of yet another valley she momentarily lost sight of Jasmine who had been riding ahead. When she reached the top of the hill with its sweeping view of the golf course to her left and the Welsh mountains rising in the distance, she spotted Jasmine speeding downhill, her legs lifted high above the pedals, which were spinning out of control.

'Be careful!' Laura shouted although she wished she could be doing the same. Her bike had got a puncture two miles back and she had told Jasmine she could ride on ahead as long as she remained in sight and she was under strict instructions to stay on the pavement and not turn down the country lane that led to the caravan park. Laura hadn't enjoyed taking Jasmine along the narrow, winding road on the way out and she was looking forward even less to the return journey, although it was true to say that it wasn't only the road that was worrying her.

She had been foolish to think that Finn's good behaviour

would last. He had promised her he would do anything and everything to keep on the straight and narrow now he had a new job, and although he hadn't gone cold turkey, he had cut back on his drinking – at first. Laura was well aware that alcohol was a depressant and she was never sure if it was the drink that pulled down Finn's moods or if his moods led him to drink more, but the end result was always the same . . . Except this time it was also different. Finn had reached new lows.

Trying to hold onto the bike with one hand, Laura loosened the scarf around her neck, which was chafing against already sore skin but didn't attempt to remove it. She didn't want Jasmine to see the marks on her neck that she hoped would fade by the next day. The deep purple fingermarks on her arms would be a lengthier reminder of the night before, but not as enduring as the memory. She could still smell Finn's fetid breath suffocating her after he had stumbled into their bedroom.

'Missed me?' he had asked as he kicked off his trainers, unbuckled the belt on his jeans and then almost toppled on top of her as he tried to take off his pants. He was laughing to himself as he got into bed, but as soon as he moved closer to her, he felt his wife freeze up, igniting the slow burning anger he had been struggling with all day.

'What is it? Would you rather have Sam in your bed?'

'No, of course not,' Laura whispered. 'I'm tired Finn. Go to sleep. Please.'

'Please, please, Finn, don't touch me,' he mimicked in a whiny voice.

In the next room, they could hear Sam and Anna moving about. There were hushed whispers and creaks as the two got into their bed. Finn was quiet for a moment as he listened. 'Do you think he'll give her one tonight?' he said and then sniggered. 'I would, but here I am stuck with you. What do I have to do to warm you up, Laura? Would it help if I talk in a Scottish accent?'

'I'm not interested in Sam. I love you, Finn, only you. You know that. You must know that.'

'Why? Because it's the only reason you could put up with a loser like me?'

'You're not a loser. Things are looking up now and we're through the worst. Please Finn, just go to sleep and tomorrow we can have a nice day together, just the three of us.'

'Yeah, but you're not so keen to be on your own with me though, are you? Show me you love me, Laura.' He started to move on top of her and that was when she had panicked.

'Don't, Finn. The others will hear us.'

His grip on her arms tightened like a vice and when he spoke, sour spittle sprayed across her face. 'Why? Are you saving yourself for Sam? Do you think he's interested in you? In *you*?' He laughed softly, taking pleasure in humiliating his wife. 'Have you seen Anna? She's stunning! She's beautiful and funny and quick witted and . . .' His slurred words slowed to a stop. In the dim light, Laura watched Finn's eyes close as he lost himself in his own thoughts and when they snapped back open, he let go of her arms only to make a grab for her throat.

Finn had held her down before and had used enough force to leave bruises, but as he squeezed her neck so hard that he constricted her airway, she really didn't know her husband any more. She had been forced to accept long ago that he was capable of hurting her, but she had thought he had limits. Apparently she had been wrong.

'Who would ever choose a shrivelled little mouse like you over her?' Finn said. He leaned in closer and whispered into her ear. 'You should be grateful I'm still interested.'

Laura could see blotches of white light against the darkness of the night and might have passed out if Finn hadn't released his grip on her neck. She gasped, which Finn took as encouragement and when he pressed his body against hers, he expected her to respond. Even if she had wanted to, Laura couldn't move because his full weight was on her chest. She was struggling to breathe again and her body tensed as panic took over. Finn noticed only her frigidity and pushed himself off her in disgust before turning away. Within seconds of his head hitting the pillow he was asleep, leaving Laura frozen in shock.

It was the heat of the afternoon sun on her back that drew Laura's mind back to the present, and when she dropped her gaze to the ground she was surprised to see she cast any kind of shadow at all. Further ahead, she spied the Crown coming into view, but the cosy pub which offered the promise of a much-needed long and cooling drink couldn't be any less appealing. Laura had become conditioned to feel nothing but unease at the sight of a pub.

'Can I ride straight back to the caravan now?' Jasmine asked. She was out of breath, having cycled back up the hill to speak to her mum.

'No, you can wait for me. We can use the shortcut through the farmer's field like we did last night on the way to the Crown.'

'We can't get our bikes over the stiles.'

'Not on our own,' Laura said. 'Which is why we need to be together. You can ride as far as the turn-off but no further.'

Jasmine looked as if she was about to argue and then thought better of it. Her sweet, innocent child had a sixth sense when it came to knowing not to argue when her mum was feeling beaten – either that or she wasn't as deaf to the raised voices as Laura would like to believe.

For the second time, Jasmine whizzed down the hill with the pedals spinning out of control and in less than a minute she had disappeared around the corner and onto the road that would take them past a scattering of houses before narrowing into the country lane that Laura wanted to avoid. A knot began to tighten in her stomach as she wondered if Finn's mood would have improved by the time they reached home. After the accusations he had been firing at her, she wasn't hopeful. The knot tightened and made her stomach lurch when she spied a figure striding across the field on the opposite side of the road. Sam was some way ahead and waved at her.

Laura's palms felt sweaty and her hand slipped on the handlebars as she picked up her pace, unsure if she was trying to outrun Sam or catch him up. Finn would not approve of the two meeting up, but Laura's anxiety was swept away by a flutter of anticipation. Sam was everything her husband was not: kind, calm, considerate. He made her feel something she hadn't felt for such a long time; he made her feel safe.

'Puncture,' she announced solemnly as Sam approached. Her voice barely quivered.

'Where's Jasmine?'

Rather than stopping to chat, Laura pushed onwards and Sam fell in beside her. 'She was supposed to wait at the corner,' she said tipping her head towards the junction that was only a few hundred yards away now.

'She won't have gone too far,' Sam replied although he didn't sound at all confident and Laura didn't argue when he took the bike from her so they could walk that little bit faster.

Laura's anxieties returned with renewed force when another thought struck her. 'Didn't Anna go out with you?'

'She wasn't feeling too good so I left her in bed.'

'Oh.'

Sam tore his eyes away from the road to look at her. 'She'll probably still be there,' he added.

Laura tried to fake a smile while imagining what her husband might be up to with the woman who, as he had been at pains to point out to Laura last night, was more beautiful than she was, more interesting and clever and infinitely more captivating. Not that Laura could care less if her husband did find the teacher more attractive. She was beyond such feelings as far as Finn was concerned. The only thing that actually mattered right now was her daughter's whereabouts.

'Phew, there she is,' Sam said with a gush of relief that suggested he had been just as worried.

Laura waved at her daughter before turning her attention to Sam and giving him a curious look. 'You really care about her, don't you?'

Sam simply nodded.

'I'm surprised you never had kids,' she said. 'You'd make a good dad.'

172

Despite the strength of the sun, it was hard to miss the shadow that crossed Sam's face. 'I'm the last person who should be a father,' he said in a way that made it clear he would say no more on the matter, not that he had the chance because Jasmine came screeching to a halt in front of them.

'Mum says we have to cut across the field, but don't you think we should use the proper road, Sam?'

'Definitely not. I think your mum has the right idea.'

It was quite a challenge getting the bikes over the stiles but Sam was as determined as Laura to avoid the country lane. Finally, when they reached the farmer's field, Jasmine jumped back on her bike and sped off.

'I worry about her,' Laura said, the words slipping out before she realized what she was saying.

'I worry about you both,' Sam said, looking just as shocked as Laura that they were speaking so frankly. He had slowed to a stop and when he turned to her, she could see he was battling with his thoughts. 'I know I'm speaking out of turn and you can tell me to mind my own business, but are you OK?'

'I'm fine,' she said as she felt embarrassment flood her chest. Nervously, she pushed a rogue curl behind her ear and didn't realize she had started playing with her scarf until she saw Sam's eyes widen. She quickly put her palm against her neck to hide any telltale signs that would prove her a liar while Sam was slower and more purposeful with his response. He lifted his hand to her neck but didn't pull her hand away. He wasn't going to force her to reveal her misery and humiliation, he simply covered her hand and his touch was so much more powerful than her husband's.

'You only have to ask if you need help,' he said.

'Mum!' Jasmine called as she did a U-turn at the top of the field.

Sam jerked his hand away and the two resumed walking even as Laura replied to her daughter. 'What?'

'Can I go straight back to the caravan?'

'Yes, of course,' she said, with a smile that she held when she glanced back at Sam. 'We'll be fine, Sam but thank you for . . .' She wasn't sure what she was thanking him for. For noticing her? For caring? 'For the offer.'

'You'll find me in Calderstones more often than not. If ever you do need me.'

As they made their way through the back of the caravan park, Laura kept her hand on the bike's handlebar, not touching Sam but close enough to feel his warmth. 'I'm glad we met,' she said, and felt an unfamiliar fizz of excitement bubbling inside her, but it took only the thought of her husband to make her emotions feel suddenly flat. What if Finn was right? Anna was a beautiful and interesting woman; if Sam saw anything in Laura, it was surely only pity. Fuelled by self-doubt, she decided she had been reading the situation completely wrong and tried to backtrack. 'I mean, today . . . with the bike.'

'Any time,' Sam said, leaving the offer floating in the air ready for Laura to grasp and, whatever Sam's motives, she felt comforted knowing it was there.

The path that took them through the caravan park followed peaks and valleys in much the same way as the surrounding area, although on a much smaller scale. When Sam reached the brow of the last hill, he could see all the way to Pat's caravan where Finn was leaning on the fence waiting for them. Laura still had her hand alongside Sam's on the handlebar but quickly let go, dropping her head at the same time. The way she extended the distance between herself and Sam was another conscious move, albeit a little less obvious.

'Looks like you're the hero of the day,' Finn said to Sam. 'I was about to send out a search party for these two.'

'I had a puncture just outside Mold,' Laura explained. 'I got back as quickly as I could.'

'You shouldn't have rushed on my account. Anna and I have been having a fine old time enjoying the peace and quiet.'

Sam parked the bike next to Jasmine's and, sensing his presence was only adding to the tension Finn could draw expertly from thin air, he left Laura standing by her husband while he went inside to find Anna.

He was surprised to find she was still in bed, although in his absence she had dressed and was now lying on top of the covers.

'Don't tell me you're still suffering?'

She peeled her eyes open and smiled at him. 'I've missed you,' she said, lifting her hand towards him. 'Sorry again about messing up your day.'

Sam sat down next to her on the bed. 'There's nothing to apologize for. I probably wouldn't have been able to concentrate with you around and I've made tonnes of sketches,' he said, flexing his fingers, which had turned numb as he worked if not his mind. He had been haunted by the startled look on Laura's face when he had stepped into the kitchen that morning and meeting her on the road back from Mold had done little to settle his growing anxiety.

She hadn't explained the mark she was trying to cover up on her neck and he wasn't at all sure he wanted to know, but it added more weight to his worries even so. His first impression of Laura had been that she seemed as lost as her daughter, but he was quickly coming to the conclusion that Finn's wife was deliberately hiding from view; hiding in fear.

Even as his thoughts lingered on Laura, Anna lifted herself towards him, putting her arms around his neck. 'I'll make it up to you,' she whispered in his ear.

She kissed his cheek softly before brushing her lips lightly over his, her breath tasting peppermint fresh. He was slow to respond and, assuming he was still a little cross with her, Anna trailed tender kisses across to the other side of his face and neck. She nibbled his ear playfully and was in the process of pulling him back down onto the bed when there was a noise behind them.

'Sorry, should I have knocked?' Finn asked. He was standing at the door with a smirk on his face.

Sam stood up and when he pulled Anna up with him, she was scowling. 'Thanks, Finn, you know how to ruin a girl's plans,' she said.

Finn raised an eyebrow. 'Speaking of appetites, I'm famished,' he said as he continued to stare at them, or more precisely, at Anna, who had the hint of a smile on her face to suggest she had picked up on the innuendo. She held his gaze until Finn blinked and turned to Sam again. 'Which is why my wife has kindly offered to nip out to get fish and chips if you want some.'

'Sounds good to me,' Sam said. 'I don't think I could take another session in the Crown, that's for sure.'

'Oh, don't be such a lightweight. She's calling in at the off-licence too.'

It was only when Sam edged his way along the narrow gap between the wall and bed that Finn finally moved and they followed him into the living area where Laura was waiting with her handbag over her shoulder, car keys in her hand. She had a blank expression on her face that gave away her disapproval.

'I don't want anything else to drink, not tonight,' Sam said.

'Then I hope you're not going to let me down, Anna.'

'Of course I'll join you,' she said. 'As long as it's orange juice.'

Finn laughed. 'But only if there's vodka in it, right?'

'Do you need help?' Sam asked Laura without thinking. He had been too keen to escape the storm clouds brewing over Finn's head.

The clouds darkened.

Laura felt it too and was already moving towards the door when she said, 'No, I can manage.'

'Oh, why don't you take your knight in shining armour? He wants to rescue you again, don't you, Sam?'

'I can manage, Finn,' she said without a backward glance at either of them.

Sam wanted to get out into the fresh air again, but he didn't immediately follow Laura. He was beginning to understand how Finn's mind worked and even watching Laura leave would serve only to antagonize him further and create more grief for Laura. During the holiday, Sam had consciously avoided letting his eyes linger on Laura, and he had thought he had done a good enough job, but Finn had obviously noticed and was threatened by it.

Outside, Laura could be heard talking to Jasmine. She didn't want to go with her mum and said she would stay to water the plants. Laura's parting remark was to give her strict instructions not to go bothering her dad and then she left. All the while, Sam, Finn and Anna stood in awkward silence.

'I'd better help Jasmine water the plants,' Sam said once he heard Laura drive off.

'I'll come with you,' Anna said.

Jasmine was nowhere to be seen and the watering can had been left untouched at the side of the caravan. Sam followed his instincts and wandered down the slope towards the far end of the garden where tall oaks and beeches were lined up along the boundary of the caravan site and the neighbouring fields, their dense boughs creating an immense canopy that let through only slivers of light. Sam peered into the shadows and at first couldn't see the little girl until he spied the familiar wisps of blonde hair from behind a beech tree. She had sought peace in the part of the garden furthest away from her brooding father and Sam and Anna went to join her.

'Do you think there are fairies living down here?' Jasmine whispered when Sam and Anna appeared at her side and she was sure her dad wasn't with them.

She was crouching down with her back against the tree and had been trying to imagine she was back in Calderstones, sitting beneath the shadow of the ancient oak that always made her feel a little less scared. It had been a nice surprise to find a different kind of magic lurking in this corner of the world, but she supposed there was magic all around if you looked hard enough.

'Where?' Sam asked when he failed to notice what she had been staring at.

Jasmine pointed towards a ramshackle section of the hedgerow where a circle of mushrooms shone out from the shadows. Their thick, creamy tops were pristine compared to the dank, rotting earth they had emerged from.

'Ah, you've found a fairy ring,' Anna said. 'That's where the fairies come at night to dance and make merry. You know you mustn't destroy it, don't you?'

'I won't,' Jasmine promised. 'Can I stay up tonight and wait for them?'

'I think you're more likely to find badgers than wee fairies down here,' Sam said.

'Don't be such a grouch,' Anna scolded. 'How can someone who believes in the Wishing Tree not believe in fairies?'

Jasmine stood up and dusted herself off. She willed Sam to say that he did believe in fairies because she didn't want him to be like her dad – but then, she already knew he wasn't. There had been times in the week when she had sensed Sam getting frustrated and yet she couldn't imagine him losing his temper. Even if he did, Jasmine knew he wouldn't take it out on someone else. He was nothing like her dad, but then her dad was nothing like he used to be.

There had been times when he was the best dad in the world; when he was so happy he could laugh himself hoarse and make everyone around him laugh too. But then there were darker times when he couldn't raise even a smile, when he acted as if he hated the sight of her, and then there were times like now, when he was somewhere in between and no one, not even her mum, knew what might happen next. It was these times that scared her most and it scared her mum too. She had been quiet all day and maybe she had told Sam what was worrying her. She had seen him putting his hand on her mum's shoulder which people did when they wanted to help. It was good that Sam wanted to look after her mum. She trusted him more than she did her dad.

'I said it would be more likely for badgers to appear,' Sam was saying. 'I never suggested fairies didn't exist.'

'It doesn't matter,' Jasmine said with a shrug. 'My dad will go mad if I start going on about them so maybe we should forget about it.'

'Are you sure?' Anna said. 'If you want to camp out here tonight then I'll tell your dad it's part of your schoolwork. He won't argue with me.'

No, Jasmine thought, but he would argue with Mum, and Jasmine would do anything to avoid that. 'It's all right. I'm a bit tired after the bike ride anyway.'

Jasmine couldn't see the caravan above the steep incline, but she looked at it anyway. She wished she could stay where she was forever. She wished the fairies were real and that they would adopt her so she would never have to climb up the slope and be afraid.

'We can always see if there are any board games you haven't played with yet,' Sam suggested. 'I could teach you how to play chess.'

Despite the shade of the hedgerow wrapping around her, Jasmine's eyes twinkled out of the darkness. 'Or you could teach me how to make one of those paper birds.' She had been watching Sam make them from pages torn out of the gardening magazines he had brought with him.

He hadn't exactly refused to teach her, but always seemed to find an excuse not to.

Sam thought for a minute, casting his gaze towards the fairy ring then back in the direction of the caravan before coming to rest on Jasmine's expectant face. 'I don't suppose your dad would have any objection to that.'

'Thank you, Sam!' Jasmine said and tried to convince herself that the butterflies she felt in her tummy were from excitement and not the fear she had carried around with her all day.

23

Thursday 20 August 2015

The following day Finn set about building a barbeque from the reclaimed bricks. Even with a crippling hangover that was making him dry retch from time to time he was doing a decent job. Sam and Anna were building a rockery in the corner of the garden nearest the road while Laura and Jasmine had disappeared down the slope and were secretly watching out for fairies while clearing enough space beneath the beech trees for a rope swing. The little girl, who had been slowly but surely emerging from her shell during the first few days of the holiday had all but disappeared again. She was no longer heard and rarely seen and as the happy holiday that Sam had imagined for her slipped from his grasp, he began to feel decidedly homesick.

'I think if we push really hard we could have it all finished by tomorrow,' he told Anna when she handed him the final rock from the pile Pat had amassed during the initial garden clearance.

'I'd say we could have Saturday off, except, oh yes, we'll be going home then anyway.'

Wedging the stone between two larger rocks and fixing it into place with dark, moist soil, he said, 'I was actually thinking we might go home a day early.'

'Really?'

Sam straightened up, and as he wiped his hands on his work pants he watched Finn pointing the final row of bricks. He hadn't slowed down, not even after lunch, which for Finn had been a liquid one.

'You have to admit, Anna, it's been a bit strained around here the last couple of days. It was always going to be a bit testing because we don't know Finn and his family very well. I was thinking maybe we should go before someone snaps,' he said in such a way that left no doubt as to who that someone might be.

'I'd agree Finn's been a bit off, but he's probably just exhausted. We all are,' Anna said and when she failed to convince even herself, she added, 'OK, maybe you do have a point but we don't all have to leave early.'

'I'm missing my own bed,' Sam insisted.

Anna thought on it for a moment. 'I am too,' she said with a smile. 'We could always let the others stay on and give them the last night on their own.'

Suddenly, the thought of being home that bit sooner lost its allure as Sam imagined Laura and Jasmine being left alone with Finn, his case of beer and his foul mood. He didn't want to abandon them, but it was too late, Finn was walking over towards them, can in hand, and Anna couldn't wait to tell him her suggestion.

At first, Finn looked almost as unenthusiastic about the idea as Sam but then he said, 'I suppose we have been living in each other's pockets and those walls in the caravan are paper thin.'

A flush rose in Anna's cheeks. She was all too aware of how easily noise travelled and their sex life had been non-existent, unlike Finn and Laura's, which was why, after the first night, Anna had been wearing earplugs religiously.

'We've still got a fair bit to finish off here though,' Sam said, backtracking as much as he dared. 'And I need to make another trip into Mold to pick up a few more plants for the rockery.'

Anna wasn't to be put off. 'We can do that now. Is there anything you need, Finn?'

'Best ask the wife,' he said, tipping his head in the direction of Laura who had appeared at the top of the slope, pulling a reluctant Jasmine with her. She was wearing her yellow cardigan, which was smudged with dirt, and when she let go of her daughter's hand, she used the edge of her neck scarf to wipe the sweat from her face.

'We were thinking of going into Mold,' Anna explained.

Laura smiled. 'Oh, all right then.'

'Not you,' Finn said impatiently. 'Can't you see the love-birds need a bit of time on their own?'

Laura looked crestfallen and not as enthusiastic as Finn when it came to the shopping list they put together which consisted of more alcohol than any real sustenance.

'We won't be long,' Sam said, and made the mistake of directing his promise to Laura. It was a throwaway comment that should have been forgotten, but an hour later when Sam and Anna arrived back from their shopping

184

expedition, it soon became apparent that it had been playing on Finn's mind.

Sam had pulled up outside the caravan, switched off the engine, and waited for the electric windows to close. The weather was scorching and once he and Anna were sealed in, the air thickened with a mixture of summer heat and damp earth smells from the trays of plants in the back of the Land Rover.

Sweat trickled down his temples and yet he was reluctant to get out, torn between wanting to return to the caravan to make sure Laura was all right and running the risk of annoying Finn if Sam so much as looked at his wife. But it was hard not to, just as it was difficult to hold his tongue. He wanted to tell Finn he should count himself lucky to have such a beautiful and supportive wife and a little girl who was crying out to be loved. He wouldn't, of course, mention how attractive he found Laura but if pushed, he could assure Finn with a clear conscience that he wasn't about to steal his wife. He had a girlfriend; someone who was caring and attentive and was opening up her heart to him. All he had to do was accept that love.

'I've really missed this,' Anna said.

She had put her hand on his arm as if she imagined he was savouring this quiet moment with her too. She had no inkling of Sam's conflicted emotions and why would she? Sam was a closed book to her. He smiled and tried to absorb just a little of the affection radiating from her face, but if he yearned for anything then it was his apartment in Liverpool: sparse, cool and empty, a place where he could be alone and isolated from feelings that might warm his heart one day and break it the next. 'You don't mind going home early, do you?'

'Not if it means we can spend some time on our own.' She leaned over and kissed him before whispering in his ear, 'I think I'm falling in love with you, Sam.'

Sam's body tensed and he wasn't quite sure how he managed to fight the urge to pull away. It was guilt more than anything that made him lean over and kiss her cheek, which at least meant he didn't have to look her in the eyes. With his lips still touching her skin, he said, 'Don't, Anna, please. I don't deserve you.'

She lifted her head. 'You can't tell me you don't care – and I won't believe you even if you try.' She cupped his face in her hands, 'Don't look so terrified, Sam. I'm not expecting you to tell me you love me too. Believe it or not I have heeded your warning that you don't want to get in too deep too soon. But now it's my turn to warn you: I'm not going to let you slip away from me, Sam McIntyre.'

Despite everything he was feeling, Anna's words soothed him and when she kissed him again he could feel himself responding to her. After years of self-imposed isolation, he had forgotten how good it felt to be loved and he wished his closed heart could open up to her, and perhaps it had in recent months which might explain why someone else had sneaked into it.

Leaving the car, his steps felt lighter despite being weighed down by two trays of alpines and bedding plants, one stacked precariously on top of the other. Anna opened the gate and, as he slipped into the garden, he heard Finn's voice coming from the open caravan door, presumably from their bedroom, but then an inner door flung open.

'Don't you walk away from me!' Finn's voice boomed but it was Laura who appeared at the door first, her face blotchy and her nose bright red.

Sam couldn't be sure if it was his sudden appearance that gave her a start or the fact that Finn had grabbed her cardigan and pulled her back into the caravan. She stumbled briefly before regaining her balance.

'Stop it, Finn!' Laura cried. 'Please, why are you doing this? Why do you have to destroy everything that's good in our lives?'

She tried again to leave by slipping off the cardigan Finn was still holding, but he quickly grabbed at her arm. His fingers dug into Laura's flesh, which was already marked by deep purple circles the size of a man's fingers.

Sam dropped the two plant trays and launched himself up the balcony steps. He wasn't aiming for Laura and even knocked into her as he forced his way into the caravan. Using his momentum to his advantage, he shoved his palm against Finn's chest and pushed him backwards. In Finn's inebriated state, it didn't take much to knock him off his feet and he fell, landing so hard it knocked the breath out of him. Sprawled across the floor, he didn't look capable of getting up again but Sam's hands were balled into fists in case he should try.

'What is *wrong* with you?' Sam bellowed.

The dazed look on Finn's face was replaced by one full of hatred and his speech was slurred and guttural. 'Want to play the big man in front of the ladies, do you? Go on then, hit me!'

Sam checked behind him before he spoke. Laura had disappeared and he presumed Anna had gone after her. 'I don't want to hit you, Finn, but I swear I will if you ever hurt Laura again,' he said, his words as tense as his jaw which was set firm to hold back the kind of fury he hadn't experienced for many years.

Finn's face contorted into a snarl. 'Don't think you're the first to come sniffing around her,' he said, flinching when Sam took a step closer and then hiding behind his hands which were shaking badly.

'I'm not interested in your wife, Finn,' Sam said, hoping the drunkard would believe him, despite the lack of conviction in his words, 'but I can't for the life of me see why she would want to stay with someone like you. She deserves better.'

Through splayed fingers, Finn's unfocused eyes flitted between the door, Sam's face and hands that were still ready to take a punch. He balled up his own fists as if preparing for a counterattack, but then his sneer began to disintegrate and his lip trembled. 'I don't want to lose her. She means everything to me and I don't need *you* telling me she deserves better.'

The pitiful sight in front of him wasn't enough to take the heat out of Sam's fury. He had seen the bruises clearly enough and the marks on Laura's neck and he had no sympathy for any man who could hurt someone he proclaimed to love. He didn't know what to do for the best but he suspected that whatever was going on between Finn and Laura was nothing new and he could only intervene so far.

'Why are you doing this, Finn?'

'I don't know.' Finn rubbed his face, hiding the tears he would never admit to shedding. 'I don't know, I don't know. I don't know!'

'Well, you'd better find out before it's too late.'

The two men didn't move for a moment. Sam was desperately trying to think of something that would bring Finn to his senses and magically transform him into a decent husband and father, but words failed him. Finn, meanwhile, had come up with his own plan.

'Did you get the ale I asked for?' When Sam looked ready to launch into a tirade, he lifted a palm towards him. 'I was only going to ask that you keep it away from me.'

He groaned as he got to his feet. 'It's the drink that does it, Sam,' he said, as if the answer was not only that simple but excusable too. 'I don't know why I let it control me. I'll be fine once I've slept it off, honest.'

Watching Finn stumble towards the bedroom, Sam wanted to say he wasn't interested in Finn's welfare, only in his family. And with that thought prominent in his mind, he picked up Laura's cardigan and stepped out onto the balcony, taking a deep breath of fresh air before making his way to the far end of the garden where he knew instinctively he would find a little girl who still believed in fairy tales and happy endings. Anna and Laura were there too, but neither was looking for a magic solution to their problems.

Laura stood with her arms wrapped around each other to cover her bruises. Her eyes looked hollow as she turned towards Sam. 'Where is he?'

Sam handed her the cardigan. 'He's gone for a lie down. He wants to sober up.'

Laura covered herself up and didn't show any emotion when she said, 'Good.'

Anna was standing next to her, close enough to put her

arm around Laura if necessary. 'See, I told you it would be all right,' she said. When the smile she offered drew no response, she looked to Sam. 'We thought there was going to be a punch up.'

Sam's body was still taut with anger and he couldn't deny that he had come close to releasing it on Finn but with Jasmine crouching only feet away, he chose a more diplomatic answer. 'There wasn't.'

'You certainly moved quickly enough,' Anna continued. 'I hope you'd come to my rescue like that.'

'I hope I never have to. Violence doesn't solve anything,' he said, looking to Laura and holding her gaze. 'It never does.'

She blinked, nothing more, but it was as if she had passed on a secret message that only he could read and it filled him with dread. Finn didn't share his view on violence.

'It's been a hard week for all of us,' Anna was saying. 'And he's worried about losing his job again.'

'It won't be the first time my husband has lost a job and it won't be the last.'

Anna refused to read between the lines. 'While you were out yesterday, he was telling me how hard he's been trying to impress Jack. Maybe you could work your magic again, Sam's, and then Finn won't be so stressed?'

Jasmine had been focused on the deepest shadows of the undergrowth but her head tilted oh so slightly. Sam had no doubt that she had picked up on the remark and could only imagine what she was thinking. But some things were beyond his power and even that of the Wishing Tree.

Taking her daughter's hand, Laura began to move away, slipping past Sam like a ghost that no longer wanted to be seen. 'You've done more than enough already and I'm really grateful,' she said. 'But there are some things that Finn has to do for himself.'

Sam watched as they disappeared. His hands were balled into fists again and he tightened them. How could Finn be such a fool not to see what he had?

Anna cleared her throat. 'The sooner we can get those plants in the ground and the rope swing up, the sooner we can go home.'

'We'll have it done by tomorrow,' Sam promised but then added a note of caution which had nothing to do with the gardening. 'As long as Finn is up to the job.'

24

Sunday 23 August 2015

Other than the distant hum of traffic and the occasional barking dog, Sam was enveloped in complete calm as he lay prostrate on the wooden floor of his apartment. His running vest was damp with sweat and his chest was heaving, but with his eyes closed, his mind was blissfully empty of the thoughts that had kept him awake for the last two nights.

The garden had been finished off on Friday as planned, with Finn emerging revitalized after sleeping off his hangover. His anger had passed like a storm and if any dark clouds remained, he hid them well and their last day together was reminiscent of the first; everyone putting in a concerted effort while trying to get the measure of each other.

Anna and Sam were home in Liverpool by that evening and it was a foregone conclusion, in Anna's mind at least, that she would stay the night. Sam didn't think she wanted to leave at all. She wanted to be held and loved, and while his arms could oblige, his heart was incapable of closing the deal. Anna's love wasn't enough to drive away guilty thoughts of another woman; for that, it had taken a two-hour run, and even then he had come temptingly close to the family he was trying to banish from his mind.

There had never been a set route for Sam's runs and although they often took him through Allerton, he had never before zigzagged up and down side streets. He had crossed the top of the road where the Petersons lived and searched for a glimpse of their car as if that alone would tell him that Laura and Jasmine were safe.

It hadn't, and Sam had faced the prospect of running until sheer exhaustion gave him the peace he was seeking, but he had been holding out for one final hope. Continuing his run through Calderstones Park, he eventually found solace in a single sheet of pink paper.

Lying on the floor now, Sam could smell the aroma of Selina's Sunday lunch coming from downstairs. He had been instructed to join her later and would no doubt share with her the latest of Jasmine's wishes, but for now he stayed where he was. The room was bathed in intense sunshine that stained his closed lids ruby red. He fought to keep his mind clear but it was a losing battle and when his thoughts pulled him back much further than he had wanted to go, his stomach did a somersault.

The sunrays dancing across his eyelids shifted, creating rippling shadows that deepened towards the edges of his vision to create a distinct oval of dappled light. Two sparkling orbs began to form, captivating him as they developed into unmistakeable eyes. A thin shadow picked out a button nose and below there was the gentle curve of lips. The child's smile broadened, sending a shudder down his spine.

He had trained himself not to recall those achingly familiar features, knowing that her cherubic face could so easily crush the air from his lungs and leave his body as broken as his heart. Except it didn't, not today. Today he was enjoying a rare sense of calm and he allowed himself to focus on the image that had been gifted to him by the afternoon sunshine. Her face rippled in the tears that gathered across his tightly closed eyelids before slipping down the sides of his face.

'Ruby . . .' he whispered.

Dear Wishing Tree

It's me again. Did you miss me? I missed you. I went on holiday with Mum and Dad and Miss Jenkins and Sam who looks after you. We saw lots of trees but Sam said none of them were as old as you.

We had a nice time at the caravan. There were lots of nice people there and Mrs Hayes has a dog called Nando who barks a lot and wouldn't stop licking me. I think dogs make you so happy that it hurts but not in a bad way. I wish Dad would let me get a dog but he won't and I am not asking you for one by the way.

My wish is for Dad to keep his job. He got really sad while we were on holiday and then he got angry. So did Sam. Miss Jenkins thought they were going to have a fight. She thinks it's romantic when men fight over you but it was horrible and scary. Mum was scared too but then Dad got better and I really, really wish that he would stay like that and that no one is frightened ever again.

I am soooo sorry for making more wishes and if

you can just manage to help one more time then I
will love you forever!!
   No! I'll love you forever anyway!
   Your friend,
   Jasmine xxx

25

Sam was still wearing his running gear and the smell of body odour was getting stronger. 'Would you mind if I changed?' he asked.

'I'd rather we finished up the interview first, if you don't mind,' Harper said as if the choice was still Sam's, which they both knew wasn't true.

'OK, what else do you want to know?'

'Was Mrs Peterson visiting you while you were dating Miss Jenkins?'

'No, and she only visited once. It wasn't like that,' Sam said.

'What *was* it like, Mr McIntyre?' Harper said in a soft tone that was meant to lull Sam into a false sense of security but had the effect of opening relatively fresh wounds that hadn't had the chance to heal yet.

'I was just there when she needed someone to turn to,' Sam said. Jasper was still on his lap, curled up with his bony legs digging into his flesh, but Sam didn't object. He ran his fingers through the dog's fur, which brought him some much-needed comfort.

'Tempting her away from her husband? Just like you were tempting Jasmine away from her father?'

'You've met Finn and you've probably met plenty of men like him. I wasn't tempting anyone – I didn't have to. Finn pushed his own family away and—' Sam stopped before he said too much.

'And?'

'And all I wanted was to keep them safe,' he said bitterly. 'But I shouldn't have had to. I don't understand the man, really I don't. He made their lives a misery.'

Harper frowned. 'You wanted to protect them and yet you were about to head off into the sunset. What changed?'

'Nothing changed,' Sam said, and was tempted to smile but under current circumstances even his cynicism couldn't raise the corners of his mouth. 'And that's why I had to get away. It was driving me crazy not being able to stop Finn from destroying his family.'

Harper surprised Sam by nodding. 'I can understand that, but whatever Mr Peterson's faults, he was at home with his wife this morning when Jasmine left the house, and there's absolutely no evidence that he is involved in her disappearance.' He took a moment to check his notes and review the evidence before quickly concluding that his current lines of enquiry were the right ones to focus on. 'So your idea of helping was to give Jasmine's dad a job, take the family on holiday – and then what?'

Sam didn't offer an answer, but the way Harper was looking at the dog suggested he knew exactly what had come next.

'What child wouldn't love a puppy, Mr McIntyre?'

'He's not my dog.'

'The Petersons seem to think he is. You were the one inviting Jasmine to take him for walks, weren't you?'

Jasper must have known they were talking about him, or perhaps it was hearing the little girl's name that made him whine softly, and the sound was mournful. Jasmine had believed a dog could bring happiness into the world, but Jasper had brought a measure of pain too. In hindsight, the puppy had been a step too far and had only helped in bringing his relationship with the family to a climactic conclusion. 'It's my landlady's dog; I just helped take care of him now and again.'

'When you needed a prop to get Jasmine on her own?'

Sam's face twisted in disgust at what Harper was suggesting, but the detective wouldn't be thwarted. He sighed and pushed away his notes. 'Come on, Mr McIntyre, let's stop playing games. What was really going on between you and the girl? And more importantly, what happened today that tipped you over the edge?'

Sam's jaw started to ache with the effort of containing his anger and frustration and Harper was only saved from the abuse Sam was about to hurl at him by the return of the detective's partner. He beckoned Harper to the door where there was a whispered exchange. When silence fell, the detective's shoulders sagged as he turned back to Sam.

'Mr McIntyre, has Jasmine ever been to the house? I caution you to consider your response carefully before replying.'

The sense of dread was ice cold and made Sam shiver. 'My previous answer stands,' he said. 'She has never been here.'

'Are you aware of any other children who may have visited? Does Mrs Raymond have grandchildren?'

'No, she doesn't have any family.'

'Then can you think of any reason why there would be a child's footprints in the front garden? Footprints that match the shoes Jasmine was wearing this morning.'

'No, no I can't,' Sam said, feeling nauseous. 'Not unless she came here while I was out running.'

The theory didn't ease Harper's mind. 'But I thought she didn't know where you lived?' Before Sam could answer, he added, 'I think I'd prefer to continue this interview down at the station, if you don't mind, Mr McIntyre.'

'You're arresting me?'

'No, this is purely voluntary, but I would like you to make a formal statement under caution. The interview will be recorded and you have the right to free legal representation. Of course, if you refuse to co-operate . . .'

Fresh beads of sweat pricked Sam's brow. 'I don't know how you think I can help you. You were here when I came home and Selina's been out the entire time too. The house would have been empty and I have no idea how Jasmine found the house or where she might be now. I swear, if there was anything I could tell you that might help . . .'

But Harper wasn't listening to Sam. His attention had returned to the bookcase. He walked over and this time not only looked at the shoebox, but picked it up. He stared for a moment at the letters cut out from contrasting pieces of coloured paper and pasted onto the lid. There were four letters. One name.

'We know about Ruby, Sam,' he said.

26

Thursday 27 August 2015

When Sam returned to work after their week in Wales, there were plenty of chores to catch up on which meant he hadn't managed to get home before eight o'clock most days, but that suited him fine. Being busy meant he had a clear conscience each time he turned down Anna's suggestion about coming over. And it was a suggestion she made on a daily basis. School was about to restart and she was desperate to make the most of what time was left. He promised to make it up to her at the end of the week, but for Anna the weekend wasn't soon enough. As he turned into the drive on Thursday evening after another exhausting day, he found her sitting on the steps waiting for him.

'What's wrong?' he asked.

Anna offered a guilty smile. 'Nothing, I just missed you, that's all.'

'You didn't have to wait out on the step. Selina would have let you in.'

'I wouldn't have had to wait outside if I had a key,' she replied. 'I did knock but she's not in.'

'Oh.'

'I know it's late,' she said when Sam continued to look underwhelmed by her surprise appearance, 'and you probably just want to crash out, but I bet you've been too tired to feed yourself properly this week which is why I brought this.' She lifted up a large paper bag. 'If we're going out tomorrow night, then I don't want you flaking out on me. You need to keep your strength up, Sam McIntyre, because I can be very demanding.'

Sam reluctantly accepted the proffered bag without a word but even the sweet, spiced aromas of the takeaway couldn't mellow his mood.

'Chinese,' she confirmed. 'Enough to feed an army – but don't worry, I'll finish off whatever you don't want.' There was only the slightest pause. 'I don't mean now. I know you're tired so I won't bother you. I'm not even going to come in, assuming you were going to invite me.'

'Sorry,' Sam said by way of an apology for his unenthusiastic welcome.

Anna gave him a forgiving smile but it was the pause she left in the conversation that allowed Sam's sense of guilt to build. He was about to give in and ask her to stay when Selina's old Mini pulled into the drive.

'Hello, you two,' she said. She had a giddy expression on her face that immediately made Sam suspect she had been up to something. 'We weren't expecting a welcoming committee.'

'We?' Sam asked.

Selina had left her car door open and leant inside. There was a bit of a scramble and then she clicked her tongue. 'Come on, boy.'

When Selina stepped away from the car, she had hold of a leash that was attached to something still inside. A moment later, a head poked out and a pair of beautiful brown eyes fixed on the old lady. They could hear the sound of a tail thudding against the car seat that could just as easily have been the quickening of a little girl's heart. The puppy shuddered with excitement but it took another tug on the leash to encourage him out of the car. His long, silky coat shone despite the waning light; a chocolate mixture of bright orange and deep russet.

'This is Jasper,' Selina announced. 'He's only six months old.'

Sam put the takeaway on the ground and, when he crouched down, the dog bounded over to him, tugging the leash from Selina's unsteady grasp. 'He's a cocker spaniel, isn't he?' he asked. 'Whose is he, Selina?'

'Ours.'

Sam had been rubbing the puppy fiercely behind one of his ears and the dog collapsed in pleasure. 'Selina, what have you done?'

'We were talking about getting a dog,' she retorted. 'And then I had an offer that I couldn't refuse. Dot's son bought him a few months ago but he's had second thoughts now that he realizes how much of a responsibility they are. So I said we'd take him.'

'Since when were you thinking of getting a dog?' Anna asked Sam.

Sam gave Selina a warning glare as he told Anna a barefaced lie. 'I might have mentioned it in passing, but I was never seriously considering it.'

While Sam had been happy to share the details of

Jasmine's wishes with his landlady, he wasn't prepared to share any more of the little girl's notes with his girlfriend. Selina was one step removed, while Anna was Jasmine's teacher. She knew the girl and the family too well, or at least that was how he was justifying his reluctance to open up to her.

The latest plea from the little girl had been a tough one and Sam had told Selina that he couldn't and wouldn't help Finn find permanent work. When Sam had phoned Jack to ask if he was thinking of keeping Finn on the books, his old friend didn't even hesitate. He wouldn't be reemploying Finn and Sam hadn't asked why. He hadn't needed to.

But Sam hadn't wanted to fail Jasmine completely and had wondered how he could grant her at least one wish, the one she had been willing to forego for the sake of her father. Yet how could he justify giving a dog to the Petersons when Finn would soon be unemployed? He sighed. It would seem his landlady had taken matters into her own hands.

'Well, if you don't want it, maybe you could ask that family you took to the caravan if they want a puppy,' Selina said, giving Sam a not-so-subtle wink. 'You said yourself how the little girl was besotted with the dog she was taking for walks.'

'Jasmine?' Anna asked.

Sam wouldn't look at her and continued to make a fuss of Jasper. 'I suppose it's an idea, but let's not get carried away.'

'Yes, Sam, let's not get carried away,' Anna said coldly. 'You've done more than enough for that family as it is and now you want to shower them with gifts? Don't you think it's time you started concentrating on your own life?'

There was a subtext to the conversation that neither Sam nor Anna would speak about directly. As long as Sam refused to open his heart to her, Anna was always going to feel excluded and therefore exposed. She had perceived a threat from his ex-wife and now she was becoming jealous of Laura too, helped along no doubt by Finn's accusations.

'It's one dog, Anna,' Sam said. He was losing patience. 'That's hardly showering them with gifts and it's not like I'd planned any of this.'

Selina squirmed under the glare he gave her but she refused to repent. 'So we'll keep him, then. I can look after him while you're at work and you can have him the rest of the time. He'll be good company for both of us – and just look at the two of you.' The puppy had been jumping up to lick Sam's face, threatening to knock him over. 'You were made for each other.'

Anna scowled but Sam was smiling when he said, 'You *are* irresistible, aren't you laddie?' He sighed, if only to let Selina know he was agreeing under duress. 'OK then, let's see how it goes.'

Presuming the matter closed, Selina said, 'Oh, and I saw Pat today. She's in complete shock. She can't believe how much work you all put into her garden and I think she'd marry you, Sam, given half the chance.'

'She'll have to wait in line,' Anna said under her breath.

Sam pretended not to hear the remark and busied himself keeping Jasper away from the takeaway bag. 'Hey, get your nose out.'

Selina laughed. 'He is a ball of energy, but you could always take him out running with you.'

'Not a bad idea. I might just take him out for a run

now and see if I can tire him out. But when I get back, we need to sort out exactly how this new arrangement might work.'

Selina was unfazed by the veiled threat and marched up the steps to the front door, leaving Sam to sort everything else out.

'I thought you were exhausted?' Anna said with a hand on her hip. 'Taking care of a dog is hardly going to make your life easier.'

Sam gave the dog one final rub along his back and then stood up and stretched. 'A good run will do us both good and I have a takeaway to look forward to when I get back, thanks to you.'

Anna tried to smile. 'It's good to know I'm useful for something. I suppose I'd better go then and leave you and man's best friend to get to know each other.'

Sam wanted to reach out to Anna, to hold her in his arms and reassure her, but he knew if he did he would struggle to extricate himself from her clutches. She deserved better, he told himself, and not for the first time.

On a positive note, Jasper was already house-trained, although there were no other apparent signs of obedience training. On their first attempt at a run together, the puppy wove in and out of Sam's legs, twisting the leash around him and tripping him up more than once. After five minutes Sam had to concede that they would have to learn to walk together before they could run – and there was another reason to start his training sooner rather than later. If there was any chance of persuading the Petersons to take him, Jasper was going to have to be on his best behaviour.

The first chance Sam had to start in earnest was Saturday morning, and because Anna had stayed over, she was dragged along for their first session too, albeit reluctantly. After completing a full circuit of the park, the puppy was showing signs of responding to Sam's voice. He recognized the harsh tone whenever he was disobedient and became deliriously happy when Sam praised him.

'I think if we go around the park one more time, he might finally get the message.'

'Again?' Anna groaned. 'He must be tired out by now. I know I am.'

Jasper strained at his leash to keep going and whimpered his own plea.

'Jasper, stay!' Sam said and the dog calmed, if only for a second. 'I tell you what. Why don't you go back to the apartment and I'll take him on my own? It's not like I've been great company anyway – I've spent most of the time talking to the dog.'

'I've noticed,' Anna replied with a sigh. Her body swayed from side to side as she waited for Sam to register her need for attention.

When he took a step closer, she nuzzled into his neck while surreptitiously using a foot to push away the puppy who was determined to wriggle between them. 'I'm jealous,' she admitted. 'I want you to myself.'

'I know.'

'So, I was thinking . . . As compensation for being half ignored, how about I don't go home today? It's the bank holiday weekend and we should be making the most of it.'

Sam gritted his teeth. 'I've got a lot on.'

'Such as?'

'More puppy training tomorrow.'

'Would you rather I found my amusements elsewhere? I can, you know. I've had offers,' she said with a pout.

Sam's first thought was that that might be for the best and briefly considered telling her so, but Anna was already backtracking. 'Look, why don't we take him to the beach or, I know, a trip to Delamere Forest? We could find a dog-friendly pub for lunch.'

'Yeah, OK,' Sam said, prepared to accept that it wasn't a bad idea. 'But then I have park ranger stuff on Monday.'

'All day?'

'I have a tour lined up in the afternoon,' he said. He also had plans for the morning, which he didn't think Anna would approve of, but while he tried to think up a way of skirting around the issue, Anna was already making new arrangements.

'Which means you'll be free until Monday lunchtime. Perfect,' she said, as if they had both decided. 'I'll stay until then and I'll even pick up a few things on my way back now so I can make us a nice meal tonight.'

Sam scratched his head as he watched Anna disappear along the path and out of sight. 'What am I to do, Jasper?' he muttered. The dog whined. 'I'm totally screwed up, I know. She's a lovely lass and I shouldn't be messing her around like this, should I?'

Jasper wagged his tail and pulled on his leash in response.

'OK, let's leave that problem for another day. Now, what are we going to do with you?' Sam asked as he turned his back on the path Anna had taken and headed in the opposite direction.

* * *

A thick blanket of dirty white cloud covered the sky and there was a chill in the air that had more than a hint of autumn despite it being August. Not that the weather put off the determined crowd who had turned up for Sam's guided tour of Calderstones Park. His final stop, as always, was at the thousand-year-old tree, and although there were a few children in the group, Sam kept to the approved script. This was the Allerton Oak, after all, a place where Liverpool's ancestors held court before the city had even existed. There wasn't a single historical suggestion that the tree might have special powers.

A few people hung back once the tour was over to ask the odd question, but soon after, there remained only one other person and a dog, both of whom had been standing some distance away from the group. The old lady's skin was as weathered as the tree, her wrinkles almost as deep as the cuts in its bark and, like the tree, her outward frailty belied an inner strength. She was perhaps a little easier to fell, as Jasper almost proved when Sam called him over.

'That bloody dog!' Selina cried, only just managing to stay on her feet.

Sam was laughing as he caught hold of the leash that had been yanked from her hand. 'He was your bright idea!'

'But he's your dog, now.'

'Maybe, maybe not,' Sam said.

'Do you think Jasmine will be allowed to keep him?'

Sam shrugged. He really didn't know. 'I suspect it'll depend on Finn's mood.'

'Are you still going, then?'

Sam had asked Selina to bring the dog over to the park

when his tour was finished so he didn't have to waste more time going back to the house. 'I would have preferred to have gone over to see them this morning, more chance of them being in,' he explained.

Sam had told Selina enough for her to understand the real reason. 'More chance of him being sober, you mean,' she said shrewdly.

'The longer the day wears on the more apparent it'll be if he has fallen off the wagon, I suppose,' he said. When Jasper jumped up to get his attention, he added, 'But if he *is* back on the booze, it's better that I know now. I don't see how I could offer them the dog in that case, even if Jasmine does fall in love with him.'

'Which she will. What eight-year-old wouldn't?'

Sam tried to smile. 'Yes, she will.'

'I just wish I could be there to see the look on her face when she sees him,' Selina said wistfully.

'You could come with me if you like.' The offer was genuine. Sam had a feeling he would need reinforcements and his wily landlady was an expert at manipulating people into doing her will.

'I don't think so,' she said. 'This is your good deed, not mine.'

Sam would beg to differ!

The Petersons lived in a tidy little terraced house that was easy to spot. The hanging baskets on each side of the front door were a mass of colour; bright pink and purple petunias, trailing red fuchsias and blue lobelia. They went some way to compensate for the narrow patch of concrete that constituted a front garden.

Sam rang the doorbell and told Jasper to sit. When the

dog obliged, he was rewarded with a treat, only to stand up again as soon as the door opened.

'Hello, Sam.' Finn looked surprised but genuinely happy to see him. 'Come in.'

'Are you sure? I've got a visitor with me and even though he's pretty well behaved, he's still in training.'

They both looked down at the puppy and, to Sam's relief, Finn reached over and stroked him. 'Oh, don't worry about that. If we were bothered about bad behaviour in this house then I'd never get over the threshold. The girls are out shopping but they shouldn't be long. I'm glad you called, I wanted to catch up with you anyway.'

Sam hadn't been inside the house before and as he stepped into the hall, all his preconceptions about the Petersons' home fell away. He had imagined a house that would reflect the women of the household, modest and understated, but the cool blue colour scheme running down the hallway was followed through into the living room where it became stronger and more vibrant with cobalt blue and silver accents that provided the perfect balance.

'This is Jasper. Thanks to my landlady, Selina, we've somehow managed to adopt him although it's only a temporary arrangement until we can get him re-homed. In the meantime I'm in charge of taking him for walks,' Sam explained, deciding not to labour the point about his need for intensive training. 'We were just passing and I thought I'd call in and thank you again for helping out with the garden. Pat was thrilled with it by all accounts.'

Finn's smile was broad. 'She was that excited when she turned up on Saturday I thought she might pee in her pants. She even had a go of that rope swing.'

Sam shook his head as he laughed. 'Why am I not surprised?'

'And she's said we can all go back again next year for a holiday if we want. There's a method in her madness, of course. The garden will need a bit of maintenance by then, but why not?' He caught the look on Sam's face, which told him exactly why not. 'Look, I know I lost it for a while there. Things get on top of me sometimes, not that that's an excuse for behaving like an idiot, but I want you to know that I've got my act together now and I'm working hard. The future's looking good, Sam.'

'How's the job going?'

'We've probably got another month's work on site and I won't lie, I'm worried that it might all come to an end then,' he said and then gave Sam a pointed look. 'Which is why I'm counting on you to put in a good word with Jack for me.'

'I'll see what I can do,' Sam promised, his face giving no hint of the lie.

'Sorry, where are my manners? Do you want a drink?' He smiled when he added, 'Tea? Coffee?'

'No, thanks. We won't stay long,' Sam said. 'This laddie's keeping me on my toes although they say dogs can be therapeutic.'

'Unless you're allergic to them.'

The thought had never occurred to Sam. 'Are you?' he asked.

Finn gave a short laugh. 'Why? If you were thinking of off-loading the mutt onto me then think again. It's hard enough providing for the family I already have. I don't need another mouth to feed.'

Sam pursed his lips. There was a part of him that was relieved. He had come to the house with a single purpose, to make another of Jasmine's wishes come true, but now that he was alone with Finn, Sam was having second thoughts. Even a puppy as cute as Jasper wasn't going to be the magic ingredient that would make a happy family, especially not with the hard times that lay ahead when Finn realized he shouldn't be pinning all his hopes on Jack keeping him on. Sam didn't want to leave Jasper here. He could hardly bear the thought of leaving Laura and Jasmine.

'I really need this job, Sam,' Finn continued.

'I realize that, Finn, but a lot of the major landscaping work is seasonal. Like I've said before, your best bet is to impress Jack as much as you can in the next few weeks and then maybe he'll take you on next year.'

'Next year doesn't see us through Christmas.'

Jasper, who had been sniffing the rich woven rug in the centre of the room, ventured towards the sound of Finn's frustrated sigh but Finn was in no mood for the pup's sympathy and pushed him away a little too harshly.

'We'd better get going,' Sam said. He would have liked to wait to see Jasmine and Laura, but he could feel the colour draining from the room until the dull grey world outside felt suddenly inviting. 'But I'll keep in touch and let you know if I do hear anything. I hate to say it, but maybe you should start some serious job hunting.'

Without even trying to persuade Sam to stay longer, Finn saw him to the door.

Sam had somehow taken on the responsibility of not only satisfying Jasmine's wishes but her father's too. Finn had wanted Sam to tell him that his job was secure, but

Sam had only succeeded in denting Finn's fragile optimism. From the little Sam knew of the man, it didn't bode well for his family so he tried again to reassure Finn. 'Look, I'll do my best,' he said.

Finn shrugged as he opened the front door. 'Thanks, mate, I appreciate it.'

The cold air held the promise of rain, matching Sam's spirits which were already dampened. When he said goodbye, both men were subdued – and then from out of nowhere there was a flash of colour and the world brightened.

Sam wasn't sure who saw who first. Jasper's body rippled with so much excitement that it forced a high-pitched whine from the pup's throat the moment Jasmine jumped out of the car that had pulled up outside the house. She dropped to her knees in front of him, gasping in surprise as Jasper licked her face and nibbled her ears. Strands of blonde hair wrapped around his snout and his shiny coat reflected the bright yellow of her jumper.

Eventually she lifted her head towards Sam, her smile too wide to hold back her giggles as the puppy continued to jump up at her, licking her chin. 'Is he yours?' she asked.

Sam nodded. 'His name's Jasper and he's a cocker spaniel. He's still got a lot to learn but he already knows a few commands,' he said proudly. 'Sit, Jasper.'

The dog ignored Sam's command. Twice.

'Sit, Jasper,' Jasmine said in a deep voice.

The dog's deep brown eyes connected with the sparkling blue of the little girl's and his back legs began to bend as he tried his best to follow her command. His excitement was all-consuming, however, and with his tail wagging ferociously, his bottom remained an inch from the ground until Sam pushed it down gently with the toe of his boot. Jasper looked up at him briefly before turning back to the little girl. If only Jasmine had been there when Sam first arrived, he thought, then perhaps Jasper would have found his new home.

'It looks like they're friends for life,' Laura said. The sparkle in her eyes was a reflection of her daughter's, although partly hidden by the lock of hair that had fallen across her face. With her arms laden with shopping bags, she tried to blow it away as she manoeuvred herself past the dog and child blocking her way.

'Here, let me,' Sam said.

Finn nudged past him. 'It's all right, I've got them,' he said, taking the shopping, and the light in Laura's eyes along with it.

Jasmine stood up, conditioned to follow her mum even though she was loath to leave the puppy. 'Can I take him for a walk?'

Sam looked up at the brooding sky but these weren't the only dark clouds he sensed looming. 'Maybe another day, if your dad says it's OK,' he said. It wasn't the gift he had wanted to offer, but having access to a dog was surely better than nothing.

'I thought you were looking to re-home it?' Finn asked suspiciously.

Jasmine gasped. 'Dad, could we—'

'No, Jasmine,' Finn said but then released a hiss of air between his teeth as he relented just a little. 'Fine, take it for walks if you want, but only on the condition you don't bang on about getting one yourself.'

'Deal!' she squealed.

'But you live on the other side of the park, don't you?' Laura asked. 'I don't want Jasmine wandering about on her own.'

'You could come with me!' Jasmine suggested before catching the look her mum gave her. 'And you Dad, we could all go.'

'No chance,' Finn mumbled.

'Jasper will be tagging along when I do my tours so that I can keep up with his training. I was even thinking of making him part of the act,' Sam said quite convincingly even though he was making it up as he went along. 'We'll be there tomorrow and Thursday from about four o'clock, so if Jasmine wants to come along then, I'd be happy for her to take him off my hands for a quick walk.'

Laura looked to Finn for his reaction before she spoke but her husband seemed more interested in going through the shopping bags. She turned to Sam with a tentative smile. 'She's allowed to go to the park with Keira and her older sister so I suppose it would work.'

'Thank you, Mum!' Jasmine yelped.

Laura's eyes narrowed at her daughter. 'But only on the condition that Leah is with you and you let me or Natalie know when you're going and when you'll be back. And you don't pester Sam and do exactly what he tells you.'

Jasmine was nodding her head and Jasper, who wouldn't take his eyes off her face, bobbed his head up and down too.

Sensing that he should withdraw before Finn had a chance to upset their plans, Sam said, 'I think the heavens are about to open so we'd better get going. It was nice seeing you all again.'

Jasmine gave the puppy one last hug, and although it was clear that being parted so soon tore at her heart, she didn't object; she had, like her mum, picked up on her father's mood and was retreating into the shadows where she hoped not to be noticed. Sam's heart wrenched too. She didn't belong there. As a gardener, he spent his life nurturing seedlings and saplings, encouraging them into the light, protecting them from the frost and propping them up when needed. But Jasmine wasn't a seedling, he told himself as he set off for home. She was a young girl, someone else's daughter and he was the last person who should be giving advice on how to care for a child.

27

Jasmine's home: Wednesday 7 October 2015

Every time the family liaison officer popped his head around the door, Laura searched for that first clue to the news he was about to impart and had become expert at reading his expression. There was the apologetic look whenever Michael came to offer nothing more than another cup of tea; the concerned look that wasn't quite grave enough to suggest the news was going to crush her; and then there was the expression he wore now. It was a mixture of wariness and curiosity, as if he wasn't sure how Jasmine's parents would react.

'You have a visitor,' he said.

No one had rung the doorbell, although with police milling around to keep press and sightseers away, they didn't need to. 'Who?' Laura asked.

'Jasmine's teacher.'

'Anna?' Finn asked.

'Do you want to see her?'

Laura remained tight-lipped. She didn't trust herself to say the right thing.

'Yes, of course we do,' Finn said. He had stood up and was straightening his clothes and raking his fingers through his hair as Anna came into the room.

'I'll leave you to it,' Michael said, and although he hadn't posed a question, he waited for Laura to nod before leaving.

Anna was also giving the stricken mother her undivided attention and didn't even acknowledge Finn. 'How are you?' she asked.

It was a question that Laura had yet to find a satisfactory answer to, and when she simply shrugged, Anna came over to give her a fierce hug. Even with her nose blocked by the dam of tears she was now too deeply in shock to let fall, Anna's scent was not only strong enough but familiar enough to be immediately recognizable.

'That's Ghost you're wearing, isn't it?' Laura asked.

Anna straightened up and smiled tentatively. 'Yes, it's new.'

'Why the hell are we talking about perfume!' Finn said in exasperation.

Laura asked herself the same question. Did she care that the schoolteacher had started to wear the same scent she had been wearing for years? Or that her husband's clothes had carried that scent recently, even when she hadn't been wearing perfume? It was a trick she wouldn't put past her husband, buying a new conquest the same scent to cover his tracks, but did it really matter to her what Finn was up to and with whom? Not any more, she realized, and probably not for a very long time.

'Have you any news?' Finn was asking Anna. 'Have you spoken to the police yet? What would Sam want with our Jazz? Do you know?'

'I've made a statement for what use it is. I'm sorry, but Sam was a closed book to me. Did you know he had a daughter? The police asked me about her – as if I'd know!' she said with a bitter laugh.

'A daughter?' Finn repeated.

'I know, it doesn't make sense, does it?' Anna said. 'You heard me trying to persuade him to go to his ex-wife's wedding when we were away at the caravan, didn't you, Finn? Did he ever mention a daughter or wanting to see her? No, not once!' She shook her head in disgust. 'I dread to think what else he's been hiding.'

Laura looked from Anna to her husband. They had it completely wrong and her pulse began to quicken as she prepared to speak up for Sam. She had spent years considering very carefully not only everything she said in front of Finn, but *how* she said it, for fear of provoking a reaction which wouldn't necessarily be immediate. He might brood on a throwaway comment for days or weeks and then attack her out of the blue with some irrational accusation or another – and this was certainly going to be a remark that would feed her husband's paranoia, only this time Laura didn't care. She wasn't that timid little creature any more. The worst might already have happened and she would gladly face Finn's wrath if it meant seeing Jasmine again. And while that particular trade-off wasn't available, she had nothing left to lose. She held Finn's gaze.

'I knew Sam had a daughter,' she said.

Finn's head snapped back to her. 'What?'

Anna made that sound again, the kind of laugh that held no mirth. 'I don't believe it! I was dating him for months and he never even suggested he had kids, but he managed to tell you? When?'

'Oh, why am I not surprised?' Finn sneered. 'I knew you two were up to something. That's why you've been acting weird lately.'

Finn opened his mouth to say something else but Michael had come back into the room. Laura's heart sank when she saw the expression on his face – this was a new one. 'What's happened?' she asked before holding her breath.

'We've found what we believe to be Jasmine's footprints.'

'Where?' Finn demanded.

'In a private garden.'

'Is it Sam's house?' asked Anna.

Michael couldn't confirm their suspicion, but neither did he deny it. He simply shrugged and that was when the ground beneath Laura's feet began to shift.

'That's it, I've heard enough,' Finn said and went to push past Michael.

'Mr McIntyre has been taken to the station for further questioning,' the officer said, blocking Finn's way.

Anna pulled Finn back and kept her hand on his arm as he shook with rage. Laura took a step away.

'Has he told you what he's done with her yet?' Finn demanded and when Michael shook his head, he turned on his wife. 'Well, I hope you're happy now. You must have fed him all the information he needed to work out where Jasmine was and when, all so he could take her any time he liked. Are you still going to stand there and defend lover boy?'

Laura's mind was in freefall. From the moment she had met Sam, he had been the hero, but was she really that

220

good a judge of character? The evidence against him was damning, and for the first time she found herself questioning his innocence. What did she actually know about his past? What was it that made him feel so guilty that he hadn't wanted to talk about his daughter? Was it possible that she had been taken in by another man who would prove to be a monster?

'I don't know,' was all she could say.

28

Tuesday 1 September 2015

Jasmine drummed her fingers on the windowsill as if her restless fingers could speed up time. She was in her bedroom, her head pressed against the glass as she searched for the first glimpse of their neighbour's silver car. Natalie had taken her two daughters out shopping for last-minute additions to their school uniforms and she had promised they would be back in time for Leah to take the girls to the park.

The day before, Jasmine had told Keira all about Sam's puppy until her best friend had complained that her ears were bleeding. She couldn't have been that fed up, though, because she had managed to persuade her sister to take them to Calderstones. Leah had had a glint in her eye when she said that a trip to the park suited her fine, which meant it suited her boyfriend too.

The strumming slowed to a funeral march as Jasmine looked at her bedside clock. It was a quarter to four and there was still no sign of them. Her stomach lurched as she considered the possibility that she might not get to see

Jasper after all. She shook her head. It simply wasn't possible. She had asked the Wishing Tree in a roundabout way for a dog, and in a roundabout way, the tree had granted her wish. She looked up at the paper crane hanging from a piece of cotton above the window and thought about the man who had shown her how to make it. Sam wouldn't mind sharing his new dog with her because she had already proved how responsible she was by taking Nando for walks and she would look after Jasper as if he were her own. But she couldn't let Sam down on the first day; what if he didn't trust her again?

Another five minutes ticked by and, with a heavy heart, Jasmine pulled herself away from the window and dragged her feet downstairs with heavy thumps. The living room door let out a groan as she opened it.

'Hi, sweetheart,' her mum said although it was more of a croak. 'Aren't they back yet?'

Jasmine had her chin pressed against her chest but it didn't stop her lip trembling. 'No.'

After a brief coughing fit, Laura said, 'Don't worry, even if you can't go today, there's always Thursday.'

'But I'm back at school then and Leah doesn't know if she'll be home in time to take us!' Jasmine said and then bit her lip to stop from asking her mum to take her instead. She was sick and hadn't left the house all day. Her dad had been quiet too when he was home and the only thing that had raised Jasmine's spirits had been the thought of going to the park.

Laura offered a weak smile. 'This means a lot to you, doesn't it?'

Jasmine nodded, but when she saw her mum pull herself

up from the sofa, she was already having second thoughts. 'You can't take me, Mum. You're not well.'

'It's only a cold and I'm not going to get any better sitting on the sofa feeling sorry for myself. I was thinking of going back into work tomorrow anyway and I could do with some fresh air. It's a lovely day out there and it would be a shame to miss out on all that sunshine.'

'But—'

'I'll take you on the condition that you don't tell your dad. He's got enough on his plate at the moment and you know what he's like.'

Jasmine knew only too well. There was nothing wrong with taking the dog for a walk; after all, her dad had said she could, but sometimes things didn't have to be wrong to upset her dad. He could get angry over nothing at all and he was most definitely in one of those moods where he was looking for any excuse to unleash the anger that was eating him up inside.

'Are you going to stand there and argue or shall we get going?' Laura asked, but she was already talking to thin air as her daughter raced to the front door.

The fresh air made Laura's lungs burn. She had started coming down with the cold on Sunday night and had made the mistake of trying to push through it on Monday. When she had woken up this morning, she had been aching all over but had dragged herself out of bed because she hadn't wanted to take time off work. Her boss was the owner of the builders' merchants, the one who had fired Finn after he had come in one day so drunk that he had crashed a forklift truck into a wall. It had been lucky that no one had been hurt, luckier still that Laura hadn't lost her job too, although that wasn't how Finn saw it, and his wife's determination to get out of her sickbed only served to fuel his suspicions further. He had suggested that the only reason Laura wanted to go in was because she was having an affair with her boss, and so she had stayed at home. It had probably been the right thing to do because she really wasn't well; it had just been for the wrong reasons.

Walking across the park in the late summer sunshine, her legs felt distinctly wobbly although she wasn't entirely sure it had anything to do with her illness. She was looking forward to seeing Sam again. He was the exact opposite to Finn in every sense of the word, in his looks and his demeanour, and it was hardly surprising that her feelings for the two men should be another contrast. She had tried her best to understand her husband, to excuse and forgive him, but he had destroyed the last vestiges of her affection for him. She hated him now. While Sam . . .

'Do you think he'll have waited for us?' Jasmine asked.

'It's only just gone four,' Laura said. 'And Sam said he had a tour organized, so we'll track him down somehow.'

They followed the path that curved around Calderstones Mansion, dipping them into cool shade before bringing them to the Coach House. There were quite a few people milling around, families making the most of the last few days before the start of term and the arrival of autumn, but there was no sign of Sam or his dog.

'Where else can we try?'

Laura gave her daughter's hand a quick squeeze to reassure her but a second later, Jasmine wrenched herself away.

'He's here!' Jasmine squealed.

Sam had appeared around the corner looking as anxious as they had. He too had scanned the crowd but it was when his eyes met Laura's that his features relaxed into a smile. Reminding herself that Sam had made arrangements to see Jasmine and that she was only tagging along, Laura took her time catching up to her daughter who was now kneeling on the ground. The puppy was jumping up and licking her face while leaving little puddles on the flagstones in his excitement.

'You made it,' Sam said, still looking at Laura.

'It was a close call,' she said, and would have smiled except she was struck by a sudden coughing fit. She patted her chest as she brought it under control. 'Sorry, I've got a stinking cold. Natalie's eldest daughter was supposed to bring Jasmine but they've been waylaid.'

'So Jasmine dragged you out of your sickbed.'

There was a smile on Sam's face as if he wasn't the least bit sorry, or was she fooling herself? 'Oh, I'm stronger than I look,' she said.

There was another cough only this time it came from behind Sam and was a deliberate one by the sounds of it. Laura drew her eyes from Sam to notice the elderly lady peering over his shoulder.

'Sorry, where are my manners?' Sam said. 'This is my landlady, Selina. Selina, this is Laura and her daughter Jasmine.'

Laura ought to have been taken aback when Selina gave her a hug, but there was kindness in this stranger's eyes and it felt comfortable.

'Sam has told me so much about you both,' Selina said. 'It's good to meet you at last.'

'And it's good to meet you.'

'It's Selina you have to thank for the dog. Not that I'm foisting him on you or anything,' Sam added quickly, 'I just meant it's clear that Jasmine must have been pestering you to bring her here.'

Jasmine was oblivious to the three adults who were now watching her with satisfied smiles.

'I'll leave you to it,' Selina said, 'I want to get home and give the garden a good mowing while the weather's so glorious.'

'But I—' Sam began, only to be silenced by a stern look from his landlady. 'Oh, OK.'

Before she left, Selina gave Laura yet another hug and then placed her weatherworn hand on Jasmine's head. Jasmine looked up and saw the same thing that Laura had seen; warmth, openness and something else. Understanding.

After Selina had gone, Laura and Sam gave Jasmine their full attention. Jasper had managed to attract every child within a fifty-foot radius and Jasmine was in danger of being relegated to the back of the crowd as groping hands scratched the puppy's ears and rubbed his back. The poor dog was spinning round and round as he tried to satisfy everyone's needs.

'Can we take him for a walk now?' Jasmine asked.

The puppy heard the concern in her voice and pulled away from the other children to reach her. Sam heard the worry too, and within seconds of handing over the leash, Jasmine was setting off along the path back in the direction of the Mansion House.

Laura hung back. 'Shall we meet you here later?' she asked him.

'Actually, my tour doesn't officially start until four thirty. I've still got twenty minutes to kill if you don't mind some company.'

Laura nodded and as they fell into step, she wondered if Sam felt as awkward. They both had their heads bowed as if they didn't want to be seen together. Laura knew she shouldn't be there – why else had she instructed Jasmine not to tell her dad what they were up to? She didn't want Finn knowing that she had met Sam because she knew what he would think and for once he might be right.

'How's Finn?' Sam asked.

Laura put her hands in the pockets of her jacket and hunched her shoulders. 'In an even worse mood than he was yesterday, and that's saying something. He texted earlier to say he's definitely being finished up at the end of the month.'

'I'm sorry there wasn't more I could do.'

'Don't be. If I'm honest, it wouldn't surprise me if he didn't last that long. He's not a good worker when he's unhappy.'

'So I've noticed.'

'Which is all the more reason for me to get back to work. I'm hoping the fresh air will do my chest some good. Someone has to pay the bills, although . . .' she said, stopping to take a raspy breath that created another tickle and a cough, 'he doesn't like me being the breadwinner. He doesn't want me to work, full stop, but unfortunately it's a battle I have to keep fighting if we're going to keep a roof over our heads.'

Laura began wafting herself to create a breeze. She wasn't feverish, simply hot from the baking sun, but there was no way she was going to remove her jacket and reveal fresh bruises on her arms. Sam was watching her and perhaps suspected as much when he asked, 'Are you sure you're all right?'

'I'm fine, Sam,' she said softly.

They walked along the path in silence, watching Jasmine and the puppy lollop across the grass in the direction of the lake. Jasmine launched herself onto the ground and the puppy began trampling all over her. They were still some distance away but Laura could hear her giggling and then her daughter yelped as Jasper began yanking a chunk of her hair with his teeth.

'Do we need to rescue her?' Laura asked.

Before Sam had a chance to answer, the two were on their feet again. Jasmine had lost her grip on the leash and she looked over her shoulder at Sam.

'You can let him run free as long as you can run fast enough to catch him,' he called.

She darted off in pursuit of the puppy. When she couldn't catch him, she instinctively changed direction and began running in the opposite direction. The trick worked and a moment later Jasper was desperately chasing her.

When Sam turned to Laura, he hadn't forgotten the question she had left hanging in the air. 'Does she need rescuing?'

The air caught in Laura's throat. She was shocked how Sam could look at her and see what she hadn't yet been able to share with family or friends. He had simply known and that made her want to love him more. That thought, that *word*, didn't scare her as much as it should for a married woman with a husband like Finn. Her growing feelings for Sam had become a secret pleasure that she felt she deserved in her miserable life. Finn could dig his fingers into her flesh but he couldn't reach her mind where she nurtured desires that she never expected to be revealed or reciprocated.

'Are you both safe, Laura?' Sam asked. 'I don't mean to intrude, but I know Finn well enough now and I'm not blind. I saw the bruises on your arm. If you need help, if you think you and Jasmine aren't safe, then please tell me and I'll do whatever I can.'

They were walking slowly and yet Laura felt the world spinning past her at a terrifying speed. She had tried many times to imagine what would happen if she left her husband, and while she could quite clearly picture the angry confrontations, the accusations and the threats, she couldn't envision a life beyond that, one that would see her escaping Finn completely. She was forever bound to her husband and, in some ways, felt a certain responsibility for him. Yes, there were times when she was afraid of him, but she feared for him too, and suspected he was more of a danger to himself than anyone else.

'We're fine, Sam,' she said. 'Finn gets angry now and again and when he has a point to make, he makes it forcibly.' Seeing the look of alarm on Sam's face, she added, 'He has bouts of depression where you can't get a word out of him unless he has a pint in his hand. He gets paranoid and jealous, possessive and cruel, spiteful and . . .' Laura ran out of damning words to describe her husband. 'He doesn't hit me, Sam, if that's what you were suggesting. He grabs me sometimes when he's desperate for me to listen to him, but he wasn't always like this.'

'How long?'

Laura thought for a moment. 'Years, Sam. Too many years.'

'And Jasmine? Does she suffer the effects like you?'

Laura gasped. 'No, of course not. I swear he's never touched her, Sam.'

'And are you as sure that he never would?'

'I wouldn't stand for it, not ever,' she said and then quickened her pace to escape the questioning that was making her feel uncomfortable. She wanted to believe Sam cared for them, that he might one day return the love she felt growing inside her, but after years of conditioning by her husband, all she had heard in Sam's voice was disapproval and pity.

They were fast approaching Jasmine who was leaning against the iron railings that sectioned off the lake. Jasper had pushed his nose through the bars and was yapping at the ducks. Realizing he couldn't squeeze through, the dog began searching until he found a gap big enough. It was Sam who realized what was going to happen first and he took off at a sprint, jumping over the railings just in time to grab Jasper's leash before the pup could dive into the water.

'Naughty boy,' scolded Jasmine when they were all back together.

Forgetting herself, Laura stared at Sam as he gave Jasmine some quick instructions about training the puppy to be a little more obedient. A comfortable smile had settled on her face when Sam noticed her watching. 'What?' he asked suspiciously.

'You're a natural.'

'Catching dogs?'

'No, engaging children, especially that one,' Laura said tipping her head to Jasmine who was absorbed in the challenge of getting Jasper to sit still. 'And for the record, I have to say that I disagree with you completely.'

Sam looked intrigued if not a little uncomfortable. 'About?'

'About not being good enough to be a father. I haven't forgotten what you said when we were in Wales—' She stopped what she was saying when she saw the look on Sam's face. 'What?'

'I was arrogant enough to call myself a father once,' he said, 'but I messed up. I messed up just about as much as any father could.'

'You have children?'

'A daughter,' he said, and then struggled as his mouth formed a word he seemed unused to saying out loud. 'Ruby.'

Laura couldn't hide the shock. She couldn't imagine someone as considerate and caring as Sam walking away from his family and never mentioning them again. 'How old is she?'

Sam raised his head to the skies as he tried to work it out. 'Let me see . . .' he said with a forced lightness in his voice that crackled with the effort. 'Eighteen.'

'Wow, all grown-up then.'

'It's impossible to imagine,' he said, shaking his head and then taking a step towards Jasmine and the dog to let her know the conversation was at an end.

'Sorry, I didn't mean to—' she began and then wasn't sure how to end the apology.

Sam pretended not to hear her and was about to say something to Jasmine when his phone began to ring.

'Hi, Anna,' he said, 'can I phone you back after? I'm supposed to be meeting up with a tour group in five minutes.'

Self-consciously, Sam turned his back on Laura and Jasmine as he continued to talk to his girlfriend who, by the sounds of it, had questions she wanted answering before ending the call.

'I'm at the lake. Jasper almost went for a swim.'

Another pause and then Sam glanced over his shoulder to look at Jasmine, but it was Laura his eyes settled on and when he smiled, her heart fluttered. 'Aye, of course Jasmine turned up. They're here now, and I need to say goodbye to them so I can get going.'

Having seen the odd hint of jealousy from Anna at the caravan and from Sam's next response, Laura guessed that his girlfriend was eager to find out who he meant by 'them'.

'Jasmine and Laura,' he said, his words clipped. 'I'll speak to you in a bit. OK?'

With the call ended, Sam looked apologetically towards Jasmine whose face had fallen. 'Sorry,' he said, 'we really do have to go.'

'We could look after him while you work,' Jasmine argued.

Laura was tempted to agree with her. She didn't like leaving Sam when there were things left unsaid but she had a feeling she wouldn't find out any more about his daughter, no matter how long they stayed. And there was another reason they had to go, which had more to do with the future than the past. 'I don't think so, sweetheart,' she said.

'We need to get back before your dad gets home. You can come back another time.'

'Thursday. You said I could come on Thursday too.'

Laura cocked her head. 'I thought you said Leah might not be able to take you?'

'I don't know, Mum. Maybe she will.'

'All right, as long as Sam doesn't mind.'

'You're both welcome. Any time,' Sam said.

Laura pulled her daughter away and hoped Jasmine wouldn't resist because Laura was only just managing to walk away herself.

29

Police station: Wednesday 7 October 2015

Sam was sitting in a windowless interview room and had lost all track of time but guessed it was mid-afternoon by now. He was wearing a grey tracksuit kindly provided by the police in place of his running gear which was now being scrutinized by forensics along with his mobile phone. Because he wasn't under arrest, he hadn't been obliged to co-operate, but Sam was more than willing to give them the shirt off his back if it meant being eliminated from their enquiries that little bit sooner. He didn't want a solicitor, he didn't want to obstruct their investigations, but he was tired of being questioned and he was especially tired of DCI Harper.

The detective had disappeared briefly only to return with two items that he had placed on the table in front of him. The manila folder remained unopened, but it was the evidence bag that drew Sam's attention although Harper was taking his time getting to it.

'What do you think has happened to Jasmine, Mr McIntyre?' Harper asked.

Sam had thought of little else in the last few hours. 'I think she's run away of her own accord and the longer she leaves it, the harder it will be for her to come home and face her father's wrath,' he said pointedly.

'And why are you so convinced she's run away from home?'

'Because I won't allow myself to consider any other option, that's why,' Sam said and then tried to add more weight to the theory, by adding, 'I think she'll be hiding out somewhere, probably helped by a friend. She might even be hiding out in the park, I don't know.'

'Where in the park? Is there somewhere in particular that you used to take her?'

'No,' Sam said.

'Not even the Allerton Oak?'

'If she was standing by the tree then I think even the most inept police force in the country would have found her by now,' Sam replied. There were no hiding places around that section of the park and, besides, Sam didn't think that Jasmine would run to the Wishing Tree, not any more. She had put her faith in the tree once upon a time but so much had happened since the day he had spun her that particular fairy tale.

Harper ignored the slight and reached over to pick up the evidence bag. 'Did Jasmine remind you of your daughter?'

'No, not at all,' Sam said as he watched the detective open the bag.

When Harper removed the shoebox, it was all Sam could do to stop himself from tearing it from his grasp. He hated the idea of something so precious being pawed over, and he watched helplessly as Harper's fingers explored the embellishments that had been pasted on the lid; those four beautiful letters encased in glue that still held impressions of Ruby's fingerprints.

'This box means a lot to you, doesn't it, Sam?'

The detective's use of his first name and the gentle tone was both unnerving and infuriating. Sam wasn't about to become Harper's best friend and unburden his soul just because he was talking softly. If it had been that simple, Sam would have done it years ago. He dug his fingernails into the palms of his hands as the need to take the box from Harper continued to gnaw at his insides. 'Yes, it does,' he said.

Sam expected Harper to open up the box to reveal the nine hundred and ninety-nine birds it contained but instead he set it to one side and opened up the manila folder instead, revealing a collection of press cuttings. He didn't need to read the headlines to know what they contained. He could see the school photograph and his daughter's smile shining like a beacon across the dark years since he had last seen it.

'Tell me what happened to Ruby, Sam.'

30

Wednesday 2 September 2015

It had been Selina's idea to start a barbeque and when she and Pat had failed miserably to get the charcoal alight that afternoon, she had phoned Sam to ask his advice. The moment she suggested using a can of petrol, he had promised to come home as soon as he could to supervise. With a sixth sense, Anna had called him soon afterwards and invited herself along.

They were all out in the garden to make the most of the rapidly fading summer while, in contrast, the reservations Anna was about to voice had the strength to persist for much, much longer.

'If you ask me, the whole thing is a recipe for disaster. He's getting far too involved with Jasmine, and her entire family for that matter,' she said. She was picking dog hairs off her dress as she spoke, sitting in a garden chair between Selina and Pat while Sam tended the burning coals.

'Oh, don't be so hard on him,' Selina countered. 'Getting more involved has been good for him. Only a matter of months ago he was a miserable, old sod who ignored as much of the world around him as he could.'

Sam was busy turning over sausages and burgers but risked a glance over his shoulder at the coven behind him. 'I can hear you, you know.'

The women ignored him.

'What about me? Don't you think I had something to do with his transformation?' Anna asked.

Selina tutted. 'Oh, don't pout. I'm not saying you haven't played your part, of course you have. But there's no harm in Sam broadening his interests, is there?'

'No, of course not, which is why I'm so eager for us to finish our children's book.'

'Oh, yes,' Selina said. 'How's it going?'

'We haven't quite got around to pulling it all together yet,' Anna replied. 'But we will.'

'Well, that's nice dear,' Selina said in a tone that was guaranteed to rile Anna further. 'But it's healthy for you both to have your own interests and your own friends.'

Sam didn't need to look again to know that Anna's pout was now a scowl and he couldn't blame her. She felt threatened by Sam's attachment to the Petersons and was still brooding over the fact that he had met up with Laura as well as Jasmine the day before. Sam had been brooding too, and Laura and Jasmine's welfare continued to play on his mind, as did the haunted expression on Laura's face. He hadn't known whether to save her or walk away, but perhaps he was meant to do neither. He had made the offer to help, and it was Laura's decision; he could only hope that she would make the right choice.

'I couldn't agree with you more, Selina.' It was Pat leaping to Sam's defence this time. 'I would never have gotten my beautiful garden if Sam hadn't been able to call on his new friends for help. Including you, of course, Anna.'

Anna wouldn't be appeased. 'It's only a matter of time before it causes trouble, believe me.'

Above the sizzle of meat, they could all hear the annoyance in her voice and still Selina wouldn't back down. 'But think of all the good it's brought. Letting that sweet little girl sneak into his heart is nothing short of a miracle.'

'Is it?' Anna sounded exasperated, and when Sam turned around to shoot Selina a warning glare, she added, 'Why do I always get the feeling that I'm deliberately being kept in the dark?'

'We're all allowed our secrets,' Selina said.

Pat lifted her glass. 'I'll drink to that.'

Anna wouldn't give up and continued to pick at the invisible wounds in Sam's heart. 'She's Finn's daughter, not yours, Sam. If you want to experience fatherhood vicariously you've picked the wrong family. Finn doesn't appreciate you coming in and taking over his life.'

'Oh, is that a fact? He's actually come out and said that, has he?' Sam was full of indignation, annoyed that Anna was using supposition to shore up her argument, but the flush in her cheeks told another story. 'You've spoken to him, haven't you?'

'I bumped into him while I was out last night,' she said, and then for Pat and Selina's benefit added, 'I went for a few drinks with some teacher friends to settle our pre-school nerves. Anyway, Finn was in the King's Arms drowning his sorrows. Did you know he's losing his job? I feel so sorry for him, Sam. He was trying to be a Jack-the-lad as usual but I could tell how much he was hurting and he was not happy at all that you and Laura had been meeting up in the park.'

'You told him,' Sam said flatly.

'Why not? It wasn't a secret, was it?'

Before Sam had the chance to reply, Pat said, 'You need to watch that one. All smiles on the outside but he's got a darker side too, if you ask me. He made a few digs at his wife when he gave me a guided tour of the garden the other weekend, the kind of comment that sounds like a joke but isn't. You know what I'm talking about, don't you, Selina?'

Selina nodded grimly but it was Anna who spoke up. 'I can't believe people are making him out to be such a demon. He's a decent bloke who happens to be going through a rough time. Leave him in peace, why don't you?'

A cloud of black smoke wrapped around them, darkening the mood further. Sam had overlooked his barbeque duties and one of the sausages had caught alight. He picked it up with tongs and tossed it onto the lawn where Jasper pounced on it. The puppy yelped, jumped back and then barked angrily at the sizzling sausage; torn between wanting to devour the juicy meat and attack a fiery enemy.

The remaining food was only partly cremated but when Sam served up it was greeted with more enthusiasm than it deserved. It was far easier to talk about the burnt offerings than continue with the conversation that had unsettled them all. An unspoken truce had been called.

As the evening wore on, the day began to empty of light and warmth and Sam found himself in Selina's kitchen helping Pat make some hot toddies to warm them up.

'Don't you be put off helping that little girl,' Pat said.

241

'You're a good man, Sam. You'll be a blessing in her life, just like you've been a blessing in Selina's.'

'I would have thought Selina sees me more of a curse than a blessing. I cause her nothing but worry, Pat.'

She put a hand on his shoulder. 'I don't believe that for a second and I hope you don't either. You saved her, Sam. You do know that, don't you?'

Sam met Pat's gaze which was slightly unfocused thanks to the vast amount of wine she had consumed during the evening, although her words had undoubtedly been full of conviction.

'I help out where I can, that's all,' he said.

'Oh, it's more than that, much more. She's had enough lodgers in her time who helped cover the bills, but that wasn't really what she was looking for.'

'You mean she needed someone who would do the chores too,' Sam said flippantly. He wasn't sure he wanted to hear what Pat so obviously wanted to share. He was getting too close to people and to life in general. Anna had said no good would come of it and perhaps she was right.

Pat refused to let him off the hook. 'She's spent the best part of the last fifty years existing but little else. We all thought that was how she would see out her days, and then you came along right at the last. She needed someone in her life she could care about and yes, someone she could worry over. But more importantly, she needed a troubled soul who she thought she could help. And that's where you came in, Sam. Not that I have any idea what troubles you,' she added with a gentle nudge to cajole him into believing the lie. 'She had such an awful time with that louse of a husband of hers. She was younger than you at the time

242

and it seemed as if it had damaged her for good, but thanks to you, I think she's mending.'

Sam stopped what he was doing to concentrate on Pat's words. 'What do you mean, damaged? I thought – I assumed Selina was happily married. She was devastated after the accident, I know that much and she never mentioned problems with her husband.'

Pat nudged him again and almost lost her balance. 'Then neither did I. Now, let's get these drinks served before that girlfriend of yours thinks I've led you astray with my womanly wiles.'

Sam didn't argue, if only because he was worried about leaving Anna alone with Selina. His landlady may have been a great supporter of Sam's new girlfriend in the early days, but given the friction sparking between the two all evening, it was becoming apparent that Anna had fallen out of favour with Selina – which was a shame, because she had been the one person who might have been able to convince Sam that the relationship was worth fighting for. But it wasn't. Sam knew it, Selina knew it, and judging by Anna's current display of insecurity, she sensed it too.

While Sam did his best to wrap up his tour, the group were far more interested in the dog wrapping himself around the park ranger's legs than anything Sam could tell them about the ancient oak. He was relaying the story of the exploding gunpowder ship and how it may have been responsible for the damage to the tree, when he caused his very own earth tremor by tumbling backwards.

'I think you'd better call it a day, don't you, love?' a woman said after her husband helped Sam to his feet.

'Sorry, Jasper was far better behaved the other day,' Sam said without mentioning how both the dog and his master had been decidedly less agitated on that occasion.

'Oh, don't worry about it. He's been great entertainment,' the woman assured him. 'In fact, I'd come back again just to see him.'

Sam tried to laugh but his heart was too heavy. 'I'm not sure about that. Bringing him along was a mistake,' he said, thinking of how his efforts to bring a little sunshine into Jasmine's life had only succeeded in darkening his own.

The sickening realization that Jasmine wasn't going to show up that afternoon had been tortuously slow as the minutes crawled by until Sam had been forced to abandon hope and rush to apologize to the tour group he had left waiting. He didn't know why the little girl hadn't appeared, although he could imagine plenty of scenarios, the most rational being that the friend who was meant to bring her to the park had let her down. But that wasn't the only explanation his imagination conjured up during the guided tour, and it was Sam's distraction that had caused Jasper to become as nervous as his master.

Sam didn't know what to do next. He knew he wasn't going to rest until he was satisfied that Finn hadn't been up to his old tricks – or learnt some new ones – and yet he couldn't very well turn up at the house again. Even if he could rationalize his concern about Jasmine not showing up, certain people wouldn't see it that way, namely Anna and Finn. The fact that the little girl hadn't met him in the park was no reason to raise an alarm or demand an explanation but his heart and mind demanded it anyway.

Earlier that afternoon he had used his car to pick up Jasper. It was parked behind the Coach House and that was where he was heading when his mobile began to vibrate in his shirt pocket. There had been a time when his phone would have remained silent and lifeless for days on end, and yet Sam was now in the habit of switching it to silent mode to avoid disruption while he was working. Its intermittent buzz felt like someone prodding him in the chest with a finger; someone insisting on being noticed. He refused to respond and eventually the caller gave up. Ten seconds later there was another vibration; it was another prod. The caller had left a voicemail message and it wasn't much of a stretch of his imagination to guess who that person might be.

During the school holidays Anna had fallen into a routine of phoning him two or three times a day for a quick hello and, in fairness, it usually was just that. Sam ought to appreciate the thought but instead it irritated him and he cursed under his breath before taking his phone out of his pocket and checking the message. It wasn't Anna. It was someone he had been avoiding for far longer and it probably surprised her as much as him when he phoned her back.

'So you got my message then?' she asked.

'No, I phoned you straight back,' Sam said, his mouth dry. He had chosen not to listen to the voicemail, which would only have negated the reason for speaking to his ex-wife and at that moment he needed to hear her voice.

'That's a first,' Kirsten said happily, and then her voice softened. 'It's good to speak to you at long last. It's been too long, Sam.'

He pressed the phone a little closer to his ear. They both

still cared for each other, although it was true to say they had fallen out of love with each other long before their fifteen-year marriage had been dealt its final death blow. They had both moved on as much as they could since then, creating an impassable space between them, and yet he would go back to the life they once shared in a heartbeat. Realizing Kirsten was expecting a reply, he managed to say, 'Yes,' and that single word spoke volumes.

'I have some good news, Sam.'

'You're pregnant.' His tone was flat, tempered with quiet acceptance.

Kirsten laughed. 'No.' There was a pause and then, 'Although it might happen one day, hopefully one day soon.'

'Sorry, I just thought . . .'

'I know and for the record, if it does happen, I promise I won't try to ram the *good news* down your throat,' she said, taking a breath before continuing. 'No, what I was actually phoning to tell you was that I've found a place for you to stay. Auntie Evie's always had a soft spot for you so if you're willing to put up with her cats, you don't need to look for a hotel, she would love for you to stay with her.'

Sam rubbed his chin as he tried to follow the conversation. 'Why would I need somewhere to stay?' he asked.

'You're not planning on doing the round trip in one day, are you? I was hoping you'd hang around long enough to raise a glass to the bride and groom.'

'Sorry, Kirsten but I won't be coming up for the wedding,' he said, now even more confused. 'I'm glad for you, really I am but it's your day, *your* new life, and I don't belong there.'

'What?' she said. It was her turn to be surprised. 'But you accepted the invitation! I thought you were bringing Anna?'

'N-no . . . I didn't . . .' Sam stammered, wondering how on earth Kirsten knew about Anna. His first instinct was to blame Selina for interfering, but even she wasn't capable of that level of meddling. There was only one other person it could be, and Kirsten confirmed it before Sam could get his words out.

'But Anna sent a lovely card saying you would both be there. Didn't you know?'

'We must have got our wires crossed,' he said quickly. 'It was a mistake. I'm sorry, Kirsten, I won't be coming.'

His ex-wife knew Sam wouldn't be browbeaten so, rather than force the matter, chose a different tack. 'How are you, Sam?'

'Fine,' he answered more harshly than the question deserved. He tried again. 'I'm fine, Kirsten. Really, I am.'

'No one blames you, Sam. You do know that, don't you?'

'*I* blame me.'

'I blame *me* too,' she said.

When Sam didn't respond, Kirsten chose to slice through the silence with the inescapable truth her ex-husband had spent six years running from. 'She died, Sam. Our little girl died, and while we can both wish we had made different decisions – even those little decisions that should have been insignificant but weren't – we didn't, and we lost her. We *both* lost her.'

Sam closed his eyes but he might just as well have closed his ears. Ruby had died and it was his fault and his alone. He knew Kirsten was willing him to say something, anything that might open up the conversation and allow them to talk about their shared grief. And in truth he had returned her call because he thought he would, only to discover yet again that he couldn't, so he filled the gap in their conversation by drawing it to a close. 'It was lovely hearing from you, Kirsten. Pass on my best to the lucky groom.'

Rather than return to his car as planned, Sam took Jasper for a brisk walk, so brisk that the puppy had to trot to keep up. They headed west through the Four Seasons Gates and towards Jasmine's house. Sam stopped short of marching straight up to the front door, but when he saw the Petersons' car parked outside and seeing no sign of emergency services along the route Jasmine would have taken to get to Calderstones, Sam's worst fears were allayed. His mind, however, continued to spin and by the time he returned to the car and drove the short distance home, he was wound up so tightly he felt physically sick.

After he was fed, Jasper made a bed on one of the brightly coloured crocheted cushions Pat had made – a present in payment for her beautiful garden with the promise (or threat) of more to come. Sam wouldn't rest until Anna arrived. He had sent a text inviting her over, not trusting himself to speak to her directly.

'I thought you would have wanted an early night tonight after the barbeque,' she said when he met her at the door. 'I wasn't exactly on top form myself for the first day of school.'

'Do you want a drink?'

'Did you get more wine in?' Anna said as she came into the living room where she spotted a collection of newly made origami cranes on the dining table. 'You've been busy.'

'It helps me concentrate,' he said dismissively. 'And I was thinking we'd have a coffee rather than the hard stuff.'

He could feel Anna staring at him, but so far he had refused to meet her gaze. 'What's wrong, Sam?'

Foregoing the drinks, he offered her a seat at the table and they both sat down on opposite sides. The curtains had been drawn to keep the apartment cool during the day and Sam hadn't bothered to pull them back or open a window to release the stale air that was growing heavier by the minute. 'We need to talk,' he said as he picked up the crane he had been in the process of bringing to life when Anna arrived.

'What's wrong, Sam?' Anna asked, more slowly this time.

'I spoke to Kirsten today.'

'Ah, is that it?'

Sam shot Anna a look that halted the visible relief washing over her. 'What the hell were you thinking?'

'I found the invitation languishing in the back of a drawer the other day while you were out training the dog.'

'And how does that explain why you would go ahead and accept the invitation on my behalf, knowing I didn't want to go, and inviting yourself along in the process?'

'I'm sorry, I should have told you sooner but I was waiting for the right moment. I was holding off until this weekend, that way you'd only have a week to fret about it. I didn't think you'd speak to Kirsten first, I thought you said you didn't talk to her.'

Tilting his head, Sam couldn't believe his ears. Was that an accusation? 'I speak to who I want, when I want, Anna. Why do I get the distinct feeling you don't like that?'

'You don't have to justify yourself to me, I know that.'

'Do you?'

She was shaking her head as she said, 'You're making it sound like I'm possessive.'

Sam raised an eyebrow but said nothing.

'If I was, then I'd hardly be persuading you to go back to Scotland to see your ex-wife, would I? I was trying to be supportive, Sam. You still have feelings for her, that much is obvious, and I thought that going to the wedding would help you draw a line under the past once and for all.'

'You know nothing about my past!'

Anna's nostrils flared and her voice had an edge to it when she said, 'No, I don't, Sam. I've been patient and I've been understanding, but there comes a point when you have to start trusting me. And I don't want to hear all this nonsense about taking things slowly. We're in a relationship whether you're ready to accept that or not. We can't go on like this. You know that, and I know it.'

When Anna reached over to take Sam's hand, he pulled away and she was left with only a paper bird in her hand. She crumpled it into a ball and flung it across the table. 'I love you, Sam, and you might be too scared to admit it, but you love me too.'

Sam stood up and turned his back on her. His empty stomach twisted and he could taste bile at the back of his throat. He had told Selina it was inevitable that he would hurt Anna and that day had come. He pulled back the curtain and watched the sun dipping in and out of a scattering of cloud. Light chased shadows across the ground without ever completely eradicating them.

'I'm so sorry, Anna. I can't give you what you want,' he said. 'And you're right, we can't carry on like this.'

There was a gasp that held back a sob. 'Don't say that, Sam! I can make you happy, I *do* make you happy. And I don't care what Selina says: it's our relationship that's seen the biggest change in you. You *need* this. You need *me*.'

There was the scrape of a chair as she stood up and a moment later she wrapped her arms around him, her head resting on his back. 'I can heal you, Sam. Let's go to Scotland. Let me be there with you as you watch Kirsten getting married. It'll help you resolve your feelings for her and give you a chance to start again – with me.'

'No,' he said and peeled her hands away so he could turn to face her. 'Let's get one thing straight: I'm not in love with my ex-wife, not any more, not by any stretch of the imagination.'

'Rubbish! You're in denial, Sam!'

'I. Don't. Love. Kirsten.'

His measured tone was a stark contrast to Anna's screeched response. 'Stop it! Stop lying to me and stop lying to yourself!' She was panting, trying to catch her breath as she waited for Sam's counterattack but he remained tight-lipped. She took a gulp of air and then continued. 'What did she do to turn you into such a heartless machine, Sam?'

'Nothing.'

There was a painful mewl as Anna struggled to hold back a scream while she thumped her balled fist against his chest. 'For God's sake, Sam, tell me why you can't move on? Tell me why you can't love me? You're breaking my heart and I have a right to know why.'

Sam tried not to react to the tears streaming down her face. He felt sick with guilt for hurting her but he refused to pity her. There were worse things that could happen in life than unrequited love. 'I know you're hurting right now, Anna, but I think this is for the best and I hope you'll see that one day. I told you I wasn't looking to settle down, not ever. I'm sorry if you thought I'd change.'

Stepping away, Anna wiped angrily at her tears. 'But you *have* changed. Even Selina said so.'

Sam was shaking his head as he considered sitting back down at the table so they could talk things through. He could tell her about Ruby, he could make her understand exactly how broken he really was and how no one could ever fix him, not Kirsten, not Anna – no one.

'Is it every woman you've closed your heart to, or just me? Have you got your sights on someone else? Is that it? How about Laura, Sam? Would you reject her?' she asked, as if the thought had only just occurred to her. 'Is that why you can't commit to me?'

'I don't know what else I can say to convince you that my feelings for you have nothing to do with Laura and they have nothing to do with Kirsten. I can't love you, Anna. I'm sorry if I led you to believe anything else. Please, cut your losses and find someone else, someone who can give you what you want.'

'That's it?'

Sam didn't even nod his head this time.

'But what about the book we were writing?' she asked desperately.

'It was only ever a pipe dream, Anna. You know that.'

'So you're dumping me?'

Sam's silence gave Anna her answer and her face crumpled. She looked up at the ceiling as she tried to stem the flow of tears. 'I can't believe I've done it again. What is it that draws me to men who are determined to break my heart? I thought if I went for someone steady and gave him all my attention then I'd get the love I deserved.' She dropped her gaze to look directly at him. 'I never strayed, not once Sam, and this is the thanks I get?'

Despite himself, Sam's curiosity was piqued. 'But there might be someone else?'

Anna continued to glare at him but refused to confirm or deny what he'd said.

'Then go to him, Anna. Stop wasting your time on me.'

'His wife might have something to say about that,' she said with a sneer. 'But why should I care about other people's feelings when no one gives a damn about mine?'

At last, Anna had provoked a reaction from him. 'Don't, Anna. You're better than that,' he said, hoping she was talking about a fellow teacher and fearing that she wasn't.

He tried to reach out but Anna was too quick. She hurried across the room towards the door in confident strides, enjoying her moment of triumph.

She turned to face him one last time. 'Oh, don't worry, Sam. I know how to look after myself. I've had to learn the hard way, haven't I?'

In her wake, Sam was left momentarily stunned until a wave of utter relief washed over him, sweeping away the minor irritations, the barbs that Anna had used to rile him and the petty jealousies that would have eventually destroyed their relationship even if Sam had felt differently about her. It was all irrelevant now, the relationship was over.

But then came the aftershock. Anna's parting shot was intended to rattle Sam and it had. Had she been talking about Finn? Had he just told her to go to him? Sam picked up the crumpled piece of paper Anna had flung across the room, straightened it out and tried to concentrate only on remaking the origami folds. He wished once again that Jasmine had turned up that afternoon. He wished – and then he worried.

Jasmine kept her eyes glued to the television. Her nose itched but she didn't want to scratch it in case her dad suddenly remembered she was in the room. Her stomach growled and she held her breath in the vain hope of silencing it – it didn't work. She hadn't eaten since dinnertime and even if her dad did remember to feed her now, she would be too nervous to swallow a single bite.

They were watching some kind of snooker match and although her dad had tried to explain it to her once, she had completely forgotten how it worked. The expression on her face, however, suggested she was taking an avid interest just in case he tried to go through it all again. He would only lose his temper when Jasmine couldn't remember what the different coloured balls meant.

The leather sofa was making the back of her legs feel hot and sticky so she tried to pull her school skirt down a bit further by shuffling back a little while giving the impression of not moving at all. Sweat trickled down the back of her knees and now she had another itch to add to her woes.

An empty beer can flew through the air with lightning speed and glanced off the top of her head. 'For God's sake, will you stop fidgeting,' Finn snarled.

The strike was more of a shock than anything and Jasmine released a sob only to quickly swallow it back again. 'Sorry,' she said. She hadn't taken her eyes from the screen.

Finn muttered something under his breath and from the corner of her eye Jasmine could see him pick up a fresh can. There was a hiss as he opened it, a loud slurp and then stillness returned to the house. She had been hoping he would nod off in front of the telly like he usually did after downing a few beers, but not today. Today he was wide awake and growing more agitated by the second.

Her dad had been in a foul mood since Tuesday night when he had come home late after Jasmine had gone to bed. She had been dreaming about playing with Jasper when her parents' argument had woken her up, although in truth she had only heard her dad's voice. He didn't like Sam any more because he thought it was his fault that he was going to lose his job. He had been even less happy about her mum taking her to the park and had said they weren't allowed to see Sam ever again. Her dad had still been going on about it yesterday and then this morning he had stormed into Jasmine's bedroom to reissue his instructions and she had been forced to promise faithfully that she wouldn't go to Calderstones. Of course she had her fingers crossed. She had only taken the puppy for one walk and it wasn't fair. She was sure Sam would let her take Jasper for a walk every day if she wanted to and she wasn't even asking for that. She *had* to see her puppy again, if only one last time. She needed to say goodbye.

Jasmine suspected her mum knew she had crossed her

fingers because she had made sure Natalie knew about the new rules. And if that wasn't enough, her mum had asked Jasmine to repeat the promise she had made to her dad before sending her off that morning. With a heavy heart, Jasmine had said she wouldn't go. She had her fingers crossed then too.

It was only when she was alone with Keira that the two girls began hatching a plan. They would pretend to play in the shed in Keira's garden and her friend would make lots of noise to cover the fact that Jasmine had dashed off to the park. She could say hello and goodbye to Jasper and be back home again in twenty minutes. It was a plan that would have worked perfectly if only her dad hadn't been waiting for her at the school gates.

Finn had tried to make it sound like it was a special treat for his daughter, but when he failed to raise a smile from her, he had ended up sulking almost as much as she had. And here they were now, watching snooker and waiting for her mum to come home. Time crawled almost as slowly as the sweat trickling down her leg.

'Mummy's home!' Jasmine said, jumping up the moment she heard her mum's keys jangling in the lock.

Laura gasped with shock when someone rushed up to her, having expected to step into an empty house. 'I was just about to go to Natalie's to pick you up,' she said. Her voice was still croaky from her cold and it sounded strained. 'What are you doing here, Jasmine? You're not on your own, are you?'

'She's with me,' Finn called from his armchair.

Jasmine and her mum shared a look and the anxiety that had been crushing the little girl was deftly transferred

256

to older and wiser shoulders. Whenever her dad was in one of his moods, it only took one wrong move to make him explode and her mum was far more practised than Jasmine at traversing that particular minefield.

Laura stepped carefully towards the living room door. Her eyes shone brightly as she asked, 'Home already?'

'Home for good, more like it.'

While her mum was swallowed up into the living room, Jasmine stayed by the front door. She didn't catch what her mum said next because she was too busy working out if she could slip out unnoticed, wondering how long Sam was likely to stay in the park and if there was still a chance she might see Jasper. She hadn't got too far with her calculations when an explosion of words jolted her to her senses.

'How can I trust you now!' her dad screamed. 'If you can go behind my back once, you can do it again! I had to leave work early to make sure Jasmine wasn't led astray and I had to be home to make sure you came back when you were supposed to!'

'You didn't have to do that, Finn. I explained what happened last time. I thought you knew we would be going to the park so Jasmine could take the puppy for a walk,' Laura said patiently. 'You were there when Sam made the arrangements. I wasn't trying to deceive you, but I understand that you don't want us seeing him any more; you made that perfectly clear. I gave you my word and so did Jasmine. You *can* trust us.'

There was a bang as something hit the wall. It dropped to the floor and Jasmine recognized the sound of an empty beer can rolling across the timbered boards.

'No, I can't, Laura! You've ruined everything. I'm unemployed again because of you!'

'You walked out on your job?'

'You gave me no choice. You never do,' he said, his voice calmer and yet all the more menacing. 'You'll never learn.'

Laura's voice trembled when she said, 'Finn, please. Don't do this.'

The living room door closed.

31

Police station: Wednesday 7 October 2015

When Harper closed the file, Sam felt a measure of relief. He had been staring at the grainy image of his daughter in the press cutting and it felt wrong that she should be in a room that had played host to all kinds of villains and reprobates. There would have been innocent victims here too, of course, but not Ruby. Not his beautiful, smiling daughter.

'You can understand our concern,' Harper was saying.

'In what way, exactly?'

'We're worried about Jasmine, Sam, and you of all people should know what her parents are going through.'

'Should I?' Sam asked. 'As your neat little file will tell you, there was never any doubt about where my daughter was or what had happened to her.' He tried not to close his eyes, not even to blink in case the darkness summoned up images he couldn't face. 'Six years ago she was alive and then she wasn't. She was taken from me and I was crushed by the awful truth of knowing that she was never coming back. I didn't have the torment of hope, or the torture of not knowing.'

'And how does that make you feel about Jasmine? Is there the torture of not knowing or do you know exactly what's happened to her, Sam?'

The crash as Sam brought his balled fist down onto the table made Harper jump. 'No, I don't know what's happened to her!'

'That's quite a temper you have, Mr McIntyre.'

'What is this, Harper? What's going on in that narrow little mind of yours? Let me guess . . . You've decided I'm a bereaved father, crazed with grief, so of course I would have taken Jasmine. I've lost a child so logic dictates that I've kidnapped someone else's? Is that really the best you can come up with?'

When Harper refused to deny that was exactly what he had been thinking, Sam continued with his rant, 'You seriously think I walked around the park as if it were a car showroom so I could pick out this year's model? Is that how you think it works when you lose a child?' His jaw was clenched so tight that his back teeth ground against each other, but it wasn't enough to hold back the anger. 'Let me tell you how it goes, shall I? For twelve precious years, Ruby was my life, my world and my reason for living, right up to the moment I had to say goodbye to her forever. Which, for the record, was just before they wheeled her into theatre – not to save her life, but to give other children the chance to live.' He waited to savour the pained expression on Harper's face, proving the detective had a heart after all. 'Yes, that's right. Less than twelve hours after seeing my beautiful, smiling daughter at the breakfast table, Kirsten and I agreed to donate her heart, her lungs and her liver so that maybe other parents would be saved from the kind of devastation we were going through. That's the kind of man I am, Harper. The kind who will endure any kind of sacrifice just to help ease someone else's suffering. So I ask you again, do you really think I've taken her?'

'Grief can do terrible things to a person,' Harper said in an attempt to justify his suspicions.

'It doesn't change who they are! Who I am! I didn't turn into some kind of monster the day my daughter died. I was a good, decent man,' Sam said through gritted teeth. 'And there was a time I even thought I was a good father. I would have done anything to protect Ruby; I would have laid down my life for her and I'll spend the rest of my life regretting the fact that I couldn't. Don't you understand yet? I may feel as if I don't deserve to be called a father, or even admit to having been one, but I'm no monster either, so for pity's sake stop looking at me as if I am.'

Harper took a moment to consider his response then said, 'You know, that was a nice speech and maybe I did jump to conclusions – bereaved father attaches himself to a little girl who reminds him of his long, lost daughter, she goes missing . . . What else was I supposed to think?' When he shrugged it was clear he would offer no apology. 'But the fact remains that we have placed Jasmine at the house of someone who was a complete stranger to her six months ago, someone who has evidently become obsessed with her and her family ever since.'

'I've had enough of this,' Sam said. 'I'd like to go now.'

'And I'd like you to stay,' Harper said. Slowly and deliberately, he pushed the manila folder to one side so he could put the shoebox in front of them. 'If you refuse then I will arrest you, Mr McIntyre,' he said, no longer pretending to be Sam's friend. 'I don't particularly want to do that because that creates all kinds of problems and not just for us. The media are a key tool in our investigations and once they hear you've been arrested, then even if we release you without charge, the press do tend to be quite tenacious. While you continue to help us with our enquiries, then their interest in you can be kept to a minimum. It's up to you, Mr McIntyre. Are you refusing to help?'

Sam met the detective's steely glare. 'No.'

Lifting up the lid, Harper rummaged inside the shoebox. 'Did you make these little birds with your daughter?'

'Some of them, yes,' Sam offered, doing his best to be helpful and not thinking how the detective's grubby fingers were defiling the sacred pieces of paper.

'We found one in Jasmine's room,' Harper said as he picked a bird up.

'I showed her how to make them while we were on holiday,' Sam said, keeping his eyes fixed on Harper and not the pink piece of paper in the detective's hand.

There was no way of knowing which of Jasmine's wishes it contained. Should he tell Harper to open it up? Would it convince the detective to direct his investigations elsewhere or would it lead to more questions such as why he was compelled not only to grant Jasmine's wishes but to keep them too. Knowing Harper, he would see them as some kind of trophy.

'She worshipped you, didn't she, Mr McIntyre?'

'No,' he said, and before he could stop himself, he added, 'If anything, she hates me for betraying her.'

Harper dropped the bird back into the box and leant

back in his chair. He knew he was breaking through Sam's defences. 'Why? What did you do?'

'I read her wishes.'

'There was more than one?' Harper asked and then actually laughed. 'Of course, the job for her dad, the holiday, the dog.' He was still chuckling to himself when his breath caught in his throat. 'And you *read* them? You mean she didn't just tell you, she actually wrote them down?'

'Yes, it was part of the story of the Wishing Tree. I told the kids to write down the wishes and throw them into its trunk.'

'Why the hell didn't you mention this before? If she has run away, she might have left another one there, for God's sake!'

32

Sunday 6 September 2015

'I haven't got a clue what I'm doing, Sam.'

Selina was a few steps ahead of him as they meandered along a narrow path that curved its way through a dense patch of fir trees and into the shadows. Jasper was supposed to be at her heel, but he was far more interested in looking back at his master. His back legs scraped along the ground as Selina tugged at his leash.

'You're doing fine. Don't give up.'

She turned and shot Sam a meaningful look. The irony of his words hadn't been lost on him either.

Sam had spent the last couple of days trying to unpick emotions that were knotted so tightly that he hadn't known where to begin, and after spending yet another restless night in a hopeless search for answers, the solution to his problems in the end was a familiar one. There was nothing he could do to change the past but he could exert some power over the present and he had already made a start by ending his relationship with Anna – something that had been reinforced during a number of painful telephone conversations. But their relationship wasn't the only error of judgement he had made in recent months.

He worried constantly about Jasmine and Laura, more so after phoning Jack to be told that Finn had walked out on his job after the pair had almost come to blows. Sam had no other information on how the family might be faring, but he imagined the worst. And there lay the problem. He didn't know and couldn't know what was happening because the closer he tried to get to the family, the more problems it caused. His involvement with the Petersons had been a mistake, for him and for them, and one he had to rectify if he was ever to stand a chance of returning to the simple, uncomplicated life that he had been a fool to turn away from.

He hadn't come right out and told Selina what he was planning, but she was no fool. She knew his reasons for leaving Scotland and she was aware that the constant need to outrun his thoughts might one day take him further away. And she was certainly sharp enough to realize there was a method in Sam's madness when he insisted on involving her in this latest puppy training exercise.

'Show him who's boss,' he urged which prompted Selina to tug half-heartedly on the leash.

'I have,' she muttered. 'And we're both agreed – he is.'

'No, he is not. I can't believe you're letting a six-month-old pup walk all over you, woman.'

Jasper chose that moment to run circles around his would-be mistress until she was tethered to the spot. With a deep sigh, Selina unravelled the leash from around her ankles and offered it to Sam.

'I thought my years of being a doormat were behind me, but apparently not,' she said.

A few sharp words and Jasper was at Sam's side. The pup looked up at his master with doleful eyes that held more admonishment than guilt. Don't abandon me, they said.

'I think you have to accept that he's your dog, Sam,' Selina said as she let him move ahead of her with the puppy falling easily to heel. 'I'll take care of him while you're at work but he belongs to you.'

'You can't go shirking your responsibility,' Sam said, realizing too late he had given Selina another opportunity to condemn him.

'Neither can you.'

'So when were you ever a doormat?' he asked if only to distract her.

'A long time ago.'

'How long? Would that be fifty odd years ago, maybe?' he said. When Selina refused to respond, he continued. 'I can't imagine you being a pushover with anyone.'

'I think Jasper would beg to differ.'

Selina had only ever given Sam the bare facts about her life with her husband. She had told him about the failed pregnancies that blighted her marriage and a little about the accident which had taken the life of her husband and their unborn child, together with her ability to ever carry another. She had talked about her sense of loss, comparing and contrasting her feelings with Sam's, but she had said very little about the man she had once shared her life with or his character. Based on his own experiences, Sam had assumed that it was the profound pain from her loss that made the subject so difficult to voice, but after Pat's comment at the barbeque, he had started to challenge that view. 'Were you not happy when you were married?'

Selina didn't reply and they walked on for a while in silence. Jasper kept so close to Sam that he bumped into his leg occasionally while Selina started to fall behind as if she were deliberately extending the distance between them. Sam slowed his pace too, letting her know he was still waiting for her answer.

'It was a long time ago.'

'You mean you can't remember if you were happy or not?'

'I remember.'

'Pat said something about Finn having a darker side and how you knew what that was like. Was that a reference to your husband, Selina?'

Selina sniffed the air as if she had detected something unpleasant. 'If Finn is anything like Alf was then I pity Laura and that little girl. She's a sweet little thing and she shouldn't have to live a life where her only ray of hope comes from sending begging letters to an inanimate object.' She stopped and looked around. 'Didn't you want to pay a visit to the Wishing Tree? We've gone past it, haven't we?'

'My days of granting wishes are over,' he said abruptly. 'And I thought we were talking about you.'

'What if it's me making the wish?'

Sam didn't answer. He knew what was coming.

'Don't go running off on me, Sam,' she said. 'I couldn't cope with this little tyke on my own.'

'He'll be fine.'

'Maybe he would,' she admitted. 'But I wouldn't. Don't make me beg, Sam.'

Sam wasn't used to Selina exposing her vulnerable side. He hadn't thought she had one. He stared intently at the path ahead and tried to work out where he was going.

'OK, let's go home,' he said, and as they did an about-turn, Sam hoped there was also a way back to the peace he had once found within the four walls of his apartment. If he couldn't, then Jasmine wasn't the only one he would be letting down.

'I see you haven't got the troublemaker with you today.'

It took a moment for Sam to recognize the woman. She had been on his guided tour the week before and her husband had helped Sam get to his feet after Jasper had tripped him up. 'I thought it was safest to leave Jasper at home this time,' he said. His lips curved to match the shape of the woman's mouth but he didn't feel the smile.

'That's a shame. You make a good double act and the tour you gave was fascinating. You know, I've visited the park for years and never knew there was so much history about the place.' They both glanced towards the Allerton Oak as it shivered in the breeze, its drying leaves trembling with apprehension for the coming season. The woman was oblivious to its fears as she continued, 'I've told all my friends that they have to book themselves on one of your tours, but I'm warning you now, they're expecting Jasper too.'

'I can't make any promises,' he warned, aiming his frown at the trunk of the tree. He could see the merest hint of pink paper, its torn edges reaching out from the shadows towards him.

Sam had been staring at it for ten minutes but so far had refused to give in to his curiosity. That week had marked the start of a whole new chapter in his life, one where he was determined that the pages would remain relatively blank. Selina needed him and he owed her too much to abandon her, but if he was going to stay then he had to strip back his life until it was as sparse and uncluttered as his apartment and that meant breaking all ties with Jasmine. She had two parents and they were responsible for her, not him. He didn't care that it was Thursday and that there was a chance she might come looking for him.

He hadn't brought Jasper to the park on Tuesday either; in fact, he was spending as little time as possible at Calderstones while there remained a risk of glimpsing flashes of golden tresses through the trees. There had been plenty of office-based work thanks to the delay in filling Jack's post and Sam had been quick to volunteer, making sure he only returned to Calderstones to deliver his tours with a handful of minutes to spare. He was going to immerse himself in his job, which had been his single source of fulfilment in the last few years and could be again.

After the woman had bidden him goodbye, the scrap of pink paper continued to taunt Sam. He made a half-hearted attempt to move away from the tree, but his feet were firmly planted in the ground. He rubbed his chin, which was as rough as sandpaper; it would be weeks before his beard looked anything more than five o'clock shadow, but, given time, it would be as if the last five months had never happened. He closed his eyes and was relieved that the dark and light playing across his eyelids didn't merge to form the image of a little girl's face, and yet he could sense

Ruby standing next to him, telling him he was better than this; reminding him it was in his nature to be a protector.

'No, Ruby, you're wrong,' he whispered. 'I didn't protect you.'

He turned and made sure he had his back to the tree when he opened his eyes. He took a step, then another and another, until he broke into a run, but rather than find a clear path, Sam headed straight for a fir tree. He slammed his hand against its trunk, hitting it with enough force to propel him back in the direction he had just come. He used the momentum to jump over the railings and, before he could even catch his breath, he had the note in his hand.

To my Wishing Tree

Please please help me. My mum's hurt and she won't go to the hospital. Dad says she's fine but I heard him crying. He's scared and so am I and it's all my fault. Mum says she fell but it wouldn't have happened if Dad hadn't been angry and he was angry cos of me.

And Sam must hate me too now cos he didn't have Jasper with him when I saw him. I let them down and he must know I can't be trusted just like Dad who said I'm not ever allowed back in the park but here I am.

I'm sorry I'm asking you this but I promise it's going to be the last wish ever. I love my mum so much so don't let her die and if you can't do that then let me die too cos I don't want to live with just my dad. I'm so so scared.

Your loving friend
Jasmine xxx

When someone knocked at the door, Laura's first thought was to ignore whoever it was, but with Jasmine upstairs, there was always the chance she would answer it anyway. It took her longer than normal to get moving and she shuffled slowly down the hallway.

Laura opened the door only a crack and her gasp of surprise was a painful one. Sam had been the last person she had wanted to see even though he was never far from her thoughts. She had been torturing herself with fantasies of what life might be like if she had married someone like Sam instead of . . . 'What are you doing here, Sam?'

Scratching his head, Sam said, 'I've been worried about Jasmine not turning up to take Jasper for a walk. I just need to know that you're both all right.'

'We're fine.'

Sam didn't look convinced. 'Can I come in?'

'No,' she said quickly, and then, 'I'm sorry, Sam. Not now.'

'Is Finn home?'

She was gripping the edge of the door and her hand trembled. 'No,' she whispered.

'Please, Laura, let me in.'

'But I told you, Sam, we're fine,' she said, sounding strong and resolute until the effect was lost when her voice cracked.

Sam inhaled deeply and the anxiety on his face deepened when he glanced over his shoulder at a spot further up the road. Her heart leapt into her throat. 'What is it?'

'The kids are playing on the road,' he said. 'I can't see Jasmine with them.'

'She's upstairs in her room.'

'Are you sure?'

'What do you want, Sam?' Laura asked impatiently.

'Can I come in?'

Realizing there was as much to fear from Sam being spotted on her doorstep as there was from Finn arriving home to find him in the house, Laura's only option was to let Sam in long enough to convince him to leave.

Slipping past her, Sam waited in the hallway and then watched her as she ushered him towards the living room. From her slow and deliberate movements, it was obvious that she was in pain, even though she was gritting her teeth so as not to let it show on her face. Sam didn't take a seat but stood facing her while Laura remained by the living room door. She pulled at the sleeves of her cardigan, then wrapped one arm around her waist, her hand covering her left side to give gentle support to cracked ribs that made every breath painful. She rested her free hand on the door to keep herself steady.

Sam's eyes swept across her body as if he could see every bruise, and when his gaze came to rest on her ashen face, she didn't want him to ask again if she was all right, so she asked a question of her own. 'What *are* you doing here, Sam?'

Sam put a hand over the breast pocket of his shirt. There was something inside, a piece of paper, and Laura thought he was about to take it out or at least make reference to it, but his response threw her completely.

'I've broken up with Anna.'

'Yes, she mentioned it to Finn. I'm sorry about that Sam, but . . .' She stopped short of asking why he had felt it important to tell her. Could there be more to Sam's feelings than pity?

Sam must have read her mind because he became flustered. 'Anyway, I thought you ought to know that she said something to Finn about us meeting up in the park last week. Anna has a bit of jealous streak and she probably made it sound . . . oh, I don't know, seedy I suppose. With Jasmine not coming back to see Jasper, I thought it might have caused trouble between you and Finn and I just wanted to apologize if it had.' He glanced at the arm she was using to cover her ribs.

Laura had already assumed that was how Finn had found out. 'I'm afraid it's not the only thing Anna's been telling him lately. He knows how your first meeting in the pub wasn't accidental, or the invite to go on holiday, for that matter,' Laura said with a weak smile that she hoped would tell Sam that she wasn't offended or disturbed by the revelation. If anything, Sam had gone up in her estimation.

'I'm sorry. I was only trying to help . . .'

'I know, and none of this is your fault, Sam. I should have known better than to take Jasmine to meet you in the park, especially without telling Finn. Anna's not the only one who can get jealous, but I guess you've already worked that out for yourself.'

'I suppose he was angry.'

When Laura shrugged, it made her wince and tears sprang to her eyes. She looked over to the window where sunlight had broken briefly through the clouds to dance across the brilliant white voile. The warmth began to evaporate her tears, but all too soon the rays of sun disappeared and the world returned to grey.

'What did he do, Laura?'

'What he always does. He drank himself into oblivion.'

She stopped short of saying how he had taken her with him, or how painful the fall had been. She didn't need to.

'Did he hurt you?'

She recalled coming home the week before to find her daughter waiting at the door. Such a greeting should fill any mother with joy but for Laura there had been only dread. Finn had started screaming at her, repeating the threats and jibes she had already heard over the previous two nights, only this time Finn had given up all sense of restraint.

'It started that night after we'd met in the park. Finn had gone to the pub after finding out his job was about to end.'

'Where he bumped into Anna.'

'He came home, steaming drunk, too drunk really to do anything more than make some pretty nasty threats. I didn't argue with him,' she said with a sad laugh. 'I've learnt the hard way that there's no point. I can't hold a rational conversation with Finn when he's like that and whatever I do say gets twisted, so I say nothing and wait for him to pass out.'

'And is that what happened?'

As Laura held Sam's gaze, she wondered if he had any idea of the effect that single look had on her. She felt protected, and for the first time in days her body relaxed until her cracked ribs made a stabbing reminder that she was anything but safe.

'Yes, he passed out, that night at least, and the next day he just brooded. He had it in his head that we were going to meet you again on the Thursday and it was eating away at him. Our life is a bit like a line of dominoes and Finn's always the first one to fall, but never the last. On Thursday he walked out on his job, or maybe he was fired, I don't know and I don't care. The net effect is the same.' She exhaled slowly to keep herself calm and then said, 'What I do know is that he was hellbent on coming home early to make sure neither of us went behind his back. I ended up sending Jasmine over to Natalie's for a couple of nights until he had calmed down.'

'You were frightened for her safety?'

Laura was shaking her head. 'No, Sam, I don't believe Finn would physically harm Jasmine,' she said, although she couldn't be so sure that there had been no emotional harm over the years. Laura tried her best not to let Jasmine see or hear anything that would upset her, and her neighbour was used to Jasmine turning up on her doorstep, especially of late. 'I've told you: I would never let him touch her, not ever. I only send her away because I don't like her witnessing the one-sided arguments that can go on for days until Finn's fuse blows out.'

'And how bad did it get before that happened?'

He was looking again at the way she held her left side and had the answer whether Laura was willing to reveal it or not.

'Finn's more dejected than angry now.'

'Where is he? Out looking for work by any chance?'

'Maybe,' she said but even as she spoke, she knew she couldn't fool Sam. 'Or he's drowning his sorrows. He's in a dark place right now, Sam and he'll stay there until he finds a reason to sober up. I've seen it before.'

'And you'll see it again, but I don't need to tell you that, do I? He'll make promises and he'll be true to his word

– until he finds a reason – or an excuse – to do all of those things he swore he'd never do again. That's how it goes in abusive relationships, isn't it?' Sam glanced over Laura's shoulder towards the stairs, as if he could see Jasmine cowering there while she listened to her parents fighting.

There was no mistaking the look of pity in Sam's eyes now. Suddenly angry, she asked, 'So you're the expert now?'

'No I'm not, thank God, but *you* are. So tell me I'm wrong, Laura. Tell me there won't ever be another crisis or another reason for Finn to raise his fist to the world.' He waited only a heartbeat. 'Or raise his fist to you.'

Laura didn't move except to pull her arm around her a fraction tighter. The anger had been fleeting; she was too exhausted to fight and even the tears she had been holding back won the day. She hated herself in that moment. She felt feeble and utterly worthless. Why couldn't she have the courage to stand up to Finn? Perhaps if she did, her husband might respect her more, or maybe Sam would.

'How badly are you hurt? Do you need medical treatment?'

'It's nothing. He didn't hit me, Sam. We had a bit of a tussle, that's all,' she said as the first tear trickled down her cheek. She couldn't admit, not even to Sam, how terrified she had been. That fear had been building since the night at the caravan when Finn had put his hands around her throat. She couldn't be sure that if he had the chance to do it again, he might just squeeze the life out of her, and so for once she had fought back, if only a little. 'I fell against the dressing table and I think I've cracked a rib. Finn helped bind it up.'

'That was caring of him.'

'Go away. Please, Sam,' she begged softly and felt humiliated as the tears flowed freely.

When Sam stepped forward, she wasn't sure if he was about to leave and, despite her words, she wasn't sure she wanted him to. He stopped in front of her and cupped her face in his hand. 'I can't leave you like this. You or Jasmine.'

Laura closed her eyes and held onto that moment. She knew it wouldn't last, but she wanted to savour it. As she felt Sam's thumb brush across her cheek to wipe away her tears she wanted to turn her face to his hand and kiss his palm. She imagined falling into his arms and making him promise never to let her go, but she couldn't take that leap of faith. She was such a pathetic creature.

As consolation, she reminded herself that she had a home, a marriage, a husband and a child. She had responsibilities, and besides, they *had* been happy, hadn't they? Finn had been desperately remorseful, he had cried in front of her when he had seen the bruises the next day. This could be the wake-up call he needed.

When she did touch Sam's hand it was to pull it away from her face. 'We'll be fine, Sam,' she said. 'We can move on from this, we can be happy again, but not if you're here. The more involved you get, the more it fuels Finn's insecurities. Please, I know you want to help but you must keep away.'

The soft click of a door being closed made them both jump as if there had been a crash of cymbals. Laura's pulse was racing and she fought off a wave of nausea as she craned her neck to look down the hallway towards the kitchen. Her hand went to her mouth.

33

Following Finn's gaze, Laura and Anna looked through the window to catch a glimpse of a policeman walking past. A moment later there were voices in the hallway and then Michael came into the room.

'They've found something else, haven't they?' Finn demanded.

'Is it Jasmine?'

Michael gave Laura a sympathetic smile. 'No, not yet, although we would like you to look at something.'

As he lifted up an evidence bag, Laura felt dizzy as the room swam around her. She didn't want to look at what the police had found, already imagining it would be a sock, a shoe, or, God forbid, an item of underwear. Please, please, no, she repeated as her eyes came into sharp focus on a sheet of pink paper. She took a shuddering breath. 'That's from Jasmine's notepad,' she said.

'What does it say?'

Finn had made a move to take the note from Michael, but the family liaison officer kept it out of reach. He turned

278

it over so both parents could read the scrawled message. The paper was damp and the ink had bled in parts but it was still readable. 'Could you confirm that this is your daughter's handwriting?'

'Yes,' Laura said, ignoring the pain in her side as she leant forward to devour every word.

To my Wishing Tree

I don't ever want to grow up not EVER. Grown-ups spend too much time being really sad or really angry. I want to stay being little cos then I can still believe in you and people won't think I'm stupid or silly. I wish I could just disappear. That's my wish, Wishing Tree. No one will miss me except Jasper maybe. I'm going over to see him now and if he wants to, he can come with me. That would be all right wouldn't it? I don't know where we'll go but far away so this is goodbye.

I'll never forget you and I hope you won't forget me too.

Your loving friend
Jasmine x

There was a hiss and a curse from Finn. 'And there you have it. I told you she went to see McIntyre,' he said to Laura. 'She knew where he lived all along.'

'But didn't you say Sam had been out running when the police turned up at the house?' Anna asked.

The question was to Michael but it was Finn who answered. 'He could have taken her with him when he went out. It wouldn't have taken much for him to tempt

279

Jazz into taking the dog for a little walk, would it?' Turning to the policeman, he added, 'You won't find her at the house, then, she'll be somewhere else. Buried in the park for all we know.'

The words her daughter had written blurred with Laura's tears as well as the rain. The note proved Jasmine had run away, but what had happened after she had reached Sam's house? Laura didn't want to give credence to Finn's twisted theories about Sam, but it didn't help that she had so little faith in her own judgement. Had she been that weak, that gullible?

'Do you think Sam could have . . . ?' she asked Michael.

'Nothing is being ruled out at this stage,' Michael said, 'but there's no evidence to suggest that Jasmine has come to any harm, either at Mr McIntyre's house or anywhere else.'

'Not that you've found yet,' Finn said. 'And he'll know how to hide the evidence. I wouldn't be surprised if he's done this kind of thing before.'

'He was determined not to go back to Scotland,' Anna added helpfully. 'I bet his ex-wife can tell you a thing or two about the wonderful Sam McIntyre.'

'We've haven't been able to contact her yet,' Michael said. 'We think she set off on holiday this morning and we're waiting for the plane to land.'

'Honeymoon,' Anna surmised. 'What about his daughter?'

Michael took a moment to consider how much more information to divulge, but seeing the distress Laura was going through, he said, 'Mr McIntyre's daughter Ruby died in an accident six years ago; she was twelve at the time.'

It took Finn only a fraction of a second for his warped

mind to use such devastating news to condemn the man. 'That's it, then,' he said. 'That's why he was so obsessed with Jasmine. He wanted someone to take her place.'

'Stop it!' Laura said, and when she began to cry, she wasn't sure if it was because she felt the horror of Sam's grief or the fear of suffering a similar fate, but in amongst those emotions there was an element of relief too. She still didn't know where Jasmine was and not knowing was killing her, but Ruby's death explained so many other things. It must have been torture for Sam to see Finn holding his own family in such contempt. He had wanted to stay away but he hadn't; he *couldn't*. There were no sinister motives; he had simply wanted to protect Jasmine, to protect them both. The doubts that had plagued her earlier were swept away. Sam wouldn't harm Jasmine and he wouldn't put Laura through the kind of pain that he knew only too well; pain she couldn't yet contemplate.

She wiped her eyes and stood up as straight as her injured ribs would allow. 'I want to go to the police station. I need to talk to DCI Harper.'

'What the hell for?' Finn demanded.

'Jasmine isn't going to come back here, Finn, not of her own accord, and I have to tell the police why. I have to stop them wasting time on this stupid theory that Sam has abducted her.'

'You still think it's a stupid theory, Laura? After everything we know about McIntyre?'

'She wasn't taken, Finn, she ran away from home!' Laura said, raising her voice to her husband for the first time in a very long time. 'She ran away from *us* and I need to speak to DCI Harper now!'

'Then I'm coming with you.'

'No, you're not. I want to speak to him on my own,' she said.

With the family liaison officer watching Laura's back, Finn couldn't stop her from leaving and he remained in the house, slightly stunned, with only Anna for comfort.

34

Thursday 10 September 2015

Jasmine had snuck in through the back door as quietly as she could. She had already taken off her trainers so she could tiptoe through the house to her bedroom and she was too busy watching every step she made to look up and notice her mum standing by the living room door.

'I thought you were upstairs,' Laura said, giving her a start.

'I wasn't out long. I just needed to go somewhere.' When her mum raised an eyebrow, she quickly added, 'For something.'

Laura glanced at someone out of sight in the living room and a knot of dread began to tighten and tighten in Jasmine's stomach until she was close enough to peer around the door to face yet another surprise.

'Oh, hello,' she said.

Sam gave her a tentative smile but still managed to look worried. 'Sorry, I didn't bring Jasper with me. He's at home with his tail between his legs at the moment. He managed to trip me up the other day while I was giving one of my tours.'

283

Rather than return his smile, Jasmine frowned. 'I should have been there to take care of him for you.'

'He needs a bit more training, that's all. Maybe . . .' he began, but then stopped and rubbed his face. The bristles on his chin made him look much older than he did when he was clean-shaven, wearier too. 'I've got my landlady Selina on the case now.'

Jasmine lowered her head although she kept her eyes on Sam. 'I'm not allowed to take him for a walk any more,' she said, her words catching in her throat.

'Yes, I know.'

Sam pursed his lips in much the same way that she was pursing hers, making her wonder what it was he wanted to say. Was he sorry too or would he try to convince her it was for the best, like her mum? Jasmine would never believe it and wished she could tell Sam that her heart was breaking. She wanted to beg him to keep telling Jasper how much she cared about him; but she didn't need to because she had already done it herself.

After pouring out her heart to the Wishing Tree, Jasmine had intended to go straight back home before she was missed, but she had been so desperate to see Jasper. She had seen Sam and knew that he must have left the dog at home and when she heard the sound of traffic coming from Menlove Avenue, it reminded her that Jasper was within touching distance. She knew where Sam lived. The piece of paper he had given her to make her very own crane at the caravan had been torn from the back page of one of his magazines. It had his address printed on it, and although she hadn't seen any use for such information at the time, she had carefully peeled apart the bird's wings after her dad had told her she would never see Jasper again and the magical bird had revealed its secret.

Her faithful friend had been waiting for her in the back garden, as if he had known she was coming. She had spied him poking his nose through the side gate, which was locked, and so she had to resign herself to stroking him through the wrought iron bars while his sad eyes questioned why she was abandoning him. Jasper hadn't wanted her to say goodbye and began yapping when she tried to leave. Suitably chastised, Jasmine had no choice but to use a wheelie bin to climb over. It was worth the risk of being caught by Sam's landlady simply to hold Jasper for a few precious minutes and let him lick her face, which had been wet with tears.

But it was her mum's wet cheeks that caught Jasmine's attention now.

'So where were you, young lady?' Laura said. 'You know you're not allowed to go sneaking out without telling me.'

'I was playing with Keira at the top of the road, that's all,' she said, then looked from her mum to Sam. 'I didn't make you worry, did I? Is that why Sam's here?'

'I was just checking that your mum was all right,' he explained.

'Did she tell you she fell over?' Jasmine said in a way that suggested her mum might not be telling the truth. Not that she wanted to even think about what might have really happened, but she wanted Sam to know that she didn't believe her mum's story. She wanted him to help her.

'I've cracked a couple of ribs in my time, mostly falling out of trees,' Sam told her. 'It's very painful, but I'm sure your mum will be on the mend very soon.'

'Are you sure she'll get better?' Jasmine asked, her eyes narrowing so that Sam would realize exactly how important this question was.

'Yes, I promise.'

All the muscles in Jasmine's face remained tense. She wasn't ready to relax. What would happen next time? Her dad was trying to be nice, but he would lose his temper again. He always did, and he seemed to get angrier and angrier these days. Jasmine had been able to feel the anxiety seeping through her mum's pores and it was infectious. She didn't know what Sam could do, but she didn't want him to leave, and yet try as she might, she couldn't think of anything else to say that might keep him there that little bit longer. Maybe, she thought, her mum would think of something, but probably not while she was there.

'Is it all right if I go to my room now, Mum?' she asked.

'Of course.'

'Take care of yourself,' Sam said. 'And when you do play out, be careful on those roads. When I saw those kids outside kicking the ball around, they were paying no attention to the traffic and it's easy to get distracted.'

'It's a wonder you didn't see Jasmine with them,' Laura made a point of saying.

Jasmine blushed and had the good sense to say no more as she scurried upstairs to her bedroom where she retreated into the shadows and hoped no one would find her.

Sam cut a solitary figure as he sat at a table outside a local café. The mug of coffee in his hand had been steaming when it arrived but was now stone cold. Summer's last breath had been spent and the days weren't only getting colder but distinctly shorter too. It was mid-afternoon and whereas Liverpool was only starting to look a little grey around the edges, Sam suspected it would already be getting dark in Edinburgh. 'Congratulations, Kirsten,' he whispered as he raised his mug in a northeasterly direction.

He had thought about getting in his car that morning to make the journey back home and was surprised how seriously he had considered it. Not that he regretted turning down the wedding invitation; there was no place for him in Kirsten's new life. What he was more interested in was an excuse to leave Liverpool so he could put some distance between himself and the people who had snuck into his withered heart. Who knew where he might have ended up or if he would ever have returned?

But while he managed to resist the urge to flee, for now, at least, he was too restless to stay cooped up at home. He hadn't ventured far and could still make out the southwest edge of Calderstones Park where the lush green canopy had faded to yellow, although the trees weren't yet dry enough to catch the spark of autumn that would set the leaves alight.

There were quite a few people strolling up and down the road, walking dogs, pushing prams or laden with shopping, but it was a man with a newspaper folded under his arm that his eyes settled on. He recognized him as a regular in the King's Arms and, as expected, saw him turn the corner in the direction of the pub.

When Sam put his hand in his pocket to retrieve his phone, Jasper jumped up. The dog had been dozing under the table but had heard the movement and was hoping for a treat.

He patted the dog's head. 'Sorry, laddie, you have to earn your rewards.'

Jasper kept his deep brown eyes fixed on Sam as he lowered his head back down. The obedience training was still a work in progress, but the puppy had certainly perfected the doleful look that melted Sam's resolve.

While Jasper crunched happily on a dog biscuit, Sam checked his mobile. Anna had stopped phoning him but she had sent a text that morning to say she was thinking of him; an act of kindness that he didn't deserve. He had treated her badly and they both knew it. There had been a mutual attraction, but on every other possible level they had been incompatible and Sam had known that from the start. Yes, he had tried to tell her he didn't want a serious relationship but she had assumed, and justifiably so, that Sam had more than a superficial interest in her. But he hadn't. He had used her.

In spite of his sense of guilt, however, he was in no hurry to see Anna again and had chosen his spot carefully. If she was planning on spending Saturday afternoon in her local, then she would come from the opposite direction. That was what made the café the ideal place to sit and watch the world go by. He checked up and down the road again before beginning to type out a text message. He took his time composing a reply to Anna's text. It was polite and very short, but he deliberated over every word, not wishing to hurt her further or give even the merest suggestion that he was interested in resuming their relationship.

His neck was aching by the time he looked up again and he rubbed away the tension while glancing over his shoulder.

Finn was only twenty feet away . . . He had spotted Sam first and was ready with a quick smile.

'Hello, Sam.'

Sam stood up and after the two shook hands, he resisted the urge to wipe his palm on his jeans. In his mind's eye, he was already ramming Finn into a nearby wall, pinning him down and not releasing him until he knew exactly what would happen if he ever touched a hair on Laura's head again.

Not returning Finn's smile, Sam balled his hand into a fist. 'I hear Laura had an accident. How is she?'

There was a flicker of uncertainty. Finn looked less sure of himself. 'She tripped over her own feet,' he said. 'How did you hear about that?'

Sam was prepared for the question. This was no chance meeting and along with imagining what he wanted to do to Finn, he had also practised what he would say. He had to tread a fine line between letting Finn know how much he knew without telling him how he had found out. 'I bumped into one of Jasmine's friends in the park.'

'Oh, right.' Finn was edging slowly past Sam. He licked his lips as if desperate for the first pint of the day.

'Sorry to hear about the job, by the way.'

'Yeah, well, we knew it wouldn't last forever.'

Sam shook his head. 'You're your own worst enemy. You do know that, don't you?'

Finn scowled. 'Oh, I get it. I suppose Jack's been going on about me. So what if I turned up late a couple of times or dared to ask to leave early? You've seen how I work, Sam. I can do the job of two men when I set my mind to it. I more than made up for the time I might have shaved off the day.'

'You're fooling yourself, Finn, if you think you can ever provide properly for your family while you let your anger rule your head, not to mention the drink.' Sam's self-restraint was fading fast.

'But that's the point, isn't it, Sam? It's *my* family, not yours,' Finn hissed.

He had taken a step closer and Sam could smell his breath, which was sour from the previous night's binge. 'Then look after them, Finn. Turn around, go home, and sober up. Protect what you have as if your life depended on it.'

To his shock, Finn started to laugh. 'You expect me to take advice from you? Where's *your* family, Sam? Oh, that's right, you walked out on your wife and now she's marrying someone else. Come on, what are you really after? I know you set me up for that job, Sam, Anna told me. What I can't quite work out is why.'

'I wanted to help, that's all.'

'Yeah, help yourself to my family because you messed up your own life.'

Sam had grabbed hold of Finn by his T-shirt before he even knew what he was doing. 'You're the one messing things up now, Finn, not me. Why the hell can't you see what you're doing?' he said, spraying spittle across Finn's face as his anger coloured his world red. His jaw clenched as he tried and failed to reel in his emotions. 'If you think I'm such a threat, then OK, I'll keep away. But I swear, Finn, if you ever hurt Laura or Jasmine then I'll come and find you and I won't be responsible for my actions.'

As Sam's fist relaxed, Finn pushed him away. There was a moment when he looked as if he was going to launch

himself at Sam but Finn was sober enough to realize that
he was always going to come off worse in a fight. 'Keep
away from me and my family or I'll have you for assault
or something,' he sneered. 'I'm warning you, Sam, keep
away!'

35

'What can I do for you, Mrs Peterson?' DCI Harper asked, his tone one of curiosity but there was a smug look on his face too. It was as if he had been expecting her.

'Do you seriously think Sam had something to do with Jasmine's disappearance?' she asked.

'Do you?'

Laura wasn't afraid to meet the detective's gaze. She listened to what her heart was telling her and the last remnants of doubt fell away. Sam had only ever tried to help them and if anything bad had happened to Jasmine then Sam was the last person to blame. 'No, I don't and I want you to stop wasting time questioning him and concentrate on finding my daughter.'

Harper took a seat opposite. 'We're pulling out all the stops to find Jasmine, I can assure you of that.'

'Then why haven't you found her yet? Why are you stuck in here talking to someone I would trust with my daughter's life more than I would her own father!'

Leaning back in his chair, Harper looked infuriatingly

unfazed by Laura's outburst. 'Is there a reason why you would think your daughter wasn't safe with your husband?'

'No, that's not what I'm saying,' Laura said, gritting her teeth as she fought back her frustration. 'Whatever I think of Finn right now, he has nothing to do with Jasmine's disappearance, at least, not directly . . .'

'He *was* home with you this morning, wasn't he?' DCI Harper asked, testing her previous statement.

'Yes, Finn was in the house when Jasmine left. He hasn't harmed her, if that's what you're suggesting,' she said. 'Have you seen the note she left in the tree?'

'Yes, Mrs Peterson and I'm glad I have the opportunity to speak to you again – alone,' he said. 'Why do you think Jasmine would want to run away? Who were these grown-ups that were sad and angry? Was that you and your husband by any chance?'

'Ours is not a happy marriage,' Laura said by way of an answer. When Harper waited for her to continue, she knew she had to tell him everything now. She didn't think it would help locate Jasmine but at least it might stop them looking in the wrong place. 'In fact we haven't been happy for so long that I can't even remember what it felt like.'

As Laura explained to DCI Harper how Finn's behaviour had gradually become more and more volatile, the expression on the detective's face remained fixed despite the fact that she was revealing the innermost detail of her marriage and humiliating herself in the process. Determined to get some kind of response from the hardened detective, Laura considered pulling down the polo neck of her dress, but the faint red marks wouldn't be enough to convey the horror behind how she had received them the day before.

Instead, she rolled up her sleeves to reveal yellow bruises that were the fading evidence of her husband's earlier abuse.

'And you didn't report the incident?' Harper confirmed, checking his notes.

'No.'

'And you didn't seek medical treatment for your broken ribs? You didn't see a doctor?'

Feeling suddenly small, Laura gave a small shake of the head.

'Did he ever hit Jasmine?'

'No!'

'You're sure about that?' When Laura couldn't bring herself to answer, the detective didn't force the issue and said instead, 'I can't imagine Mr McIntyre being the kind of man who would take kindly to a man hitting a woman.'

'Yes, because he's a *good* man,' Laura said pointedly. 'He and Selina didn't need to involve themselves in our lives and clearly it would have saved them a whole lot of trouble if they hadn't, but I'm glad they did.'

'Selina Raymond,' Harper said with a nod. 'What do you know of her?'

'I've only met her a few times, but she's an interesting lady. She looks small and frail but appearances can be deceptive.'

'Can't they just,' Harper said, mostly to himself. 'And did Jasmine ever meet her?'

Laura was about to say no, but then remembered the one and only time Jasmine had taken Jasper for a walk. 'Yes, but only briefly in the park.'

'When I saw you earlier, you said that Jasmine didn't know where Mr McIntyre lived.'

'She didn't – I honestly don't know how she could have got there.'

'But *you* knew where he lived, didn't you?'

Laura was annoyed at the blush that rose in her cheeks. 'Yes, I visited him – once, but not with Jasmine.'

'No, I appreciate that,' Harper said, making a note in his file that was little more than a tick against something. He tapped his pen on the page then asked, 'Would you say that Jasmine trusts Mr McIntyre?'

'Yes,' Laura said, albeit reluctantly. She was aware that this was not only a testament to the man's character, but evidence that could be used to incriminate him. 'But I still don't think—'

'And if Jasmine trusted Mr McIntyre, it would be reasonable to assume she would also trust his landlady.'

'Oh,' Laura said, her response not even beginning to register the shock. 'Do you think Selina might somehow be involved?'

'We're having some trouble locating her at the moment.'

'I don't see how Jasmine could be with Selina, but I wish she was,' Laura said, her voice catching. 'At least I'd have some hope that she was safe, but like I said, they met only once and besides, Selina's in her eighties. Do you really think she would have taken her?'

Harper shrugged. 'I'll happily point the finger of suspicion at every harmless old lady I see if it brings Jasmine home.'

Laura shook her head. 'No, I'm sorry, but I think you're wrong. Sam and Selina have each faced unimaginable traumas in their lives and neither of them would inflict that kind of misery on someone else, not without . . .' she said then stopped.

Harper pounced on the sentence Laura was loath to complete. 'Not without good reason? But there was good reason, wasn't there? I'm sure I don't need to remind you that your husband was physically abusive and perhaps they thought it was only a matter of time before he harmed Jasmine.'

Laura shook her head although she had no argument to make. She could only confess her own culpability. 'I was living in denial for too long, I know that. At first I thought that with enough support and patience, Finn would learn to control his moods. And even when I realized that wasn't going to happen, I still imagined I could contain his temper. If he took his anger out on me then at least Jasmine would be safe, but I was always afraid that tactic wouldn't last forever. I knew I had to do something. If only I'd held my nerve!'

Harper leaned forward in his chair and rested his elbows on the table. 'Tell me what happened, Mrs Peterson. Tell me why you're here. What is it that you couldn't say in front of your husband?'

She took a deep breath, then, 'Selina came to see me not long after I'd hurt myself,' she said before correcting herself. 'I mean, not long after Finn had attacked me.'

36

Tuesday 15 September 2015

Although she spent most of her working day processing orders in a tiny office, Laura did enjoy her job. Unsurprisingly, it wasn't the work itself she liked but the freedom it brought with it. Now that Finn wasn't working at the builders' merchants, she didn't have to worry about him until she clocked off and went home. She didn't have to worry about Jasmine either, because even though her unemployed husband was now free to do the school runs, Natalie had been as reluctant as she was to hand over that particular responsibility.

She was humming to herself as she tapped another requisition into the system, and if it wasn't for the pain in her side every time she inhaled, Laura could imagine that life was, if not perfect, then at least normal. She had a smile on her face as she looked up as one of the receptionists popped her head through the door.

'You have a visitor, Laura.'

'Oh, really?'

Laura had deliberately isolated herself from the rest of

the workforce after Finn's dismissal and although there were a couple of spare chairs in the room, they were rarely used. She discouraged visitors, especially Finn's old workmates because she didn't want reports getting back to her husband that she had been fraternizing. It was rare for customers or suppliers to visit her in person and she was about to ask who the visitor was when an old lady peered over her colleague's shoulder. Laura couldn't quite place her face at first and when she did, her heart skipped a beat. 'Aren't you . . .' She couldn't remember her name.

'Selina. I'm Sam's landlady.'

'Is he with you?'

'No, just me, I'm afraid,' Selina said. 'Can I come in?'

When Laura offered her a seat, the receptionist gave them both a curious look but said no more and left. 'What can I do for you, Selina?'

'How about putting a certain someone's mind at rest?'

'Tell Sam I'm fine,' Laura said. Her words were clipped. She could only presume that Selina had been told all about her sorry life, which irritated her. Her secrets weren't Sam's for the telling.

'He said you'd say that – and I think I believe you even less than he would,' Selina said and then narrowed her eyes when she saw Laura purse her lips. Although Laura was far too polite to say anything, the old lady read her mind. 'I know, it's none of my business, but you have to understand, I have a vested interest. I live underneath Sam's apartment and I can hear him pacing up and down, night after night, worrying about you, and I'd like some peace for both our sakes. Did you know he went to see Finn?'

The shock on Laura's face told the answer. 'When?' she asked.

'On Saturday. Sam bumped into him accidentally on purpose when Finn was on his way to the pub. He told your lovely husband exactly what he thought of him and warned him about . . . Well, you can imagine,' Selina said, skirting around the truth. 'But then he was worried that he might have made Finn angrier than ever.'

'Not that I noticed,' Laura said. 'Actually, Finn didn't come home on Saturday night.' She had presumed he had found somewhere else to lay his head, or another shoulder to cry on. She certainly hadn't asked him about it when he reappeared on Sunday in a relatively good mood. Whoever she was, Finn's new dalliance had managed to tame him – for the time being at least.

'Oh, right then, that's good to know,' Selina said.

Laura felt as awkward as Selina. 'Yes, erm, well, thanks for dropping by.'

Selina might have been about to get up but then she slapped her leg, startling them both. 'I'm sorry, but do you mind if I speak openly? At my age I don't have time to dilly-dally.'

Doubting that she could stop her anyway, Laura nodded.

'Your husband is a bully, Laura, and you might think he's reached new depths but believe me, once they start hitting you about, it can only get worse. He'll tell you he's trying his best and then blame you when he fails, and the lower he falls, the angrier he'll get and, as I'm sure you already know, you'll bear the brunt of it. And if not you, then that sweet little girl of yours.'

The bright little office where Laura had created a safe

haven felt as if it were under attack. Her body shook as her defences were breached and reality came crashing into the room. She fought off the urge to cry as she admitted her worst fears to someone else for the very first time. 'I – I think you might be right. But I don't know what to do.'

Selina fixed her with a stare. 'Yes, you do, Laura. What you don't know is if you have the courage to do it.'

Laura went to nod but it was more of a wobble.

'You're not alone.'

'But you don't know what it's like,' Laura said, and only when she sniffed back her tears did she realize she hadn't been able to staunch them after all.

'I'm afraid I know *exactly* what it's like.' Selina sat back in her chair and gathered her courage before continuing. 'I've never really spoken to anyone before about what happened during my marriage. My friends know a little, but they weren't around much back in the day. I had become isolated from pretty much everyone.'

'Because of your husband?' Laura asked, having recognized a parallel in her own life.

'Alf,' she confirmed with a smile that didn't reach her haunted eyes. 'He was a lovely bloke, very entertaining and generous too. He'd insist on buying the next round of drinks when everyone else was talking about going home. And if it was last orders then they could always come back to the house to carry on the party, maybe have a game of poker. "Oh, Selina won't mind," he'd tell them. "She'll even get up to feed us all."'

When Laura nodded, Selina added, 'Does it sound familiar?'

'Yes, but if you don't mind me saying, I can't imagine you being ordered about by anyone.'

'Oh, this was over fifty years ago and I wasn't the person I am now,' Selina said and laughed bitterly. 'Nor was I the young, misguided woman who walked up the aisle expecting to live happily ever after. When I promised to love, honour and obey my husband, Alf made it clear soon afterwards that was exactly what he expected from me. I was . . . How can I put this? Beaten into submission.'

'I'm sorry,' Laura said, and wasn't sure she wanted Selina to continue, but the old lady was determined to share her history, blow by blow.

'It was always *my* fault if his friends didn't want to know him any more, it was *my* fault if he lost at cards, and it was even *my* fault if he had a hangover.' Selina exhaled fifty years' worth of pain before adding, 'And it was absolutely my fault that we couldn't have children. Yes, I might have suffered a miscarriage because he'd kicked me in the stomach, but surely it was my fault for getting him angry in the first place. Wouldn't you agree?'

Laura could feel the colour draining from her face. 'I don't know what to say.'

Selina wasn't listening, she was lost in her own thoughts and it took a shake of her head to free herself from them. 'It's hard to believe now, but Alf had me convinced. He had been the perfect gentleman before we married, so of course I had to take at least some of the responsibility for the change in him.'

'Finn isn't that bad,' Laura found herself saying. 'He never sets out to hurt me.'

Selina raised an eyebrow. 'Alf didn't only use his fists to

persuade me of my failings as a wife. He was manipulative; he played with my emotions and eroded my confidence until there was nothing left. Does that sound more familiar, Laura?'

When Laura refused to answer, Selina's jaw set in grim determination. 'While I've still got breath in my body, I won't sit back and let another woman and her child's life be destroyed.'

'I can't leave him. He wouldn't let me,' Laura said. 'And even if I could, I have nowhere to go.'

'Why? Because you've become isolated from your family and friends? I hate to say this, but things are about to get a lot lonelier for you.'

'What do you mean?' Laura asked, wondering if this wizened old lady had a crystal ball in her handbag. She had certainly summed up Laura's life perfectly so far.

'He's going to leave, Laura. He's going to leave us both.'

'Sorry?'

'Sam,' Selina said. 'I've begged him to stay but I can see it's become too much for him – seeing you and not being able to help.'

Laura's breath caught in her throat. 'No, he can't!' she said. She had told Sam to stay away but she didn't want to lose him.

'Then I'm afraid you're going to have to give him a reason to stay,' Selina said.

Sam knew his every move was being closely monitored and even a simple task like mowing the lawn was viewed with suspicion by his landlady. She had been loitering close by and he could feel her eyes on him as he unplugged the mower and began cleaning the blades with an oiled rag. He rubbed the metal to a dull shine, which immediately dimmed when a shadow blocked out the watery sunshine.

'What are you doing that for?' Selina asked.

'I'm hoping I won't need to mow it again.'

'Oh,' she said simply.

Sam looked up and frowned. 'The grass isn't growing so unless we have a sudden warm spell, it won't need another cut until next year.'

Jasper had been hiding from the deafening bray of the mower but padded over now that his master had killed the beast. He jumped up and licked Sam's face in gratitude and when Sam stood up he was confronted with another type of onslaught.

Selina's face was set in a grimace. 'At which point, I suppose, you'll start all over again.'

'Will I?' he asked, squaring up to her.

Her eyes narrowed. 'Will you?'

It was a question she had posed almost daily and as always, she never asked him outright if he was going to leave her, but rather forced from him his plans for the future. His answer was, as always, evasive. 'If you include all the grass I've cut at work, I've probably mown an area equivalent to the size of a small country. I don't want to think about starting all over again just yet.'

'A small country,' she mused. 'About the size of Scotland would you say?'

Sam wound the power cord in tight circles around his lower arm as he replied. 'Too many mountains.'

'Where then?' Selina asked.

At that moment, they both heard the distant chime of

the front doorbell. When Jasper barked, Selina was so tense it gave her a start, but she didn't follow him when he rushed into the house.

'Aren't you going to get that?' said Sam.

'It'll be for you.'

Realizing Selina was in no mood to be argued with, Sam handed over the coiled lead and set off into the house. He was getting tired of his landlady's constant needling. If she wanted him to stay, then nagging him wasn't going to work. He needed his mind and his emotions to settle and he wasn't there yet, he wasn't even close.

It was still a tempting thought, moving away and starting over. He would continue to worry about Jasmine and Laura but at least he didn't have to face the possibility of opening the front door and coming face to face with one of them, which was exactly what happened next.

'Hello, Sam,' Laura said, while Sam remained frozen in shock. 'Didn't Selina tell you I was coming over to see you?'

Of course she hadn't. If he had known in advance then he might have taken flight a little sooner and Selina had known it. 'No, she didn't,' he said. 'How are you?'

Laura managed to smile. 'I'm fine. It hurts when I laugh, but that's not very likely these days.'

Sam started wiping his hands on the rag he was still holding. He refused to look at her; he was trying not to let her back into his heart. 'Good,' he managed to say.

Laura's shoulders sagged and whatever courage had brought her to his doorstep was failing fast. 'You look busy, maybe I should go,' she said.

'No,' Sam said. 'Please, come in.'

He stepped to one side and a moment later they stood

304

facing each other in the hallway where he had no choice but to soak in every detail of her. Even draped in shadows, Laura was beautiful. Her cheeks were flushed with embarrassment but there was a subtle touch of make-up too.

'Hello, Laura,' Selina said as she scurried down the hall towards them.

Sam assumed she was about to tell him her plan but instead she gave Laura a kiss on the cheek and said simply, 'I'll leave you both to it.' She winked at Laura, gave Sam a meaningful look, and then disappeared into her own flat.

With no other choice, Sam led Laura upstairs and motioned her to an armchair while he remained standing, holding onto the back of the other chair as if it were a shield from the emotions Laura evoked.

'Selina came to see me,' she said which was something Sam already knew. 'She told me you might be leaving soon.' This was something Sam hadn't known but as Laura glanced towards his bookshelves that were all but empty after a recent clear out, it was something he couldn't completely deny.

'I haven't decided yet.'

Laura looked as if she were consumed by her own indecision and played nervously with the hem of the lace blouse she was wearing.

'What is it, Laura? Why are you here?'

'I wanted to say thank you. For trying to help us.'

Sam focused on one word. 'Trying,' he repeated. 'That doesn't sound promising.'

'You found Finn a job and you brought some light into our lives for a while – that meant a lot to me and to Jasmine too.'

305

'And now?'

Laura leant forward, wincing a little as her injured ribs objected to the movement. With her elbows resting on her knees, she played with her wedding band. 'It's never been this bad and what happened the other week has made me take a good long look at myself. I'm so ashamed, and I'm still trying to work out how I got here. You must look at me and think I'm so pathetic – beyond hope, beyond help,' she said.

'That's not what I see.'

Sam dared himself to hold her gaze even though his cheeks had begun to warm beneath his thick bristles.

'It's not what your landlady sees either,' she said. 'Perhaps it's just me who needs convincing.'

'Why do you put up with him, Laura? Why do you not see that you deserve so much better?'

She looked down at her fidgeting fingers, inhaled deeply and then tried to explain herself as best she could. 'I was in my mid-twenties when I started working at the builders' merchants and, as you can imagine, any woman in a place like that attracts a lot of attention. Despite appearances, I could handle myself. I wouldn't let them wind me up, Finn included. I refused to fall for his charm, or at least I refused to let on that I had, so he changed tactics. Instead of the constant innuendos and suggestive comments, he told off the other lads who were still trying to embarrass me.' She smiled at the memory, then shrugged. 'It worked, obviously, and we were happy for a while. I didn't mind that he continued to be the charmer with other women because he was *my* charming man.'

She stopped playing with her wedding ring and rubbed

her forehead but her frown couldn't be smoothed away. 'Finn was always a heavy drinker but he knew his limits. He knew how much he could get away with and still turn up for work the next day relatively sober, or at least he thought he did. When Jasmine came along, he struggled to adapt. I think the baby was a puzzle to him that he couldn't solve. He could chat up women, carouse with the blokes, but kids? He simply couldn't relate to a baby and I'm not sure he ever bonded with her.'

Sam dug his fingers deeper into the upholstery of the chair. He had wanted to forget about the Petersons. They weren't his problem to fix, Finn had made that perfectly clear and so had Laura.

'I don't suppose Finn is the first man who didn't take naturally to fatherhood,' she continued and then for Sam's sake, added, 'I'm sure it wasn't plain sailing for you, either.'

'Me? You're comparing Finn to *me*?' Sam shook his head and could feel the colour in his cheeks intensifying.

'No, I didn't mean that. I don't know what kind of father you are to your daughter and I'm not excusing Finn by any stretch of the imagination.'

'I'm sorry, Laura, I don't know why you're telling me all of this, really I don't.'

Laura looked mortified. 'You're right. I don't know either. I should go.' When she tried to move, she gasped out loud and put a hand against her side, the pain making her eyes water.

'Wait,' Sam said and then pursed his lips until he could summon up the right words. 'I care about you and Jasmine. I care about what happens to you, Laura – it's just that I don't understand Finn. I don't understand how he can treat you the way he does.'

Laura appeared as reluctant to justify her husband's behaviour as Sam was to hear it, but she tried anyway. 'Finn found himself in a role he was never meant to take up, not as a father and maybe not even as a husband. If I'm honest, it's why we never had any more kids. He tried his best, he still does try, but every once in a while it gets too much for him.'

'And what does he do when it gets too much?'

'He goes off the rails,' she confessed, 'but eventually he rights himself.'

'So is that why you're here? To tell me life gets a bit too much for Finn and that's why he abuses his wife and terrifies his daughter in the process? I suppose you're going to tell me everything is fine now and not to worry?'

Laura covered her face with her hands. 'I know that's not true, not any more. When Finn's in one of his moods, he can spend the whole day God knows where, and when he eventually staggers home, it's me who faces the inquisition about where I've been and who I've been seeing. He'll go on and on at me, grabbing my arms so I have to give him the attention he thinks he deserves.' She took her hands from her face only to place one across her throat. 'It doesn't matter what I've done or not done, he'll find any excuse to vent his anger. It's an awful cycle that's been spinning faster and faster out of control.'

'So should you be here right now?'

'He has a new distraction, I think,' she said with a bitter laugh. 'He's had affairs before and I know the signs. He's being nice to me.'

'And you're going to accept that?' Sam asked, only just stopping himself from wondering out loud if Finn was seeing Anna. Her behaviour was no longer any of his business and he hoped that, one day, Finn's would be nothing to Laura either.

'Is it bad that I'm actually relieved?' Laura asked. 'I keep thinking that maybe he'll leave and, even if he doesn't, if she makes him happy then we all see the benefit.'

'And this is the kind of life you've settled for? This is good enough for you and Jasmine, is it?'

When she lifted her head, the colour drained from Laura's cheeks. 'I want to leave him, really I do but it's not that easy. Selina tried to convince me, but I'm not her. She might have had the courage to leave, but I didn't.'

'Selina didn't leave her husband.'

'But I thought . . . She said she had a lucky escape.'

'Only if you can call a car crash that kills your husband and your unborn child lucky.' Realizing that Laura was even less likely to stand up to her husband now that she knew Selina had been unable to do it either, Sam added, 'What do you want from me, Laura?'

'I want you to stay, Sam,' she said. 'I know it's unfair of me to ask, but just knowing that you're here, I don't know, watching our backs, makes things bearable.'

Sam was shaking his head. 'I'm sorry, but, if anything, you've just given me all the more reason to go, Laura. You can't expect me to stand back and wait for you to fall.' He thought of all the cruel and vicious ways that Finn might harm his family both now and in the future. Even if Laura could endure the abuse, what would become of the little girl whose life had been blighted by insecurity and fear? What would the future hold for Jasmine? He couldn't stand back and watch. It would destroy him long before Finn had dealt his last blow. 'You think I'll catch you but I'm not that strong. Really I'm not.'

These were not the words Laura wanted to hear but Sam couldn't stop now even if he tried. 'You have two options, Laura. You can fool yourself into thinking that Finn will come to his senses, that he won't get progressively worse and that he won't hurt Jasmine in the same way he's already hurting you, or you can cut your losses and run.'

'I have nowhere to go. I could stay with my sister but she doesn't have the space for us, or the patience, for that matter.'

In the pause that followed, Sam was acutely aware of the four walls closing in around him, four walls and a roof that could be offered to a mother and her daughter. He could always move in with Selina for a while and sleep on her sofa; she'd be happy just to have him stay. But was that the offer Laura wanted him to make, or did she want more? The very thought terrified Sam, not because he didn't care enough about Laura and Jasmine but because he cared too much. 'I can't . . .'

Flustered with embarrassment, Laura didn't let the pain in her side stop her this time when she stood up. 'Sorry, I didn't mean – I wasn't suggesting that we stay *here*.'

'I can't . . .' he tried again.

'It was wrong of me to come here. I shouldn't be burdening you with our problems.'

She headed for the door and left Sam holding onto the back of the armchair for dear life. 'What will you do?' he asked, his voice strangled with concern.

310

'We'll be fine, Sam,' she said without looking back at him in case he saw the lie.

Sam's heart was hammering in his chest as he stood staring at the empty space Laura had left. Hadn't he just told her how much he cared? How could he, if he was willing to turn his back on her, or to be more correct, allow her to run away from him? Self-preservation was all well and good, but at any cost? What if this was Laura's only chance to get herself and Jasmine away from Finn?

As Sam listened to Laura rush downstairs, he reminded himself of all the times he had wished he could go back in time and change even the smallest of decisions; the times he had taken hold of Ruby's hand and the times he had let it go. Such a small decision that had had unimaginable consequences.

The decision he was being presented with now was by no means small or the consequences unimaginable. He had already painted a picture of Jasmine's future in his mind and if he continued on the course he was thinking about, he would be condemning her to that life of misery.

Sam's feet moved faster than his thoughts and he still had hold of the armchair as he lurched towards the open door. By the time it toppled over, he was already out of the room. Laura had reached the front door and she was fumbling with the catch when he grabbed her shoulder and turned her around.

Tears were running down her cheeks in muddy lines of mascara. 'Let go, Sam!'

'Please, Laura, come back in. Let's talk about this. If you want somewhere to stay you can stay here. You can't live in fear all your life – and Jasmine can't either. Let me help you. I *want* to help you.'

'No, I can't. There's no knowing how Finn will react. You're best keeping out of it, Sam.'

'I'd say that's all the more reason to accept his help,' came a voice from behind Sam. Selina was standing at the far end of the hall. 'I wish someone had made the same offer to me once upon a time. My life could have been so very different. Don't make the same mistake I did.'

'But I've left Jasmine with Natalie. I should get back.'

'How about a nice cuppa first?' Selina asked. 'I bet Sam didn't even offer you a drink.'

Sam tried to keep his tone light. 'I'm a little out of practice at playing hostess,' he said.

'All he needs is a bit of training,' Selina said. She had crept up on Laura and slipped her arm around her waist. 'So, what do you say?'

Accepting a cup of tea is such an unremarkable decision to make, but sometimes they are the most dangerous . . .

37

Police station: Wednesday 7 October 2015

When Harper returned to the interview room, his face was like thunder. 'By rights I should charge you with obstruction.'

Sam supposed it was an improvement on abduction, but at that precise moment, he couldn't have cared less what he was charged with. 'Have you found her?'

'No, but we've found a note in the tree.'

Harper had sat down with what was now a familiar manila file. It had grown thicker during the hour Sam had been left waiting for his accuser's return, and he waited for Harper to open it up and reveal the note, but the detective simply sat and glared.

'You could have saved us a whole lot of time if you'd mentioned the notes earlier.'

'I didn't think she would leave any more.'

'Because she thought you read them?' Harper asked, recalling their previous conversation.

Sam wanted to close his eyes but he was afraid his mind would summon up the image of the last time he had seen Jasmine. 'Because she caught me reading one. Because she

313

realized the Wishing Tree was nothing more than a story spun by a grown man who should have known better,' he said, his voice fading to nothing until a spark of hope set it alight again. 'What did it say?'

'It suggests she has run away.'

Sam had spent the last hour chasing shadows of his own making and searching for Jasmine amongst them. He had been clinging to the hope that she had run off of her own accord, but the confirmation from Harper didn't completely dispel his darker fears. Jasmine was a sensible girl and he wanted to believe that she would keep herself safe. But then Ruby had been sensible too . . . .

Why hadn't the police found her yet if she had only run off? Could Finn have stumbled upon her first? What if his temper had got the better of him? Sam would never forgive himself if something had happened. He could have saved her. He *should* have saved her.

With so many questions still unanswered, Sam was certain of only one thing. He had to get out of there. 'So are you going to arrest me or not?' he demanded.

'Not, Mr McIntyre,' Harper said.

The certainty in his voice took Sam by surprise. 'Then I've given you my statement and I'd like to go home. I came here voluntarily so I presume I can leave any time I like.'

'If you could just bear with me a little longer.'

'For pity's sake man, why?'

Harper put his hand on the manila folder but didn't open it. 'I've just had an interesting conversation with Mrs Peterson.'

'Laura's here? Is she all right? Is Finn with her?'

Always one to offer no more information than was absolutely necessary, Harper ignored the questions and continued with his own. 'I'd like you to tell me about the plans you were making with Mrs Peterson. She tells me she was intending on leaving her husband and that you and your landlady were going to help her.'

'If that's what she says,' Sam answered churlishly.

'She does, and now I'd like you to go through exactly how you and Mrs Raymond intended to help, right up to the point where you decided to leave Liverpool this morning.'

It was clear that Harper already knew the full story from Laura; in fact, he probably knew more now than Sam did himself. The detective was looking for holes in their stories, that was all, and as Sam drew a deep breath, he considered refusing to answer. But then an image of Jasmine came to mind – an image that was fading fast – and so he released his frustration with a sigh. 'Laura had called around to let me know that she was all right after she had a *fall*,' he said, hoping the detective would pick up on his intonation.

'Mrs Peterson has told me about her injuries and how she got them.'

'Good,' Sam said. 'Although I don't suppose you're at all interested in charging Finn with assault.'

'I'll be honest with you, Mr McIntyre. I couldn't care less right now. My only priority is finding Jasmine.'

'And you don't think the two events are related? Did she tell you how Finn didn't take to fatherhood naturally?'

'I should imagine that's something you would find difficult to reconcile.'

Ignoring the attempt to bring the focus back onto him,

Sam said, 'Selina and I managed to convince Laura that, if not for her own well-being, it would certainly be better for Jasmine in the long run if she left Finn.' Sam gave a bitter laugh and added, 'We were scared that Jasmine might face a troubled future if Laura didn't do something; I just didn't realize how soon that future would catch up with them.'

'So you invited them to stay with you?'

'Not with me, as such,' Sam corrected. 'The idea was that Laura could move into my flat and I would sleep on Selina's sofa for a while. Laura took some convincing. She was scared of Finn, scared of what he would do to her and to Jasmine,' Sam said pointedly. 'But Selina wasn't taking no for an answer by that point.'

'Mrs Raymond is an interesting character by all accounts.'

'Have you spoken to her yet?'

'No, she hasn't been seen by us or any of her friends.'

'Really? What time is it?'

Harper looked at his watch. 'Five thirty.'

'I should go home. Jasper's been on his own all this time,' Sam said, more determined than ever to leave, although it had little to do with the pup.

'Are you sure you don't know where Mrs Raymond might be? Is it usual for her to stay out all day?'

Coming to the conclusion that the more he shared the quicker he would be released, Sam said, 'We had an argument last night. I'm guessing she's gone off somewhere to let off steam and she'll be in no hurry to come home to what she expects to be an empty house.'

'An argument?'

'In case you hadn't noticed, Laura didn't follow through with her plans to leave Finn. And as you've already worked out, I had become heavily involved in the Petersons' lives, far more than I ever intended. I came to Liverpool to escape emotional ties. I wasn't looking for a new family and I didn't want to hang around to see the people I cared about follow a path to self-destruction. I tried to help and I failed. That's why my bags were packed. That's why I was going to leave.'

'And Mrs Raymond wasn't happy being left to pick up the pieces?'

'Selina was determined to help Laura, come what may. She's had her fair share of heartache in her time, but I don't think she appreciated how badly this whole mess was affecting me.'

When Harper opened the manila folder in front of him, Sam glimpsed a photocopy of what looked like a very old, handwritten police report, the scrawl indecipherable from where he was sitting.

'Mrs Raymond had to deal with a lot more than heartache by the looks of it.' Harper lifted up one page, then another, and another.

'She has a police record?'

'Of sorts,' Harper said, closing the file abruptly.

'What do you mean?'

'Right, Mr McIntyre,' Harper said, dismissing the question. 'I think you've helped as much as you can for now so I'm happy for you to go. But,' he said, emphasizing the word, 'if you do hear from Mrs Raymond or think of anything that will help us locate her, then I suggest you contact me as a matter of urgency.'

Sam had been desperate to leave but now he didn't want to go. 'You think *Selina* took her?'

'The duty officer will return your wallet and mobile phone, but you might have to wait a bit longer for the rest of your personal effects. There are some formalities to go through, the usual paperwork, but other than that, I'd like to thank you for your co-operation and we'll be in touch if we need anything else.'

'But—'

'Go home, Mr McIntyre.'

38

Saturday 26 September 2015

The leaves were tinder dry and crunched under foot when Jasmine veered off the path. Her pace slowed as she approached the old tree which had managed to cling onto most of its foliage for now, although the yellow and brown leaves made her old friend look a little more weary and weatherworn. She silently apologized as she clambered onto the overhanging branch that rested on the railings, too weak to hold itself up but still reaching out, inviting her to come a little closer.

Keira was waiting for her by the swings so she couldn't stay long. Leah was there too, but she had been too busy with her boyfriend to notice Jasmine sneaking off. Not that Leah would be able to make much of a fuss because none of them were meant to be there. Everyone knew Jasmine wasn't allowed in the park any more and so Leah had told her mum she was taking them to her friend's house to pick up some homework. Jasmine was surprised that Natalie believed her because Leah was only interested in one thing and that was the boy her face was currently glued to. It was disgusting the way they snogged and Jasmine couldn't help wondering if her mum and dad had ever done that. She didn't imagine they did it now because they struggled to even talk to each other and that worried her. It worried her a lot.

That morning, Jasmine had been sent over to Natalie's for the day. She was used to being shipped off to her friend's house whenever her dad was in one of his moods, only this time it was different. There had been no sign of the brooding monster that often took over her dad's body; in fact there hadn't been much sign of it or her dad for the past week or so. He was spending a lot less time at home than he had when he had lost his job before. He generally disappeared before Jasmine came home from school and either turned up later smelling of beer or he didn't bother coming home until the next day, just as Jasmine was heading off to school again.

Her mum had been acting strange too. She didn't smile and some days her eyes looked red and sore. That was why a knot of worry had begun to twist Jasmine's insides and she found herself more scared of the silence than she had ever been of the loud, angry rows. Something bad was going to happen. It was probably happening now, which meant she had to act fast. Taking the note she had already written out of her pocket, Jasmine read it again. Was she sure this was what she wanted? Once she had made her wish there would be no going back.

The breeze above her head rattled the leaves and one landed on her head. The tree was telling her to get a move on so she quickly dropped the note inside the trunk and then scrambled back over the railings before she had a chance to change her mind.

She was a little out of breath as she turned to face the tree. 'Right, let's do this,' she said and then lifted her head back, opened up her arms and closed her eyes. The tree shivered and then there was a strange scrambling sound that didn't sound like her Wishing Tree at all. She prised an eye open and searched the sprawling branches for signs of a squirrel but the noise wasn't coming from above. It was a much bigger animal and when she turned around, Jasper's chocolate coat shimmered in the autumn sunshine. He was on a leash but Sam had let it extend fully to allow the puppy to race towards her. Jasmine's heart leapt with joy, but then she pulled herself up short before she could give into her excitement.

'Get away, Jasper!'

As Sam tried to retract the leash, Jasper twisted his body in an effort to reach Jasmine's side.

'Sorry, did he frighten you?' Sam asked.

Jasmine began sidling along the railings to put as much distance between them as she could. Her blue eyes sparkled with a mixture of fire and ice as she stared at the dog. She wanted so much to wrap her arms around her puppy and let him lick her face. Her fingers tingled with the need to stroke his fur and her heart broke when he began to whimper. He didn't understand how it hurt too much to even look at him and how she couldn't risk getting close. 'I'm not allowed to go near him,' she explained. 'And I don't want to get dog hairs on my dress in case my dad finds one.' What she didn't add was that she had already said goodbye to him and couldn't face it a second time.

Sam nodded. 'Fair enough, I understand. So, are you

here on your own?' he asked, trying too hard to sound casual.

Jasmine's eyes narrowed as she worked out just how much information to share. She trusted Sam, and since he wasn't likely to talk to her dad or her mum, she thought it would be safe to tell. 'I'm with my friend Keira and her sister. We're not supposed to be in the park but we won't be staying long. I was just on my way back to them.'

Jasmine watched as he rubbed his face nervously. 'All right, as long as you're OK.'

'Yes, I am,' she said confidently as she listened to the tree swaying in the breeze, as it considered her wish.

'Good.'

Neither moved and in the pause, Jasmine couldn't help staring at Sam. 'You've shaved your beard off again,' she said at last when she realized what was different about him.

The park ranger smiled. 'I keep changing my mind whether I should keep it or not.'

'I'd go with the *not*,' she told him. 'You look kind of scary with all that hair over your face and you might frighten people off.'

Sam gave a soft chuckle. 'I think that was why I kept it.'

Jasper had stopped trying to reach her and was momentarily distracted by a smell he had picked up. He pushed his nose into the ground and scratched at the earth, raking up dry leaves to reveal a damp layer of mulch. Jasmine took advantage and started inching her way along the railings away from him. Sam was watching her.

'I'm sorry,' he said.

She stopped moving. 'What for?'

Sam had to think for a while and then he simply shrugged. 'Just for being here with Jasper when I can tell how desperately you want to give him a hug.'

At that moment, Jasper lifted his grubby nose and wagged his tail so energetically that his whole body swayed. Jasmine did her best to ignore him and kept her gaze on Sam.

'OK. Bye then,' she said, and turned on her heels. Heading through the trees towards the playground, she kept her legs moving. If only she could put enough distance between herself and Jasper, it might stop the ache in her heart that was making her chest heave and her breath come out in sobs.

Jasmine sprinted between the trees with a trail of blonde hair and then she was gone. Jasper pulled on his leash and whined, but try as he might, he couldn't persuade his master to follow the little girl. Sam had wanted to visit the park to take his mind off Laura but now he was more anxious than ever. A week had passed since she had sat in Selina's kitchen building up the nerve to leave her husband. He had wanted her to go back home and tell Finn there and then that their marriage was over, but Laura had needed time to prepare. No one was under any illusions that Finn would make it easy for her – he was unlikely to give up his home and she expected to be the one who would have to leave.

Where Laura would go was still under debate. If Finn made threats then she might have to leave Liverpool and one option was to hide away in Pat's caravan. If her husband were more magnanimous, if, for instance he was minded to trade in Laura for the newer model he was seeing, then Laura felt more able to accept Sam's generous offer of moving into his flat while he stayed with Selina. There were other things she would need as well as lodgings, like clothes and other personal belongings, and of course, money. She had given herself a week to get her life in order so she could pick it up and move out. A week wasn't very long, not compared to a marriage of ten years, but for Sam it was an agonizing delay.

Stretching his back, he looked up into the spider web of gnarled branches. Through the brittle canopy of leaves, holes had begun to appear and sunlight flickered across his face. He ought to feel good about himself. Up until now he had been forced to watch helplessly as Finn destroyed his family. The man had wrung every last drop of hope and joy from their lives and if Sam could help Laura and Jasmine to make a fresh start then that was something to be proud of – wasn't it? But with so much uncertainty ahead of them, he found no joy in breaking up a family, even a dysfunctional one. He looked at the hollow of the tree that had swallowed up Jasmine's latest wish and knew he couldn't ignore it.

Tying the dog to the railings, Sam jumped over and created a small cloud of dry, crisp leaves when he landed with a thump. Jasper yapped then pushed his head between the iron bars where he promptly became stuck. Sam sighed as the puppy began to whine. 'You'll have to wait,' he said. 'Now, sit.'

To his surprise, the dog somehow managed to sit down despite being trapped. His head was bowed and his brown eyes looked up at Sam with a mixture of embarrassment and desperation. Sam ignored him while he retrieved the note from the rotting splinters of wood that had gathered in the hollow of the trunk. He felt a twinge of guilt as he always did taking the letters that Jasmine only intended to share with the tree, and jumped when he heard scraping leaves close by. He jerked his head just in time to see a squirrel scampering up a nearby fir. Jasper whined again.

'Just a minute,' Sam said while carefully unfolding the piece of paper. His heart sank as soon as he read the first line.

Dear Wishing Tree
    I can't remember what happy felt like. I'm glad mum didn't die (thank you for saving her) but I still think something bad is going to happen.
    I don't want my mum and dad to get divorced—

'What are you doing?'
The sound of dry leaves was thunderous as Jasper became delirious with excitement. He pulled his head free from the bars with an almighty twist of his body and began straining at his leash again. Sam paid him no attention, like the dog, he saw only the figure of an eight-year-old girl with flowing blonde hair and eyes that sparkled with angry tears.

'Jasmine, I thought you'd gone.'
'You've read my note?'
Sam folded up the paper and was tempted to hide it in his pocket but it was clearly too late. 'I was just—'
'Did you read all of them?'
Judging from what he had read, her worst fears were about to be realized and the only hope Jasmine had left was

325

in the power of the Wishing Tree. He couldn't take that from her, not today. 'It's my job to look after the tree and clean up around it,' he explained. 'I see scrunched-up bits of paper in the Wishing Tree. I didn't read all of it,' he said.

Jasmine eyed him with suspicion.

'Can I have it back?'

'But what about your wish?' Sam said. He didn't want to read it, not any more but he wanted Jasmine to still believe in the magic of the story he had sold her.

'It doesn't matter,' she told him. 'It was hopeless, anyway.'

Sam climbed back over the railings and, ignoring Jasper, walked with slow and deliberate steps, the pink piece of paper held tightly in his grasp. The willowy child held out her hand and Sam placed the wish into her upturned palm.

'It still matters, Jasmine,' he said.

'I came back because I felt guilty about ignoring Jasper, but I think I should just go,' she said, stuffing the note in her pocket.

'Whatever happens, Jasmine, you'll be OK. I know I'm not the Wishing Tree—'

'There *is* no Wishing Tree, not any more. I won't ever make another wish.'

'Maybe not, but there are still plenty of people who care about you. I know I don't have the power to give you what you want,' he said honestly, 'but I'll do what I can to help. I promise.'

They stood staring at each other for the longest moment and then Jasmine turned away. He heard her whisper, 'I wish,' but the rest was drowned out by the sound of the wind as it became tangled in branches above their heads, making the wise old tree tremble.

Jasmine rubbed her arms as if she felt the shiver too. She seemed to panic and took a few stumbling steps but then Jasper let out a pitiful whine and she couldn't ignore him a second time. When she rushed over, the pup launched himself at her and knocked her to the ground. He licked her face furiously and tempted a smile that Sam had all but given up hope of seeing.

When Jasmine pulled herself away, she didn't pause to say goodbye or look back and Sam was left reeling. He had spent years perfecting the art of feeling nothing and yet this child, who was so insubstantial he ought never to have noticed her amongst her classmates, had managed to slip through his defences. He had known Jasmine needed saving even then and she had haunted his thoughts ever since.

But *was* he saving her? Jasmine didn't want her family torn apart, her note had made that clear, and yet Sam was complicit in the break-up of Laura and Finn's marriage. He was convinced it was the right thing to do, but his motives weren't as noble as they should be. Despite spending so little time with Laura, he felt a strong attraction that he wasn't yet ready to fully admit or accept. How could he, while Laura was still sifting through the wreckage of her marriage? And even if she would be willing to take a chance on life again one day, would he?

The tree shivered in the breeze again, making Sam wonder what Jasmine's whispered wish had been. Was it for Sam to leave them alone? If that was the case then it was a wish he couldn't fulfil. He couldn't let Laura down. It was late morning and she would be at home in the midst of a heated discussion with Finn. She had phoned earlier after dropping

Jasmine off at Natalie's to confirm that she was going ahead with the plan. She would tell Finn she was leaving and the moment he stormed off to the pub she would pack her things and let Sam know she and Jasmine were on their way. The pubs were about to open so Sam expected the call at any moment.

Nine hundred and twenty-eight.

Nine hundred and twenty-nine.

The latest additions to Sam's collection of paper cranes were strewn across the dining table. The afternoon had faded into evening and with the day all but exhausted of light, Sam's fingers turned and folded the paper by touch alone. He felt the sharp point of a neck and pressed firmly to create a valley fold for the head before opening out the bird's wings and releasing it into the cold, lightless world, only to hear it drop onto the table a fraction of a second later.

Nine hundred and thirty.

The shoebox had been retrieved from its hiding place under his bed and was now on the bookshelf, ready for the new additions that might just complete the set. As he reached for another piece of paper, the screen on his phone glowed, its soft light casting ghoulish shadows off the carcasses of the paper birds. His eyes stung as he adjusted to the light, but there was no mistaking the name on the caller display.

'Laura? Are you all right?'

'Yes,' she whispered. 'Sorry for leaving it so late but this is the first chance I've had to ring you.'

'What's happening?'

'I'm on my way over to pick Jasmine up from Natalie's.'

Sam closed his eyes and let the relief wash away the tension and fear. He had gone through countless scenarios in the last few hours, most of which involved Finn losing his temper or Laura losing her nerve. At last it was happening. At last they could be removed from harm's way.

'Do you need me to do anything? Do you want me to pick you up?'

He could hear Laura's footsteps along the pavement. They faltered and then there was silence.

'Laura?'

'I told Finn,' she began. 'And he surprised me, if I'm honest. He took it – well, maybe not well, but much better than I expected. He recognized that he has a problem and what happened the other week when I cracked my ribs was a wake-up call for him.'

Sam was leaning on the table, a hand propping up his head as he listened to Laura with growing dread. Don't do this, he begged her silently. Don't fall for Finn's twisted reality.

When he gave no response, Laura filled the silence. She sounded a little less sure of herself now. 'He doesn't want me to leave, of course he doesn't. There were the inevitable accusations about me seeing someone else but I hit back with some of my own. He didn't admit to an affair, and I didn't expect him to, but I think we're both agreed that it doesn't really matter. The problem lies with our relationship and his behaviour, irrespective of who else may or may not be involved.'

Still Sam refused to ask the question that was crying out to be answered. For the first time since meeting Laura he felt no desire to make it easier on her and that realization was destroying him.

'He wants me to stay in the house, Sam. He thinks it's unfair to uproot Jasmine when she's had such a hard time of late. I told him I was thinking of booking into a bed and breakfast.' She tried to laugh as she said, 'That's partly true, isn't it?'

Again Sam gave no response.

Laura took a deep breath. 'We *are* splitting up, Sam,' she said. 'I've told Finn the damage has been done and it's too late to repair our relationship. I wasn't interested in hearing promises that I know he'll break the moment the going gets tough and he goes on another binge. He made some noises about going to the AA, but I'll believe that when I see it. And like I said, it doesn't matter any more.'

Breaking his silence at last, Sam asked, 'So if you're staying in the house, does that mean Finn's the one who's leaving?' He thought he could already guess at the answer.

'Not yet,' she said. 'I wasn't ready to up and leave on the spur of the moment and I wouldn't expect Finn to do that either. We've agreed that he'll move out next weekend, which gives him enough time to find somewhere to stay and then, in the long term, we have to look at how to split up the assets. That's what we spent most of the afternoon discussing. I can't afford to keep the house on by myself so we'll probably sell it. We'll have to involve solicitors eventually but for now I can't believe how amicable he's being.'

'Me neither.'

'There's no going back, Sam. This time next week, Finn *will* be moving out.'

330

Sam sat back in his chair. 'It's your decision. This has nothing to do with me, Laura. I was offering you a place to stay, that's all.'

The conversation had stalled to a stop. Sam pressed the phone a little harder against his ear, wanting to feel Laura close but realizing that was never meant to be. He wasn't convinced Laura, and especially Finn, would follow through with their plans, and if he had any sense he wouldn't hang around long enough to find out. When the call ended with awkward goodbyes, Sam shuffled into his bedroom. There was a holdall on top of the wardrobe that was big enough for all his worldly possessions. His running shoes were on the floor. He debated long and hard which to pick up first.

39

Tuesday 6 October 2015

Allowing only a week for Finn to find a new place to live was probably a little optimistic, so when the weekend of his supposed departure came and went with more excuses than action, Laura wasn't too worried. Finn's behaviour was otherwise exemplary, and although she knew it wouldn't last, the important point was that it didn't have to. All she had to do was help him stay on the straight and narrow long enough to find a place to stay and maybe a job too. He had already sent off half a dozen applications and had been for an interview which sounded promising, so there really was no reason to worry when she found herself doing the weekly shop and buying enough to feed three hungry mouths as usual.

Her cracked ribs were healing, but as she carried the shopping bags from the car into the house, she felt a twinge and grimaced. Finn was standing at the kitchen door watching her and there was a moment when she thought he was going to offer to take the heavy load from her.

'Is that the look I can expect every time you walk in the door?' Finn said.

With a sinking heart, Laura tried to keep her tone light. 'These bags are breaking my arms . . . could you help?'

'Why yes, I'd love to break your arms, dear.'

Laura chose to ignore the remark and shuffled past Finn with the bulging bags. She was keenly aware that she was being watched as she began unpacking. 'Where's Jasmine?' she asked.

'In her room.'

'OK,' she replied in a cheery tone. 'How about I make a start on the tea?'

She was in the process of emptying the last bag when Finn grabbed it from her and searched the contents. 'What's this? Can't you even trust me with one can of beer? Is that what we've been reduced to?'

'We agreed, Finn. You didn't want me to get any. What's wrong? What's happened?'

Finn's face twitched as if her soothing words were a swarm of angry bees. 'I'm going to the pub.'

In that moment, Laura knew what a terrible mistake she had made. She should have left Finn when she had the chance, but she had felt sorry for him. She had thought she had spied some remnant of the man she had once loved, someone she could still reason with. She had been prepared to be proved wrong and that day had come, but Laura wasn't going to let things return to the way they were before. If she allowed that to happen then there really was no hope for her.

Straightening up to face her husband, a sudden calmness descended over Laura. 'No, Finn,' she said.

'What?'

'If you go to the pub then don't expect me to be here waiting when you get home. I won't live in fear any more, and I'm certainly not going to face another night waiting for you to come home, not knowing what kind of mood you'll be in.'

Finn's reaction was mocking. He laughed until the tears were rolling down his face and then that face changed. 'OK, Laura, you go,' he said coldly and quietly. 'Go now. Shall I pack your bags for you? I know what, I'll call a taxi. Where would you like to go? Is Sam keeping his bed warm for you?'

Refusing to be intimidated, Laura said, 'I can manage on my own.' She tried not to let her fear show as she stepped past Finn and into the hallway.

'Yeah, you do that. Don't worry about me and Jasmine. We'll manage just fine without you.'

Laura stopped. 'No, Jasmine's coming with me.'

'Oh no she isn't. Do you think I'd let you take her so you can play happy families with the weirdo who talks to trees for a living?'

'It's not your choice,' Laura said, trying to sound stronger than she felt.

Finn reached her in two strides, grabbing her by the throat and pinning her against the staircase. 'It *is* my choice,' he hissed. 'If you go, Laura, then you go on your own.'

He began to tighten his grip around her neck and she sucked what little air she could into her lungs. With his face only inches from hers, Laura could feel his breath on her face. There was a faint hint of coffee but nothing else. Finn was stone-cold sober which made his attack all the more frightening. She clawed at his hands as her vision transformed into flashes of light and dark. She thought she was going to pass out when Finn relaxed his grip just enough for her to speak. He was playing with her but she wasn't ready to give up the fight, not yet. 'Please, Finn, no. You can't keep Jasmine. You don't want a child dragging you down – isn't that what you've always told me?'

'I've changed my mind,' he said casually as he let go of her neck and stepped away. 'We need to stay together, Laura; I've decided that's the best thing for our daughter and I can't believe you'd consider anything else. You really want her to be holed up in some grotty bedsit, whether that's with you or me? I can't believe what a heartless mother you are, but if you *do* try to take her,' he said, 'then I think I can produce enough evidence to prove what an unfit mother you are.'

Laura was gulping air as she asked, 'What evidence?'

Finn shrugged. 'The way you left Jasmine to roam free – don't you remember how I lost my job because I was so worried I had to go home without permission? I didn't want my daughter racing off to the park to see some loner who's a little bit too obsessed with our family, and all with your encouragement. And now I've been turned down for yet another job because I had to be honest with my potential employers and tell them I have dependents and an incapable wife.'

'You didn't get the job,' Laura said, more to herself than to Finn. It only ever took one setback for Finn to relapse into his old ways and that had been it.

Finn shrugged off the comment. 'That's not what's worrying me now; it's Jasmine's welfare. I've already mentioned to Anna how worried I am for her safety. Schools have a lot of influence with social services, you know. You may think you can take her, Laura, but I promise you, I'll get her back if you do.'

Laura was too stunned to move and even if she could, she didn't know which direction to turn.

'Now,' Finn said, bringing the conversation to a swift conclusion, 'you stay there and I'll go out. If you want to leave, by all means go, but at least be responsible enough to phone and ask me to come home to look after Jasmine. I can trust you to do that, can't I? You wouldn't completely abandon her?'

When Finn left the house, Laura managed to move but only as far as the living room. She watched Finn's shadow dance across the window in the direction of the King's Arms and there was nothing she could do except wait for its return. She was utterly defeated.

While Laura paced the floor waiting for Finn, Sam was preparing to shave off another millimetre from the soles of his running shoes. In the last ten days he had been out running every day, only returning home when he was sure he would be too tired to give into his much stronger compulsion to pack his bags. For the first week he had clung to the vain hope that Laura would contact him at the weekend to say Finn had left home. She hadn't, and in truth he hadn't expected the call and he certainly didn't expect it now.

He had come home from work and changed straight into his running gear as usual but he hadn't been able to leave the apartment. Jasper looked at him in confusion and wagged his tail slowly in expectation that for once Sam wasn't going to go straight out again. Unfortunately for the pup, Sam was still intent on leaving, only this time it would be for much, much longer.

Sam was slow and deliberate when he pulled the holdall down from the top of his wardrobe; it was as if he couldn't quite believe what his body was doing. His decision wasn't a conscious one but it didn't need to be. He had rehearsed what he was about to do so many times in his mind that he didn't need to think, he only needed to act. Gradually, he built up speed and in no time at all he had thrown everything he needed into his holdall and the remainder into bin bags. He took the rubbish downstairs where he bumped into Selina who had heard him moving about and was ready to pounce.

She knew immediately what he was up to but there was still a note of disbelief when she asked, 'You're leaving?'

'I can't stay,' he said. 'I can't live like this, Selina.'

'Have you spoken to Laura? Has she said what's happening?'

Sam couldn't hold Selina's gaze. He shook his head.

'Then you can't leave, not yet. I won't let you.'

Lifting a bag of rubbish, he said, 'Let me get rid of this and then we'll sit down and have a talk. Have you had dinner yet?'

Selina folded her arms. 'No.'

'I have a couple of ready meals to use up, if I can tempt you.'

'Our last supper?'

Sam didn't answer but went outside to throw out the rubbish. When he came back into the house, Selina was waiting for him at the bottom of the stairs. She had her house phone in her hand.

'Phone her.'

'I can't do that, Selina. If she needed me she would have called, and besides, I can't just ring her when there's every chance that Finn will be home too. I don't want to put her in an awkward position.'

'Then I'll phone her. What's her number?'

Sam considered telling her he didn't know without looking at his mobile, but it was committed to memory and denying it would only delay the inevitable. 'It's a waste of time,' he said. His body tensed as he punched in Laura's number as if he were turning to stone. 'There's nothing that you or Laura for that matter could say to change my mind.'

His landlady sniffed the air and put the phone to her ear. As she waited for the call to be answered, her confidence began to wane. 'She's not picking up. Should I leave one of those message things?'

'No,' Sam hissed. 'Finn might hear it.' He was about to grab the phone before Selina caused untold trouble when his landlady's face brightened.

'Hello? Laura?' she asked. 'It's Selina. Can you talk?'

Presumably Laura said yes because in the next moment, Selina was handing Sam the phone he no longer wanted to take from her. He took it reluctantly and said, 'Hi, Laura, it's me. How are things?'

He held his breath and, despite himself, hoped that by some miracle she would say Finn had gone, or that they were leaving and she wanted to come over straight away.

'There's been a change of plan,' she said.

'You're staying together.'

'Yes, I think it's for the best. For Jasmine's sake,' she said.

Sam listened to the intonation of her voice, searching out the slightest clue that might give away her thoughts. Was she absolutely sure it was for the best, or was she waiting for Sam to give her that final push to leave? He heard neither suggestion; her voice was calm, cold even.

'Maybe you're right,' Sam said and kept his eyes cast down so he couldn't see Selina glaring at him.

'Divorce can be really hard on the children, can't it?' Laura asked.

'I'm the last person you should be asking, Laura. It's your choice and I hope it works out for you, really I do,' he said. 'We all have decisions to make, and we have to live by them I suppose.'

Laura didn't ask what decisions Sam might be about to make, but she could probably guess. The conversation and their friendship had run its course and what remained was a long, uncomfortable pause which Sam didn't want to end, not when the only alternative was to say goodbye.

'I'd better let you go then,' she said.

'Yes.'

Another pause filled with longing.

'Bye, Laura.'

Sam cut the call and handed the phone back to Selina. 'Dinner will be ready in ten minutes,' he said and went upstairs without another word.

While the microwave hummed, Sam paced the floor, closely shadowed by Jasper. He didn't want to leave Laura and Jasmine to their fate but what could he do? He had to accept Laura's decision, it was hers to make, not his. He refused to feel guilty for turning his back on them. He couldn't be expected to live like this. He was leaving and no one would stop him this time, although the octogenarian who knocked on his door ten minutes later had a somewhat different opinion.

'So this is it, then?' she asked, taking a look around the empty room.

'In case you hadn't worked it out, Laura has decided to stay with Finn. I wish them well – but that's about all I can do. There's nothing left to discuss, with her or with you,' he added, hoping she would take the hint.

Selina put down the shopping bag she had brought with her and sat down heavily at the dining table which had been set for two. 'What's for dinner then?'

Sam didn't press her for any further reaction; it would come soon enough, so he kept quiet and served up.

Selina pulled a face at the defrosted shepherd's pie on her plate. 'What's for dessert? Rice pudding out of a tin?'

'Sorry, I know it's not up to your standards but it fills a gap,' he said.

'And empties your cupboards,' Selina said as she watched him chase garden peas around his plate. 'What are you doing about your job? Don't you have to work your notice?'

He stabbed at a pea, crushing it. 'I don't suppose they'll be too pleased when I phone up tomorrow to say I'm not coming in, and God knows what kind of reference I'll get, but I'll manage.'

'Tomorrow?'

Sam nodded.

'And what about him?' Selina asked. She was looking

at Jasper who was sitting on the floor watching them. Sam's training was finally paying off and when he had told the dog to sit, that was exactly what Jasper had done. He would wait there forever if Sam asked.

'He's a good dog,' Sam said and then tried to ignore the sound of Jasper's tail thumping against the floor. 'He'll keep you company and I don't mind paying for a dog walker if it's too much for you.'

'There's always Jasmine.'

'No, I don't think so.'

'Did she say why?' Selina asked without needing to explain the shift of focus in their conversation.

Sam continued to reorganize the food on his plate rather than eating it. 'Laura doesn't have to explain anything to me, Selina.'

'Are you sure it was her choice, Sam?' Selina said, more firmly this time.

'Of course it was. She had options, didn't she? If she wanted to leave then she could have done.'

'Don't you dare think it's as easy as packing a bag and walking out, Sam McIntyre.'

Sam played with his food, using his fork to create a long, winding path through his mashed potato. It would have been far easier to have left as soon as his bag was packed, without phoning Laura, without explaining to Selina, but he deserved to be punished by at least one of the people who had made the mistake of getting close to him.

'You have no idea how hard it will be for her,' Selina continued. 'She's spent years fighting to hold her marriage and her life together. It's going to take a lot for her to admit defeat.'

'But why, Selina? It's not exactly her failure, it's Finn's.'

'This isn't about Finn. This is about her own battle to resurrect the person she used to be. She's trying to remember what it's like to have a free will and to take charge of her life again. She will do it, Sam, she has to – she has Jasmine to think of.'

'What makes you think she isn't thinking about Jasmine? She said it was because of her that she's staying with Finn.'

'She said that?' There was a new note of concern in Selina's voice. 'But she was *leaving* for Jasmine's sake. We all agreed the child would be better off away from Finn. Why would she change her mind?'

'You tell me,' Sam said sullenly. 'Maybe it's Laura's turn to grant one of Jasmine's wishes.'

'No, I don't like this, Sam. I don't like it one bit.'

Sam remained silent, not wanting to open up the conversation further. He had enough questions of his own – along with a gnawing fear that Laura and Jasmine still needed his help and that he shouldn't abandon them.

Selina held her tongue too, but only as long as her patience would allow, which wasn't long at all.

'It might be half a century ago, but I remember what it was like being in Laura's position as if it were yesterday.'

Giving up on his pretence to have an appetite, Sam pushed away his plate of food and waited for Selina to continue.

'I could have left too, Sam,' she said, 'but it was as if I had stopped being a person in my own right. I was only an extension of my husband's life and I couldn't escape. I could pack my bags and leave, but while Alf was alive I was never going to be free. He wouldn't have let me go without a fight and I knew if I tried to leave he would find me and then there would be hell to pay. Even when I was pregnant for the fourth time and managed to get beyond the third month, when my baby's survival was in my hands as much as it was in Alf's fists, I still didn't have the courage to leave. As long as he was alive, we would always be in danger.'

'I can't imagine what it must have been like for you after the accident.'

'I can remember coming around in hospital and being told that Alf had died. I could have hugged the poor doctor who thought she was delivering earth-shattering news. Even when she told me how I'd lost the baby and they'd had to perform an emergency hysterectomy, it didn't diminish that feeling of pure elation. Of course, I was being pumped full of drugs at the time and it was only later, once I began to rediscover the person I had once been, that it hit me. I'd lost my babies, past, present and future and, in the end, Alf was right. It was all my fault.'

'I can't believe you're even saying that, Selina. You may have been browbeaten into believing that once, but you can't think that now.'

'Can't I? I'm responsible for the life I went on to lead. It was my decision to close my heart and keep the world out, wasn't it?'

Sam's only response was to clear away the food that had become as indigestible as the point his landlady was trying to make. 'Do you want pudding?' he asked.

'I'd prefer a glass of whisky.'

When he returned from the kitchen with two glasses, Selina had placed her shopping bag on her lap. She reached in and took out a clear plastic bag. 'I found these in the wheelie bin,' she said, lifting it up so Sam could see its contents.

'That's where they belong.'

She reached in and grabbed a handful of origami cranes, their wings neatly folded. 'There are nine hundred and ninety-nine of them by my reckoning.'

'I'll take your word for it.' Sam took a sip of whisky and let it warm his throat as he swallowed. His heart meanwhile remained ice cold.

'One more and you could have your heart's desire,' she said. 'Just out of interest, what would you have wished for?'

'I don't believe in wishes.'

'What would you wish for, Sam?'

From the tone of her voice, Sam knew she wouldn't relent. He shook his head. 'I'd wish for the impossible.'

'If I had a wish, then I think I'd ask for another go at the last fifty years. I'd already lost so much; my innocent babies together with my chances of ever being a mother, but I shouldn't have kept on punishing myself. I didn't have to give up my future happiness to prove how deeply I felt my loss.'

'Very subtle,' Sam muttered.

'I wasn't talking about you, Sam,' Selina said.

'I don't believe you.'

Selina drained her glass in one gulp. 'And I think Laura has made her decision under duress. She was determined not to give Finn another chance. Something's happened and you have to find out what.'

'I'm leaving tomorrow, Selina. It's not my problem any more.'

344

Selina glared at him. 'You can't leave her like this!' she hissed.

Sam glared back. 'I can, and I am. Don't you see—'

'Well, if you won't help her then I will.' Selina stood up.

'And do what? Go around and invite Finn to break one of your hips?' Sam asked. This wasn't the farewell dinner he'd had in mind and although he hated the idea of their last evening together ending with a row, he wouldn't give in. 'Leave them to their own fate. Leave us all to our own fate, Selina.'

His landlady grabbed the plastic bag full of birds and rummaged inside until she found an unused square of paper. She slammed it down on the table. It was dark green with yellow flowers and a pure white underside. 'I tell you what, Sam. Why don't you make it anyway and wish that Laura and Jasmine survive the next few years with an abusive husband and father. At least then you can say you did something!'

Sam jumped up so fast that his chair fell backwards, narrowly missing Jasper who yelped anyway. 'Don't you dare lay that guilt on me! This is the reason I have to go, Selina! I don't want to be responsible for them. I won't have them on my conscience, do you hear me?'

40

Police station: Wednesday 7 October 2015

'Why didn't you tell me?'

Sam had stepped out into fresh air to find the light draining rapidly from what had been a very long day, and promised to be an equally long night until news came that Jasmine had been found safe and well, if that news came at all. He turned to see Laura emerging from the gloom of the police station. Close behind, there was a police officer and Laura gestured to him, letting him know she wanted some time on her own with Sam.

'Tell you what?'

'About Ruby. Why didn't you tell me she had died?'

Sam exhaled and his whole body deflated. 'So you think I took Jasmine too.'

'If I believed that, Sam, then I wouldn't have come down here to convince DCI Harper that you wouldn't harm Jasmine. I understand now more than ever how you were only trying to protect her.'

There was a chill in the air, and as the autumn wind wrapped around them, Sam wondered if Jasmine were exposed to the elements; cold, alone and abandoned. Laura didn't move; she seemed not to feel the cold and the wisps of hair that had escaped her ponytail wrapped around her face, sticking to the fresh trail of tears on her cheeks.

'I shouldn't have been so quick to accept your decision yesterday,' Sam said. 'I should have done something.'

He didn't ask why Laura had decided to stay with Finn but she gave the answer willingly. 'Finn said he would fight to keep custody of Jasmine if I left. I couldn't risk that.'

Sam was about to tell her that no court in the land would grant Finn custody of any child, but the argument was a moot point when the child in question was missing. 'I'm going home to see if Selina's back yet. Apparently the police haven't been able to track her down.'

'Yes, I know. Do you think they could be together?'

The police officer who had been shadowing Laura was standing on the other side of the door and Sam couldn't be sure if he could still hear them but he dropped his voice anyway. 'I swear I don't know, Laura. I can't even explain why Jasmine's footprints should be by the house. I never told her where I lived.'

'She went to see Jasper according to her note,' Laura said. 'I don't know how she knew where to go either but clearly she did. Do you think Selina might have got to Jasmine somehow and invited her over? Do you think she might have planned to take her?'

'I can't believe it, but it is possible, I suppose. Selina was as desperate as I was to get you and Jasmine away,' Sam said before correcting himself. 'More so, given that she wasn't about to abandon you.'

'I don't blame you for not wanting to hang around, Sam. I'd put you in an impossible position, dragging you into this sorry mess and then pushing you away,' she said, and sensing that neither of them wanted to trawl over the past when there were more pressing matters to deal with, she added, 'I know Selina had an abusive marriage, but if she was trying to help us escape then why would she take Jasmine without at least telling me or you?' She wrapped her empty arms around herself before adding, 'If they are together, do you think . . . Is there any possibility that Selina would harm my baby?'

'Selina's a good person, Laura, and if Jasmine is with her then she'll be safe. Selina cares a lot about you both.'

'Then why would she put me through this!'

'I wish I had an explanation but I'm sorry, I don't,' Sam said. He was momentarily distracted by his mobile ringing in the pocket of the grey sweats the police had kindly let him keep while they kept hold of his running gear. When he checked the number it was withheld. 'I wonder if the press have my number. I don't suppose it would take them long.'

'The police are organizing a press conference now. They want me to make a plea for information and I think that's when they'll announce they're looking for Selina too. It's going to be hard to keep you out of the spotlight I'm afraid.'

'And I'm sure Finn will make sure I stay there,' Sam said as he ignored the short vibration on his phone that told him he had a voicemail message.

'It might not come to that if you can track down Selina first. And hopefully Jasmine too.'

There was desperation in Laura's face as she looked to him for answers, but it wasn't in his gift to give. 'I'm sorry, Laura, I've told the police all I know. I'll go home and change, then I'll phone around Selina's friends and after that I'll scour every inch of the park in case Jasmine's there.' He shook his head. 'I don't know what else to do. I don't know what else to say. I'm so sorry.'

'I want her back, Sam. I just want her back,' Laura said, her voice breaking. She took a gulp of air and held it. When she spoke again, it was to beat herself up with her own words. 'She's been scared for such a long time. I knew that, I just didn't want to see it. I was too busy convincing myself that I could be the buffer between Jasmine and her dad.'

'I should have done more,' Sam added.

'No, don't you dare blame yourself, Sam.'

'It's hard not to,' Sam said, thinking of another little girl and the weight on his conscience.

'I'm sorry . . . About Ruby, I mean. I can't imagine . . . Oh, God, Sam, I don't *want* to imagine what it might be like.'

Sam wanted to reach out and take Laura in his arms, but he was being watched closely so instead he offered only words which were cold comfort to both of them. 'And don't you blame yourself either. If anyone is responsible for this, it's Finn.'

As Laura stood with the wind pushing against her, she didn't sway; in fact she grew in substance. 'Yes, it is, and even though it's too late, I'm going home to do what I should have done a long time ago. I'm going to throw him out, Sam. I dread to think what the press will make of it, or the police for that matter, but I'm beyond caring.' She laughed then. 'Actually, what better time to do it than when I've got a police presence?'

'Let me know if there's anything I can do,' Sam said.

It wasn't until he was safely in a taxi cab on his way home that Sam listened to the message left on his mobile.

'What have I done, Sam? Oh, dear Lord, what have I done?' Selina cried out into thin air because Sam hadn't had the good sense to answer his phone.

41

Wednesday 7 October 2015 – Early morning

The first thing Jasmine noticed when she awoke was the hiss of rain hitting the window; the second was the knot in her stomach. It took only a moment to remember why it was there, and when she did, the knot tightened and she wanted to be sick.

Slipping out of bed, Jasmine was torn between rushing into the bathroom to be sick and not wanting to leave the security of her bedroom at all. Home didn't feel so safe any more. She had heard her mum and dad arguing the day before which proved she had been right to think that they were getting divorced – only it was much, much worse than she had feared. She had thought she would be living with her mum and spending some weekends with her dad like Keira did. She had never considered the possibility that it might be her mum leaving – without her.

It was all because she hadn't been able to make her wish properly. If only Sam hadn't found her note and spoiled everything. She had been angry at Sam and had thrown the wish away, not because she had stopped believing in the tree but because she didn't want to risk anyone else reading it, especially her dad who now had plans of bringing up his daughter on his own. It wasn't what Jasmine wanted. It wasn't what she had asked for at all!

Jasmine had told the tree she didn't want her parents to get divorced, but then she had thought about how horrible their life had become lately and especially how frightened she had been when her mum had had the accident. Jasmine hadn't been there when it happened and while she didn't want to believe that her dad could hurt her mum, Jasmine had heard enough and seen enough to know that was entirely possible. How many other knocks and bangs had her mum had and how many times had Jasmine been woken up by her dad staggering into the house in the middle of the night? She had often heard him talking to her mum in the next bedroom and although she couldn't always make out what he was saying, the tone was enough and it terrified her. It must have terrified her mum too.

When she wrote her note, she had been less concerned with saving her parents' marriage than she was with what would happen afterwards. She didn't want to be like Keira. Her friend liked going to stay with her dad and his new family, but then Keira's dad was really nice and he liked children, he must do because they had a new baby. Finn, on the other hand, didn't like kids and he especially didn't like her, at least not all the time. She was scared of spending time alone with him. She wouldn't be hearing his ugly threats through a bedroom wall any more because he would be taking it out on her instead. And that was why her wish had been never to see her dad again after her parents got divorced. And the tree would have made it happen, if only . . .

A wave of nausea crashed into Jasmine as she realized how much worse it was going to be if she had to live with her dad full time. Why did Sam have to find her note? And if he had read it, why wasn't he helping like he said he would? Her mum couldn't stand up to her dad on her own, but Sam could, and he could have helped them run away. Anything was better than pacing the floor waiting for her dad to come home, which is what her mum had done.

Jasmine had been waiting too and had barely slept, but as far as she knew, her dad hadn't come home. He would eventually, of course, and that thought was enough to send her rushing to the bathroom. Kneeling in front of the toilet bowl, she dry retched. Her hair fell forward and brushed the surface of the water until her mum came in and swept it over her shoulder and started rubbing her back.

'Are you all right?' she asked when Jasmine had pulled herself up and taken a sip of the glass of water waiting for her.

'Think so.'

'Will you be OK to go to school?'

It was normally a tempting proposition to exaggerate her ailments and stay at home, but Jasmine had no desire to spend any more time than she had to waiting for that first sign that her dad was back. There was something in her mum's voice that suggested she didn't want her to do that either.

'You'll be here when I get back home, won't you, Mum?'

Not realizing Jasmine was frightened that her mum might

leave for good, Laura said, 'No, I'm going into work soon but I'll be home at my usual time. Is that OK?'

Jasmine nodded.

'Go and get dressed and I'll make you some dry toast. It should settle your stomach.'

'I'll be fine,' Jasmine told her. 'Honest.'

The thin line of Laura's mouth tightened and for a moment she tried to curve her lips into a smile but failed miserably. She swept her hand across her daughter's cheek. 'You're a good girl.'

Jasmine was still upstairs shoving school books into her backpack when the front door opened then closed again. At first, panic set in when she thought her mum had left without her, and then fear bloomed when she realized it was her dad returning home. Jasmine could hear a mumbled exchange between them and decided to go onto the landing so she could hear better, but even as she started to move, she could hear Finn coming upstairs. She opened the door a crack.

'You can piss off now, Laura. Go where the hell you like,' Finn was saying in a sing-song voice that was slightly slurred. 'Don't you worry about Jasmine and me, we'll be fine, just fine.' He stumbled into his bedroom and then there were two thuds as he took off his shoes. The bed creaked and in no time at all he was snoring.

Jasmine had to think fast. She wanted to go back to the Wishing Tree and make another wish, only she wasn't sure now what she should ask for. She couldn't simply repeat her last wish – it was too late now, things were moving too fast. And even if she could think up something new, getting to the tree was going to be a challenge in itself and then it struck her. What if that was her wish? To escape once and for all. Could she run away on her own? Jasmine didn't think so. She needed help, and given how all the humans in her life were letting her down, she was counting on a certain four-legged friend.

It didn't take long for Jasmine to get ready, and when she left her bedroom, her school books were hidden beneath her bed out of sight to make room for some travel essentials in her backpack. She kissed her mum goodbye and tried not to dwell on how much she was going to hurt her, concentrating instead on the conviction that if Jasmine wasn't there to worry about, her mum would be free to leave too.

On her way to Keira's house, Jasmine turned to check that her mum had gone back inside. She had, and so Jasmine's next challenge was to get past Natalie's without anyone seeing her. She was hardly inconspicuous with her red polka-dot umbrella with Minnie Mouse ears, so she folded it up before shoving it in a nearby hedge where she hoped her friend would find it later – Keira always did like that umbrella and could have it as a keepsake of their friendship. Thankfully, Jasmine's navy-blue jacket had a hood which she pulled over her head before crouching down and stepping out onto the road to use the parked cars as cover while sneaking past.

As she crept away, Jasmine asked herself what on earth she thought she was doing. She didn't have an answer, not a proper one anyway, and knew she would end up in a lot of trouble if her dad ever caught up with her. But while Jasmine didn't know where she was going, she was prepared for anything. In her backpack she had her pink notebook, her packed lunch, an extra jumper, half a packet of chocolate biscuits she had sneaked out of the kitchen when her mum wasn't looking, and eight pounds and fifty-four pence for emergencies.

It was still scary stepping into the unknown, but when she turned the corner and headed towards the park, she felt surprisingly calm. The knot of tension was unravelling and the more distance she put between herself and home, the better she felt.

After leaving her note in the Wishing Tree, Jasmine left the park and turned right along Menlove Avenue towards the pedestrian crossing. It was rush hour and she didn't want to draw attention to herself by darting across the busy road. As she waited at the traffic lights, Jasmine kept her head down and her hood up to conceal her face, imagining herself as a spy in the kind of films her dad liked to watch. She was on a secret mission.

Crossing the road, she could still feel the warmth of the bark after she had pressed her palm against the Wishing Tree and connected with her old friend. It had heard her wish, she was sure of it and now she was putting her plans into action.

Her hope was that Sam would already have left for work and she would only have Selina to worry about. The old lady might not let the dog out of the house in the rain, but Jasper would need a toilet break at some point. She would wait in the garden until her patience paid off. Her plans beyond that were fluid to say the least. She didn't know how long it would take for anyone to notice she was missing. Natalie might assume she wasn't going to school with them, and it wouldn't be until the register was taken that anyone except Keira would notice she wasn't in class. She hoped the school secretary wouldn't ring her mum at work but if she did, Jasmine still had at least an hour before the alarm was raised.

As she approached Sam's house, her legs began to feel a little wobbly. It might be the steep incline of the road or it could be nerves, which secret spies weren't supposed to feel. She concentrated her mind on imagining what it would be like to be running free with Jasper somewhere. It was only when she reminded herself of all the walks she had taken with Nando that the next piece of the plan came together and she wondered how much a train ticket to Wales might be.

Suddenly pleased with herself, Jasmine stepped onto Sam's driveway without hesitation or caution and was nearly knocked down by the red Mini reversing towards her. Hoping the driver hadn't seen her, Jasmine darted into the evergreen bushes that bordered the front garden. She peered out again through the dense foliage of a holly bush which tore at her jacket sleeves while her school shoes dug into the sodden, muddy earth. The car had continued out of the drive but instead of moving off, the driver parked and got out.

'I know you're in there, young lady,' Selina said.

Sam sat at the dining table with the paper square lying exactly where Selina had slammed it down the night before. The blinds were still drawn but the grey dawn had slowly revealed the intricate pattern on the paper; tiny rows of yellow primroses lined up in perfect symmetry across the forest green paper. His life was not so ordered, and since the call he had made handing in his notice with immediate effect, nor was it as busy.

Squeezing his eyes shut, he could still see the lines of primroses burning into the back of his eyelids. He heard the front door open and close downstairs, and a moment later Selina's Mini reversing out of the drive. He stood up and went to the window, but refused to open the blinds and watch her leave. He wished they had been able to say goodbye properly and didn't relish the idea of their argument festering over the vast distance he was about to put between them. Selina wasn't getting any younger and there might never be another chance to make amends, but he had made his decision and there was no going back now.

Jasper had been dozing on an armchair, but seeing his master move for the first time in hours, he had scampered over and drew Sam's attention away from the window. Crouching down, Sam rubbed his ears and watched the pup's eyes roll in pleasure.

'I'm going to miss you,' he said.

Rather than weaken his resolve, the catch in his voice made him all the more determined. He was getting too attached – to everyone. Laura had made her decision, and although Sam's misgivings were as strong as Selina's, there was always a chance that Finn was capable of being a faithful husband, devoted father and reliable employee; a small chance, but a chance all the same. And it wasn't his problem now. His holdall was full and the only other item left to pack away was Ruby's shoebox. The nine hundred and ninety-nine paper cranes were back inside it but he had yet to decide on what to do with the green square of paper lying on the table. He had thrown out the paper birds for a reason; he no longer had the appetite for making wishes.

He was ready to leave and yet it felt wrong not telling someone he was going, someone who didn't have four legs and doleful eyes. In the absence of Selina, there was only one other person and so he picked up his mobile and dialled quickly.

'Sorry,' was his opening remark.

'Wow, this is getting to be a habit,' Kirsten said. 'I can't so much as get you to answer my calls and now *you've* called *me*. Twice in one year.'

'Sorry,' Sam repeated.

There was a long-drawn-out pause and Sam couldn't be sure if Kirsten was wondering what to make of this latest contact from her ex-husband or if she was simply finding somewhere private to talk. He thought he heard movement and imagined Kirsten mouthing an apology to her new husband. He had seen her do the same to him often enough.

'Have I called at a bad time?' he asked.

'No, but you're lucky you caught me. We're waiting for the taxi to take us to the airport. We're off to the Maldives.'

Realizing Kirsten was about to set off on her honeymoon, Sam considered ending the call there and then, but Kirsten had other ideas. 'OK, Sam, tell me what's going on.'

'I just thought I'd let you know that I'm moving on.'

'You're . . . Sorry, Sam, are we talking figuratively here?'

Sam's laugh was hollow. 'No, not in that way. I mean I'm leaving Liverpool.'

'And going where?' There was a pause, and even though

Kirsten couldn't see him, she sensed the shrug of his shoulders. 'You're running away again, aren't you? Does this have something to do with your new girlfriend? Anna, isn't it?'

'No, I can honestly say it has nothing to do with her and, for the record, she's my ex-girlfriend.'

'Then what are you running away from?'

Sam put his hand on top of the shoebox, his fingers warming to the touch of four letters that he had watched his daughter cut out while her tongue poked out of the corner of her mouth. 'I thought . . .' he began, then stopped. He had never really opened up to Kirsten about Ruby. He had been happy enough to listen but not to talk about his own feelings and he didn't think he could do it now, but then why had he phoned? 'I thought I could do it, Kirsten. I thought I could put it behind me and start afresh like you.'

'Like me?' Kirsten repeated and he sensed her bristling. 'Is that what you think I've done, Sam? Do you think by getting remarried and giving my future to someone new that I'm letting Ruby go? Do you think that's how it works? Really?'

'No . . . I don't know . . .'

He was at a loss and didn't know what to say next so went with what his heart told him. 'I miss her, Kirsten. I miss her so much that it kills me a little more every day and I think I've reached the point where I'm not even living any more.' He took a deep, juddering breath as he questioned again what he was doing telling his ex-wife all of this. 'Sorry,' he said, 'I shouldn't have phoned. I had no right to drag you into this mess.'

'You're not dragging me into anything, Sam,' Kirsten said. 'Back when Ruby died I never felt more alone, wondering why I was barely able to function while you hadn't even spilled a tear. This mess, as you call it, has been around for a long time: I've just been waiting for you to let me know you were in the middle of it too.'

'But it's been six years, Kirsten.'

'Oh, Sam,' she whispered. 'I wish you'd gone with me to see the bereavement counsellor when you had the chance. If you had, maybe you wouldn't be where you are now. He made me realize that there are a lot of hurdles to jump over before you can start putting your life back together. One is accepting that the life you're rebuilding isn't going to look anything like the one you once planned. Another is to accept that, despite that, you can still allow yourself to be happy. But those are just the obvious ones; there are plenty more hurdles and some you don't see until you wake up one morning and run straight into them. Do you know what I think your problem is?' She didn't wait for an answer. 'You're stuck at that very first hurdle, Sam. You want to get over your grief. You want to get over losing Ruby, our sweet, precious baby, but you can't. And do you want to know why you can't?'

'I have a feeling you're going to tell me,' Sam said. It was a flippant remark, but in his mind Sam was counting on Kirsten to tell him where he was going wrong.

'Because it doesn't exist. I haven't got over losing Ruby and I never will. I've survived the last six years by taking her with me, by making her a part of my new life, and I don't just mean in my heart and my memories. I'd like to think it's Ruby pushing me on to do things I never would have attempted or even thought of if she hadn't been a part of my life.'

'But I don't deserve a new life, especially not a happy one! It's my fault she died, Kirsten.'

'What do you want me to say, Sam? That I don't blame you? Of course I do!' Kirsten said, keeping her voice as low as her sudden anger would allow. 'You could have picked her up from school that afternoon, but then so could I. We both have to live with the knowledge that if we had taken different decisions then Ruby would still be alive and that eats me up too. But do you know what? I hope it always will, because that's what I deserve and it's what you deserve too.'

Sam's ex-wife's hurtful words were wet with tears and he wished he could reach out and hold her. She must have sensed it because her voice softened again. 'The pain we feel is the price we pay for having had our beautiful angel in our lives and it reminds us how much she was surely loved. We were good parents, Sam. We're good people, and despite all that pain and guilt, we also deserve to feel good about ourselves again.'

After a long pause, Sam said, 'There is someone . . . *was* someone I thought maybe I could build a new life with if only I'd been brave enough, if she'd been brave enough, but it's complicated. I think she wants me to save her, Kirsten. I think she needs me to save her but . . .' Sam closed his eyes and tried to summon an image of Laura and Jasmine but they had all but disappeared. 'I can't do it. Caring too much about someone is a risk I can't take. I just can't.'

'I won't tell you what to do, Sam,' Kirsten said. 'All I will say is that if Ruby taught us anything it's that life is precious. Don't waste your chances. You really should talk to someone.'

'I'm talking to you.'

'A professional, Sam,' she answered sternly. 'Don't waste your life, for Ruby's sake.'

Kirsten couldn't see him shaking his head, but she knew when to stop pushing. The next step was for Sam to take alone and to his surprise, instead of picking up his car keys, he picked up his running shoes and Jasper's leash.

They started off at a slow jog so Jasper could work out for himself that this was a pace he was expected to maintain. At first the pup alternated between trying to run ahead and trailing behind until Sam corrected him with a tug on the leash.

Sam cut through the park without so much as a passing glance at the Allerton Oak. He would normally continue south across Liverpool until he reached the river and then turn east or west. The destination had never been important to Sam, his only goal was running until he felt completely spent, at which point he would work out a route home. But Jasper's stamina would not allow such an epic journey today and perhaps that was why Sam had brought him along. Despite his ex-wife's wise advice he was still planning on reserving enough strength to begin another journey that day, one that would have no return leg.

He deliberately avoided the area where the Petersons lived and after about half an hour they reached Springwood. Sam was only just warming up but he slowed to a walking pace as they diverted through the cemetery which would eventually bring them back onto Menlove Avenue.

Sam wasn't one for visiting cemeteries and had never understood why Kirsten had gone over at least once a week to visit Ruby's grave. He refused to accept that a headstone could ever replace his daughter's physical presence. It wasn't the kind of mark he had expected her to stamp on the world. Sam had said his last goodbye when he and her uncles had carried Ruby's coffin into the crematorium and had spent the rest of the day comforting distraught family members while trying not to think about the flames that would reduce her young, broken body to ashes and remove any last hope of seeing her face again. He could spend the rest of his life staring at that piece of granite etched with his daughter's name but he wouldn't find her there. She was gone.

And yet now, as he walked amongst the graves, he felt an unexpected sense of calm. There were other visitors going quietly about their business, each one immersed in their own private moment of reflection, unaware of Sam's presence as decaying bouquets were replaced with fresh flowers, fallen leaves were swept away and gravestones were polished, patted and kissed.

Sam spied a water tap and waited patiently for an old man to finish filling up a plastic bottle. He had a bunch of flowers under his arm which Sam guessed would be for his wife's grave. The man took as much care filling the bottle as he might have once done with a kettle to make a pot of tea for the two of them.

After the man had left, Sam cupped water in his hand and let Jasper lap it up greedily. 'Don't worry; you won't have to do this again. I can't imagine Selina dragging you out on a run any time soon.'

When the dog looked up, his tail drooped as if he understood what he was being told. The guilt Sam was trying to escape had caught up with him and, rather than hurry back to the apartment, he took a seat on a bench. The name engraved on it matched the headstone of the loving husband and father buried a few feet away. Although he felt as if he were imposing, Sam bowed his head, closed his eyes and, to his surprise, allowed himself to remember what it had felt like to have those labels.

There was only a moment of trepidation where Sam feared he would be pulled back towards memories too chilling even for his nightmares: walking into a sterile room to see his daughter's crumpled body hooked up to machines that would keep her alive that little bit longer; or God forbid, the time he and Kirsten had held onto Ruby as if their own body heat could stop the coolness of death enveloping their precious child.

But as the harsh wind bit at his neck, freezing the sweat on his back, Sam felt warmth flood his heart as he recalled memories of happier times that had also been locked away; Ruby toddling towards him and wrapping her chubby arms around his neck; watching as she tried on her mum's shoes and lipstick and thinking how his baby was growing up too fast; and walking with her through the forest as she absorbed everything her dad was telling her about the flora and fauna, not to mention the woodland's more magical inhabitants with their toadstools and fairy dust. The memories just kept coming. Ruby playing football and scoring a goal before taking a lap of honour; Ruby's first day at high school; holding Ruby's hand tightly as he walked between queuing traffic instead of teaching her to use the pedestrian crossing . . .

Sam's eyes snapped open. A wave of self-loathing smashed into him and obliterated the sense of calm. He needed to leave and thankfully Jasper was rested enough to be able to keep up when he broke into a run the moment they cleared the cemetery. They wouldn't stop until they reached home, where an unexpected welcoming committee awaited them.

42

Jasmine's home: Wednesday 7 October 2015

While Sam was debating what to do about the message he had received from Selina, Laura had no such misgivings about what her next move would be.

'You might want to stay outside for this,' she said to Michael when they pulled up to the kerb. An area outside the house had been cordoned off and continued all the way up to Natalie's where the press were congregating.

'Is there something I should know about?' the family liaison officer asked. He was eager to prepare Laura and Finn for their press conference within the hour.

'Watch this space,' was all Laura would say.

When she entered the house, Laura felt a crushing sense of loneliness. She willed her heart to believe that Jasmine was still upstairs in her room, but the moment her mind conjured the image, she saw only a vulnerable little girl, head and heart full of fear, cowering in the shadows while listening to the painful disintegration of her parents' marriage, a fear that had become so intense that it had made her physically sick that very morning. How could

Laura have not seen what they were doing to her? How could she have not considered the effect their behaviour was having on their daughter in the last few months, if not years?

If she had looked, Laura would have seen her own fear and trepidation reflected in Jasmine's face the night before. After ending the call from Sam, Laura had been pacing the floor, waiting in vain for Finn's return, when Jasmine had brought her a glass of blackcurrant juice which she had promptly spilled on the rug. Laura had been wound up so tightly that she had snapped at her daughter rather than being grateful for the comfort being offered. She had been too wrapped up in her own world to realize the little girl had been reaching out for comfort in return.

Holding her breath, Laura tried to sense a connection with her daughter now, hoping it wasn't too late, but all she felt was cold fear. She couldn't be sure if it was her own or Jasmine's.

'You're back.'

Finn was standing at the living room door. He had showered and changed since she had left, presumably because he wanted to look his best for the cameras, although there was a scratch mark on his face that didn't look like a shaving cut. 'Is Anna still here?'

'No, she's gone,' Finn said with undisguised contempt. 'More trouble than she's worth, that one.'

'Had a lovers' tiff, have we?'

Finn shook his head. 'Now is not the time for your paranoia, Laura. A child is still missing, in case you've forgotten. Have you recovered from your histrionics, then?' he asked. His look was scathing, but there was doubt in his eyes, perhaps a little fear too. 'Are you going to tell me why you stormed off?'

'I told DCI Harper how you've been abusing me for years.'

Finn laughed. 'And he believed you? Where's the evidence? Where are the police reports with photos of a bruised and battered wife? Ah, yes, there aren't any, because I never touched you. You're losing it, Laura. I know these are testing times but you're an embarrassment, you really are.'

Laura pulled up her sleeve to reveal yellow bruising. 'Remember these?'

Twitching, Finn shook his head. 'You can't prove that had anything to do with me.'

'I don't have to,' Laura said, surprisingly calmly. 'This isn't a police matter, it's a personal one. I want you out, Finn, and I want you out now.' She was already moving before she had finished speaking, heading upstairs to the spare room where she'd been sleeping and grabbing an empty suitcase. When she came out, she had to shove past Finn to get to their bedroom.

Finn followed her and then stood at the door to block her exit. 'I'm not going anywhere,' he said with his arms folded and his legs spread wide.

Flinging the contents of drawers into the suitcase, Laura wasn't particularly concerned with what she was packing. It was the act alone that mattered. It was only half-full when she zipped it back up and she held it in front of her as she rammed into Finn, knocking him back before he realized what she was doing.

Her eyes were wide as she yelled, 'Get out, Finn! Get out!'

Finn stumbled but then managed to hold his ground and he glared at his wife while keeping his voice low and menacing. 'I told you, Laura, I won't let you keep Jazz.'

'In case you haven't noticed, Finn, she's not here! Our daughter has run away because she's frightened of you. She's terrified of you, just like I am! No, just like I *was*!' Laura said with a gasp when she caught a flicker of recognition in her husband's expression. Her injured ribs were aching but it was a new, painful realization that had taken her breath away. 'You know, don't you? You *know* how much you scared her. Did you hurt her, Finn? When I wasn't around, did you ever hit her?'

'I'm her father, Laura, I have a right. And in case you've forgotten, this mess has nothing to do with what *I've* done. If you don't start behaving then I'm going to have to tell the police how you helped Sam groom her.'

Laura let out a yell as she pushed Finn back again, and this time he couldn't stop her. 'If you don't leave now then I'm going to stand up at the press conference and tell everyone what's been going on!' she screamed at him. 'I want the world to know what you're like, Finn, but more importantly I want *Jasmine* to know she doesn't have to put up with you any more.'

They were stumbling downstairs in the next moment, Finn grabbing hold of the banister to keep himself from falling. 'Please, Laura, think about what a fool you're making of yourself!'

She had him pinned to the front door now, the suitcase wedged between them and their eyes locked. 'I'm no fool, Finn, I know what I'm doing. The only way I can get Jasmine back is if you're not here, so go. Get out!'

'You're a stupid bitch and I don't know what I ever saw in you.'

'Get. Out. Now!'

There was a look of utter confusion on Finn's face, then flashes of anger, then fear. His mouth moved, but the words wouldn't come. Laura stepped back calmly to give him enough room to turn and open the door. It was only when it slammed shut again that she realized she was still holding the suitcase.

When the taxi pulled up outside, the house was dark and deserted. Sam hadn't been expecting to see Selina's car parked on the driveway but his heart sank anyway. After listening to the message, he still didn't know where she was or exactly what she had done, but he had wanted to give her one last chance to explain herself and put things right. Now, he had no choice: he would have to phone the police.

After paying the cab driver, he glanced only briefly at the holly bush where the police had found Jasmine's footprints. Had she been hiding there that morning when he had taken Jasper out for their run or had Selina already taken her by then?

He wasn't sure why he crept into the house, but supposed it was an instinctive reaction to having his home raided earlier in the day. The police had left their mark, most notably on Selina's door which had been opened forcibly and left ajar. He peeked his head around to check what kind of state it had been left in. The cluttered apartment was still cluttered, her ornaments remained lined up in a haphazard order, although not necessarily the same order that

Selina had left them in. He didn't step further inside, he didn't need to. The police would have taken anything they considered incriminating and Sam didn't need to find proof of her guilt: he had all the evidence he needed but he wanted to hear the message one more time before handing it over to Harper. He sat down on the stairs to listen.

'What have I done, Sam? Oh, dear Lord, what have I done?' Selina said. 'And what do I do now? I can't go to the police, I just can't. They won't believe me this time. Oh, Sam, you have to help me get away before they realize what I've done . . .' There were mutterings then as Selina cursed under her breath. 'My money's running out. These stupid machines. I'll explain everything—'

The call had ended abruptly and Sam could only presume that she had been using a payphone and it had got the better of her. It was about the only thing he could be certain of because Selina had told him precisely nothing except in a roundabout way to confirm that she had taken Jasmine. She hadn't even said that the little girl was still with her or what they were going to do. It didn't seem likely that she was coming home. He could phone the police and let Laura know, but would it end her misery or only compound it? Selina had the child and while Sam couldn't consider any circumstance where Selina would let harm come to Jasmine, he couldn't be sure. He recalled the file Harper had on Selina Raymond and wondered what Selina had done that would make her think the police wouldn't believe her *this time*?

Heaving himself up, Sam groaned in sympathy with the steps as he made his way upstairs. Even before he turned the lock, Jasper was scratching at the door.

'Come on, let's get you out,' Sam said without looking inside his own apartment. He didn't care how the police had left the place. This was no longer his home, it was simply somewhere he would lay his head until Jasmine had been found and he could resurrect his original plan.

After taking Jasper downstairs to stretch his legs in the back garden, Sam returned to his apartment. There had been little for the police to disturb and even the green square of paper had been left on the dining table. The shoebox had remained with Harper for the time being and Sam hated to think of it languishing on a police shelf in an evidence bag, but it was a *thing*, not a person. It didn't matter in the grand scheme of things. It wouldn't bring Ruby back and neither would it bring Jasmine home.

He stared at his phone and, with enough effort, he found another reason to put off making the call. Once he told the police, Sam would have to return to the station and who knew when they would release him again. He had to at least get cleaned up first. He knew he smelled of stale sweat which was also making his skin itch. He grabbed a change of clothes from his bedroom, where the police had already emptied his holdall, and headed for the shower.

Although it was growing dark outside, Sam didn't switch on the lights. He was imagining how Jasmine must be feeling. She might not be alone, but she would be as scared as her mother. Harper had been wrong to suggest that Sam would understand what Laura was going through. If anything, Sam felt envious. He was aware how perverse that was, to be jealous of Laura because she stood a good chance of being reunited with her daughter, and it was cruel of him not to share Selina's message, but they had both been plunged into nightmares and for a few more minutes at least, he didn't want to feel so alone.

As the water trickled down his back, Sam closed his eyes and pushed Jasmine and Laura from his mind, which was all the encouragement Ruby needed. Not only could he see her smiling face but he could hear her too. Above the hiss of the shower, he caught the sound of laughter and a little girl's squeals of delight. It sounded so real that when he switched off the water, he strained his ears but his daughter had had her fun.

Sam towelled himself off and dressed quickly before returning to the living room, barefooted. He had left his mobile on the table and, before picking it up, he looked out of the window to check one last time. The space where Selina's car ought to be was still empty. He returned his gaze to his mobile phone and stared at it while the distant sound of laughter made his skin prick with goose bumps. He stopped and held his breath but again the ghost of his daughter eluded him.

Stepping away from the table, he moved towards the two armchairs. A cushion had been left on the floor and Sam picked it up and stared at the bright multi-coloured covers that Pat had lovingly crocheted for him. His grip on the cushion tightened as he asked himself what on earth he was doing. Why was he allowing himself to be distracted by searching for a child whose earthly presence had been stolen years earlier when another needed his help?

Every nerve in his body tensed and he felt ready to explode. A familiar sense of impotence wrapped around him, pressing against his chest. He trembled until he could hold it back no more and with a yell, sent the cushion flying across the room. He saw, too late, that Selina had appeared at the door and the cushion hit her square in the face and she stumbled back.

'Ow!' she cried. As she tried to recover from the direct hit, her lip quivered. 'I suppose I deserved that.'

'Selina!' Sam reached her in a handful of strides and took hold of her shoulders. 'What did you do to her? Where's Jasmine?' he demanded. 'Where is she?'

'She's downstairs.'

Sam was torn between rushing out to see Jasmine for himself and grabbing up his phone so he could let Laura know. He did neither because the sound of laughter rooted him to the spot.

'She's reacquainting herself with Jasper, the little minx,' Selina said with a reluctant note of affection. 'So what are you doing here anyway? I thought you would have left by now.'

'What am I doing here?' he cried. 'Let's just say my plans have been messed up by someone who should be old enough to know better than to abduct a child.'

'She's really dropped me in it, hasn't she Sam?'

'You're blaming *Jasmine* for this?'

'No, of course not, but it's not as if I planned any of this. It was just that, well, when I was leaving this morning I practically ran her over. I was about to give her an earful, but she burst into tears. She was terrified, Sam, terrified. She had it in her head that Finn was going to throw her mum out and that she would have to live with her dad. Whether it was true or not, I couldn't send her back to them, and you were set to leave so it was down to me to save her.'

'Which you thought you'd do by going on the run with her?'

Selina looked offended by the suggestion. 'Of course not! I was worried that Finn might come looking for her so I bundled her into the car. Jasmine wanted to go to Wales, so that's where we've been. At Pat's caravan.'

Sam stared at her in disbelief and simply waited for an explanation of how she could knowingly put Laura through such anguish.

'On the way, I left Laura an answering machine message thing.'

'You mean a voicemail?'

Selina sniffed. 'Call it what you like, but it turned out to be no message at all. I wasn't to know Jasmine's phone didn't work, was I?'

'But you've been missing for the entire day, Selina. Weren't you worried when Laura didn't ring back?'

'Well, I knew there was no mobile reception so I wasn't surprised that we didn't hear anything, not at first. But by this afternoon I was starting to worry that something bad might have happened and so we took a quick trip into Mold. I put the radio on in the car and that was the first I heard about the missing child who just so happened to be sitting right next to me with a guilty expression on her face.'

Sam glanced towards the rear of the apartment and the small window which looked out onto the garden. He was desperate for his first glimpse of the little girl who had caused a wide-scale search but there was something he knew he shouldn't put off any longer. He went to pick up his phone.

'What are you doing?' Selina asked. 'You can't tell anyone, not yet.'

The phone was already in Sam's hand when he asked the question. 'Why on earth not, Selina?'

His landlady's expression hardened. 'It's best not to ask. All I need, Sam, is for you to put off the call until I've had a chance to get away.'

'And go where? You can't go back to Pantymwyn,' he said before realizing he was asking the wrong question. 'What is it you're running from, Selina? Why can't you simply tell the police what you've told me?'

'I can't take the chance,' she said with a shake of the head that let loose a tear. 'They'll want to rake up the past, and I can't face that, Sam. I only came back here to pack a few things. I parked the car around the corner in case someone saw me and my next step was to drop Jasmine off at Pat's before I hit the road, but I can leave her with you instead.'

Given Sam's experience with Harper, it was entirely possible that Selina's fears would be realized, but he couldn't let her go on the run. 'I'm sorry, Selina, but if Jasmine is going to have to face the music, then so should you.'

'I dread to think what Finn will do when he lays his hands on her,' she said. 'Or me, for that matter. Maybe we should all do a runner. We could go anywhere. I've got savings and I could sell some jewellery.'

'Stop, Selina,' Sam said firmly. 'It'll be all right, I promise, and you don't have to worry about Jasmine. Laura was going to throw Finn out last I heard and the police will be keeping a careful eye on them. They'll be safe enough and so will you.'

Selina gritted her teeth as she tried to come to a decision. 'I'll stay on the condition that you do too.'

Rather than answer, Sam moved towards the rear window and Selina followed him. 'What does Jasmine think of all the fuss she's caused? Is she scared?' He pulled back the net curtain only to find the garden deserted.

'I think she was more interested in being reunited with Jasper than she was her parents. She was worried about Laura, but by thinking of her mum she also had to think of her dad and she's so scared of him, Sam.'

Pressing his forehead against the window to get a better view, Sam still couldn't see Jasmine. 'Let's go down and find her.'

Selina couldn't keep up and by the time she reached the bottom of the stairs, Sam was rushing back in from the garden. He hurried past her and into Selina's apartment only to reappear a moment later. He looked over at a side table by the front door which was where he had left Jasper's leash that morning. 'She's gone – and she's taken Jasper with her.'

Selina released a whimper. 'You have to find her, Sam. They really will lock me up and throw away the key if something happens to her now.'

Sam handed Selina his mobile. 'Phone the police,' he said as he flung open the front door and literally ran into Anna.

He grabbed her arm briefly to steady her. 'Have you seen Jasmine?' he demanded.

She shook her head and might have been about to say something else but Sam didn't give her the chance. His bare feet slapped against cold concrete as he rushed out onto the street, looking up and down the road but Jasmine was nowhere to be seen. He called Jasper but to no avail. Jasmine had gone.

43

Jasmine: Wednesday 7 October 2015

Jasmine knew, deep down, that she ought to be worrying about where she was going next but she was so happy to see Jasper that she could think of nothing else, and besides, the Wishing Tree was watching over her; she could feel its branches reaching out, calling her to it.

She had set off at a trot and was surprised how much better behaved the pup was than the last time she had taken him for a walk. Knowing it was only a matter of time before Selina and Sam realized she had gone missing again, Jasmine slipped down a side street so they wouldn't be spotted so easily.

Her adventures so far that day had taken her to Wales and back, and while she was glad to be returning to the ancient oak, she wasn't so keen on being closer to home. Her dad would be furious by now, but if she regretted anything, it was worrying her mum so much. She hadn't imagined she would cause so much trouble, especially for Selina, although in her own defence she hadn't deliberately set out to mislead her, it just seemed to happen that way.

'What are you doing here?' Selina had asked the shrubbery that morning. 'Shouldn't you be on your way to school?' After a protracted silence, she had added, 'Don't make me wrestle with a holly bush, Jasmine. Come out of there.'

Reluctantly, Jasmine had left her hiding place. 'You won't tell anyone you saw me, will you?'

'That depends on what you're doing here.' More silence had followed. 'So, are you going to explain yourself?'

There was something in the old lady's face, something that made Jasmine believe she could trust her. 'My mum's leaving home,' she had said, her lip quivering.

'Oh, thank God for that!'

'No!' Jasmine had cried. 'She's leaving me behind and I don't want to live with my dad!' Her body had started to shake uncontrollably as she thought of life with her dad and everything that would entail. 'I'm running away and you can't make me go back. I'd rather *die* first!'

Selina had rushed over to wrap the trembling girl in her arms, making escape all the more impossible. 'I won't make you do anything you don't want to, Jasmine, I promise. I'd rather run away with you than hand you back to your dad.'

Jasmine's spirits had soared. 'Can we? Can we run away together? I was going to go to Wales.'

Selina had looked back towards the house as she considered their options. 'I was planning on making myself scarce so spending the day at Pat's caravan might not be a bad idea. She's given me the spare key for emergencies.'

'And this is an emergency, really it is!'

'I suppose . . .'

'Can we take Jasper too?'

'It's probably best not to,' Selina had said, still looking at the house. 'That would mean telling Sam, and I should think he'll have other ideas about what to do.' Before Jasmine had a chance to object, she had added, 'He doesn't think we should be interfering in your mum and dad's affairs, Jasmine. If anyone were about to make you go home, it might just be Sam.'

With a heavy heart, Jasmine had been forced to agree and if her spirits weren't low enough, there was another problem looming.

'We'll stop off at a phone box on the way and let your mum know what's happening,' Selina said as they drove off.

'No, please, Selina. She'll make me stay. She won't stand up to Dad, he's too scary.'

'Let me worry about that.'

And that was when an idea had struck her. Jasmine's phone had been in her backpack and Selina was easily convinced that it worked. At first, Jasmine had tried to explain that her mum wasn't answering the phone, but the trick hadn't lasted long. Selina had been worried that the reason Laura wasn't answering the phone was she had already realized her daughter was missing and was out looking for her so Jasmine got her phone to make a beeping noise then held it to Selina's ear, convincing her she was leaving her mum a voicemail message.

'Now don't be mad at me, Laura,' Selina had started, 'but Jasmine is with me. You might already have worked out that she's run away, and while I had nothing to do with that, I can't bring her back. The poor child is terrified and she says she'd rather die than be left at home with Finn. I don't know what's happening there, but according to Jasmine you are still leaving him. Well, I hope you are because you're not getting Jasmine back unless you're prepared to follow through with your plans this time. Leave him, Laura, and get yourself to Pat's caravan as quick as you can. We'll be waiting.'

And if it hadn't been for that stupid radio report they would still be in Wales. That morning Selina had almost convinced Jasmine that she would be able to persuade her mum to run away too, but not now, not with the police hunting them down. Being forced to come home had been the worst feeling ever and Jasmine had been inconsolable, but at some point she had realized that perhaps she was going back for a reason. The Wishing Tree was still working its magic and all Jasmine had to do was bide her time before making another bid for freedom; this time with Jasper. That time had come and she was determined not to get caught again. Lifting up her hood to cover her face, she kept moving.

Sam rushed back into the house and ran up the stairs two at a time. He was in his bedroom, struggling to lace up his old work boots with shaking hands, when Anna appeared. 'You knew where she was all this time?' she asked him angrily.

'I haven't got time for this, Anna,' Sam replied with a growl.

'What is *wrong* with people?' she said, then let out a sigh. 'At least she's safe now, I suppose.'

There was something in Anna's voice that was crying

out for attention but Sam didn't have the time or the inclination to worry about anyone except Jasmine. 'She won't be safe until she's back in her mother's arms.'

'Not her father's, then.' It wasn't really a question.

It was only when Sam stood up that he had the chance to look at Anna properly, if only because she was blocking his exit. Tears had carried a river of mascara down her face, almost washing away the concealer she had applied to cover up an angry bruise around her left eye. She looked utterly bereft, more so when Sam tried to get past her. When she leapt into his arms, she clung on tightly.

'Please, Anna, I have to find Jasmine.'

She began sobbing loudly. 'You should have talked to me about your daughter, Sam, instead of doing something crazy like this.' When Sam tried to pull away, she grabbed his arm. 'I know I don't deserve your sympathy. I know I shouldn't have got involved with Finn, but he could be a good laugh in the right mood – and he gave me the kind of attention that would turn any girl's head,' she added, not yet so distraught that she couldn't manage to give Sam a cutting glance. 'And yes, he could get angry, but I thought he was a tortured soul and all he needed was the right woman to help him sort himself out. Stupid cow that I am, I thought that could be me.'

'Until he started knocking you about,' surmised Sam as he forcibly peeled her hands from him and pushed her away.

Anna cradled the injured side of her face. 'My parents have been staying at their villa for a few weeks so Finn and I were spending more and more time together. When he told me Laura wanted a divorce, I suggested we might set up home together. I was really excited and I thought he was too. But I knew something was wrong last night when he stayed over because he refused to talk about any plans for us.'

Sam was making no show at listening to her as he headed out through the apartment with Anna in hot pursuit.

'I went round today to offer my support and I was there when Laura stormed off to the police station to defend you. Finn wasn't just furious, he was – he was jealous,' she said as she followed Sam down the stairs. 'I confronted him about it and when he had a go at me, well, I'm not Laura and I gave as good as I got. I didn't think . . . The police were only outside and he didn't care, he just didn't care.'

With his heart pounding, Sam stopped at the foot of the stairs to catch his breath. Selina had remained in the hallway, clutching the mobile phone. 'Have you phoned the police?' he asked, already suspecting the answer.

'Can't we find her first?'

'No, Selina,' he said losing patience as he looked from his landlady to his ex-girlfriend. 'Can the two of you stop thinking of yourselves for once and help me find Jasmine!' There was real terror in Sam's voice that appeared to come out of nowhere but it had been lurking there for six whole years. 'Anna, make sure she phones the police. Tell them Jasmine has Jasper with her so she'll be easier to spot.'

As Sam rushed outside, he considered only briefly taking the car. He didn't want the sound of an engine drowning out the dog's bark when he called to Jasper, so now all he needed to do was decide which direction to take. He tried to put himself in Jasmine's shoes. Who would she run to now? He glanced back over his shoulder to see Anna and

Selina at the door. 'Tell them to go to the Wishing Tree,' he yelled before sprinting off.

Although the street lights weren't yet on, it was growing dark by the time Jasmine reached Menlove Avenue. Through the gloom she spied the red sandstone wall that marked the entrance to the park directly opposite. She could see very little of the actual park itself because her view was obstructed by huge trees running along the thirty-foot wide central reservation that was a miniature park in itself.

Rather than attempt to weave between the steady stream of traffic coming from both directions, Jasmine turned left and headed towards the pedestrian crossing. She knew she couldn't take risks and she needed to stay calm, although Jasper was another matter entirely. He had sniffed the air and picked up the unmistakeable scent of damp, decaying leaves and sodden grass that were the park's hallmarks and he began straining on his leash.

'Come on, we're nearly there,' Jasmine told him as the green man flashed into life.

The dog pulled harder and this time Jasmine didn't attempt to hold him back. They both ran across the road and turned back on themselves towards the entrance. The dog was faster than Jasmine and she giggled as she tried to press the release button on the leash so it could extend and give Jasper more leeway, but it was jiggling in her hand and she couldn't engage the button.

'Jasmine!'

Jasper came to a stop almost as quickly as the girl. It might not have been his name, but the pup recognized the voice. His ears flapped as he moved his head from side to side and tried to work out where the sound had come from. It took him a while to realize Sam was standing on the opposite side of the road. Two carriageways, a central reservation and a wall of trees, not to mention the speeding cars, all separated the dog from his master.

Oblivious to the dangers, Jasper was ready to dart across the road, but Jasmine gripped the plastic handle of the leash as tightly as she could. 'No, Jasper!'

The little girl stared at Sam, neither of them knowing which way to turn next. She could try to disappear into the park, but Sam knew the place far better than she did and he was a pretty good runner for an old man. And even if he didn't catch her, they would send out police helicopters with beams of light that would track her in no time at all.

As she stood frozen in indecision, a hand clamped around her shoulder and gave her a start.

'Where the hell have you been?' Finn roared.

Jasmine looked up into her dad's face in terror. His eyes were bulging and there was a scratch running down one of his cheeks. There was also the smell of beer on his breath. She tried to pull back but her dad's grip was painfully tight.

'I – I was just – just . . .' Her mouth was dry and the words choked the breath out of her, but eventually she managed to say, 'I was just taking Jasper for a walk.'

'Do you have any idea how much trouble you've caused? Your mum's gone crazy with worry. Crazy! I've had to get all the lads from the pub to help with the search because the police are hopeless. I told them *he* would be involved,' Finn said, releasing his grip on his daughter to jab an accusing finger in Sam's direction.

Jasmine's reaction time was faster than her dad's and the moment he let go, she turned and ran back the way she had come, away from her dad and away from Sam. Unfortunately, Jasper didn't have the same escape plan in mind. As she tugged one way, he pulled in the other – so hard that the leash was yanked from her hand.

The plastic handle clattered along the ground as the dog bolted across the road. He might have reached the central reservation, but he had to change direction when the driver of a speeding red car in the outside lane almost hit him.

At the sound of horns blaring and screeching brakes, Jasper came to a juddering halt, as did the traffic, which gave Jasmine the chance to lunge towards the trailing leash. The driver of the red car shouted some expletives out of his window, aiming them at Finn who responded with some choice words of his own while Jasmine pulled the dog back onto the pavement and safety.

'You stupid cow!' screamed Finn as he grabbed her again. 'You should have just let the mutt go. If it gets knocked down it's its own stupid fault!'

Jasmine began to cry. The knot in her stomach she had felt that morning had returned, twisting so tightly that it made her heart and chest hurt. Her dream of escaping was in tatters and she was going to have to live with the consequences of her actions for a very long time. Her whole life was going to be one long, miserable mess and she wished she was dead. She wished she had been the one to jump in front of the car and that the driver hadn't slammed on his brakes.

Sam watched from the opposite side of the road and it was as if he had fallen into his worst nightmare. He hadn't been there with Ruby on what would be her last trip home from school, but he had relived that moment so often in the early days that it had formed a false memory in his mind that was as real to him as any other. There was a part of him that was there now, back in Edinburgh. There was a part of him that had never left.

They had lived only a short distance from Ruby's high school and it was Sam who had insisted that she was old enough and sensible enough to get herself to and from school. There was one main road to cross which had a pedestrian crossing, albeit one that was at the opposite end of the road to where Ruby needed to cross, but they had told her in no uncertain terms that she had to use it, even if it did add an extra five minutes to her journey. It hadn't mattered that Sam never bothered to use it himself. Not then.

And while those thoughts came to the fore, he was forced to watch helplessly as a new nightmare unfolded. Jasmine had been on his side of the road when he had first spotted her in the distance and he had run at full pelt to catch her up. He had prayed she would use the crossing while his mind conjured up that false memory of a white van with a smashed windscreen and his daughter's blood blooming across the tarmac.

In her dark jacket, with the hood pulled up, he had lost sight of Jasmine for a while. When the traffic came to a stop, logic told him it was the traffic signals and not the scene of an accident, but his mind wouldn't release him from his fears until he spotted her again on the other side of the road. A sigh of relief exploded from his lungs and he had to put his hands on trembling knees before he could regain composure. When he straightened up again, he was so focused on calling out to her that he didn't notice Finn until he was at Jasmine's side.

Even in the fading light, Sam could see that Finn was seething with anger. Had Laura finally had the courage to throw him out? If she had, who would Finn blame for the dissolution of his marriage? Fear stabbed at Sam's heart while Finn pointed an accusing finger towards him. And that was when all hell had broken loose.

There had always been that question in Sam's mind. What would have happened if he had been there shadowing Ruby as Kirsten had at first suggested? They had chauffeured their daughter in her first year at high school, or, to be more precise, Sam had because he worked relatively flexible hours. He enjoyed that time alone with his daughter, just the two of them talking about their day, complaining about too much work, or people who didn't work as hard as they did. But Sam had reared enough fledglings in his time to know that there came a point when a parent had to let their child go, not that he intended to do that for many years to come, but he wanted Ruby to experience a little independence. It would be good for her.

Taking a couple of steps towards the kerb, Sam knew he wouldn't get to Jasmine in time. As he waited for a break in the traffic, on the other side there was the screech of brakes and Jasper came to a trembling stop, giving Jasmine a chance to catch hold of him again.

The little girl was safe for now, even though it looked as if her dad was reading her the riot act. Not caring what Finn might think of the intrusion, Sam had to reach them, but he refused to dart across the road in full view of Jasmine so made his way towards the pedestrian crossing. He kept looking back over his shoulder to see what Finn and Jasmine were doing and had just reached the crossing when he saw Finn raise his hand to his daughter. Sam couldn't believe his eyes. Finn slapped Jasmine and she stumbled back.

'Finn!' Sam screamed. 'Get your hands off her!'

Forgetting his resolve to use the crossing, Sam ran back the way he had come, looking for a break in the traffic as he went. He stepped out into the road in the hope that a driver would slow down enough to let him cross. A car horn blared but didn't stop. Trapped on the wrong side of the road, Sam could only ball his hands into fists and watch, powerlessly, as Finn made another grab for his daughter. Jasper had his hackles up and, sensing another assault on his friend, the puppy lunged at her attacker. Jasper's jaws locked on the sleeve of Finn's jacket, but he was so light that when Finn flung out his arm, he sent the dog flying into the air.

Sam was too far away to hear Jasper's yelp or the clatter of plastic as the leash dropped to the pavement again, but Jasmine heard. Finn lunged at her, but Jasmine was too fast. She chased after poor Jasper who was now terrified and only wanted to reach Sam. With his ears down and his tail between his legs, the pup ran along the edge of the kerb, barking at the traffic that was preventing his escape.

In the distance police sirens could be heard, but they wouldn't reach Jasmine in time. They would be too late.

'Jasmine! Stay where you are!' Sam shouted with such a power of emotion that his voice crackled. He felt the kind of pure terror that could bring a grown man to his knees and almost did, but then it was as if a switch had flicked and fear was replaced with superhuman determination.

He would have been there for Ruby. He would have jumped in front of the white van before it came into contact with her fragile body. Like a superhero, he would have held out his arms and pushed against the windscreen that was capable of shattering a child's skull. The van would have been brought to a screeching halt to the applause of all of those helpless onlookers who might otherwise have been traumatized for the rest of their lives.

Sam stepped out into the road again and held out his hand to an oncoming car which braked so hard there was the smell of burning rubber. A car in the second lane whizzed past him with a blare of its horn, but the car behind had already started to slow, giving Sam enough time to reach the central reservation.

Jasper had found his own gap in the traffic and, before Sam could order him to stay, the dog darted across one lane with Jasmine in hot pursuit. She was less interested in the traffic than she was in the plastic handle trailing along the ground after the dog.

'Jasmine, no!' Sam shouted, an instruction that was echoed a fraction of a second later by Finn.

The two men were directly opposite each other. They made eye contact briefly as both ran towards Jasmine. Sam stepped into the road and narrowly missed being hit by a silver car. He began waving his hands frantically to warn oncoming traffic but the van driver coming up on the outside lane had already seen the dog in the middle of the road. He swerved to avoid Jasper without realizing he was steering towards another hazard. He didn't have time to react and couldn't avoid the girl in the navy-blue jacket. Her blonde hair didn't shine like a warning beacon because she still had her hood up.

Sam's superhuman powers failed him and he didn't reach her, but he was close enough to hear the sickening sound of screeching brakes, skidding tyres, shattering glass and metal hitting flesh.

44

Endings

The few belongings that had been taken out of Sam's holdall since his first attempt to leave had been returned and there would be no more delays. Even Selina had given up trying to change his mind. Like Sam, she had been forced to weather the media storm surrounding their private lives during the last week or so, and he suspected that if she were ten years younger she might have suggested riding shotgun when Sam rode off into the sunset.

Selina was clearly unhappy about his departure and had taken to deep sighs and wringing her hands whenever she saw him, which was what she was doing now.

'It's a nice day for it,' she said as she looked out of the window.

Sam was sitting at the dining table holding a familiar piece of paper that had been transformed into a soaring bird. It was as green as the fresh buds that had peeked out from gnarled branches on the day Sam had first set eyes on Jasmine; young leaves that would soon be no more than rotting mulch. 'Better than driving through the rain,' he agreed.

'I meant for a funeral.'

When Sam looked up, it was impossible for Selina to gauge his feelings. They were hidden so deeply that even Sam couldn't feel them. 'I wouldn't have thought there was such a thing,' he said, thinking back to a glorious summer's day when the sun had no right to be in the sky.

To this day, there were still huge gaps in Sam's memory of his daughter's funeral. He knew the crematorium had been packed but he couldn't remember who had attended. He recalled a sea of faces staring up at him as he read a speech which he and Kirsten had written together. She hadn't been able to say a word so he had braved the lectern on his own. He had been the strong one and it had taken all of his strength to stand next to the white coffin that was too small and too damn soon for Ruby. He had wanted to run at full pelt out of there and to keep running. He wanted to run now.

Selina's next sigh was so loud it made Jasper lift his head. 'I suppose I'd better take him downstairs,' she said but didn't move.

'Aye, I'll bring his bed.' Sam didn't move either.

'What are you going to do with that?'

He turned the bird over in his hand but didn't even try to answer the question. When he had made the one thousandth crane that morning, he hadn't been sure if there was a special ceremony. It was something he hadn't considered when explaining the myth to Ruby because neither of them had been thinking that far ahead. His daughter was taking a pragmatic approach and had told him she would take her time making the cranes, possibly saving her wish until she was an adult when she would have a better idea about what she truly wanted from life. She had believed that wishes were too precious to be wasted and when he had sat on Ruby's bed on the day of her funeral and counted the ones she had made so far, there had been twenty-three.

The latest and last crane looked no different to its brothers and sisters and he had considered simply slipping it into the shoebox which had been released from police custody the day before. But this one was different. If you looked hard enough, there were telltale indentations on the paper from when he had written down his secret wish on its white underside. Technically, it hadn't been a single wish and Sam wondered if the crane might need a little extra help from an old ally of his. 'Maybe I should take Jasper out for one last walk.'

'To the park?'

'Maybe,' he said.

Sam hadn't been near Calderstones since the day of the accident. He didn't work there any more for one thing, and when he had been called upon to drive Selina to the police station, he had taken a circuitous route to avoid Menlove Avenue completely. They had made several trips to see Harper and his team and there had been countless questions, but eventually Selina had been let off with a caution. Sam wasn't sure if it was because Harper had mellowed following the accident or if Selina had simply worn him down.

Keeping his head down as he walked, Sam didn't look up until he felt soft mulch beneath his feet. The road was to his back and the scene of the accident was hidden from view as he slipped between the fir trees and startled a couple of squirrels, but it was Sam who was the one truly shocked when he caught a glimpse of blonde hair that shone beneath dull skies – only this time it was the mother and not the child who had paid a visit to the Wishing Tree.

Laura wore a black dress and jacket and was standing on the path that led directly past the Allerton Oak. Her head was bowed and her long blonde hair fell loosely over her shoulders, covering her face until she was startled out of her reverie by their approach.

'How are you?' he asked, knowing it was a question Laura was surely tiring of by now.

There was a pained expression on her face and when she said, 'I'm fine,' it convinced neither of them.

In spite of the dark circles under her eyes, Laura looked far better than the last time he had seen her. She had been in the police car that Sam had heard approaching as he watched Finn strike Jasmine, and while she hadn't been near enough to see the accident, she had been quickly subsumed by its aftermath.

'Selina was going to visit you,' he offered, 'but she wasn't sure if you'd want her to.'

'Tell her she's more than welcome, you both are,' Laura said before catching the look in Sam's eye. 'You're still leaving?'

He considered giving her a full explanation of his feelings, telling her how he wasn't brave enough to live in a world where joy and happiness were ultimately paid for with debts of fear and grief. But today was not about him and so he simply said, 'Yes, I was just taking Jasper for one last walk.'

'And so you ended up here,' Laura said, turning her attention to the Wishing Tree.

When Sam could draw his eyes from her, he looked over

to the tree that had cast its shadow much further than the length of its sprawling branches. Its trunk looked dark and damp, a stark contrast to the thin strands of light that danced in the breeze to the side of the tree. They were no more than a hair's breadth.

The spark of light ignited Sam's memory and he was returned to that heart-stopping moment when he had watched the van swerve into Jasmine's path. He couldn't have reached her, even if Jasper hadn't been wrapping himself around his legs at the time. Sam had held up his hand but he couldn't stop the van in its tracks and he couldn't protect Jasmine from its impact. He had been only feet away and still he hadn't been able to save her. If Finn hadn't been there to shove his daughter out of the way then . . .

'How is she?' he asked.

'She won't talk about what happened, Sam, in fact she barely talks at all. I wish I knew what was going on inside her head but then, maybe I don't want to know,' Laura admitted. 'She was like a little statue all through the service and when she did speak, she insisted on coming here. The wake's at the King's Arms so we've just nipped out for half an hour. I thought it might help. It can't be good keeping all of those feelings bottled up.'

'I suppose not,' Sam said, feeling obliged to agree when what he really wanted to say was that Jasmine would be terrified of letting go, that it would feel like she was standing on a precipice, and that once she took the plunge there would be no going back. He knew how that felt and supressing his emotions had been a survival technique he had perfected over the years.

'She's going to miss you, Sam. We both are.'

'You'll be OK,' Sam said if only to appease his own conscience. 'You're stronger than you give yourself credit for, Laura. You were going to go it alone, remember. You still can.'

'I don't suppose I have a choice,' she said, waiting for Sam to respond to what she wasn't saying. When he didn't even blink, she shook her head. 'I wanted to be free of Finn but not like this, Sam, not like this.'

There was nothing more either were prepared to say but when Sam made a move to leave, Jasper pulled him towards the tree rather than away from it.

'Will you at least say goodbye to Jasmine?' Laura asked. 'I think she'd appreciate it.'

Jasmine was sitting on the ground with her legs crossed. She was wearing a red tartan pinafore with a white blouse and had used her school coat as a mat to sit on. She wasn't the least bit startled by Sam's appearance because she had recognized the sound of Jasper panting long before they came into view.

Sam tied the dog's leash to the railings before taking hold of the overhanging branch that would give him the purchase he needed to leap over. 'Can I come in?' he asked.

She nodded.

Sam groaned as he jumped over, landing with a thud. 'I'm getting too old for this,' he complained then waited only a heartbeat before adding, 'There's no easy way of saying this, Jasmine so I'll say it straight out. I've come to say goodbye. I'm going away.'

'Is it because you're mad at me?'

Sam kicked away a couple of fallen twigs and sat down on a patch of damp leaves in front of her.

'Why on earth would I be mad at you?'

The little girl narrowed her eyes into slits as she forced back tears and did her best not to look at Jasper. She would definitely cry if she did that. 'Because I'm nothing but trouble and everyone would be better off without me.'

'I think your mum would disagree with that.'

'No,' Jasmine said, thinking of the moment the van had smashed into her dad and how the world had then gone eerily quiet. She had watched Sam holding his hands up to her, warning her to stay away while he knelt on the ground, his jeans soaking up the pooling blood in dark, purple patches. And then she had heard her mum screaming and before Jasmine knew what was happening, she had been pulled off her feet. Desperate arms wrapped around her and hands covered her face. They were her mum's hands shielding her from the gaze of her dad's dead eyes but Jasmine could still hear her screams. She would never forget them. 'Mum would be better off most of all.'

'Oh, Jasmine,' Sam said, 'there's nothing you could ever do that would make it better for your mum not to have you in her life.'

'I think I must have been born bad.'

Sam took his time before he gave his reply. 'I can think of some people who that might apply to but not you, Jasmine. You are not a bad person and don't ever let anyone tell you otherwise.'

Tears stung her eyes now. Her dad had thought her a nuisance, always getting under his feet or spoiling the fun and nothing she ever did was good enough. He *hated* her

– and that was before the accident. What would he think of her now? 'It was my dad's funeral today,' she said to remind Sam of what she was capable of.

'Yes, sweetheart, I know.'

His voice was soft and lulling, as if he thought she deserved comfort and not blame. She couldn't let that go unchallenged. 'I killed him,' she said, and when it looked like Sam was about to correct her, she scowled and added, '*And* I stole Jasper, who nearly died too.' She still wouldn't look at the pup who was whining now. 'Is that why you're taking him away? In case I do hurt him?'

'I'm not taking Jasper with me. He's staying with Selina,' Sam said. 'You'll have to speak to your mum, but I'm sure you can arrange to take him for walks, when you're ready.' If Sam had been expecting Jasmine to jump up and down with excitement then he was left disappointed. He sighed before adding, 'I saw what happened, Jasmine. It wasn't your fault.'

Jasmine had heard it all before and was tired of the lies and the sympathetic looks. She dropped her head and concentrated on picking at the skin around her fingernails which had been bitten to the quick.

'Have you talked to anyone about what happened?'

There was a shrug. 'A police lady keeps coming around but I get upset and she goes away.'

Sam was quiet for a moment and all Jasmine could hear was the gentle soughing of the tree and maybe the sound of the park ranger scratching his head. 'Hmm,' he said. 'Are you saying she makes you upset and you can't talk about it, or you make yourself cry so she goes away?'

With her head still bowed, Jasmine looked up through

401

her eyelashes. Sam had a suspicious look on his face. 'I don't want to talk about it.'

'You could always write it down. Tell the tree.'

'Keira showed me the newspaper. Everyone knows about my wishes now and how it was you who made up a silly story about the tree having magical powers. It *was* you who made my wishes come true, wasn't it?'

When Sam spoke, his voice cracked. 'It was a really bad thing to do, I know that now.'

Jasmine wanted to lift her head, not to look at Sam but to raise her gaze to the sprawling branches above her head, reaching towards her in what she had been foolish to believe was a loving embrace. She still wanted to feel that connection but instead she was only aware of sapped wood so weak that it needed metal props to keep it from collapsing into a pile of kindling.

'I wish I still believed.'

'I do,' he confessed. When he tapped his chest she wasn't sure if he was patting something in his pocket or feeling his heart. 'Sometimes there's nothing else left.'

'Did Ruby believe in wishes?'

'Yes, she did.'

'You miss her, don't you?'

'Yes . . .' Sam said, his voice trailing off into nothing.

The autumn wind became tangled in the branches above them. Drying leaves scraped together and one or two fell to their death. Jasper pounced at one and in the process trapped his head in the railings. When he cried out, Jasmine pulled harder at the skin around her fingernails, ignoring the tearing pain and the thin trickle of blood as she concentrated on holding back the flow of tears.

Her nose was blocked and her voice strained when she asked, 'Is Jasper all right? He fell so hard when my dad knocked him away and he was limping when he ran across the road.' A vision flashed in front of her eyes of the dog running straight into the path of the oncoming van. 'I didn't think he'd move fast enough.'

Sam was quiet for a moment. 'He *didn't* move fast enough, Jasmine,' he said, speaking slowly and deliberately. 'That was why the van swerved, the driver was trying to avoid him.'

Jasmine's nostrils flared as she looked up and glared at Sam. Her head was pounding as she continued to dig her fingers deeper into her flesh, although she couldn't feel the pain any more. She was only aware of the fury. 'It was *not* Jasper's fault! He's only a puppy and he was scared, Sam! He didn't know what he was doing!'

'No, I don't suppose he did,' Sam said softly. 'He ran away instinctively. You saw he was in danger and you reacted on instinct too. You put your life in danger to save him. That was pretty brave of you.'

Jasmine shook her head and teardrops splashed down onto her hands, the salty water stinging her wounds. 'Daddy was the one who was brave,' she said in a hoarse whisper.

'Yes, he was,' Sam replied, sounding surprisingly envious. 'And I know today is a day to remember your dad and all the good things he did, but I'm sorry Jasmine, I can't let you spend the rest of your life blaming yourself while your dad is turned into some kind of saint. He wasn't always a good person, was he?'

Sam was waiting for Jasmine to agree but she couldn't

hold his gaze and pushed her chin against her chest as she brought her knees up close.

'No one is all good or all bad,' he continued. 'We all make mistakes, we say things to hurt other people for no better reason than because we're hurting too. Your dad was no different and neither are you. He was very angry when he found you and he didn't just hurt Jasper, did he? He hurt you too. He hit you, Jasmine, and he shouldn't have done that. You can't blame yourself for wanting to run away, just like you won't blame Jasper.'

When Jasmine spoke it was only a mumble. 'But it was me who made him angry.'

'I'll tell you something, Jasmine. You're making *me* angry now,' Sam told her, momentarily lost for words: there were things he wanted to say but couldn't. When he found his voice again, it was full of bitterness. 'Your dad chose the life he lived. He chose to be a husband and father and he ought to have made you and your mum the centre of his life. He didn't. He thought only of himself and blamed everyone else when things went wrong, even when it was his fault – like losing his job. I wish he'd faced up to his responsibilities. I wish he'd seen how precious you were and how his one and only job was to protect you.'

When Jasmine looked at him again, his eyes were glistening.

'He should have felt like that from the moment you were born, not seconds before he died,' Sam told her.

Jasmine's tears began to surge and she tipped her head back and looked up at the branches reaching out over her. She couldn't tell if the tree was trying to protect her or ensnare her. 'What if it is still magical, Sam? What if it heard me the other day?'

'What do you mean, Jasmine?'

'When we were here last time, I spoke a wish out loud,' Jasmine said, although at the time she hadn't thought the tree was listening. 'I wished that you were my dad instead.'

Sam took a breath that caught in his throat. 'And if you had been my daughter,' he managed to say, 'then I would have gladly laid down my life for you. I'm glad your dad did what he did because believe me, if he hadn't saved you, Jasmine, then he wouldn't have been able to live with himself.'

Jasmine could feel her heart pounding. It was as if she could see into his soul and he into hers. When she blinked, a tear trickled down her cheek. 'Do you think he ever liked me?'

'I think he loved you, Jasmine.'

'But why did he shout at me all the time? I *must* have been so bad.' Jasmine was gasping for air now as she tried to hold back the pain. 'If I was a good girl—'

'Stop that!' Sam scolded. 'Stop blaming yourself. Think how much your dad must have loved you to do what he did. Think about all those times when he wasn't angry. I saw you at the caravan playing together with those board games, you were like two big kids sometimes.'

Jasmine's body was heaving now and when she let go of the first sob it was quickly followed by another. Sam leaned over and placed his hand firmly on hers, stilling her bleeding fingers if not her tremors. 'Remember him, Jasmine. Not just the good times, and not just the bad. It's OK to remember.'

Her lip was trembling as she tried to speak but the words wouldn't come. She swallowed back the pain in gulps until she was drowning in it. When she pulled her hands free, for a moment she was tempted to scramble backwards and let the yawning hole in the tree trunk swallow her up whole, but instead she flung herself towards Sam and almost toppled him over. She buried her head into his neck and clung on to him. It took only a moment to realize that Sam's arms were still hanging by his sides. His body had tensed and she could feel the tendons in his neck bulging. Sensing his rejection, Jasmine went to pull away.

Sam wasn't simply frightened of returning Jasmine's hug, he was terrified. The last little girl he had held in his arms had been limp and lifeless and even though that memory haunted him, he needed it to remain intact. He wanted his daughter to be the last child he would ever hold. He couldn't help Jasmine, he told himself but when she began to move away, it felt as if she were falling. He panicked and closed his arms around her.

He expected to feel a cold shiver as Ruby slipped further from his grasp, but when Jasmine hugged him back, it felt so right that it made him gasp. He squeezed his eyes shut and time slipped backwards so fast that his body tensed for the impact. He could smell the musty damp earth around the Allerton Oak, but there was something else there too, something sweet like popcorn and candy floss. It was the smells of the circus where he had taken Ruby when she was the same age as Jasmine. Halfway through the show, a clown had run up the aisle and stopped right beside his daughter who had jumped onto his knee in terror, her arms wrapping tightly around his neck as the monster with the painted smile threw a bucket of confetti over the crowd.

Desperately holding his breath to keep the vision intact, Sam's lungs began to burn. He prised open his eyes carefully to see autumn leaves rather than the brightly coloured strips of paper falling around him and above his head crooked boughs had formed cracks in the sky. Ruby was gone and he would never hold her again. He should have had the sense to push Jasmine away but he clung to her as he released his breath with a strangled sob. In desperation, he held his next breath in a vain attempt to regain composure but the sobs just kept coming until he simply stopped trying. It took a moment before he realized that Jasmine was gently rocking him back and forth. Her grip on him had loosened and when she lifted her head, she cupped his cheek in her small hand and said, 'It'll be all right, Sam.'

Reappearing from around the tree, the first thing Laura noticed was how red and swollen her daughter's eyes were. Before returning to her mum, Jasmine glanced back over her shoulder towards someone or something out of Laura's eye line.

'Sit, Jasper!' Jasmine said, pointing a finger towards him. With a broad smile she added, 'There's a good boy. Now stay!'

When she skipped over to her mum she kept the smile on her face. 'Sam says he's not taking Jasper with him so do you think I could take him for walks sometimes?' she asked. 'Only with you though. I wouldn't want to go on my own.'

Laura was too stunned by her daughter's transformation to digest fully what she was asking but she nodded anyway. 'Of course, honey.'

Happy with the answer, Jasmine took hold of her mum's hand as if to lead her away.

'What about Sam? I need to say goodbye.'

Jasmine yanked on her arm. 'No, Mum, it's best that we go. Sam's going to be fine and so are we. Come on.'

Laura didn't want to leave but her daughter spoke with such authority that she found she couldn't argue. She assumed it was what Sam had wanted them to do, but the more distance she put between them, the more she wanted to ignore what Sam McIntyre might want and put herself first. It was a concept she was still getting used to and so she continued walking.

'Do you think Keira will still be at the pub?'

'I should think so,' Laura said. Finn had never been so popular since his death and along with all his drinking buddies, there had been countless other friends and acquaintances who wanted to raise a glass to the hero of the hour. And he was a hero, she knew that. She hadn't seen the accident, only the chaos and there had been a moment when she thought the fear that had shadowed her all that day had become a reality. She had thought she had lost Jasmine and when she discovered how Finn had saved her, she had loved her husband again. The shock had been slowly wearing off, however, and now that they had said their final goodbyes, she was finding it more and more difficult to grieve that old life.

'Finn's mum's looking for you,' Natalie said when they walked into the pub.

'Could you do me a favour?' Laura asked. 'Could you ask her to look after Jasmine for an hour?'

Natalie raised an eyebrow. 'You're leaving again?'

'Please, Natalie,' Laura said, her expression adding a second plea for her friend not to ask why. 'Will you ask her for me?'

'I'll do better than that,' she said, 'I'll look after Jasmine myself. Your mother-in-law is already a little worse for wear and you're probably doing the right thing keeping away. You don't need another drunk to deal with after only just burying the last one.'

Laura and Natalie shared a smile laced with guilt and honesty. Now may not be the most appropriate time to acknowledge Finn's faults but a noble death didn't absolve him from his past deeds.

'Thank you, Natalie,' Laura said and left as soon as she was sure Jasmine was happy for her to go. Her daughter didn't question what she was doing either; it was as if she knew what her mum was going to do. Laura was thankful that at least one of them did.

Her heart was in her mouth when she pressed the door-bell and when Sam answered the door, her voice was shaking. 'Can I come in?' she asked.

Sam's mouth was agog and he too struggled to speak. 'Yes, of course. I was just—'

'Leaving?'

He led her into the house and up to his apartment without answering her question. Seeing the holdall by the door, he didn't have to.

'I'd offer you a drink, but I'm a little short on supplies.'

'Will you be going far?'

'I expect so,' he said.

Laura sat down on an armchair and watched Sam do the same. He was waiting for her to say something but other than coming over to see him, she hadn't thought about what might come next. She was waiting for him to look at her, to see the woman who had emerged from the traumas of Jasmine's disappearance and Finn's death; the woman who wasn't afraid any more. She waited, but Sam refused to look.

'Why, Sam? Why are you going?'

'Why not? I only stayed last time because I thought you needed help getting away from Finn.'

'And you don't think I need you now?' she asked bluntly.

'I can imagine it's going to take some time for you and Jasmine to adjust, but I don't see how I could be of much help. I'm the last person to give advice on how to rebuild your life, Laura.'

'If it wasn't for you, Sam, then I would never have stood up to Finn, I would never have recognized how weak and pathetic I had become.'

From the look on Sam's face, it was plain that he didn't have the faintest idea of the effect he'd had on her. Should she tell him? She had learnt to face her fears head on but was she brave enough to tell Sam how much she wanted him to stay?

'It might not mean anything now,' she stumbled on, 'but I won't forget how empowered I felt standing up to Finn. Don't get me wrong, Finn's death was and is devastating. I didn't want him in my life, but I still cared about him. I never stopped hoping that one day he would find the strength to beat his demons and be the kind of dad to

Jasmine that she deserved. It's going to take a lot to come to terms with everything, harder still for Jasmine, but I keep thinking back to that moment when I pushed him out the front door.' When she smiled, her eyes brimmed with sadness. 'Although it's not the greatest memory to have of our last conversation together.'

Sam had been looking more and more uncomfortable but it was her final comment that tipped him over the edge. He stood up so quickly that it gave Laura a start. 'I can't do this,' he said and moved towards the window as if searching for a means of escape.

Laura asked herself again how brave she was feeling. In answer, she followed him to the window and put a hand on his back.

Sam immediately pulled away. 'Don't, Laura. Please, don't,' he begged.

She couldn't and wouldn't give up, not yet. She understood why Sam was so afraid – she could see how tempting it could be to cocoon yourself from the rest of the world, but she imagined it would be a very lonely place. She didn't want that for herself or her daughter and she didn't want it for Sam either, but she suspected that telling Sam how she felt could send him flying out of the room and out of her life for good. She had one chance and she had to get it right.

'Tell me what's going on inside your head right now,' she demanded, thinking that together they could confront his fears. 'Talk to me, Sam.'

Sam shook his head slowly, as much to free himself from the thoughts Laura had provoked as it was to refuse her

411

plea. It had taken years of self-discipline for Sam to stop himself dipping into the past. He had created an imaginary chest in his mind and had visualized placing his most precious and painful memories inside where he could keep them under lock and key, or so he had thought. But in recent months the chest had rattled, demanding his attention, and then, when he had held Jasmine in his arms, its lid had been flung open wide. He couldn't repress his memories any more and when Laura talked about her last conversation with Finn, Sam immediately recalled the last time he had spoken to Ruby. Her cheeks had been bulging as she shoved another spoonful of cornflakes into her mouth, and when she smiled at him, milk had trickled from the corner of her mouth.

'You're getting milk all over your uniform,' he had chided. 'Now stop messing about and eat up or you'll be late.'

Ruby had wiped her mouth with the back of her hand. 'Can you pick me later? I'm allowed to bring my violin home tonight.'

Sam raised an eyebrow. 'Are they making violins out of lead these days? Too heavy to carry, is it?'

Ruby had shovelled in another mouthful of cereal before replying. 'I just thought you might not be able to wait to hear your super-talented daughter play enchanting melodies,' she had said wistfully as her eyes danced with mischief. 'You will fall under my spell and you will do my bidding.'

'Like picking you up from school, I suppose?'

She had tried a less subtle approach next. 'Pleeeease, Daddy.'

Sam had made a play of looking as if he was thinking

about it and then said, 'No chance. Now get on with you or you'll be late for school.'

She had sulked after that, and the last expression he would ever see on his daughter's face was a scowl rather than a smile.

'I'm not as strong as you think I am, Laura,' he said, his voice trembling. Sam's chest was tightening and there was a sharp pain at the back of his throat as he struggled to contain his emotions. 'I'm of no use to you.'

'Yes, you are, Sam. In fact, one of the reasons I came here was to thank you for helping Jasmine,' Laura said.

He shook his head and refused to look at her.

'Yes, Sam. I don't know what you said to her before but as we walked out of the park, she was a different girl. Not quite the Jasmine of old, and I'm not fooling myself that she's still not scared and desperately unhappy deep down inside, but she *is* stronger. You did that, Sam. You brought Jasmine back to me, in more ways than one.'

The sob came from nowhere and tore the back of Sam's throat. 'Stop it. Please. Laura, please just stop.' Running his fingers through his hair, he dug his fingernails deep into his scalp. He tried to concentrate on the pain, but there was a far deeper and inescapable agony that was all-consuming. Sam was still reeling from having made a fool of himself in front of Jasmine and he was about to do it again. At last he caught hold of an emotion he could handle; humiliation. 'I didn't say anything to her, Laura. I didn't help her. *She* helped me!' He turned to face her, stepping back so he could fling his arms wide. 'If you want to see what pathetic and weak really looks like then take a look at me! I was crying in Jasmine's arms like a baby, Laura!'

413

'I am looking at you,' she argued gently, 'and I'll tell you what I see, Sam. I see a man who can be strong and caring and selfless – someone who puts other people before himself – but most of all I see someone who wants to be loved if only he would stop torturing himself.'

She reached out again, taking hold of Sam's arms and this time he didn't recoil. The flash of anger had left him as quickly as it had arrived, and what little strength he had left was focused on holding back the tears.

'Don't run away. Please, Sam.'

He took a deep, shuddering breath as he fought one urge to run and another, equally strong, to put his arms around Laura. He did neither and dropped his hands, balled into fists, at his sides. 'I ran away from my life in Scotland so I could start again with a blank page.'

'Yes, and keeping it blank by the look of it. But is that any way to live? Is that ever going to make you happy?'

'But that's the point, Laura,' he said quietly. 'I don't want to be happy. Selina convinced me to give it a try and I did, I swear I did, but I'm not ready, I'll *never* be ready. I lost everything when Ruby died. There's no going back and there's no going forward. Holding Jasmine today was like having my heart ripped in two. I can't do it, so please don't ask me to.'

'Not that long ago I thought I was consigned to a life of hopelessness and insecurity and then you came into my life, Sam. You have no idea what kind of impact you had on me.' Laura had begun to weep silently as she spoke, but even through her tears she smiled. 'I can remember the first time I met you at Jasmine's school play. You looked at me, Sam,' she said, her words choked with emotion.

'You looked at me when I thought I'd all but disappeared. You *looked* at me.'

They stood staring at each other, and for one solitary moment the chaos inside Sam's mind stilled. He wasn't thinking about Ruby and the guilt he would never truly escape from, nor was he aware of the holdall on the floor ready for him to pick up or unpack. He relaxed his hands and placed them on Laura's hips, pulling her to him as she slipped her arms around his neck. Their faces were only inches apart and Laura's breath felt warm against his lips. He had stepped out across a chasm and was walking along an emotional tightrope. One wrong step would see him slip and he might fall – or then again, he might fly. He didn't know which and so he froze.

'Kiss me, Sam,' Laura whispered. When he didn't respond, she pulled him closer until their lips were almost touching.

Heat rose through Sam's body and he took a leap of faith. He kissed her with such force that their teeth knocked together and they stumbled back against the wall. Laura wrapped her arms tightly around him as he lifted her off her feet. He kissed her deeply, and then desperately, as he tried to hold on to the pureness of his desire for her, unsullied by memories or the fears that had begun to flock around him. Fear of what Laura was offering him, fear of wanting too much, of loving too deeply and of living in constant terror of losing it. But it was that last thought that taunted him as they both stopped for air, and he was peeling her arms from his neck and pushing her away before either of them realized what was happening.

'I'm sorry, Laura,' he gasped. 'I can't do this.'

She blinked as if his words were a slap across the face.

She pressed her hand briefly over her mouth, holding tight the memory of their kiss and then said, 'I can't change your mind, can I?'

Sam was backing away, slowly shaking his head. 'I hurt Anna and that was bad enough. I can't risk doing the same to you. I won't do it.'

Laura didn't look convinced, which must have made what she said next all the more difficult. 'OK, Sam. If I have to, then I'll respect your wishes, but can you do one thing for me? Will you stay in touch with Selina? She's a lovely lady and she'll be heartbroken if . . .' She glanced towards the holdall waiting by the door. '*When* you leave.'

'I know she will,' Sam said. 'I'll try.'

Laura pursed her lips as if to say more, but there was nothing left to say. Sam wasn't the only one who had an urge to flee, and a second later she was rushing through the door and stumbling blindly down the stairs. She was about to open the main door when Sam caught up to her. When he put his hand over hers, she didn't turn around nor did she pull away.

Resting his head on hers, Sam whispered into her ear, 'If anyone could have given me a reason to come back into the world of the living then it would have been you. Actually, for a while it was, but I can't do this, Laura. I'm sorry.'

'I love you, Sam,' she said.

When his only reply was silence, Laura pulled the door open and ran out of his life.

'You bloody fool!'

Sam didn't turn towards the sound of Selina's voice until he had watched Laura disappear out of sight. He closed the door. 'I know.'

416

The fury in Selina's eyes rooted Sam to the spot. 'Do you have *any* idea what you've just thrown away?' she demanded.

'Yes, a wife and family,' he said flatly. 'But they're not mine, Selina. I don't want that.'

'*Them*,' she corrected. 'They're *people*, Sam. People with warm hearts and open arms.'

Sam shook his head. 'Don't you get it yet? Hasn't what's happened over recent weeks, if not months, been proof enough that I am not the kind of man everyone wants me to be? He doesn't exist any more, Selina. He's gone, and all I want now is to be left alone. Is that too much to ask, woman?'

'I don't suppose I have much choice, do I?'

'I'm going upstairs to get my things,' he said, and at long last Sam had the courage of his convictions.

Selina pinched her lips but it didn't still the tremble in her voice. 'Don't do this, Sam. Did you not hear what Laura's just said to you? She loves you, for God's sake!'

'And what happens next, Selina? We start a relationship? I slip into Finn's shoes while he's still cooling in his grave?'

'I thought he was cremated.'

Sam glared at her, or at least gave it his best shot, knowing how much he was already hurting her. 'Laura and Jasmine have been through a traumatic experience, in fact they're still going through it, and take it from me, they won't really know how they feel for a very long time yet.'

'You think I don't know that?'

'Of course you do, which is why I'm asking, no, *begging* you, Selina. Stop wasting your breath trying to convince me to stay. If you want to help, then help Laura. Interfere in *her* life.'

Selina's laugh was hollow. 'She doesn't need me telling her what to do any more, Sam. Did you not look at her? Laura's taking control of her own life although it must have taken such a lot for her to come here. And this is how you repay her bravery.'

'Don't blame me for this! I never once suggested I could offer more than I already have. After the debacle with Anna, I made damn sure I didn't.'

'You didn't have to, Sam. I could see it and so could Laura.'

'See what?'

Her voice softened, but she hadn't given up the fight. 'The potential,' she said. 'You could make each other so happy if only you weren't so determined to keep everyone trapped in their own individual miseries.'

'Stop it, Selina, please. Haven't I enough guilt on my shoulders already?'

'Haven't we all,' she muttered.

The two stood facing each other, neither willing to back down and more especially, neither willing to end what could be their last conversation. It was only when Sam felt angry tears stinging his eyes that he was forced into action. He was sick and tired of hurting.

'I'll bring Jasper down in a minute,' he told her before bolting up the stairs and grabbing his holdall.

It took only one trip to put his belongings in the car and then a final trip to collect Jasper. Sam took one last look around the apartment which appeared only marginally less lived-in than it had earlier. He picked up Ruby's shoebox which held all but one of the one thousand cranes and, as he left, he wondered if there was magic in the air.

He could recall quite clearly what he had written on the underside of the forest green paper that was now nesting deep inside the trunk of the Allerton Oak. What he might never know was if his wishes would be realized.

I wish Laura the strength and courage to love someone who will give her the love she deserves in return.

I wish Jasmine the strength and courage to remember how to be a child again, to leave the shadows behind and bring sunshine into the lives of the people who love her.

And I wish Selina the courage and strength to continue to interfere in Laura's life so she can have the surrogate family she craves.

'At least I tried,' he told himself. 'There's no more I can do.'

When Sam led Jasper downstairs, he found Selina waiting for him. She had a carrier bag in her hand.

'Some bits and pieces for your journey,' she told him.

Along with containers of food and a flask, there was another bottle which took Sam by surprise. 'Bleach?'

Selina sniffed the air. 'There's no knowing what kind of hovel you'll end up in, so make sure you give it a good clean as soon as you get there.'

'I will.'

'I know this is where we're supposed to make our peace and I'm supposed to wish you well, but I still think you're a bloody fool.'

'Aye, I know, but this way I stay a sane one.'

'You will phone, won't you?'

'Yes, I'll even phone tonight to let you know where I've ended up.'

The conversation stalled. Everything had been said except goodbye. 'You will keep an eye on Laura for me, won't you?' he asked. 'I know it's asking a lot but you have so much in common and besides, without me around, you'll need someone to fuss over. The world lost out by not making you a mum.'

Tears were starting to brim in Selina's eyes which she concealed by grabbing hold of him and giving him a fierce hug. 'I'm going to miss you, Sam.'

After peeling himself from her arms, Sam crouched down to see to Jasper. 'And you be a good boy for Selina,' he said, spending just enough time stroking the dog for Selina to dry her eyes.

'Now stay, Jasper,' he said before straightening up.

The pup looked confused as he watched Sam open the front door. The brooding sky had turned slate grey but the rain was still holding off for the time being at least.

'Wait!' Selina said when he took that first step over the threshold. 'I need to tell you something.' There was panic in her eyes and she spoke urgently. 'I never told you the whole truth about my life with Alf and if I don't say it now, I never will, not to anyone.'

'Say what, Selina?'

'Some people believe in wishes, Sam,' she said, glancing at the shoebox tucked under his arm, 'but some of us learn the hard way that we have to do the dirty work ourselves. I was the kind of person who, when I cooked a chicken, didn't keep the wishbone, I served it to my husband in the hope he'd choke on it. Not that he did, of course, he was virtually indestructible.'

Selina began wringing her hands as she continued with her speech. 'The night of the accident we were driving home from a family wedding and my darling husband was accusing me of flirting with my brother-in-law of all people. As he drove, he took great pleasure in telling me what he was going to do to me when we got home. I was sitting next to him with one arm wrapped around our unborn child, our little boy, while he told me how I didn't deserve to be a mother. Maybe he was right,' she said with a sigh. She was looking at Sam, watching for his reaction as she bared her soul. 'What kind of mother chooses to end her son's life and that of his parents there and then rather than . . . ? Well, I'll never know if either of us would have survived the beating my husband had in store for me, will I?'

'*You* caused the accident?'

She nodded. 'Like I said, Sam, for good or bad, sometimes we have to take matters into our own hands.'

'Did the police know?' he asked, thinking of the file Harper had been poring over.

'They knew what Alf was like because my neighbours called them out often enough. Not that they did anything – it was a domestic matter as far as they were concerned and I was too scared to press charges. Judging by the questions DCI Harper was asking, I'm sure the police had their suspicions about the cause of the accident at the time but they didn't pursue it.'

'How could they when they had already failed you?' Sam took a step closer to kiss Selina's forehead then said, 'You are one gutsy lady.'

Selina snorted. 'To do what I did? No, Sam, I was simply ruthless.'

'I mean to have lived with that knowledge for all this time. And for the record, you weren't ruthless. You were backed into a corner and you stood up to a mindless thug the only way you knew how.'

'There could have been other ways, but that's my guilt and my burden. Do you understand now why I can't sympathize when you tell me how you feel responsible for Ruby's death? Life is unpredictable and you can't take responsibility for the things you couldn't have foreseen. I, on the other hand, knew exactly what would happen when I pulled on the steering wheel and drove us down an embankment. The only thing I didn't foresee was that I would survive. You have the luxury of being able to forgive yourself one day, whereas what I did was unforgiveable. Think hard on that, Sam.'

And with that, Selina ushered Sam down the steps. 'I only told you that because you're leaving, so go on, sod off,' she said with the kind of false bravado that had helped her through the last fifty years. 'Live a good life, Sam.'

Sam was still in shock as he drove away from the house and he didn't give a thought to where he was heading next, but wherever it was, he knew the motorway would get him there by the fastest route. He had to get away from the people he had come too close to caring about, but his heart wouldn't be released so easily. He found himself imagining what it must have been like for Selina to reach the point of despair where she saw death as her only escape. He couldn't imagine how she had dealt with the aftermath, the relief of escaping a cruel husband only to face the devastation of losing her unborn son and the possibility of ever conceiving another.

She was right: his own guilt was nothing compared to hers, but Sam had played his part in Ruby's death and he wouldn't be convinced otherwise. Words couldn't stop him from torturing himself, time certainly hadn't eased his conscience and neither would he want it to. He deserved the pain. And if it was a hurdle that didn't exist, as Kirsten would have him believe, then why did it hurt so much every time he hit it?

In the mood to torment himself further, Sam turned his thoughts to Laura. This was a new beginning for her too and he hoped she would make the right choices. Would she become fiercely independent like Selina or would she find someone new? After Sam's cruel rejection, her confidence would surely be dented. What if she never trusted another man again? What if she fell for another charmer like Finn who would ultimately let her down? The very thought made him feel sick to the stomach but Selina had been right. Laura was in control of her own destiny now, not him.

A motorway sign flashed past. He was already approaching the junction for the M6, at which point he would have to decide whether to travel north or south. Was it time to head back towards Scotland or should he continue to put more distance between his old life and his new? Whichever way he chose, it would be a fresh start, and he thought about the imaginary chest at the back of his mind where he would lock away his memories again . . . but some were refusing to return to the darkness.

Somewhere between the grey tarmac and the leaden skies on the horizon, an image of Ruby's face appeared. She looked like thunder.

'What's wrong?' he remembered asking. They were on their way back from a shopping trip. He had dropped Kirsten off at the bakery where she worked and had asked Ruby if she wanted to sit up front, but his daughter, who would have been eleven at the time, remained on the back seat, her arms folded across her chest.

'Nothing,' she said.

'Come on, it's just you and me now. Tell.'

They had stopped at a junction and Ruby continued to sit in stony silence.

'Don't you like your new uniform? Is that it?' In his rear-view mirror he saw her shrug. 'I thought you couldn't wait to start high school?'

Just before she turned her head to look out of the window, he thought he saw tears brimming in her eyes. 'Don't want to go.'

Sam had suspected as much. The traffic lights changed and, as he drove off, he said, 'I know it must feel daunting. You're going from being a big girl in a little school to a wee lass in a big one. It'll take a while to get used to it, but you will, I promise. In no time at all you'll be all grown-up, feeling sorry for all those new starters and wondering where the time went.'

'But I don't want to grow up,' she said as she turned back to her dad.

'So you want to spend the rest of your life being bossed around by me and Mum?'

'Don't mind,' she muttered.

He raised an eyebrow. 'Can I remind you of that, Ruby, the next time you tell me to stop nagging?' When she didn't reply, he tried a different approach. 'I had you down as being your own boss, running your own business like Mum.'

'I don't want to be a baker, stuck in a hot kitchen all day covered in flour.'

Sam could have asked her outright what she did want to do, but when Ruby was in a certain frame of mind, asking a direct question rarely received a direct answer. He gave her time to ask herself the question.

'I want to be a tour guide. I want to spend all my time outdoors, come rain or shine, with a crowd of tourists hanging onto my every word. Not one of those boring ones carrying a flag and pointing out all the obvious stuff – I want to make it fun. I want to get everyone involved and excited so that even if they're shivering cold and wet they won't want the tour to end.'

'A bit like what I do,' Sam said.

'Not at all,' she said, shocked that her dad could make such an assumption. 'I'll be getting people interested in history.'

'Oh, I see. Yes, that's completely different from my tours around the estate.'

'OK, maybe a bit like what you do,' she conceded.

'But different.'

She nodded. 'You keep telling me I should work to my strengths and it's not my fault that the thing I'm good at is talking to people. Just like you.'

Sam tightened his grip on the steering wheel as this latest memory played out in his mind. At any moment he expected to feel the full force of the hurdle he was about to ram into. He braced himself for the impact but it didn't come. He was being reminded not only of the man he had once been, but the man his daughter had seen. People were his strength; being around them, talking to them, taking an interest in their lives. His training had been in horticulture, his expertise lay in flora and fauna – but his job satisfaction came from sharing his love of nature with people.

Rubbing his chest, Sam glanced at the next motorway sign. The junction for the M6 was only a mile away and he still hadn't decided. He wondered what he might do if he did turn northwards. Would he go back to Edinburgh? He still had family and friends there who would welcome him with open arms, even Kirsten; perhaps especially her, and an apology to his ex-wife was well overdue. When Ruby had died, she had turned to him, expecting to see a reflection of her own grief, but instead he had put up a wall. By isolating himself he had isolated her too.

If he were to head south, then Sam would be re-establishing his isolation. He would learn from his mistakes, though – he wouldn't let anyone sneak into his heart again. He would cut himself off completely.

The car indicator clicked rhythmically as Sam turned onto the slip road which would quickly give him the choice of two opposing directions. North or south? He still didn't know. The gnawing sensation in the pit of his stomach was still there, but so was the residual warmth left by Ruby's memory. He summoned an image of her face. He was out of practice and it took so much effort that he drove past the northbound exit before he knew it. The tension building in his body made him feel sick and his mouth watered as he fought the urge to vomit.

Sam's eyes darted to the next road sign and one word bored into his brain. South. He had run out of options. The traffic was carrying him along and he dug his finger-nails into the steering wheel as he went with the flow.

He looked into his rear-view mirror and, for a split second, Ruby was there in the back seat. 'People,' she said. 'Work to your strengths.'

Car horns blared and brakes screeched as Sam swerved and he just about managed to get to the outside lane and avoid the southbound exit. His heart was racing and beads of sweat pricked his brow, but when he saw the sign for Liverpool he released all his pent-up anxiety with a sigh of relief. He couldn't wait to get home.

To my amazing, wonderful tree,

Your new leaves look very nice and I pologize now for the noise. I've tied Jasper to the railings and he keeps barking. He's trying to squeeze his head through the bars but he's big now and he'll get his head stuck if he's not careful. Then I'll have to fetch Sam and he won't trust me to take Jasper for a walk on my own again. He really does worry about me though he tries not to show it. He's in the park now and I know he's probly watching me. I'm not as daft as I look, that's what Sam says.

Sam's a full-time park ranger now and will be showing you off all the time. It looks like the wish I made at Christmas to get Sam a job worked, but maybe you could grant me just one more???

Soooo what I'd like is sort of for Sam and most definitely for Mum. The other night Sam was staying over and he was telling Mum that the lady he used to be married to is having a baby. He told Mum he was happy about it but I know he's always going to be sad about Ruby and I am too. I think it would have been nice for her to be my stepsister when Mum and Sam get married, which course they will once Sam is brave enough to ask.

I also think he's a bit jealous about this baby and it was soooo obvious that Mum wanted him to say something but he didn't because he's probly worrying that he doesn't want to rush things, that's what Natalie said to Mum, and Mum doesn't want to push Sam, that's what she said to Natalie, but I'd like a baby brother or sister before I turn into a teenager and decide I don't like anyone any more, like Keira's sister has.

I think a little baby will help everyone. Sam can tell his new baby all about Ruby, and I can tell him or her all about my dad, or the nice bits about him anyway. I do miss my dad but there are some things I don't miss.

Jasper's whining is hurting my ears now, so I'd better go. I'll leave this note in the tree and I hope Sam doesn't come along and find it!

I love you.
Jasmine xxx

Acknowledgements

The Allerton Oak is a real tree in Calderstones Park, Liverpool, and although the magical powers I ascribe to it are pure fiction, I must confess there came a point during the writing of this book when I wanted to believe it was true. I had been working on one of the final drafts when one of my closest friends became gravely ill, and I found myself beneath the thousand-year-old tree willing it to give her the strength to pull through and return home to her family. It brought me some comfort at the time, but ultimately the Wishing Tree's powers failed.

This book is dedicated to Donna Hall for a very good reason. She was thoughtful, generous, kind-hearted, patient, and she certainly knew how to have a good time. She made friends easily, and not only kept them but shared them too. My life is richer for having known her and I'm privileged to have amazing support from the friends she brought together. My love and thoughts remain with John, Luke and Dylan Hall, and Tracy, Lee and Jonathan Wood.

As you can appreciate, it was tough finishing this novel and I would like to thank my editor, Martha Ashby, for her support, and for not putting pressure on me to meet deadlines even when I was putting that pressure on myself. Thank you to Kim Young and all the team at HarperCollins for your amazing support and making me the writer I am today. And thank you to my agent, Luigi Bonomi, who believed in me as a writer long before I ever believed in myself.

Thank you as always to my family and especially to my daughter Jessica, who has always, always been there when I needed her most.

An interview with

AMANDA BROOKE

1. Tell us about the inspiration for this novel.

The inspiration behind *The Child's Secret* came after hearing about the 'Whispering Gallery,' in New York's Grand Central Station. Apparently two people can stand in opposite corners of an archway and the acoustics allow their whispers to be carried to each other. I began playing around with various ideas for a story where my main character could 'listen in,' to the innocent wishes of a young child, and then go on to fulfil them. It took a while to think up a story that really fired my imagination, and it wasn't until I was standing in front of the Allerton Oak in Calderstones Park, Liverpool that it all came together. The Wishing Tree was born and it became the perfect device to connect my characters.

2. A missing child is surely most parents' worst nightmare. How did you deal with such an emotionally fraught storyline?

I should think most parents have experienced that sickening feeling when you lose sight of your child, even for just a few moments. Your imagination runs wild as you go through countless scenarios but thankfully for most of us, there's a swift resolution when the child in question reappears wondering what all the fuss was about. With *The Child's Secret*, I had to take that situation so much further and describing those scenes with Laura and Finn was intense at times. It was tough trying to put myself in the position of a parent whose child is missing, and even as a bereaved parent with my own personal experience of loss, it was a challenge to imagine how they must feel.

3. **As you wrote the book, how much did you want to play with reader's perception of Sam, as a potential hero or villain?**

I didn't want to make Sam's intentions clear from the outset, but there was more to it than simply playing with the reader's perception of him. In the initial planning stages, I hadn't intended for Sam to be a bereaved parent because it was his relationship with Jasmine that I was focusing on first and foremost. His past life became a way to explain both his hesitance to become involved in the little girl's life, and also his strong desire to protect her. It also provided a reason for other characters to question his motives and here I was playing on what seems to be an all too common portrayal of bereaved parents as the villains. I've lost count of how many TV dramas I've seen where a parent's loss has seemingly justified heinous crimes and I've always found this a little unfair. In my experience, bereaved parents are an incredible force for good and that's why Sam was always going to be the good guy.

4. **Do you think that fears for missing children are prevalent in our society? And with the rise of social media and the speed which information can change and distort, do you think this is true more so now than ever before?**

We're all more aware of the darker side of life these days and with historical cases of child abuse hitting the headlines on a regular basis, it's natural for parents to have their fears heightened. I'm not sure that's such a bad thing: it's a small price to pay if such cases can be prevented or at least detected quickly. Social media and increased awareness has made it difficult for any parent to ignore the perceived dangers of child abduction and abuse, and because it's impossible to quantify those risks, we've all become overcautious and children therefore have less freedom. Eight-year-old Jasmine wasn't allowed to go to the park on her own and readers might even have thought it unwise for her to be allowed to go under the supervision of her friend's sister. I grew up in the seventies so I was always going on treks to the park with my friends, but if my parents had known then what we know now, I'm pretty sure I would have had a completely different childhood.

5. **The themes of your books tend to echo the shocking stories we read about in the newspapers and cause readers to think 'there but for the grace of god…' Do you think that's an accurate description of your writing? And are the headlines sometimes a source for inspiration?**

I think my latest books are moving in that direction and it's a style of writing I'm thoroughly enjoying. My previous novel, *The Missing Husband*, was a perfect example of how I drew inspiration from the headlines because I came up with the idea while watching an evening news' piece about a man who had been missing for twelve months. It's human nature to want to peer into someone else's life and be thankful that we're not facing the same kind of trauma. It's stories like *The Child's Secret* that make us appreciate what we have and prompts us to hold those we love a little closer.

6. **How did you find writing dual narratives, from an adult and a child's perspective? Did you face any difficulties in creating these very different voices?**

In *The Child's Secret*, I tell the story from the view point of Sam, Laura and Jasmine and they were all very distinctive in my mind because of the difference in their ages, their sex and their characters. Sam's voice was the strongest and most determined, while Laura's was the quietest because she was so unsure of herself. I especially loved writing from Jasmine's point of view because she had such an innocent and at times, simple view of the world. She was someone xs

7. **Did writing *The Child's Secret* differ from your experience writing your previous novels? In what way?**

The structure of this book was something that was completely new to me, having two separate timelines running concurrently. The story essentially starts when Sam meets Jasmine for the first time, but I open the novel on the day she goes missing and then look back at her past. The present day chapters threaded through the novel were a challenge because in those scenes all my characters knew each other very well. It took a lot of planning and during the rewrites I had to track very carefully who knew what and when, as well as deciding how much to reveal to the reader. There were times when my head throbbed as I tried to connect it all together, but I loved the end result and it's a structure I'm planning on using again.

8. **How do you plot out your novels when you've got an idea in your head?**

It can take some time for that initial idea to evolve into a story with substance, but when I'm ready to commit it to paper, I'll start by writing a synopsis. That outline will only be a couple of pages long and at that stage I won't really have considered sub-plots or minor characters but I will have captured the essence of the story. My next task is to cut up the synopsis into about twelve sections which in theory will be the chapters and, if nothing else, it gives me some reassurance that I have enough of a story for a full length manuscript. When I'm ready to start writing the book, I tend to have a very clear idea of the opening and final scenes but the rest is still relatively fluid. I enjoy getting to know my characters and they're the ones who fuel my imagination as I go along, creating situations and conflict I never could have imagined from the start.

9. **What are you reading at the moment? And do you find it hard to read for pleasure when you're in the middle of writing?**

I'm currently reading *The Husband's Secret* by Liane Moriarty and even though I'm really enjoying it, I know it will take me quite a while to finish the book. I work full time and writing fills much of my free time so unfortunately I tend to only find time to read last thing at night. My reading experience has most definitely changed since becoming an author because I'm more conscious of other writers' styles, but I think that's a good thing as it helps me develop my own writing.

10. **Will you tell us a bit about your next book?**

My next book is called *The Goodbye Gift*. It's about three friends who are all going through intense periods of change. They each have a story to tell but one story is about to end abruptly and that's where my novel begins. In the opening scene, I introduce a young girl called Lucy whose survival is dependent on a heart transplant. There's been a devastating accident involving the three friends and someone is about to give Lucy a fighting chance for life.

Reading Group Questions

How did you feel about the ending? How did the accident leave you feeling about those involved?

Compare and contrast Sam and Finn's differing approaches to fatherhood. Was Finn's final heroic deed enough to forgive his failings as a father?

Discuss the way that Sam dealt with his grief.

What was your opinion of Laura? Do you think she could have done something sooner to protect Jasmine and herself?

If you had one wish, what would you ask the Wishing Tree for?

Was DCI Harper right to immediately direct suspicion towards Sam? Were you ready to believe a bereaved father was capable of abducting a child?

What do you think motivated Anna's actions after her and Sam broke up?

Do you think Selina can be forgiven for her actions, both in the past and her involvement in Jasmine's disappearance?

Discuss the role of the Wishing Tree as a device.

Out of all the complex characters, whose actions were the hardest/easiest to understand and why?